THE RUBBER ROOM

VOLUME 2

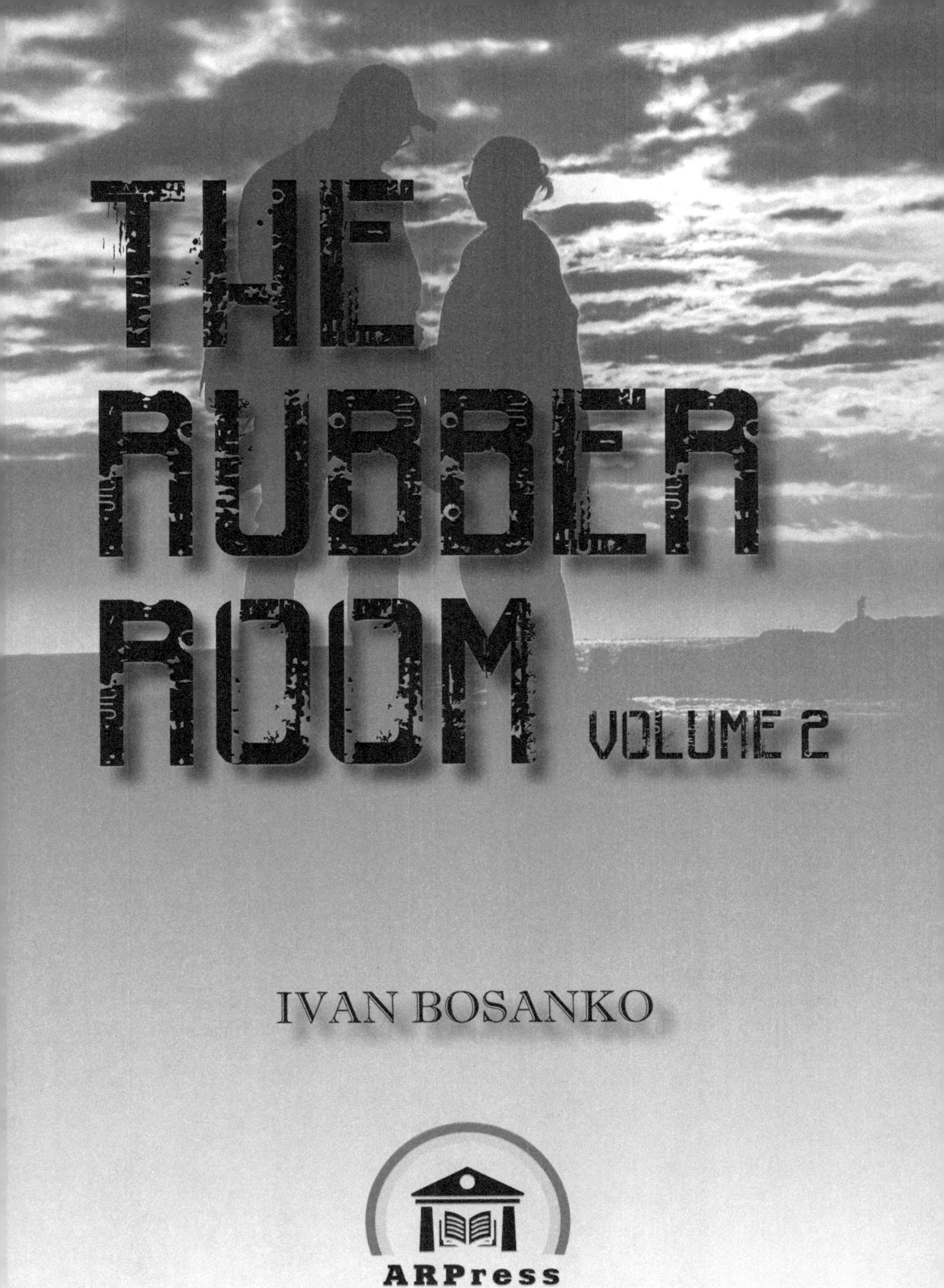

THE RUBBER ROOM

VOLUME 2

IVAN BOSANKO

ARPress
45 Dan Road Suite 5
Canton MA 02021
Hotline: 1(888) 821-0229
Fax: 1(508) 545-7580

Ordering Information:
Quantity sales. Special discounts are available on quantity purchases by corporations, associations, and others. For details, contact the publisher at the address above.

Printed in the United States of America.

ISBN-13:	Softcover	979-8-89330-807-5
	Hardcover	979-8-89330-808-2
	eBook	979-8-89330-809-9

Library of Congress Control Number: 2022913695

To my wife, Margie, who always stood by me through thick and thin.

CONTENTS

PROLOGUE

I t's 1950. It's graduation time for KateLynn "Katey" McCray, the only daughter of strict Irish Catholic parents. Katey's every wish and prayer comes true when her boyfriend, Jerry Landis, proposes to her after the senior prom. Katey risks her virginity to prove that she's shed her tomboy image and is ready for intimacy. Her wedding plans backfire—she's pregnant! To keep from trapping Jerry into marriage and to hide her family's shame and disgrace, Katey must tell the big lie and live the big deception by leaving for Chicago. There, she gives birth to Kristianne Marie (Krissy). Then she completes business college.

Katey leaves Krissy in her aunt's capable hands while she returns home to win back Jerry's affection and reset their wedding date. Jerry no longer trusts her since he's never received one letter from her—those letters that Katey promised to write. Later, he learns that his alcoholic mother has deliberately burned them to break them up. Finally, their wedding date is reset. Three days before they speak their vows, Jerry brings the worst possible news. He's been drafted into the Korean War. He does not want to risk Katey being a young widow, so the wedding is postponed once again.

Jerry is seriously wounded in Korea and is rushed by air ambulance to a special army hospital near Seattle. In a life-and-death struggle, he survives, thanks to expert medical help and Katey being by his side, complete with whiffs from her sensual perfume. Months later, following a very rigid rehab schedule, he is medically discharged. At the Sacramento Airport, he meets Krissy for the first time. What an emotional reunion for all the family members! Katey insists that they receive church counseling before their brief ceremony. Everything blows sky-high over church pledges, church doctrine, and church laws.

Little Krissy tries her best to solve the dilemma in her own way. She tells Grandpa McCray that her daddy can make it all better "'Cause he's my daddy…and my daddy can do anything…but I don't know where my daddy is. Grandpa, where's my daddy?"

CHAPTER 1

Rushton, California, was in the throes of change, so much a part of the 1950s.

This tight-knit community, a scant fifteen miles east of Sacramento, had shed the "company owned" image so long associated with its history. True, the local merchants still depended on the rise and fall of the California Central Railroad (CCR) fortunes. One had only to look at the CCR Headquarters Building. Its ten-story structure of concrete, steel, and glass was the only significant landmark that rose above the one- and two-story businesses and the simple dwellings where twenty-five thousand people called their home.

Despite the heavy commuter traffic headed west to Sacramento each workday, strong reminders of the railroad's grip were still evident. Katey Landis's father, Aaron McCray, was a railroad maintenance foreman. After finishing business college in Chicago, Katey was hired as a professional secretary at CCR. Greg Hibbard had strong ties with the CCR hierarchy. After college, he immediately completed their management trainee program. Now he was ready to climb their corporate ladder. Ricco Petrocelli wanted to be firmly entrenched as the railroad operating engineers' union representative. And last but not least was Jerry Landis. He, too, would be striving for railroad recognition. His pride, stubbornness, and independence meant only one thing —his soul was not for sale…at any price!

For the next five months, Katy and Jerry's religious impasse went exactly nowhere. While Jerry pursued his college studies, Katey continued her secretarial job at CCR Headquarters as though there would be a way out of their predicament. They met four times during these months near the college campus because Jerry did not have transportation at that point. Each time Jerry pressed Katey for an answer, her patent reply came into play: "I'm still hopeful there's a way we both can live with."

On their last meeting, both sensed the futility of their situation. Again, Jerry pressed Katey for an answer to legalize their marriage outside of her Catholic faith. Katey could only swallow hard and look away from their table.

They barely pecked each other on the cheek when Katey dropped him off at the co-op building where he had taken up residence on the campus of Sacramento State University. Somehow, the passion, too, had dried up, right along with their enthusiasm over a way out. They were now resigned to the inevitable. Despite all the doom and gloom surrounding her personal life, Katey still found comfort in her wedding band. It was her one solace, her one bright light, and her one shining hope that somewhere, somehow, a way would be found. To that end, she hung on with tenacious resolve, those inherited traits so much a part of her Irish ways.

Two weeks later, Krissy celebrated her third birthday. In honor of that special occasion, Jerry was invited to her birthday party, complete with ice cream, candies, cake, and all the decorations. He showed up, and everybody had a good time. For an hour, the McCrays made a special effort to get along. Jerry finally excused himself, and Katey followed him outside as they stood on the front steps, facing each other, both keenly aware that they indeed were treading on troubled waters.

"Thanks again for coming, dear. Krissy really appreciated that fold-up blackboard."

"I'm glad punkins liked it. She'll really put it to use. The box of colored chalk didn't hurt either. Now she can draw and color and erase to her heart's content."

Katey touched his arm. "Tonight she didn't mind you calling her punkins at all. Never forget the first time at the airport when you called her that. Wow! She really let you know her name was Krissy, not punkins. She hasn't forgotten you, love. And she still calls you her daddy. Do you have to leave so early, Jerry? Gee, I hardly ever get to see you anymore."

Jerry hooked his cane over one of the handrails then turned to her with all five feet, ten inches of solid build. His deep blues were never more serious so much a part of his makeup to go along with good looks, complemented by his blond hair. "Got two finals tomorrow morning. Probably stay up all night with a pot of coffee. Don't know what the problem is, Katey. I can't seem to keep focused on my lessons. Either that, or maybe I forget how to study in the first place. I know one thing for sure. Being away in the army for almost two years does make a difference. My classmates are two years younger, and they're sharp.

They're leaving old Jerry sucking up their exhaust."

Katey laughed. "Don't worry. You'll catch up to them. And when you do, they'll be the ones left sucking old fumes."

He looked down to her, a full seven inches shorter. He was still full of love for his one and only. "Thanks, Katey. You were always my old confidence builder. Guess I'll always have you to thank for that. Goes way back to grade school, doesn't it?"

Katey's wistful smile came into play, her blue greens just like her mother's, Mary. She truly was the reincarnation of Mary with two differences. Both had oval-shaped faces with pixie-like noses. And both had wisps of reddish-brown hair along each side of their head just above their ears, which complemented dark brown hair. The difference was that Katey was ten pounds lighter and now sported a chic professional business woman's hairstyle. Its short cut was so much a part of the fifties. "Gosh, that seems like a million years ago. So much has happened."

"I'm going to look for some wheels soon. I need to get out more. Can't keep borrowing my friend's car every time I need to leave campus."

"That reminds me! Don't leave! I'll be right back!"

Katey returned and handed Jerry a savings passbook. "This is yours. It was our emergency fund money. I meant to return it to you. Don't really know why I held onto it this long."

"I do, Katey. You still had high hopes that we'd get together somehow… even it if hasn't worked out that way."

"Jerry, if you need extra money, I can help out now. I'm in pretty good shape."

"Thanks, Katey. This money will do just fine. Should see me through till I get my degree." A twinkle greeted Katey as his slow smile set her up. "Yes, you certainly are, Katey. Even better tonight, I'd say…"

"What are you talking about?" Katey questioned.

"Said you were in pretty good shape. I couldn't agree more!"

She gave him her old tomboy jab. "Darn you, Landis. You never miss a trick, do you?"

Jerry picked up his cane, ready to say goodbye, then leaned it against his pant leg for one last thought. "Well, we tried, Katey. We certainly gave it our best shot."

"Please don't ask. I know your question is coming, and you already know my answer. Let's change subjects please! How come we never talk about our feelings anymore? How come we never say how much we miss each other?

How come we don't call each other and say I love you over the phone? How come we don't kiss like we mean it and hold each other close anymore?"

"Katey, why do you torture yourself with questions when we both know you're avoiding the hard choice? The one only you can make?"

"Please, please, can't we just have a conversation about something else?" "All right. What happened to all that furniture your folks bought for us?"

"Oh, guess I never mentioned it, but Dad and Mom talked the furniture people into taking it back. After all, it was still new…never used. They finally did get their money back."

"Good! I didn't want them to lose a dime over us. Suppose all that other stuff is gathering lint back in your hope chest, right?"

"Yes, sure looks pretty hopeless too! I've meant to ask you before, when we got together off campus, how does this co-op work where you're living now?"

He smiled. "Kinda like the army. Each of us has a duty assignment for a week straight. My job this week is dish duty. Next week, I help do the cooking. We save a lot that way. Lots cheaper than living in a dorm because we do all the work!"

"Right up your alley, Jerry. If there's a way to save some bucks, you'll find it! Nobody—and I mean this sincerely and as a compliment— nobody I've ever met can get more out of the same dollar than you do."

He laughed. "I never had any for so many, many years that when I did finally accumulate a few bucks, I decided I'm going to get my money's worth. Come all heck or high water."

Suddenly, the talk stopped. Katey didn't wait for Jerry to find her lips. She reached up then pulled his head down before he realized what was happening.

They feasted on each other's lips as though they were at their last supper. Their hunger, their passion stimulated their desire like never before. Jerry broke the embrace just as Katey moved her hips into his. "We shouldn't do this anymore, Katey."

"Why not, my love? We both want to."

"It gets things started, and it's so hard to put out the fire." *Better switch gears,* he thought. "Let me tell you about what I've done this past week, Katey."

Katey kept her body pressed against his as she held him tight, her hands clasped around his waist. "Okay, what have you done, dear?"

"I… I've kept my promise to God by joining a nondenominational church on the north side. We have about two hundred fifty members from all walks of life, even a couple of agnostics. People just like me… dissatisfied with what the big churches are doing or offering, looking for a grassroots way to really help those in need with action and not words."

"Go on, dear. Sounds good to me."

"It's a hands-on type of church. Nothing pretentious like your Catholic church, but I can really see what's happening and where the money's going."

"That's you all over again, Jerry."

"Like I said, it's a nuts-and-bolts operation. No, better make that bailing wire and pliers. That'd be more like it. But I love it! It's my type of church.

They're really committed to doing something!"

"Tell me, sweet, why do you always try to belittle yourself and your accomplishments? Like you're never going to be accepted for who you are, not where you come from? And look at you now! A war hero! You're head and shoulders above any man I've ever known, with the possible exception of my father. You're still selling yourself short…far short of your potential."

He moved away from her, out of her clasp, bent on walking away. His hand knocked his cane down the steps as he stood and watched it, in utter futility, land on the lawn next to the steps. It gave him time to utter his parting shots. "Let's do a little switch and talk about you, Katey. Your D-day is here! Two weeks early, but it's here. *It's now or never!* What's your decision?"

Katey scooted down the steps to pick up the cane. As she handed it back,

she held up her wedding band as close to his face as possible without touching him. *"Were still married. Nothing's ever going to change that!* How dare you put a time limit on our lives and our marriage! Don't you see it, Jerry? We're missing something. All we need is a little more time…that's all."

"Oh, really? C'mon, Katey, time to fess up! Our marriage is going nowhere! How can you say we're still married when another couple lives in our duplex on campus, the one we vacated? And what kind of marriage do we have when I have to live with seventeen other fellas in a co-op on campus? And what kind of a marriage could we possibly have when the last time we were intimate, the last time we…no, make that you made love to me, was nearly fourteen months ago up in Madigan General, when I was flat on my back? Does any of this sound like a marriage that's working?"

"Just a few minutes ago, we were in each other's arms. And nobody, not even you, Jerry Landis, can deny that anything is missing between us. The passion is there, the feelings are very much alive, and our love for each other is nonstop."

"But you didn't say one word that our marriage was there! Katey, don't fill your mind and heart with what ifs, regrets, or what might have been. One more time, the last time! Make your decision tonight, or slip the ring off, and we agree to release each other from all vows and commitments!"

She shook her head in disbelief, unable to accept his demand, let alone his words. "Still don't get it, do you? There'll be no taking this wedding band off! Never, Jerry! Never! You made that commitment to me and to God up in our mountain honeymoon cabin just before you shipped off to Korea, and I'm going to hold you to it till doomsday. The mere thought that you're even thinking about backing out sickens me!"

Jerry grabbed his cane and turned his back on her while he gingerly dragged his left leg down the front steps to the car. Katey got to the car first then put one hand on the car door handle, blocking his attempt. "Don't you dare think of running out on me! Do you hear me? When will we see each other again? I demand an answer! And it better be darned soon! Jerry?"

Katey saw his hand shake. Then he forced her hand off the car door latch, more to keep from unleashing his anger on her than to open the door. Twice he seemed ready to say something, then when the right choice of words came, he let her have it, full bore. "Under the circumstances between us, Katey, I'm doing us both a personal kindness and a great favor when I say never plus ten years!"

CHAPTER 2

For the next thirteen months, Katey went into a protective shell to keep her sanity. So devastating and so complete was Jerry's adamant denial of any marriage bond still existing between them. She badgered Greg at work to find out how Jerry was doing, not daring to pick up a telephone to confront him with the rumors that he'd been dating again. It was something she refused to believe until Greg swore to her it was true.

Graduation time for Jerry came, and Katey was keenly aware of the date. It was circled and underlined on the kitchen calendar. How proud she still felt regarding him and all his personal accomplishments, even though she was certain that there would be no invitation from him to attend his graduation exercise. She took some comfort in the fact that even Jerry would have to admit she had played a major role in his maturing and his development into what he had become—a most remarkable young man.

He showed up one day during her lunch break with her good friend, Mora Woodson, at the corporate headquarters' cafeteria. Mora conveniently excused herself, and the two tried their best to maintain some semblance of reasonable conduct toward each other. Jerry made the first overture for a truce between them by offering to refill Katey's coffee cup. She accepted, so he complied by not only refilling hers but also picking up a fresh cup for himself.

She watched him return with two cups on a tray and was amazed at the dexterity he exhibited using his cane to weave between tables, chairs, and the luncheon crowd. He pulled up a chair, hung his cane on the back of another, and promptly poured sugar straight into his coffee without bothering to use a spoon. He glanced up, noticed her surprised expression, and said, "Started using sugar when I joined the co-op. Another bad habit, but what the heck? Lost count of them."

"Aren't you a bit early, Landis? Thought the next time you wanted to see me was…oh yes, it's a gem, a real Landis classic—never plus ten years!"

Katey's sarcastic needling pricked a very sore spot. Jerry put his cup down, reached for his cane, and got up. "You're right! Better make that *never plus twenty!*"

Two tables away, she caught up then grabbed his right arm with the cane. "Come back! Please sit down with me! Jerry, I'm sorry. It's just that you show up out of the blue, thirteen months later…no phone calls, no nothing! Couldn't hardly forget the way you nearly ripped the car door handle off when you left last time. Came plenty close to really telling me off, didn't you? Any of that changed, Jerry?"

"Yes, some! What I stopped by to tell you is that I just finished my job interview, and they've hired me. I'll be working down the street in the CCR Support Services Building in the accounting department. We'll probably run into each other from time to time, so I thought maybe we could bury the hatchet and stay friends. What do you say, amigo?"

Katey motioned for a reluctant Jerry to follow her back to their table. They sat down.

"You want us to be just friends, right, Jerry? Not good friends, dear friends, or maybe something more?"

"Still got that communication problem going full blast! Time for one last adios! This conversation is just like all the rest—going nowhere!"

"No, no, Jerry. I get your point! Friends it'll be! Now where do we go from there?"

"Well, I could tell you about my new job. That is, if you'd care to listen?" "Please, go ahead!"

"I was hired specifically to eliminate waste and duplication, make recommendations and changes, and reduce paperwork, forms, and reports wherever necessary. The bottom line is, they're convinced our whole accounting systems needs a drastic overhaul. That's where I fit in. I'm excited about the challenge and the responsibility. The short and long-term picture for me looks good if I can show them I'm worth my salt. There's plenty of opportunity for good pay raises and promotion. What do ya think, Katey?"

"I'm sure CCR picked the right guy for the job. Nobody—and I mean this sincerely—can spread a buck better than you can. You've always had a nose for waste and duplication and saving money!"

For once, he had an attentive ear from someone who still cared. He held his head high to help spread a smile a mile wide across his face. If he had a vest, it'd pop the buttons!

He felt pumped by Katey's compliment. "I really believe I got the job because I'm a few years older than the usual accounting grad. I also believe I show a bit more maturity in that regard. Plus I'm sure they took my veteran and disability status into consideration."

"You always showed a lot more maturity for your age, Jerry. That's one of the things I first noticed about you. And when Mother and Father got to know you much better, they said the same thing."

"Thanks. You always did back me, and I'm here to say thanks, regardless of our personal differences." Jerry tried his best to return Katey's compliment. "Gosh, you're looking great as usual. Sure like that powder blue jacket and skirt! Me?" He glanced down. "I'm just what you see, faded old jeans and a wrinkled sports shirt. Sure hope they don't require a dress code on my new job.

That a new outfit, Katey?"

"Yes. Decided to go out and splurge a bit. I've had two merit raises since we last saw each other. First one was small, but my second one was a dandy."

"No doubt there. You deserved them, Katey."

"Thank you, Jerry Landis! You know, you sure left a pretty big impression on Krissy. And the more I think about it, the more remarkable it is, considering you only spent less than two days with her after your army discharge. Just this morning, she asked me if I'd seen her daddy. She asks about you all the time. I never went into detail with her about us, about our differences. When she's older, I'll try to explain more fully."

"Bet she's grown like a weed! Hope she still has that beautiful long blond hair and that her eyes keep their deep-blue sparkle!"

"She won't let me touch her hair. Still keeps it in a ponytail. Her eyes are more of a deeper blue than ever." Katey laughed. "If that's possible. Before long, she'll be five. Right now, she's in preschool and really likes her teacher. You ought to see the colorings and drawings she brings home to me and Grandpa and Grandma. They really are very good. There must have been an artist somewhere in her family's background. Hard to believe it, Jerry, but next year, she'll be starting the first grade at old Public School [PS] Fifty-Nine.

That's where we first started out! Remember?"

"Punkins in PS Fifty-Nine? Wow, Katey, time really flies!"

He finished his cup then put it back on the tray. "Times change. People sometimes change when circumstances change. Who knows, Katey?"

"Yeah, real life sure doesn't turn out much like those 'and they lived happily ever after' stories we read in grade school. Pity real life doesn't always have those wonderful storyline endings."

"That reminds me, Katey, my graduation is set for two in the afternoon this coming Saturday. I don't have any family to invite, so I thought that since you've been such a big part of my getting this far in life, maybe you and punkins would care to attend?"

"We'd be honored, Jerry. Wait'll I tell Krissy tonight. She'll be so excited to see you again!"

Jerry opened his billfold and fished out two tickets. He handed them to Katey. "They are almost worth their weight in gold. Seating is very limited. One thing, though."

"What's that?"

"I've invited another friend to attend, so please don't have Krissy call me Daddy. It could be a bit embarrassing."

Katey fought hard to keep her temper under control. "Oh, of course, Jerry. We wouldn't want anybody, especially Carol Kingman, to think that now, would we?"

"Cut out the sarcastic crap, Katey! How in the world could you possibly remember her name?"

"Jerry Landis, I make it a point to know what's going on in my husband's life. Just because you walked out on me and your commitment to God, that hasn't changed one thing with me as far as I'm concerned. I'll give you this. Your openhanded about it. At least you're not keeping your affair a secret! How many married men do you know who have the guts to trot out their mistress for their wife to sit beside on graduation day?"

Jerry poked two fingers deep into Katey's shoulder. "Gimmie those tickets back! Forget the invite. This isn't going to work! Let's set the record straight one last time. Carol isn't my mistress, and you and I were never legally married! I want those tickets back now!"

Houdini on his best day couldn't have done better. Two tickets disappeared into her purse in nothing flat. She rose from the table with her not-quite-so- warm goodbye. "Krissy and I will be there! Thanks for the invite!"

CHAPTER 3

Because of a week's worth of inclement weather, Jerry's graduation exercise was moved from the outdoor football stadium to the sports field house on campus.

The building was so jam-packed with graduates and faculty members on stage that there was barely room for the invited guests and friends on the main floor. Katey and Krissy arrived early and were quickly ushered to their seats. Her dark-blue dress with its thin red waist belt blended in perfectly with the rainbow of colors scattered among those attending. Krissy looked adorable in a lightly starched yellow dress. The traditional processional and recessional marches were waived in favor of a few strains of classical music provided by a college string ensemble, tucked away in one corner next to the stage.

Following a short opening prayer by one of the local clergy, the main guest speaker, CCR President Appleton, delivered a stirring speech in which he challenged each graduate to go out into the world and use the tools his training had prepared him for. "These are trying times," he added. "The job market is weak, so make the most of every opportunity that comes your way."

Carol Kingman arrived late and found her empty seat beside Katey. They exchanged cool greetings, each well aware of the other's role in Jerry's life. Little Krissy gave Carol a friendly and innocent dimpled smile, and she received a scowl and a stare for her trouble.

Then came the presentation and awarding of degrees, a lengthy and somewhat tedious part of the graduation program. When Gerald Landis's name was called out, a full sense of pride overcame Katey. She decided to do a little spadework of her own on Carol. "Are you still connected with real estate sales?"

Carol surveyed her competition. The medium-sized brunette's rust-colored dress went well with her disposition along with sharp brown eyes. Her haughty head toss gave Katey fair warning. "Oh, yes, I've stayed with commercial properties. The residential market is flat. It means fewer sales, but the commissions are much better."

"What are your plans for the future? Do you intend on staying in the area for some time?"

Carol sensed Katey's question was double-loaded, and she was right. She blushed a bit and then regrouped her thoughts. "Yes, I plan on staying here for quite a while. I like it here. And of course, Jerry's been a big influence on my future plans."

Katey accepted the answer with the coolness of a casino card dealer. "Oh, I hadn't realized that." Then Katey boldly shook hands with Carol. "I want to thank you, Carol."

"For what, Katey?"

"For being there with Jerry when I couldn't, for being his friend when he needed one, and for letting him lean on your shoulder. I'm surprised he hasn't told you more about us, but I'm getting ahead of myself. He's probably waiting till after his graduation today to tell you the good news himself."

"Tell me what?"

"Our marriage has been going through a difficult time. There were some misunderstandings, partly his fault. And in all fairness, I'm to blame too."

Carol came unhinged. "He never said one single word about being married.

I don't understand. Why didn't he mention it?"

Katey made sure Carol saw her wedding band as she patted Krissy on the head.

"Then there's my daughter, Krissy, here. She's been crying quite a bit lately. She misses her daddy an awful lot. We're all going to be so glad to see him back home with us again. We've patched things up. We're both going to work a lot harder to keep our marriage. We promised each other that. And in the meantime, I have you to thank for helping us save our marriage. We were planning on going out for a big dinner in honor of our reconciliation, and we'd love to have you come join us."

Carol got up, tensing to blend in with a very stern looking face. She exploded. "Tell Jerry he can go you know where! This all was one big mistake!" Katey looked downhearted. "Please stay, won't you? I brought my Polaroid, and we were counting on you to snap a picture of Jerry in his graduation gown, reunited with his family once more. Surely you'll stay for that, won't you?"

Carol never bothered to answer Katey. Two minutes later, nobody ever knew she'd been there.

After the benediction, Jerry came racing down the platform as fast as his cane would allow, sure that he'd arrive just in time to either arbitrate a shouting match or referee a possible slugfest. To his astonishment, he found Katey with her camera poised. "Smile, dear. Make sure you look your best!" He stopped long enough for one flash.

"Where's Carol?" he demanded.

"Carol decided she had better things to do with her life, so she took off."

Krissy leaped into Jerry's arms. "Daddy! Daddy! You sure looked neat up there."

He scooped her up and kissed her cheek. "Hi, punkins! My, how you've grown. Betcha got a new dress on, huh?"

"Yup, Mommy said we both had to look extra nice for you today."

He let her cling around his neck while he looked at Katey. "Mommy's right.

Both of you sure do!"

Katey asked a bystander to take their picture together. The woman obliged as the threesome posed for their family picture. After thanking the lady, Jerry resumed his grilling. "Okay, Katey, spill it. What did you do?"

"I told Carol like it is. I told her we were still married. And, Jerry, we have tender ears with us today, so watch your language."

"I'm sorry, Katey. Guess I wasn't thinking. I was expecting—well, you know what I mean."

Katey touched his arm and kissed him on the cheek. "Please, Jerry, let's be a family for today. It'll mean an awful lot to Krissy and to me. I promise, no more shouting or giving you a hard time. Let's be the best friends we can be. Okay?"

Jerry put Krissy down then put his arm around Katey's waist. With Krissy just a step or two ahead, they headed for the main aisle.

"All right. I still want to be best friends with you no matter what, Katey. Like you've always said, there's too much between us not to be. You mentioned doing something as a family."

She kissed him on the lips. "For starters, my congratulations kiss. We're both so very, very proud of you!"

"Daddy, can I kiss you too? Mommy did!"

He dropped to one knee. "Of course, punkins. Here, pucker up!"

Krissy planted a juicy smack on Jerry. Katey laughed. "She'll get better. Just give her time!"

They continued down the aisle, Jerry in his gown still and carrying Krissy. "She gets any bigger, old Dad here better forget 'bout carrying her. What do you have in mind today, Katey? Anything special?"

"Let's go where the uptown crowd eats. Let's go to Templins for a real dinner. I mean dinner and wine with all the trimmings. It's on me. I feel like celebrating."

"Hey, you burn a twenty just opening the door to talk to the maître d'. Sure you want to do it?"

"You bet! Let's go!"

And go they did for the most elegant dinner they ever had. They dined on fresh Dungeness crab flown in from the icy cold waters of Washington State's Puget Sound. It was served on decorative seashell china. The crabmeat was dipped in a special butter sauce. The taste? Out of this world! Krissy was not only fascinated with the beautiful linen tablecloth but how their linen napkins had to be slipped out of their sterling silver ring holders before using. And the finger bowls continued to be great fun and games for her. When it came time for dessert, they chose mousse, a house specialty of a slightly chilled concoction of egg whites and whipping cream combined with the house special ingredients. Their service was fantastic to the point of almost being smothering. When the bill was finally presented to Katey, she nearly went into sticker shock. Before paying it, she gave Jerry his graduation present.

Krissy clapped her hands together with glee. "Open it, Daddy! Hurry!"

Jerry opened the small box that contained a very expensive wristwatch. He was touched as he turned to her. "Oh, Katey, this is so beautiful. So expensive."

Katey fairly beamed. "Turn it over, dear. Read the inscription." He did. "My bean counter extraordinaire. All my love, Katey."

Their kiss was so long and tender that poor Krissy thought sure that they were stuck together. After Katey paid for dinner, the threesome rode in the Chevy back to the parking lot outside the field house where Jerry had left his car. Katey turned to Krissy. "Mommy'll be back in a minute, dear. I need to talk to Daddy alone."

They walked over to Jerry's car, hand in hand. "Thanks again, Katey. Today we truly were a family again. I want us to be together more. I really miss that!"

"How about Sunday dinner tomorrow? No Catholic church service required and no strings attached."

"You're on! What time?"

"Dinner's at six in the evening, but come early if you can. We still enjoy your company."

Jerry unlocked the door to his clunker. Katey teased, "Wait till that monster eats up your paycheck like the Chevy did mine. Then you'll wonder why you bother working!"

They both laughed. Then Katey turned serious. "I'm sorry about everything.

The way I acted. I refused to understand that, in your mind, you saw our commitment differently. What happened in Korea changed a lot of things. I see it now. Before Korea, you would've gone along as before. No problem attending mass with me on Sunday mornings. That's the part my folks don't understand. I'm beginning to think more and more about what you said about the lion's share of contributions going to line the pockets of the church, leaving very little to do God's work. That part, my parents will never accept either. I had a real hard time with that at first."

"Katey, I know your folks can't change. You and I have to. We have to make some changes or else there's no future for us together. That's why I asked for my release from our commitment. Can you possibly see or understand my thinking on that?"

"I do, if I put myself in your place. For me, I could never accept that because of my close ties with my church and my parents. Also, my commitment to our marriage vows cannot be changed. Maybe it's old- fashioned, but that's me. From your standpoint, you see no hope of us ever working this out, do you? That's why you want your freedom again."

Krissy would say they stuck like glue again before Jerry finished his thought. "There's no hope for us ever bridging those problems. Each of us is too set in our ways and what we believe in, even for the sake of our marriage. I've gone without sleep till I've had headaches, agonizing over this, and I see no answer, no way out."

She looked up into his eyes. "I've said this before, but somehow, someway, we're missing something. Like it's in front of us and we're too close. We have too many common interests, have known each other too long to see it. Jerry, I really believe that knowing each other like we do doesn't help in this case. That it may actually be the reason were apart."

"I've thought about that too, and I've come up with nothing. Absolutely nothing."

"Jerry, kiss me goodbye. Kiss me again like you used to. Lord, how I miss that and everything that went into our relationship. I'd give anything to have it back, to be one with you again."

He held her close. Their bodies moved together as one for a few precious wonderful moments. There was no hiding their want, their desire for intimacy, while two young innocent deep-blue eyes curiously watched every gesture, every move.

"Lord, Katey, you make it awful hard to stay just very good friends," he whispered in her ear. "Especially when we've had it all… the pleasure we've given each other."

"Jerry, we'd better break this up. Krissy doesn't understand yet."

"She will someday. Just give her time. Oh, by the way, next time I see Carol, I'd better apologize to her for you running her off. What should I say?"

"I told it like it is. Just remember, as far as I am concerned, the only thing on loan from my husband is his friendship. Nothing else!"

They drove off in different directions, Jerry back to his co-op and Katey the dozen or so miles to Rushton. Krissy was awfully quiet, too quiet for Katey's liking. "C'mon, dear, scoot over by Mommy and tell me about your big day."

"I can tell you like Daddy an awful lot 'cause you give him lots of big smooches!"

"That all right with you?"

"It's okay, 'cause he gives me smooches too!"

Katey put one arm around Krissy. "Oh, my precious, I love you so very, very much!"

"Why doesn't Daddy come home anymore? Gabriel told me her daddy comes home all the time at her house."

"I'm so glad you have such nice friends at preschool like Gabriel. Punkins, with your daddy and me, it's different. We have to work out some grown-up things. When you get a little older, I'll try to explain."

"That's what you told me when Daddy went away last time."

"I know, I know, Krissy. You'll just have to wait a bit longer. Maybe those grown-up things between your daddy and me will work out, and then he will start coming home to us like Gabriel's daddy does."

They reached the outskirts of town. Krissy, again, seemed unusually quiet. "Mommy, what does a big mistake mean?"

"Oh, you remember that lady who sat next to us saying that, don't you? A big mistake is when somebody does something that later on they wished they hadn't done."

Krissy wrinkled up her nose, scratched her ear, then her dimpled cheeks. And with all the charm and innocence a near five-year-old could possibly muster, she sweetly asked, "Was I a big mistake, Mommy?"

Her question so unnerved Katey that she pulled out of the traffic lane to stop the car. She hugged poor Krissy so hard it was a wonder she didn't break. Her eyes watered. Then she kissed Krissy again and again. "A big mistake? Hardly! You're the one miracle in my life, the one reason I believe God is going to help us find a way to bring your daddy back to us for good!"

CHAPTER 4

The following four months, Jerry, Katey, and Krissy were a family. That is, they did things and shared the good times. And in the process, they became nearly inseparable. The effect Jerry had on Krissy was nothing short of phenomenal. Each weekend, they went somewhere and did something. If it wasn't visiting the zoo, it was taking in a drive-in movie. If pizza wasn't their thing, a picnic basket and a game of softball catch was the order of the day. Then the county fair came along with its cotton candy and carnival rides. It was as if he was trying, in his way, to make up for the weeks, months, and years he'd been absent from the scene. It was payback time for Katey having to raise Krissy on her own.

There was a downside too, and Katey, only too well, read the inevitable signs. Jerry was equating his success with Krissy on his own terms. He was ready to father his own children. All he needed was the right woman to be his wife with the same family values and commitment he once shared with Katey. No less than a dozen times, Katey saw Jerry and Krissy do something together.

Then afterward, she watched Jerry look away as though he was visualizing what it might be like romping or playing with his own son or daughter instead of Krissy. On at least three of those occasions, Katey was sorely tempted to tell him the whole truth and let the chips fall where they may. And as always, the answer rang back in her mind louder than a grade school recess bell. *If you can't solve your own religious problems, adding Krissy to the mix will surely turn a bittersweet dilemma into another unsolvable mess.*

Four months to the day, Jerry came busting in on Katey and Krissy on Friday night. "C'mon, you two. Time to celebrate. I sold my recommendations in the accounting department! You're looking at Mr. Seelig's accounting assistant!"

Katey rushed up to hug and kiss him. "Tell us all about it. I'm as excited as you!"

"Got all evening to shoot the bull! Let's stop by the Colonel's for takeout chicken and play some softball catch till dark! Krissy, grab those three gloves and bring the ball!"

"Okay, Daddy. Let's go!"

They wound up at Ormandy Park down by the Sacramento River. Katey brought along some pop and potato salad from the refrigerator. They spread out a big blanket and dived into the food. Afterward, Krissy spotted the swings and slide, so she took off to join a dozen other kids in the park playground. Jerry and Katey moved their blanket a bit closer under a tree so they could keep a watchful eye on Krissy's whereabouts.

"Okay, Mr. Hotshot, tell me about your big day before I hug and squeeze it out of you! I'm dying to hear it. Don't leave out a single detail!"

Jerry picked up a blade of grass and put it between his teeth. "I can tell you, Katey, I was smoother than a snake oil salesman making my pitch. First to Seelig, then up to the ivory tower to the big cheese himself, old Carlson, the comptroller."

"How did Carlson receive it?"

"He bought it all the way! Made two hundred fifty-seven recommendations and changes. And between Seelig and Carlson, they signed off and approved two hundred fifty-one of them! How's that for really getting the job done? Huh?"

"So now what's up? I assume CCR will be keeping you on permanently now."

"Keeping me? Katey, Monday morning I write my own job description. And if Carlson approves it, I wind up with a hefty thirty percent raise and a new job title. Hey, Katey, try this on for size— CCR accounting administrative manager!"

Katey's enthusiasm spilled over. She kissed him again and again. "Katey, please sit down. People are starting to stare!"

"I don't care. Oh, Jerry, I just knew that once they turned you loose, there'd be no stopping you! Here, lay down on my lap! Tell me more!"

He removed the blade of grass then looked up. "One of my biggest money- saving recommendations was over the paper products we use. Such things as check blanks for payroll, paper supplies for fiscal reports and statements, things like that. Mr. Seelig opposed me at first, but when I showed him the seven proposals I had by going out for competitive bidding each year for our paper goods alone, he had to go along. Katey, there's over a million dollars saving there alone by going my route. Know what? Now that I get to thinking about it, I'll bet Seelig has a connection with our longtime paper goods supplier, Lentz Paper. He tried to shut me down 'cause he's probably picking up a pretty good chunk of loose change by sticking with Lentz all these years."

"Jerry, you'd better watch your back. You're the young upstart rocking the corporate boat! What other big changes did they buy?"

He looked up into her face. She ran her fingers through his haircut. "Miss my army crew cut?"

"Not in the slightest, dear. Now I've got something long enough to work with!"

He smiled then laughed. "Gee, Katey, I've heard it called a lot of things, but long enough to work with…yup, that's a new one!"

She slapped him lightly. "Landis, get your mind out of the gutter!"

"Last time you said the same thing about me, you only had it up to about one hundred fifty things about me that needed changing or correcting. And since we're getting along so great, well, shucks, I thought your list should be at least down to one hundred ten!"

She roughhoused him all over the blanket. "Darn you, Jerry Landis! I know you're setting me up, and I fall for them every time!"

"This one's a dilly! It'll cost us a bundle now!"

"I thought you were hired to cut down expenses, not spend more."

"That's right. I was. But I showed them some brochures on a whole new line of automated equipment that will pay for itself in the first year alone! From then on out, it's another two million savings each year! How'm I doing, Katey?"

"No wonder you got their attention, dear! Just the same, watch your back. Seelig's probably going along because he wants to take as much credit as he can and still look like he's on your side. I assume you submitted your own report and projections to Carlson, and Seelig initialed it or signed it, right?"

"Not exactly."

"What do you mean not exactly? Didn't you do all the spadework to come up with all the changes? Why allow Seelig to horn in and grab some of the credit?"

"Seelig retyped my report…said his format was really better for presenting it to Carlson. He signed it and had me initial the smaller changes. Of course, he had me present it and explain it to Carlson and answer most of the questions. Said that would be my job from now on as his new assistant. I was satisfied."

Katey was upset. She waved a cautionary finger over Jerry's face "From now on, you blow your own horn. Don't let Seelig blow it for you. That's the only way you'll ever be recognized for your contributions. And knowing you, there'll be lots more coming! Right? Oh, Jerry, not too far in the distant future, I expect you to be there on the seventh floor, taking Carlson's job as comptroller. You're going to be recognized in this railroad. I just know it!"

"Katey, I'm a hands-on type of guy. I like to see firsthand the changes I want to make, not from some corporate think tank or some ivory tower. Just give me a little recognition and the bucks to go along with it. That's all I want.

They can have the credit and glory. That's not for me!"

She stopped stroking his hair. "Yeah, dear, I still have your Silver Star and Purple Heart to prove it. You're low-key, so laid-back, but, boy, do I ever love you!"

He sat up. Then he pulled another blade of grass and pointed it at Katey. "You know, Katey, it's a whole different world up there where Carlson is…a lot like the Catholic church in a way. No wonder the overhead and administrative costs are killing this railroad. They're borrowing millions to keep their heads about water. It's only a matter of time till this railroad goes under or else merges with another to survive."

"You've been here just four months and already you see what's going to happen, don't you?"

"Yeah, a blind man with no Braille training at all should be able to follow our railroad's fortune. It's all downhill unless we make more drastic cuts and changes."

"And you still insist you're not corporate management material? Jerry, if you don't make a real concerted and conscientious effort to get to that seventh floor, I'll never speak to you! What a waste of talent! You already have the common sense, logic, and rare insight to financial operations that most executives would drool over just to get the chance to pick your brains!"

"But, Katey!"

"Yeah, I know. Just a low-key, hands-on-type of guy. Give Landis a few bucks, he'll be happy and let the other guy get all the credit!"

They watched Krissy at play for a minute. Katey said, "Maybe she'll meet a good-looking blond boy in the fourth grade. And who knows, they might develop a bad case of puppy love and let it all grow right on up through high school and college. Isn't that what happened to us, my love?"

"Yes, but I hope if that happens to punkins, it turns out a lot better for her." He shook his head in dismay. "Your dad keeps harping on it, and I know it's true. We're a mixed-up, messed-up generation. We don't know up from down or sideways."

"So where is this all going? How do you see it ending up for us?"

"One of us has to make the break. Then maybe, at some class reunion, we'll sit down and rehash old times. I'll probably drag out some snapshots from my billfold and show them to you. Later that night, you'll snuggle up to your strong Catholic hubby and say, 'Gee, dear, just think. I nearly ended up with that jerk, Jerry Landis.'"

"I don't care for your ending one bit, and I never want you to say those things to me again. Do you understand? I won't settle for anybody but you. Surely you must see that by now."

"I do, Katey. And that bothers me a lot. You have a daughter to raise, and I think we can both agree she really does need a full-time daddy. The best I can do for her is be a part-time daddy. The sooner I'm out of punkins' and your personal picture, the better off both of you will be. Then maybe, just maybe, you'll see that I did the right thing and you'll start to look around. There's bound to be fifty guys out there who'd kiss where you walked just to get close to you."

She cupped his face between both hands to make sure he stayed focused on her words. "That will never happen, my love, and we both know it!"

CHAPTER 5

The next couple of weekends, Katey noticed a big change in Jerry. The inevitable had come true, just as she feared it would. In his logical, rational Landis way, Jerry was comparing and gauging her. Not only her physical and emotional characteristics but also her worth as a companion and dear friend against those possibilities and potential Carol Kingman offered.

She had always treasured their goodbye embrace and kisses. They were the barometer to his heart and to his mindset. Oh, how she reveled in and relished them, controlling him as she pleased, drawing from them such immense pleasure and satisfaction. Now his kisses were less passionate. Some of his desire was lacking along with his usual drive to possess her. For in the Jerry Landis equation of love, there was no room for two women in these matters. He could never be a Ricco, one who could turn it on or off with equal passion and ardor. No, for Jerry, the equation must always be in balance. If you give to one, you must take from the other.

On this particular Friday night, the threesome had gone to a drive-in movie theater. Krissy was dressed in her pajamas so that when they arrived home, Katey had only to open the car and house doors, and Jerry would deposit his sleeping bundle of blond hair and blue eyes into Krissy's bedroom.

They walked quietly out of the bedroom. "I could go for a sandwich and a cup of coffee," he said. "Let's drive downtown. Shamrock's is open all night. What do you say?"

"Sure, hon. I'm not ready for bed either."

They finished their sandwiches, and the waitress refilled their cups. "Katey…"

"Don't, Jerry. Please don't. I know what's on your mind, and I don't want to hear it. Please, dear, not tonight."

"I have to, Katey, or else I might not be able to for a long time. It needs to be said."

Katey started pouring more sugar, stirring vigorously, trying to choke back the tears, trying to stave off the words she knew were coming. "Being around Krissy these past months has helped me arrive at a decision. Remember up in the cabin when you told me you had to fly back to Chicago to get Krissy and that I had to trust your judgment?"

Katey turned away and blinked for a few seconds. "Yes, I said I had to have her. I needed her all the more since you were leaving for Korea."

"Now I know what you were trying to tell me. I'm in the same boat. I need to start a family. I'm ready, and you'll have to trust my decision too."

"But, Jerry, this is different. Way different."

"I want that feeling of real fatherhood, just as you wanted motherhood with Krissy. Can you understand, Katey? I have the same need you had."

"Yes, I can, Jerry. But there's really one big difference! How can you love me and be my husband the way it used to be between us and then tell me you want that with somebody else?"

"I'm a realist. I know my marriage will never be like it was between us. Don't worry, I'm not kidding myself on that score. But what I do believe is that I can be a good husband and father and make a successful marriage with Carol. It happens every day somewhere in this big country of ours. Not perfect marriages, but good and solid relationships built upon mutual commitment, trust, and respect. That's all I ask or expect! Nothing more!"

They both sipped their java for what seemed an eternity, each holding their cups high, waiting for one of them to make conversation. Katey's cup rested on their tabletop first.

"You're wrong, Jerry. You're dead wrong about this! It'll never work! There's too many pieces missing in this for you to succeed. All your life, you've never failed at anything you've ever tried. This time, I won't be in your corner to make sure you succeed. This time, you'll fail miserably. There's still time for us to make some changes. We've both made mistakes. People who do real honest- to-goodness living make mistakes. I accept that now. It's called maturing. It happens to all of us sooner or later. In our case, it happened sooner. Almost before we were ready for it. Don't make the biggest mistake of your life!"

Tight-lipped, Jerry let Katey stew awhile over their conversion. He appeared deep in thought, trying to piece together, in typical Jerry Landis fashion, his logical approach. She could tell he was carefully choosing his next words. He wouldn't listen. He only heard what he wanted to hear.

"Katey, I'm doing this as much for you as I'm doing it for myself. Last week, I went to a marriage counselor. Believe me, I've really thought this through. I tried to be objective about our problems, and I think I was fair about what I said regarding the both of us. This counselor told me we have irreconcilable differences between us because of religion, culture, and family ties. Katey, we're stuck in neutral. Our relationship is going nowhere! And it never will!"

Katey made a run for the restroom. She couldn't fight the emotion tearing her apart. Jerry appeared relatively calm under the circumstances, playing a steady drum roll with his fingers on their booth's table next to his cup, waiting for Katey to compose herself enough to return.

Five minutes later, Katey sat down in their booth again. Her eyes were red, cheeks drained of their color. She tried her best to put on a brave smile. "I'm going to proposition you, Jerry. I'm going to agree to something I would never, ever agree to under any other circumstances. I'm willing to do this if it'll keep you from marrying Carol."

Jerry opened his mouth. No words came to cover his shock and disbelief. "Katey! Not you! I don't believe you'd ever agree to such a thing. How could you?"

"That give you a clue about how much I love you, Jerry?" "How often would you be willing to do this?"

"As often as we need each other." "That's a sin in your church, isn't it?"

"It sure is! I'll deal with that. It's a small price I'm willing to pay if it'll keep us together and you out of a disastrous marriage."

"I can't, Katey. I won't change my mind, no matter how tempting your offer is. Oh, one last thing. As a favor to me, please remove your wedding band and go back to using your maiden name. That band still haunts me."

"And it will, Jerry Landis, because I'll never take it off. My conscience and my God wouldn't allow it."

It was late when Katey quietly entered her home. She stopped to slip off her shoes then tiptoed down the hallway. Just outside Krissy's door, she heard a squeak from the hardwood floor that gave her away. She paused a second then continued to her bedroom. She finished undressing then slipped into bed. She backed into her extra pillow, still thinking about their honeymoon when Jerry's warm body filled that space. Tears came as she turned away just as her bedroom door opened, and there stood Krissy in her Mickey Mouse pajamas, still rubbing the sleep out of her eyes.

"Are you crying again, Mommy?"

"Yes, sugarplum." "Why?"

"Daddy won't be coming on Friday nights anymore. Or any other nights again."

"Can I come over to your bed, Mommy?"

"Sure, punkins. C'mon over. Mommy needs you tonight like never before."

Krissy pulled back the covers and slipped in beside her mother. Katey wrapped both arms around Krissy and gave her an extra big hug and long kiss. "Now go to sleep, Krissy."

"I don't ever want to grow up, Mommy."

"Why not, Krissy? Last week, you told me that you can hardly wait to grow up!"

"'Cause grown-ups must get an awful lot of hurt bumps! Way too many to kiss 'n make them all better. That's why they cry all the time."

CHAPTER 6

For one solid year, Katey watched and waited for Jerry's marriage to develop or fall apart. She made it a point to stay in contact with him on an average of one coffee or lunch break each week. At first, he was excited. Carol had made a steal in the housing market, and they set up housekeeping in this practically new bargain home. Still no mention of fatherhood, but Katey figured she'd be privy to such good news any day now.

More months dragged by, and little by little, Katey found Jerry spending their time talking only about his job, not even a slight hint or mention of starting a family. She sensed the futility slowly eating away at him. She also realized he was indirectly admitting to her that she'd been right all along. He, indeed, had made the biggest mistake of his life. While inwardly, her heart rejoiced, she knew Jerry would doggedly hold on to whatever shreds of marriage were left, his pride mortally wounded, his tenacity intact. She was convinced he would not desert the marriage. It would amount to the same thing his father had done when he was six, and Jerry Landis would do anything to escape that comparison, no matter what the consequences.

So Katey knew it would be up to her if she was ever to get Jerry back.

Though she didn't have a definite plan at present, she only knew she was going to be there to pick up the pieces, if and when. Like Jerry, she was willing to put her bulldog tenacity to work. But she needed a break. Something had to happen for her to have any chance to win him back.

In its way, the financial crisis the CCR was going through provided the break. For weeks, rumors circulated through the corporate headquarters building that the railroad was on its last leg. Heavy short-term borrowing had so eroded its operating revenues that in order to meet those obligations, the railroad was running the risk of not even taking care of current expenses, including payroll, let alone pay anything toward reducing its long-term debt. Merger talks between CCR representatives and the Colorado Western Railroad were going on around the clock, trying to hammer out an agreement that would meet Interstate Commerce Commission (ICC) approval and still leave

the two railroads' stockholders with a reasonable chance of getting some return on their investment somewhere down the line.

Wall Street, too, was well aware of this development. A collapse of the California Central Railroad could trigger an avalanche of distrust in the railroad transportation industry, creating a domino effect and sending other railroads in the same predicament into bankruptcy or, even worse, into government receivership with the taxpayers ultimately footing the bill to bail out the bankrupt railroads.

Even Congress had been alerted, through several of its powerful subcommittees, to cast a wary eye toward the Golden State and its transportation problems. It became a political football. Federal takeover, it seemed, was at best a Band-Aid approach to an ever increasing long-standing problem brought on by even more truck and airline competition. Both of which were heavily subsidized through millions of federal dollars poured into new and improved highway construction and new airport facilities. Railroad lobbyists were quick to point out that on heavy tonnage items over long hauls, the railroads still maintained a very sizable competitive edge and that the railroads, if given time, would dispose of nonprofitable short lines and remain a very viable industry. Many in Congress became doubting Thomases on that issue, feeling the time of the railroad's major importance had expired. They should be allowed, at best, a few more years to languish in their death throws and then pass on into history and oblivion.

While worried, Wall Street investors and members of Congress waited and watched. The CCR formed an ad hoc management group to dig itself out of its financial woes. All members of the group were agreed upon one thing. Merger with the Colorado Western offered both companies the best chance of survival as each road offered trackage and markets the other had long coveted. The CCR had long sought a way to ship its central California fruit, produce, and light industry products to the intermountain west regions, while the Colorado Western would bring mineral and timber resources over CCR trackage to the California markets with their ever-expanding population, economy, and coastal ports for international trade.

Other important events thrust Greg, Katey, and even Jerry into the thick of the CCR problems. Mr. Carlson, the CCR comptroller, was diagnosed with prostate cancer and had taken a medical leave of absence. Bill Seelig, Jerry's boss, was promoted as interim comptroller and also took over Carlson's spot on the ad hoc group. Needless to say, Seelig brought Jerry along with him. For Gerald Landis offered a fresh approach to the financial part of the company's problems. Seelig's job depended upon his assistant's expertise, and this rankled Katey to no end. While Seelig fattened Jerry's wallet a little, he took the lion's share of the credit by rubber-stamping Jerry's reports, recommendations, and modification in the financial arena.

Greg, too, was about to make his mark. The chubby blue-eyed blond six- footer had displayed enough usable and recognizable talent so that it caught the attention of the upper echelon with whom he was firmly entrenched with, both socially and professionally. A few phone calls here, a little arm twisting there, and those in control could see their way clear to make room for him at the top as headquarters division manager. He was welcomed into that elite circle with open arms. He had arrived.

Greg's promotion opened the door for Katey. They made a good team, as she became the consummate personal secretary, always protecting his weaknesses while displaying her own proficiency and planning capabilities to the utmost. None of the other seven personal secretaries on the seventh floor ever doubted for one split second that Katey didn't belong. She, too, had arrived.

Katey's big promotion couldn't have come at a better time. She not only enjoyed the many perks and privileges, but she immediately purchased a new wardrobe, one that enhanced her looks and effectiveness greatly. For only fifty feet away stood Jerry's desk, moved temporarily outside Seelig's office, so he'd be available at Seelig's beck and call. Needless to say, when Jerry wasn't inside the comptroller's office or attending ad hoc meetings with Seelig, Katey spent a lot of time around his desk. Her only regret was that Jerry would be back at his old job at the CCR Support Services Building once the ad hoc group disbanded.

Katey pressed her advantage to the hilt, making sure she did the little things. To be there when Jerry needed last-minute typing support or have lunch with him. A casual touch here, an overtly friendly smile there, and the right words when he needed cheering up. She knew firsthand, from the little things he did and didn't say, that his marriage was in shambles. But Katey was also keenly aware of Jerry's innate stubbornness, his refusal to admit failure in the face of overwhelming circumstances to the contrary. He adamantly refused to concede he'd made the big mistake, something Katey knew he would never admit. It was up to her to make it happen if she was ever to get him back. What she desperately needed was an incident to topple his marriage—one that would leave Jerry no choice but to end it.

Friday night came, and no one on the seventh floor remotely thought about going home. Not with the final ad hoc group meeting and management review scheduled for that evening.

And not with the survival of the railroad at stake, including their very own jobs. Jerry spent two hours in Seelig's office, reassuring him he'd done his homework. A part of the railroad's proposal package to be submitted for ICC approval was the company's financial position, which was of real concern.

Jerry's bold financial decision had more than his share of detractors, but as he so candidly put it to the ad hoc group, "There's no other way. There's no other game in town."

Strapped for operating capital to sustain railroad operations and meet payroll, Jerry had come up with a solution, albeit a previously unheard of and definitely unpopular one. Tap the corporate pension and retirement accounts to fund the railroad's operations until ICC approval is gained. It was a calculated risk for sure, yet when combined with current revenue projections, it offered a way to cross CCR investors' financial desert with at least enough water to keep those on camels from dying of thirst.

For two days, prior to the Friday night meetings, Jerry camped outside Seelig's office, sleeping on Katey's couch inside her rest facility. He looked haggard and rundown. The endless hours he'd put into Seelig's proposal were having their effects. Katey would come in each morning, rouse him, and order breakfast from the corporate kitchen on the eighth floor. Then they'd eat while Jerry would discuss what strategy to pursue or what he had to get accomplished for that day.

Katey ordered two dinners sent down to her office while Jerry shaved in her rest facility and washed up a bit. "Hey, Landis, you stay here any longer and they'll probably bill you for motel time. Don't you have a home to go to anymore?"

Katey's joke brought out a surprise. "Yes, I do, but Carol's so wrapped up in her real estate career she's hardly ever home till late at night."

"Don't you at least see her then?"

"Not always. We sleep in separate rooms."

Jerry's nonchalant answer stunned Katey. "Oh, guess I never realized."

"Don't read into it more than it is, Katey. Lots of married couples sleep alone."

His answer bothered her. She just couldn't imagine being married and not sleeping with her husband. Not if he was Jerry Landis with all the passion he'd shown her in the past.

They ate their dinner together. Katey was unusually silent. Her feelings and anxiety were in check, but she wanted so badly to comfort Jerry. He, on the other hand, thought of only one thing. Could he keep CCR from going under? Greg joined them for a cup of coffee and pie dessert. "I think we're in pretty good shape on ninety percent of our proposal regarding trackage, rolling stock inventory and maintenance facilities, location, and net worth evaluation. How's your part shaping up, Jerry?"

"That's the big sixty-four-dollar rub! I've got two meetings tonight instead of just the one you have to go to. It's going to be a long, long night. Seelig and I have to get final approval on the finance portion from the ad hoc group, and then we have to resell it all over again before the management team."

Katey added her nickel's worth. "Now, Greg, don't you see why Jerry should get the comptroller's job? Heck, he's doing all the work and making the decisions. It's his proposal that's going to bail us out till we get ICC approval."

"If we get ICC approval, Katey!" Jerry corrected. "Don't forget our competition will be filing their briefs and objections to the merger, and that could delay the final ICC decision until we run out of operating capital."

Greg handed his plate to Katey. "How long do we have moneywise, Jerry?" "No more than seven months at best. That's what I've told Seelig, and I have the figures to back the projection."

"You mean your projections, Jerry. Seelig's going along 'cause he has no choice. He'd be out in the wilderness if it wasn't for Jerry."

"His proposal, my proposal, it won't make a difference whose it is if it doesn't sell and we're all pounding the pavement looking for another job."

Greg looked at Katey. "Where'll you go, amigo, if the roof falls in?"

"I've been giving that some thought, boss. Think I'd try to work again for the Jackson Law Firm. They always liked my work, treated me right. I'm really spoiled here—new rental Buick, big raise, expense allowance. Sure would miss all those perks and bennies."

"Don't get out your resumés just yet," Jerry replied. "The night is still young."

Katey took the dinner dishes back up to the eighth floor. Greg had gone on down the hall to chat with a couple of the other managers waiting around for the second meeting. She returned just in time to see Bill Seelig stop in front of Jerry's desk. He was nervous, blinking his eyes, shifting from one stance to the other.

"You're sure! You're sure, Landis, this thing will fly? Remember, we're up front of our own firing squad on this wild idea. I don't want any screwups! Make sure you've got your data with you, so if I need a quick answer, you can cover. Right, Landis?"

Greg returned just in time to hear most of Seelig's comments. Jerry, cool as ever, let Seelig calm down before he gave his reassurance. "I've done my homework. My projections will fly. They won't like it, but they'll buy!"

Seelig glanced down at his watch. "C'mon, bring your slides so we can set up early. Never show up late or just on time. It leaves a bad impression. Makes a hard sell even harder."

"Jerry, I'll stay if you need any late help after the first meeting."

"Thanks, Katey. I'll be all right. Go on home. Krissy's probably waiting up for you. Tell punkins…"

He never finished his statement but picked up his briefcase of backup data, the rack of slides, and followed Seelig, cane touching hard in the deep plush carpet. Greg and Katey watched them till they boarded the elevator to the president's conference room up on the tenth floor.

"Now do you see why Seelig should be working for Jerry, not the other way around?"

"Yeah, Katey. I'll do everything I can to get him up here where he belongs." "Yes, and his marriage is going nowhere too! Of course, Jerry will never admit it."

Greg took Katey by the hand. "That's where you and I come in, amigo. We both know his marriage is on the rocks. That's why he practically lives here.

There's nothing to go home to. His work and you are all he's got going for him. If you ever get another chance, Katey, please don't blow it!"

"I won't. Believe you me, I won't! Don't know how or when or where, but I'll stick by him. And when it does, I'll make the hard choices if I have to. The kind Jerry said I'd never make."

"Never did fully understand what split you two up. Jerry's no help. Thinks he's Mr. Noble by doing what he did. Now look at the mess he's in!"

"Don't be so hard on him. I'm as much to blame as he is."

Greg saw the resolve in Katey's eyes. "Had a lot to do with your religion and your parents, didn't it?"

"Yes, but no more. Like I said, I'll do whatever it takes to get him back, including making those hard choices."

"Since you're going home, Katey, how about doing me and maybe yourself a favor?"

Katey nodded.

"Jerry told me earlier this evening that Carol has some big out-of-state client interested in purchasing that old Safeway property up on Norris Avenue. I think he mentioned the guys holed up at the Excelsior Hotel. Oh, yes, now I remember. His name's Carpage. Could be with Jerry pretty much out of the marriage picture, Carol has extended plans? Get the picture? How 'bout checking the hotel restaurant? Maybe there's more than dinner on the menu? As his friend, I want him out of this mess as bad as you do, Katey."

Katey called home to tell her mother to go ahead and get Krissy ready for bed. It could be a long night, and when she got home, she'd be sure to kiss her daughter good night. She had her Buick valet-parked and checked the hotel registry. Yes, a Mr. Paul Carpage was registered in room 314.

"Is he around?"

"Yes, indeed," the hotel clerk volunteered. "He's having dinner in the restaurant. Shall I have him paged? Your name, please?"

"I'll just wait in the hotel lobby and speak to him later. Don't want to interrupt his dinner. Thank you anyway."

Katey retreated to the hotel lobby, finding a fairly secluded spot where she could keep an eye on the elevator yet not be too recognizable should Jerry's wife, Carol, decide to extend the evening menu beyond a business dinner.

She didn't have to wait long. Carol, slightly tipsy from too many before- dinner cocktails, was hanging on his arm, ready to show her client something else besides commercial property. Katey could hardly wait for the elevator door to close before she grabbed a pay phone. Greg was still in his office.

"I don't care what you have to do or tell him. Just get Jerry down here! Have him check out room 314. The rest will take care of itself!"

"But, Katey," Greg answered. "He's in the middle of the finance package pitch. I couldn't yank him outa that. Seelig would can him!"

"I did the agenda handouts for the management meeting. Seelig and Jerry's pitch is the next to last item, just before the big cheese himself, President Appleton's summary. There's plenty of time if you collar him the minute the finance pitch is over for the ad hoc group."

"But, Katey, what should I say? How should I handle it?"

"That's your department. You're supposed to be the great communicator! So communicate!"

On Monday morning, Katey arrived nearly an hour early and had coffee with Mora Woodson. The middle-aged lady was completely in the dark as to why Katey acted like she was ready for some big news.

"Boy, are you in a chipper mood, Katey. Haven't seen you this excited since you got ready to meet Jerry at the airport when he got his medical discharge."

"I'm expecting some real good news from my boss, Greg."

"Oh, you think the merger proposal review got off the ground, right?"

Katey laughed. "Gosh, I haven't even thought about that. No, it's something else."

"Why don't you take your lipstick and write his name on this table? It's got to be about Jerry!"

"Shows pretty bad, doesn't it?"

"Shows? Oh, Katey, I've never seen anyone holding the torch like you do for Jerry. How or why you let him go is still a mystery to me. You're so darned private about him in certain respects. I'll probably never know."

"I've always been that way about certain things. They're just too personal. And when I get him back again, it's going to stay that way—our marriage, our love, our commitment."

"Aren't you forgetting one small detail? He's still married." "He won't be for long. Not anymore."

The two women deposited their cups on the conveyor belt, and each went to their respective work areas, Mora on the fourth floor and Katey back up on the seventh. Greg was surprised to find Katey waiting for him.

"Well, how did it go? Tell me everything! Don't leave out a single detail!"

Greg sat on one corner of Katey's desk. He held up both hands in a cautionary position. "I pulled him outa the meeting, all right. Had to lie to him about Carol to even get him down to the Excelsior. Told him it was an emergency."

"It was! His marriage is kaput!"

"Well, Katey, that's the strange part. Oh, he was mad, all right, when Carpage opened the door and he barged in to find her naked in bed. He took one look at her, marched straight back out, and never even stopped to punch the guy to kingdom come! And, Katey, he was mad enough for it. Plenty mad!"

"Go on! What next?"

Greg acted like he hardly believed what was he was about to say. "Here's the strange part. Instead of yelling and screaming about getting a divorce or something like that, he takes a whack at the padded elevator door to let off some steam. When we get down to the lobby, he's calm as a cucumber. He says, 'Drive me to my house. I want to pick up some clothes.'"

"That's good! What happened next?"

"Then he says, 'Drive me over to Ricco's apartment. I'll be staying with him. And when you get back to the management meeting, tell

Seelig to go to H. Katey, there's not a darned thing I'll be able to do about the corporate comptroller's position when it comes up for discussion after this merger business is put to bed. And by the way, they bought Jerry's pitch. Seelig buttonholes me and tells me he's going to put a note in Jerry's file that says under no circumstances is he ever to be considered for any upper-level management position in the future. Katey, Seelig blackballed him for good because he didn't show up for that management meeting. And the other part? Telling Seelig to go to H instead of his own wife in bed with another guy? No, Katey, there's something very different here. Almost strange. Not like the Jerry Landis we know at all."

"I sure don't have a clue either. Wonder why he had you drive him over to Ricco's. You know Ricco, always chasing stray skirts. That's not where I want him!"

"Get ready for some more strange news. Ricco's changed. I swear he has! He really lucked out in the Air Force, got a real sweetheart of a deal. Got in three and a half years of college while he was stationed at SAC Headquarters in Nebraska. Majored in labor relations, and he finished up out here at Sacramento State after his discharge. He's running for the local union business agent. Gonna be a tough struggle. Even his old man's support may not swing enough votes to get him in. Too many people in the union remember his wild parties and all the different women he's scr…you get the picture."

"You bet I do! Does a leopard change spots? No, I'm going to Jerry as fast as I can and tell him."

"What are you gonna tell him, Katey? That he's Krissy's father?"

Greg stayed camped out on the corner of Katey's desk, sure beyond any doubt that she would divulge what Ricco and he already knew. Seconds passed…long seconds. Nothing! Katey colored a tad but kept tight-lipped. He finally stepped away. At the open door to his office, he turned around. "Jerry's going to bail us out…and all he'll get for being such a financial wizard is a big fat nothing out of management, especially from Seelig! See if you can do something more for him! I think you know what I mean."

CHAPTER 7

Week after week went by with no outward changes in Jerry's marital status. He calmly remarked to Ricco and Greg that he and Carol were separated. That's all! This development played havoc with Katey's plans. Should she force the issue by telling him about Krissy? How would he react, especially since he considered himself still married? Would he get a divorce so they could marry and he assume his biological role as Krissy's father? It was an enigma without visible solution. It perplexed her day and night. Up till now, she would've bet her last dollar she knew him like a few, if any woman ever knew their man. Now she was anything but sure about him in light of what had transpired.

Then suddenly, Ricco went to San Francisco with Alfredo, the cousin of the Italian lady he'd been corresponding with the past year. It was to be a no- obligation look-see for each. With Alfredo as an interpreter, it was time to ask still unanswered questions, to remove any lingering doubts on either's part. And if all signs were go, then a contract of marriage would be signed then and there. Theresa would then accompany Alfredo to his home until the formal wedding and reception took place.

How strange, Katey thought. It was almost bizarre that in the year 1958, such an arrangement could possibly happen in America. It was a throwback to old times, old ideas, and old country tradition. If anything, Ricco was more handsome than ever, possibly a screen test away from a movie or television contract. He now sported a thin mustache to go along with his five-foot-ten- inch frame, similar to that of Jerry's. And when he used his usual scintillating smile, he broke unsuspecting hearts whenever he chose to. Add in those soft dark eyes and olive-toned skin, he more than fit the "Italian Romeo" image to a T. It was a most un-American way to be a husband and father. Was the world going crazy? Or was it just another nail in the coffin of proof about the social upheaval taking place in the 1950s?

Greg brought Katey more news about Ricco. The wedding was set, and all arrangements had been agreed to and the contract signed. Now all that remained was the Catholic church wedding and reception, to which she had been invited. Curiosity got to Katey. She would attend, especially after Greg assured her that Jerry would be there with Carol. It was a last-gasp attempt Katey believed to salvage something out of their marriage.

Mary was delighted when Katey broke the news that Andy Stephens was escorting her to the wedding reception. She came into Katey's bedroom far more excited than her daughter. "Katey, my love, you must give up this notion that you will ever get back with Jerry." Up came her cautionary finger. "Don't forget, he's a married man. You must never do anything to encourage him to leave his wife. That is sinful, and it cannot be allowed."

Katey finished dressing. "Mother, the only reason I've asked Andy to escort me is that I need a partner to dance with. He's been pestering me for months. He understands the ground rules. That's it, period!"

"But, Katey," she continued, "he's from such a fine Catholic family, and I'm sure if you gave him just the slightest bit of hope, you can never tell, many a good marriage can come from just such a beginning. Hear me out, lass. Jerry's the finest young man I've ever met, but you must—"

Katey jumped all over Mary. "You mean finest non-Catholic you've ever met, right?"

"I never said that."

"Didn't have to. I can tell your little pitch a mile away! It won't work, Mother, so drop it!"

They stood toe to toe and eyeball to eyeball, each letting their five-foot- three frames size each other up. She Bashed her wedding band in front of her mother.

"I'm still married, Mother! Nothing's going to ever change that! Not you, not Dad, and not even Jerry. As for Krissy's needing a father, she already has one. Now where are my high heels?"

The Sons of Italy Hall in Sacramento was the scene of Ricco and Theresa's wedding reception. It was to be a gala afternoon of feasting, lots of drinking, old-world dancing, and old-world music complete with old-world charm and attitudes. The hall was decorated with brightly colored crisscrossed streamers held up to the ceiling by multicolored bells and hearts. On stage was a five-piece dance band appropriately dressed in native Italian costumes, courtesy of a local rental agency.

Andy looked ready for an evening of dancing. His dark slacks and silver- colored tie with a light-blue dress shirt made his own fashion statement. He escorted Katey to the guest of honor table. There, Ricco jumped up to greet her. "I'm so glad you decided to come, Katey. Please let me introduce you to my bride."

Andy surrendered his dance partner and took a chair at one end of the table. Katey was amazed. There before her sat a lovely lady in a stunning white wedding dress. She was the picture of loveliness, with beautiful long black tresses of hair crowned by a custom-jeweled tiara. Her creamy-smooth olive skin and dark Bashing almond-shaped eyes accented her beauty. She was breathtaking!

Ricco spoke again. "The man to her left is her cousin, Alfredo. She understands most of our English. However, please forgive her English. She is eager to learn, but sometimes the words don't come out just right. That's why Alfredo is there for now."

"Theresa, this is my good friend, Katey McCray. One of the amigos I told you about."

Katey and Theresa shook hands. "What a beautiful bride you make,

Theresa. I hope you and Ricco will be very happy! Congratulations!" She blushed and tried to speak. "Katey, old country name maybe?" "Yes, it's really KateLynn. My parents are from Ireland."

"I want." She turned to Alfredo and spoke in Italian. Then, satisfied, she continued, "I want, how you say, I want us to be good friends. Yes, very good friends. Okay, KateLynn?"

Katey had made a friend for life. She sensed the loneliness in Theresa, yet she also admired her attitude and her willingness to change her life completely. "I'd like that very much, Theresa. When you come back from your honeymoon, we'll get together."

Theresa flashed her smile. "You come, you come…a…to my beautiful home. My Ricco, he buy for me. You come. I cook much Italian food for you, and we drink wine. Have good time. Be good friends. You say yes, please?"

"Yes, Theresa. When you get back?"

Ricco escorted Katey back to her place by Andy. "Katey, please save a couple of dances for me. We need to talk."

She caught Greg's and his date's attention and waved to them. "All right."

Then she surveyed the other guests at the bridal table. "Where's Jerry? I don't see him!"

"Jerry didn't show at my wedding, and he was supposed to be there. Said if he couldn't get Carol to come with him, he wouldn't be here. Katey, he's too proud and stubborn for his own good. Still trying to prove to everybody he's got a wife and marriage worth saving."

Katey stomped her feet. "Darned that man! I know he's miserable, but what does my Jerry do? He's so hung up on proving he didn't make a mistake that he's making a bigger one!"

The music started up. Katey turned to Andy. "Let's dance. Nothing else seems to be working out." They swung out on the floor to a lively beat and disappeared into the crowd.

An hour slipped by, and still no sign of Jerry or Carol. Andy and Katey exchanged partners with Greg and his new lady friend, Victoria, who looked like Fifth Avenue's best dressed. Her black evening dress was stunning with silver sequins that ran full length along her thighs and up to the shoulders. Her jewelry also looked like more of Fifth Avenue, complete with a small fortune's worth of beautiful diamond clusters draped around her neck. Her earrings matched the sequins perfectly. A beautiful diamond-clustered tiara adorned her jet-black hair. She stood barely an inch shorter then Greg. The "Old Communicator" was his old self, charming most of the guests at the bridal table with lots of jokes, backslapping and fun, along with more than his share of champagne and old vintage wine, courtesy of Theresa's relatives from Italy.

Greg guided Katey around the floor. He was a masterful dancer. "Don't look so dejected, Katey. You and Jerry will iron it out later. Just give it time. His marriage can't last."

"I sure hope you're right. I'm beginning to think it's already too late."

They reached the far end of the dance floor. "What do you think of my date?"

Katey smiled, her first at the reception. "Well, boss, judging by her looks, her clothes, and all that jewelry, I smell money. Am I correct?"

"There's nothing wrong with money marrying money now, is there?"

She laughed. "One thing is for sure. That kind of marriage will certainly produce one thing—more money!"

They passed the band and moved out into the center of the Boor, keeping time with a snappy beat. Twenty-five other couples also liked the music's beat, judging by the way they whirled around the highly polished hardwood dance Boor. At the far end of the Boor, Greg looked down at his partner.

"Ya know, Jerry's a different sort of duck. By that, I mean he's always trying to prove to everybody he belongs. Lord almighty, Katey, he's head 'n shoulders above the herd. A decorated war veteran, and I mean a genuine war hero, yet he won't talk about the war. Never mentions the medals he's earned.

"I still have his medals, citation, and campaign ribbons, all packed away in my hope chest. He's never once asked about them. As far as not talking about the Korean War, just watching him drag that left leg twenty or thirty feet says more than all the words or medals in the world. You've never seen his back, have you?"

Greg shook his head.

"It's a mass of scars, Besh punctures, and long sore-looking red marks. Doctor up in Seattle told me that's what saved his life. His back absorbed most of the explosion. His left leg wasn't so lucky."

Katey and Greg passed Ricco and Theresa's table. "Oh, let me tell you about another thing with Jerry. He will not, I swear this is the honest-to-God's truth, but that man will not sign a pledge! He'd rather lose his right leg than sign one. Even if it's only for the United Good Neighbor Fund! Can you beat that?"

"I know. *Boy*, do I know! Tried to get him to sign a contribution pledge for our church! He blew his stack over it! That's what started our hassle over religion and the whole bit. He thinks by signing, you've sold your soul forever and a day!"

Greg roared, "Boy, there's no changing his mind either! Take the UGN. He says the administrative cost per dollar of contribution and the ratio is way out of whack, especially for a few big-name charities on our list. That's why he won't sign it."

"Knowing Jerry, he's done all his homework. So how did we get one hundred percent enrollment for all our headquarters division management?

That was your goal, remember?"

"I had the lowest possible contribution taken out of my check. It's a small price to pay, I figure, considering what he's done for our country and for this railroad. Another thing, I have two more of his cost saving ideas sitting on my desk right now. They're darned good ones too! Just waiting on merger money so I can pay the guy! Isn't he something?"

They circled again. This time, they waved to Victoria and Andy out on the dance floor. "Tell me this, Katey, and think about it before you give me your answer. Can you honestly say Jerry was ever eight or ten or fourteen or even eighteen years old like the rest of us?"

"He never was, not like we were. He was always there, but not one of us. He never seemed to have the fun we had either. Jerry was our class watchdog, our guardian. He made sure we didn't get into too much trouble or do too many silly, stupid things. He was our class conscience day after day."

"Exactly what I told Ricco. Remember when they started our hot lunch program down in the third grade?"

"Yes."

"Never saw a kid so hungry looking, so skinny, and so poor. Always wondered where or how he ever scraped up the twenty cents."

"You can thank me. I brought him lunch money and slipped it to him at morning recess. I'd leave it on his desk just before the other kids got back in the room. Newhouser saw me do it and never said one word. She told me years later that was probably the only meal he'd get that day."

They fell silent. They were deep in thought as they danced on. Fifty feet later, they met Andy and Victoria again and exchanged partners.

Andy said, "Wow, is that gal ever loaded. Betcha her perfume must run at least a couple hundred smackers an ounce! They really dance well together, like they were made for each other." Katey and Andy circled the Boor several times then exchanged partners once more. Jerry was very much on both their minds. "One last thing, Katey, about Jerry. I know you've always kidded him about his career choice, but looking back, it was the only logical field for him."

"Yeah, I called him my bean counter. Even had his wristwatch inscribed that way. The one I gave him for college graduation."

The music stopped just as Greg and Katey passed the dance bandstand.

Greg started to escort Katey back to her chair. "Katey?" "Yes, boss."

"Just want to say thanks for watching my backside at work. If Jerry had that kind of support, neither of you would be the mess you're in today."

CHAPTER 8

The caterers arrived and wheeled in four food carts loaded down with every kind of Italian sausage, pastry, and delicacy imaginable. The band took a much-deserved break while the caterers served the wedding reception crowd.

Thirty minutes later, the band appeared on stage, ready to play.

Ricco claimed Katey for the first dance after the intermission. Neither spoke as they circled around the floor twice. He then cleared his throat. "Katey, I know things between us have been strained for quite a while, since Molly, but I want to prove to you I've changed. I want us to be very good friends again like before. For starters, I've signed a ten-year contract of marriage with Theresa. I've purchased a house. It's in her name, and I've agreed by contract to support any children born of our marriage until they're eighteen. Theresa has already picked out their names. We will have four children. That's what she wants."

Katey could hardly believe her ears. "When Greg told me about your marriage contract, I still didn't believe it until today. And yes, Ricco, I do believe you've changed. But why, Ricco?"

"I needed some direction to my life. Theresa is the direction I want and need. I promise to you and to God that I will honor and respect her. Katey, I worship the ground she walks on. That's how much I care for her. Her cousin, Alfredo, will be my watchdog. I will not stray from the straight and narrow. I will keep and honor every last word in my commitment to her and God. For me, it's the best thing that's ever happened to me. I don't see it as a heavy burden at all. Instead, I chose to see it as my way to respectability and to where I want to go."

They circled and started back. "Wow, Ricco, you've really taken a giant step backward into real old-world ways and traditions. How did this happen anyway?"

"Alfredo is my neighbor, so while I was home on leave from the Air Force, I first saw her picture at his house. I started writing to her, and she corresponded back. While I finished my hitch, I had him write to her. He'd write down what she said and forward her letters to me. I'd answer, and he'd translate my English into Italian and write to her. Well, from just being pen pals, we started to get serious, and then it blossomed into a full-blown marriage proposal at San Francisco International Airport. The rest you probably know through Greg."

"What did she do over in Italy?"

"Theresa had her own dress shop. Made a pretty decent living at it too. That wedding gown she has on, that's her creation. Makes all her own clothes. Already made me a couple of shirts."

"Her dress is out of this world, I know. It's as nice or nicer than the one I bought and almost got to wear."

"I'm sorry it didn't work out for you and Jerry. Still don't really understand about you two. Can't get a decent answer out of him. Keeps saying you wouldn't make a choice so he had to. Yeah, and look what a mess he's in. Katey, you're all he talks about. Then he catches himself and says a word or two about Carol for all of maybe twenty seconds. Then it's back to you again. I've never seen him so depressed."

They reached the opposite side from the band. "I was sure hoping he'd show up today. I'm willing to do whatever it takes to get us back together."

"Glad to hear you're going to make a move. For a minute or two today, I thought you'd thrown in the towel, too, when I saw you walk in with Andy."

"Andy is a friend. Nothing more."

Ricco waved to Theresa as they danced past her table. She smiled graciously and waved back. Katey let out a silent prayer.

Please, dear Lord, let this day be extra special for me. Help bring my Jerry back to me.

"She's such a beautiful bride. I hope your marriage is a happy one." "Thanks, Katey. You know, thinking back, it was a given if ever there was such a thing. Molly used to tell me you had your future all mapped out. Heck, it was better than a road map. You two knew what you wanted and where you were going. We all knew you'd go to business college then marry Jerry and help him get his degree. What happened?"

"Too darned many detours, Ricco. Way too darned many!" The music stopped. Ricco signaled them to replay the last song. "Hope you don't mind another dance. Still more on my mind."

They resumed the beat and moved out on the floor again. "Don't mean to bring up an old subject, Ricco, especially on your wedding day, but this day could've belonged to you and Molly. She would've walked through fire for you, but you didn't or wouldn't see it that way."

"I doubt this day ever really belonged to Molly or me. She wanted marriage and a family right out of high school. I wasn't ready. Think that's where it all went wrong. The more she insisted I make an honest lady out of her, the worse it got between us until, well, you know the rest. Why repeat? Just brings up hard feelings. Not many pleasant memories either."

"Greg tells me you're running for the local union business agent vacancy." "Yes, it's going to be a tough, tough fight. I've got to live down a pretty wild and wooly reputation. So you see, I'm already paying the price for my past." "I know a bit about that too!"

"Katey, why haven't you told Jerry about Krissy? He wants a family so bad. He'd kiss your toes all the way into the shower if he thought for one second he was her father."

"I've only asked myself that same question a million times. I was afraid, and I still am, to some extent. I wanted him to marry me because he loved me, not because he felt obligated to. Can you understand that?"

"Maybe a few years ago, but you're running out of time, Katey. It's a stroke of luck his marriage fizzled, or else you'd be out of time right now!"

"I know, and I'm going to do something about it first chance I get." "Don't wait too long, amigo!"

They circled the floor once again before Ricco spoke up. "With this railroad merger about to hatch, I'm going to be gone a lot on the campaign trail. Lots of new ground to cover. This election means a lot to me. Theresa wants to get pregnant right away, even on our honeymoon. She doesn't want to wait till either the merger goes through or the election is held."

"What do you want?"

"She's calling the shots, and it's okay with me!" "Boy, Ricco, you've changed! And how!"

Ricco dipped her. "Hey, Katey, you remembered!" Twenty feet on down the floor, he continued their conversation. "Katey, you should've seen Theresa's eyes light up when I handed her the keys to her new home. She and Alfredo have been busy furnishing it for the past week. Every night, Alfredo and I go over for dinner, and she proudly shows me what she's bought and where she's put it. Oh, she's fussy. Everything has to be just so or, boy, there's heck to pay. And can she cook! Man, oh, man! Already have one room fixed up for our nursery." He laughed. "After she buys something, then she always asks Alfredo if it's all right because she's not used to spending money like that. She's a saver! Every curtain, every drape in her house, she's already made!"

Katey laughed. "I notice you keep calling it her house. Isn't it yours too?" "No, not ever, if she wants to keep it that way. Part of the contract. After ten years, if she tears up the contract, that means I'm off the hook, and she could add my name as co-owner to the house. That's her decision."

They danced on. "I still can't get over what you've done, Ricco! All these changes! You're under the gun, and I've never seen you happier."

"Maybe some of my happiness will rub off on you, amigo."

"Sure hope so. Mine and Jerry's life has been a real roller coaster. Such highs followed by such disappointments. Beginning to wonder, I really am!"

"It'll happen if you both want it to happen. Theresa has taught me that."

Katey looked up at her handsome partner. There was something very much on his mind, something that needed saying. "When we started dancing, you said for starters, you'd convince me you've changed since you've met Theresa. What else are you trying to prove to me?"

Ricco stopped dancing. He couldn't hide the tears. "I want to see my son." "Well, that's a switch! Last time we had this conversation, you weren't at all sure Molly's baby was yours."

"I know, I know. I was angry because she tried to trap me into marriage. Katey, I want to be a part of his life. I want to spend time with him, let him know now he does have a father who cares."

Katey took the hankie out of his pocket and handed it to him. "Does Theresa know about this?" "Yes, I've told her!" "And?"

"She says my son will be welcome any time in her home!"

"Okay. Based on that, here's what I'll try to do for you. No promises, mind you, but I'll try. When you come back from your honeymoon, stop by. I'll show you the latest pictures of Little Ricco. He looks just like you. Then you write a letter to Molly and him, explaining just what you want. I'll include it in my next letter to her, and the rest is up to her. Got a deal, amigo?"

"Deal! Has she married?"

"Yes. Married a landscaper, a widower with two small sons. He's branched out into his own business, and Molly's taken a couple of bookkeeping classes so she can do the paperwork."

"Have you seen her or Little Ricco lately?"

"Three months ago. Took Krissy along with me. Had a good visit. He's a very nice boy. Ricco, people are staring at us. Let's finish the dance."

He blinked hard several times, trying to blot out the mist in his eyes. He flashed his usual scintillating smile as they moved down the floor, where they were swallowed up by the other couples. When the music stopped, they found themselves at the far end of the hall. Ricco turned to Katey then laughed.

"Theresa's mother gave her this advice about keeping a marriage happy before she flew to San Francisco. It loses a little in Alfredo's translation, but I think you'll get the point. She said if a wife will always remember to keep her husband's belly full and his balls empty, there'll be no problems."

Katey gasped then roared. "Wow, some advice! Darned good advice too!

Hope I get to practice that on Jerry!"

"You will, Katey. Just make your move!"

They started back to their seats when Katey stopped. "Now what, amigo?" "When Theresa arrived in this country, what impressed her the most?" "Our department stores, like Penney s, Sears, and Monkey Wards! She said just going up and down the aisles is like Christmas every day."

CHAPTER 9

Another fifteen minutes slipped by before Katey's eyes lit up. New color rushed to her cheeks. She turned to Andy. "Jerry's here, and I need to talk to him. First, slow dance. You get to his wife and ask her to dance. Don't take no for an answer!"

Jerry and Carol were still fifty feet away from their empty seats when Ricco and Greg jumped up to greet them. They shook hands, exchanged pleasantries, and then made their way back to the bride's table. They sat across from Andy and Katey. Jerry wore a dark-gray suit. Carol looked a mess. Two stains on the front of her light-blue evening gown were very noticeable. Hard alcohol lines appeared on both sides of her mouth. She reeked of liquor.

Greg stood up and raised his champagne glass. He was in rare form. "It's been eight long years since the original four amigos have gathered together again. It took a beautiful bride from another country to make it happen, but it did happen! Here's to the amigos! A toast, amigos!" The other three stood up and raised their glasses. "Let's make sure it doesn't take another eight to get us together again!" Four glasses clanked together as one. Greg remained standing. "And now to our lovely Theresa. Ricco has promised to drink wine from your slipper. C'mon, Ricco, do your thing!"

Everybody in the hall gathered around the bride's table in the rush of excitement to watch. Flashbulbs popped all over the place as Theresa turned in her chair and raised her beautiful gown a tad, exposing a soft black leather slipper. Ricco kneeled down, removed it, then filled it with wine. He raised it toward his mouth. "To my love, Theresa, my beautiful bride, I salute you!"

The guests shouted their approval. This old-world tradition was kept alive in 1958.

The music started up, a fast-paced beat as the bride and groom kissed. Then they beckoned for everyone to come join them on the dance floor. Jerry's and Katey's eyes feasted on each other while Carol did a slow boil. Katey broke the spell. She grabbed Andy, and they joined the dance. Jerry's eyes never left the couple as his head slowly traveled the entire floor, keeping track of Katey.

Carol, seeing this, turned her back on him. She downed a full glass of champagne in one swallow, already more than a bit unhappy that her husband had talked her into coming.

The next dances were too fast-paced for Katey to ask Jerry to dance. Meanwhile, Carol hit the champagne trail nonstop, trying to drown her obvious displeasure. She was one unhappy camper, to say the least. What a sight they made, totally ignoring each other yet seated side by side.

The first few strains of a slow waltz drifted down from the stage. Like a shot, Katey came around the end of the table, dragging Andy right on her high heels. "Jerry, will you dance with me, please?"

He looked at her then Carol. Carol saw red. "One step out on that floor with your precious Katey and I'm history! You promised!"

Andy interrupted, "I would like to have this dance with you."

Andy's invite cooled the fireworks. Carol looked at Jerry, then Katey, and finally back to Andy, with his arm extended in her direction. The hard liquor lines around her mouth softened. "All right, my good man, you're on!" She leveled a real shot for Jerry's benefit. "Notice I said my good man. Something you sure as heck aren't!"

The entire table breathed a collective sigh of relief, feeling sure they'd dodged one heckuva donnybrook.

"Katey, I don't dance anymore. The leg after thirty feet…you know that." "C'mon, Jerry. I'm willing if you are. It'll give us a chance to talk."

He finally rose then hung his cane over the back of his chair. "All right, but I'll be all over your toes, so don't say I didn't warn you."

Finally, they moved together, and Jerry tried to lead. "Oops! See, I warned you!"

They stood a second, each not quite sure how to get started. Finally, they moved out on the floor.

"You're doing fine. Let me lead and follow, like we used to slow dance.

Remember?"

Gradually, they adjusted to Jerry's leg, and fifty feet out on the floor, they kept the beat. "Glad you finally took my advice. Andy's a fine fellow!"

Katey didn't answer right away. "Andy's a fine fellow, all right, but he's only my dancing partner. And no, I didn't take your advice. Jerry, come back to me!"

They moved on slowly. "Stay out of my life, Katey. There's nothing either of us can do about it now."

"Yes, there is, if you'll end it with Carol."

"And then what? Back to square one or at best a stray weekend on some hit- or-miss affair with you? No, thanks, Katey. I'll pass on that."

They stopped dancing. Katey stood on tiptoes. "Do you still love me the way you used to?"

Jerry thought it sounded like the same old rerun. "You mean after all we've been to each other, all we've shared, and you still don't know? No wonder our lives are so screwed up!"

"Say it, Jerry! Say it! I have to hear it!"

"Oh Lord, Katey. I can smell your hair and your perfume again and feel your body close to mine. I want you so bad I could practically eat you. And you're still asking? Okay, I'll say it. I love you! That answer your question?"

"I'll do anything! Make any changes you want if you'll divorce Carol to marry me!"

The full impact of Katey's candid acknowledgment took a full thirty seconds to hit Jerry.

"Are you saying what I think I heard? You really mean it, don't you?"

"Yes, and it has nothing to do with who's right or wrong. It simply means I'll do whatever it takes to get our life back together again. Where it should've been all along."

"Okay, suppose I do file for divorce. Then what?" "We get together and we get married on your terms."

"No matter what?"

"No matter what!"

They resumed dancing. Jerry's left leg hardly dragged now, let alone slow them down. He held her close. His heart was on fire. "A second chance, Katey. Your giving me a second chance! I can hardly believe it! You won't be sorry. I promise, I'll love you and respect you like no other. Wait a minute, what about your folks?"

"That's for me to handle when I get back home today. Now are you willing to do your part? The divorce, I mean?"

"Carol can't contest it. I have her dead to rights with Greg as my witness if it turns ugly."

"Either way, I'll wait for you. Starting Sunday, Krissy and I expect to see you every weekend from now on till your divorce is final. Agreed?"

"Yes, yes, my Katey. No ifs, ands, or buts!"

Oh, what a beautiful reunion of the heart, body, and soul when they kissed on the dance floor. Several couples stopped to witness their tender embrace then moved on. The dance stopped, and they walked back to the bride's table, hand in hand, not caring what Carol did or didn't see. Their spirits and their hearts soared as one, for indeed they were.

Carol returned with Andy, unaware of the tender and passionate love scene played out on the dance floor. All she could think about, all she wanted was to cozy up to some more liquor to bury her marital problems with Jerry. At the table, Katey let go of Jerry's hand and sat down again next to Andy.

Carol took note of them separating and commented tersely for anyone within listening range, "Still chasing my husband, I see! Good thing the lights are on. No telling what she'd try to pull off if they weren't!" Nobody seemed interested in her tactless remarks. Finally, she nudged Victoria, Greg's date, seated next to her. "Get it? No telling what Katey'd pull off." She cackled at her own joke, the one she'd just laid an egg on.

Carol chug-a-lugged two more glasses of wine, then her head bobbed and weaved. Twice she belched, then she made a belated dash for the women's restroom. It was a race to see who or what got there first, Carol or her vomit.

Katey saw what happened. "I'd better see if she's all right." She grabbed her purse and disappeared toward the ladies' restroom.

To her surprise, all the stalls were empty. It was a perfect chance for her to have a woman-to-woman talk. She flushed the toilet Carol was hugging, not wanting to endure the sight of vomit a second more than she had to. She slapped Carol on one side of her cheek. "Hey, wake up! Don't you dare pass out on me yet! Got a few things that need sayin'."

Carol, still down on her knees, rolled her head to one side. "Yeah? Says who?"

"Says me! Get out of Jerry's life and stay out. He's filing for divorce Monday morning."

Carol slowly rose, clutching the face of the toilet tank for support to steady her dizziness and her legs. The two glared at each other, contempt for each other a mile high.

Carol spoke first. "Who said I'm gonna give him a divorce?" She took a half swing in Katey's direction, missing badly. "I'll fight him every step of the way. I'll—"

"You'll shut up and listen. You're the poorest excuse for a wife I've seen come down the pike in a long, long time! You've been married for almost two years, and you don't have a clue what Jerry wanted out of your marriage, do you? He's always wanted a family. That's why he married you! To start one!"

Katey's revelation nearly floored Carol. "He…he never said…he never told me. I could've given him that. I… I…could've!"

"But you didn't! Didn't you two ever talk to each other? Don't bother answering. I can plainly see you're neither barefoot nor pregnant. If you were pregnant, I'd be betting my next paycheck it wouldn't be Jerry's now, would it? How could you have done such a thing to him by sleeping with another man? Don't bother answering that either. You're beyond help, or hope, for that matter."

Carol leveled her best shot at Katey. "Well, *Ms. Know-It-All*, I've got a news flash for you too! Your precious Jerry ain't the man you've cracked him up to be. Ask him sometime. Go ahead, ask him!"

"I don't need to. I know the kind of man he is!"

Carol's voice rose to another pitch as she ridiculed and mocked Katey with a string of filthy, vulgar language that'd put a drunken sailor to shame. Katey's eyes narrowed, and her lips tensed. She squared away, jaw set. Her head bobbed and weaved as she gamely tried to get her mind working again. "That daughter of yours, Jerry keeps telling me you adopted from Chicago! That's a lie and you know it! That's Jerry's baby. Somewhere along the line, he knocked you up, didn't he? That little blond-haired girl he keeps talkin' about when he's not trying to compare me with you. Well, Katey, I'll call it the way I see it. No matter how you slice it, your wonderful little Krissy's nothing but a little blond blue-eyed bastard!"

With eyes blinded by tears and rage, Katey found her mark as she beat a steady tattoo of backhands across Carol's chops. Carol, dazed by Katey's vicious attack, buckled down to her knees. Katey kept her fist cocked in midair, poised to finish her off. "You get the H out of Jerry's life and stay out!"

Carol came charging out of the restroom like a wounded bull in a china closet, bumping and careening off people, tables, and chairs. Through bleary eyes, she finally staggered to the right table then sat in a heap for a minute, rubbing her forehead. On wobbly legs, she rose. Jerry tried to intercept his estranged spouse. She brushed by him and bellowed, "Everybody here can go straight to H!"

"Wait up!" he called after her. "You're in no condition to drive." He shot a quick glance back at Katey, who coolly sat down as though nothing had happened. "Thanks, Katey, for taking good care of her."

Katey finished her drink. "Anytime."

Two minutes passed, and the celebration continued as though nothing had ever happened. Andy noticed Katey rubbing her hands. "Your hands are all red! What happened?"

"Had a little difference of opinion, that's all!"

CHAPTER 10

Katey returned from Ricco and Theresa's wedding reception in high spirits. Andy, ever the gentlemen, proved that chivalry was not dead by opening the car door and walking her to the front steps.

After three steps inside, Aaron met her. "How did everything turn out? Has Ricco really changed?"

"Yes, Dad, he has. It's hard to believe, but it's true." She looked around. "Where's Krissy and Mother?"

"We didn't know what time to expect you, so your mother let Krissy go over to Gabrielle's to play. She's on her way to pick her up. What do you think of Andy?"

"We need to talk."

Aaron sensed Katey had more on her mind besides Andy and Ricco's wedding reception. "Let me get my pipe, lass, and I'll join you at the kitchen table."

Katey watched her father take the lid off his tobacco humidor then pack his pipe carefully. She still marveled at how with 175 pounds, he could still look like he could step into a boxing ring despite his age and the growing threads of silver gray in his hair. He lit his pipe then strode into the kitchen, his blue-gray eyes waiting on his daughter's first words as he sat down beside her.

"Dad, Jerry's going to divorce his wife, and I've agreed to marry him. It has nothing to do about right or wrong. Also, there will probably be other changes."

A ring of smoke circled about Mr. McCray's head. He moved his five-foot- nine-inch frame and returned from the front room with the newspaper. He opened it and pointed to the full page spread in the real estate section. "Jerry's wife's picture is there. She's one of the top two producers for the last six months. She has no intention of raising a family, does she?"

"No, and there's another thing you should know. She's been unfaithful to him."

"Katey, you've been meddling in a married man's life, which doesn't concern you."

"But it does, Father. It does! Jerry's made a terrible mistake by marrying her, and I'm as much to blame as he is. I forced him into it because I wouldn't make a hard choice."

He sat down, trying to get a true read. "You've changed, Katey. Are you trying to tell me you think it's all right to marry Jerry now? A divorced man?"

Katey took her father's hand. "I'm here to tell you I want Jerry. I'll never want or love another man. Listen to me, and try to see it as I do, even if you and Mother don't agree. I have a seven-year-old daughter who doesn't understand why all the other boys and girls in the second grade have a father and she has none. I'm twenty-six years old, and I've never cooked a meal, washed a dish, emptied my own garbage, used any of my own silverware or appliances, or waited for my husband to come home to me after work. Call it blind luck, coincidence, or fate, but I've been handed a second chance, and I will not let it slip away again."

"Even if it means going against your promise to your mother and me and to your church?"

"I can only say this. When Jerry and I marry, you and Mother will always be welcome where we live. If you two choose not to visit, I will be very hurt and sad, but I will share whatever happiness I have with Jerry. Happiness with my husband is better than no happiness with my life as it stands now. Once we're married, Jerry is a reasonable man. He will let me go to my church and continue to raise Krissy in our church's ways."

Aaron walked to the kitchen sink, pipe still stuck in his mouth. He drew down on it hard. "There's no man, young or old, that I admire more than Jerry. Can there be, lass, still a chance he would consider having our church recognize your marriage?"

"Don't expect that, Dad. It was one of the sticky points he would never accept before."

Aaron McCray pulled down on his pipe again. He paced back and forth. "Your generation, everything comes so hard. Why, I'll never know or understand! I'm a simple man. I work with my hands. Jerry works with his head, and he's a smart man, yet he cannot accept our ways, our traditions. Why is that, do you suppose?"

"He does, Daddy. He does! It's our religion he won't accept."

"Do what you feel you must do, Katey. Your mother and I will neither approve it nor condemn you for it. We must consider our granddaughter in this too!"

"Then you'll understand and come see us? You won't disown me or Krissy?" "We'll see you, but it's a bit much to expect us to understand or agree. Let's

leave it at that."

Katey hugged him. "Thank you, thank you, Father! Oh, I feel so much better, so much better!"

"When will Jerry be free to marry you?"

"Carol will not contest the divorce. She and I came to an understanding. It should only take a few months."

For the next few months, two people watched certain proceedings very closely—the ICC merger and Jerry's divorce.

With the certainty of their approaching marriage, Katey's personal life entered a whole new phase. It was nothing short of spectacular.

Jerry, too, felt the importance of Katey's decision to marry him on his own terms. He was a kinder, less embittered person. He now could accept his station in life on terms he was prepared to deal with. True, he'd severed what opportunity he had to make a serious challenge for the corporate comptroller's position. Bill Seelig had made sure he was out of that competition. Yet he remained openly optimistic about his future, more so now that Katey and Krissy were a part of it.

It was a hot, muggy day in early June, even for the Sacramento region, which was no stranger to soaring temperatures at this time of year. Through sweaty palms and foreheads, perspiration-soaked dress shirts, and light dresses that clung to sticky and shapely female bodies, everybody watched and waited for the news, good or bad, from the ICC proceedings.

Jerry looked up. No, he wasn't mistaken. Katey was hotfooting it down the hall in his direction.

"Hey, amigo!" she shouted, out of breath. "Guess what?"

Jerry could see the excitement oozing out of her face. Something momentous in her life had happened, though he hadn't a clue. "Okay, I'll bite.

You're here before coffee break time, so it must be something special! What's up?"

Katey raised her cool light-blue cotton dress a tad and settled on the corner of his desk. She squealed with delight at her own news. "I did it, Jerry! I did it for us! It'll be our wedding present to each other."

"Whoa, there! Slow down! What did you do for us?"

Her eyes danced a jig. She did all she could do to keep from launching herself in his arms. "I bought the cabin in the Sierras! Our honeymoon cabin!"

Jerry rocketed out of his chair into Katey's arms, startling several coworkers at their desks next to his area. "How, Katey, how? How'd you swing it?"

Embarrassed by all the nearby attention, Katey released herself from their embrace. "Jerry, people are… I remembered how much we both liked the cabin and how we fell in love with the area. So after you left for Korea, I kept contact with the management company, and when this chance came up to buy it, I went for it!"

He settled back into his chair. "Oh Lord! Not now!" "Why not?"

"The timing's all wrong, Katey. We could be bounced out of our jobs any day now."

There's something about an Irish smile. It can bedevil, it can beguile, and it can absolutely beautify great news. "Well, Mr. Doomsday! Mr. Beancounter, for your information, the ICC approved the merger! You ought to see 'em celebrating up at headquarters. They're going crazy!"

They whooped, they hollered, and they did impromptu dances up and down the aisles in the Support Services Building. It was one great big New Year's Day celebration in June.

"Feel like doing something crazy, amigo?" "Like what?" he asked.

"Let's take off, just you and me, and see our cabin! My Buick needs to blow the carbon clean out of its engine."

"Anything else on your mind?"

"Yes. It's time we worked out our marriage plans as soon as possible. No more waiting!"

"Katey, my divorce was final only last weekend!"

"Now you're a free man! We can celebrate that, too, when we're up there!" "Have you been up to the cabin lately?"

"Two months ago. Drove Krissy and my folks up there when I first saw the For Sale ad. Oh, Jerry, they loved it! Tell you what, let's take a couple days off. Both of us have lots of vacation time coming. Give us a chance to be alone again, really alone. I think we need this time together, love. I really do."

"All right, you're on! Do you have the key?"

"The management company still has it. Need to stop by the bank to sign the loan papers. They'll telephone the company, and we can stop by then to pick up our keys. Isn't it great! Oh, I'm so excited!"

"We'd better let your folks know where we'll be, and Krissy too!"

"They're off to Disneyland. Punkins has been bugging them for months. Dad's using his railroad pass. Figured he'd better, in case the merger didn't go through."

"How's the cabin look? About the same, I suppose?"

"It's a little rundown. Deck boards need replacing, probably a dozen."

"If I remember right, those were the two-by-eights. Got an idea, Katey! How about going two for one? I'll borrow Ricco's pickup. He's got the tools we'll be needing. I'll swing by Atlas Lumber for the deck boards and nails. We can make the trip count both ways. Work on the deck and our marriage plans. Okay?"

"Boy, you don't miss a trick, do you? Okay, I'll go for it. Let me pack some jeans and things since this is gonna be a work detail. I'll bring groceries for a couple of days' stay. Meet you at Ricco's house in about an hour. We'll stop by to get the keys on our way out."

"Fine by me! See you in an hour."

"Jerry, one other thing. No bedroom activity till we're married. I want that understood. We're only going to the cabin to replace some decking and to work out the details of our marriage."

"No problem, lover. I didn't figure on it being any other way."

Sixty minutes later, they headed east toward the foothills of the mighty High Sierras, happier than either had been for a long, long time. Behind them, the Sacramento Valley sweltered with its bake-oven temperatures The Sacramento Star headlines read *California Central Becomes California, Colorado and Western.*

They walked through the cabin, making a quick inspection. Everything appeared in order. Together, they unloaded the lumber, stacking it in the center of the deck so it would not have to be moved much by working around it. First thing Jerry did was take off his T-shirt.

"It's warm out, even up here," he called out to her. "Hope my back doesn't bother you. Carol always made me wear a shirt. Said she couldn't stand the scars!"

Katey set up the sawhorses. "Your back never bothered me. Leave your T- shirt off all you want too. Good Lord, you've earned it!"

They worked together well. Katey helped to hold the boards while Jerry cut them off. Finally, Katey called out, "Hey, Landis, how about a break? Boy, once you get started on something, you forget there are other words in the English language like slow down or stop!"

Jerry sat on one of the picnic table benches, mopping his brow, while Katey disappeared into the cabin to get a bottle of Coke. Together, they split the Coke and admired their progress. "We should finish replacing the rest tomorrow morning easy."

"Aren't we gonna sleep in, slave driver? Got two more days! What's the hurry?"

He didn't answer her tease. Instead, he got up with the Coke in his hand and leaned over the deck rail, peering down the canyons to Lake Tahoe far below. "I can still hardly believe it, Katey. This is ours! Oh God, you're so wonderful, so good. Everything about you says it over and over. Hope you don't mind the praise and compliments!"

She joined him at the rail and put her arms around him. "I could never get tired of you saying nice things about me."

"Soon as Greg comes up with my cost savings money, I'll pitch in and really put a dent in that loan principal. Or maybe you'd rather I put that in with the GI loan on our home? There's a new housing development going in above Thornton Avenue on the north side. We could go back day after tomorrow and have a look-see."

Katey took a sip of Coke. "Let's call it quits for today. Your leg's starting to bother some. And like you said, we can finish in a snap tomorrow. Maybe by then, we'll know where we stand on a lot of things, like GI loans, homes, and such."

CHAPTER 11

Over breakfast and two coffee refills the next morning, they tackled the biggest hurdle of their young lives—their upcoming marriage plans. Katey led in very cautiously. "Tell me a little about your church, Jerry. I need to know since I'm going to belong. Maybe we should start with that."

Jerry could see they were indeed opening Pandora's box. "Katey, do you really want to know or are you trying to feel me out?"

She never flinched a second. "Both, really. But I'm interested most in what role you play in your church. Knowing you, you have to be involved in its operation, or else you'd never belong."

"You really have me pegged, Katey. Sometimes it's almost scary the way you know me. Okay, for openers, I'm on the mission committee."

"Is that something like the Mormons do? You know, send their young people out?"

"No, only the name is similar. This committee I'm serving on picks out three or four worthwhile goals or missions to do each year, depending on our budget. Well, after almost two years, they're going to try one of my ideas."

"Knowing you, you've put a lot of thought into it. And of course, you've crunched the numbers, so you know exactly what can and can't be done."

"Exactly! Hear me out! Welfare isn't working. Never has, never will. So I've come up with a plan through the church to get four families off welfare."

"Oh, Jerry, it sounds exciting!"

"We're going to help these families get on their feet all the way. We've rented two duplexes with all utilities and groceries to be provided by the church. We'll also pay for day care for the children while they're parents are learning a trade or skill. To further spice up the pie, after their training, we've already contacted employers who will hire them and give them a temporary job because we will supplement their pay for four months as an incentive for the employer to keep them. Now here's the rub. Two of the fathers are ex- alcoholics, and one single mother was hooked on drugs. So we pay for counseling and follow-up to help make sure they stay on course. The single mother is going to secretarial school and has three kids in day care. The two ex- alcoholics are taking carpentry and plumbing through vocational training schools. The third father is now doing on-the-job training with the local telephone company as a repairman. How'm I doing?"

Katey hugged him. "Oh, Jerry, that's a tremendous idea and program. I'm so proud of you!"

"It took a lot more budget than we've ever tackled before. I had to do a real selling job to the other members. Right now, we're only three months into our mission. Anything could snafu the whole idea, but it's worth the gamble."

"Besides being a committee man, are you involved in any other church activities?"

"Yes. Once a month, on a weekend, I and three other adults chaperone eight young high school age kids while we work on the serving lines at the Gospel Mission in Sacramento. Every kid that volunteers must turn in his or her report to us on how we can do a better job of serving, preparing food, saving money, or anything else that matters to our volunteer operation. Katey, we've got something for our young adults to do. Believe you me, they're involved!"

"Oh, Jerry, what great ideas!"

"Katey, everybody helps out. Our treasurer for this month is a high school junior. She pays the bills. And believe you me, she knows what's going on!

Those that aren't on the mission serving line have to do the janitorial and maintenance work at the old bingo hall. Of course, we all pitch in too. We have a schedule posted each month for job assignments. A bit of army delegation there, I'm afraid, but it works! Young people like responsibility if the older people will just let them have it. Of course, there'll be some flub-ups along the way. It's the experience that counts, and what better way to get it and learn at the same time?"

"Do you have Sunday school classes for the young kids?"

"For all ages. Katey, we're terribly short of good teachers for Sunday school.

That's where we really need help to improve. I'm out of my realm, but I do my best if we run short of teachers."

"Could I be a Sunday school teacher and bring Krissy?"

He put his hand in hers. "Would you? Oh, Katey, you're a natural. Just look how you handle Krissy. Come on down with me any time. We'll put you to work!"

"When you work on the serving lines with those high school kids, I want to help serve beside you. Is it okay?"

He hugged her hard. "All right, but it'll be you who gets an education." Katey got up to walk outside to the deck, pacing slowly.

"Okay, Katey, so far so good. What's next?"

"I know there's at least three things you won't budge on regarding church, religion, and marriage vows."

"The first is never, but never will you sign a church pledge. Okay, I can live with that."

"Will you let me continue to contribute to my church as you do yours on a when-you-want-to and how-much-you-want-to basis?"

"I have no problem with that. Fine by me."

Katey wasn't sure what tack to take regarding the next issue. She opened up slowly. "You said you could never belong to something you don't believe in. I now respect that even though it has hurt me deeply when you refused to be a member of my church. Yes, I know now you made the right move for you by joining your nondenominational church. You also said our church needed a complete overhaul! That hurt too! Some of your messages must've gotten through 'cause our church is changing for the better, I believe. We now have an English-only mass once each Sunday. No more mumbo jumbo, as you called it. It's attracting lots of young married couples, probably for the very same reasons you stated. Would you be willing to see for yourself if I invited you to attend with Krissy and me?"

That required a lot of soul-searching on Jerry's part. He squirmed and fidgeted a bit then stroked his chin, trying to decide how to answer. "You're talking compromise here, Katey. You go to my church if I attend yours?"

"It's more than compromise, dear. I want to join yours because like you, I believe they're doing God's work, and I can feel very conformable with that situation."

"All right, we agree to attend each other's church, but don't expect me to join yours because I won't, even if you join mine. Deal?"

"You got a deal!"

Suddenly, they both realized they had but one hurdle to clear, the big one— their marriage ceremony. Again, Katey took the initiative. "I said I'd marry you anywhere so we can get our lives back on track."

"Katey, your forgetting now I'm a divorced man, and I know your church is dead set against divorce. And with you, that's double poison because you and your family will not accept divorce. How do I fit in with either situation?"

"Better than expected. I've already talked to Dad about your divorce. They don't like it, but they won't oppose me marrying you on that basis. Krissy was the reason, plain and simple. They did not want to give up seeing her because they've really become attached to her. Our church's position on divorce has changed somewhat. I can marry a divorced man and still stay a member of my church and have our marriage recognized if we marry within my church and you attend, which you've agreed to do as a visitor."

"That's a mighty big if, isn't it, Katey?"

"I don't expect you to change on that, Jerry. After all, you backed out on that part before, so let's just concentrate on getting some justice of the peace, okay?"

"Not so fast, Katey. Maybe there's room for compromise here too. Isn't it strange twenty-one months ago, neither of us could see or find a way to do and say the things we've just settled?"

"Darling, twenty-one months ago, neither of us were willing to give in on anything, no matter how miserable our principles made us feel. I'm sure you felt the same way."

"I do, Katey. And as you've always known, family comes first with me. You were willing to compromise all the way to get us back together, so I'm willing to meet you halfway. I'll agree to your church-recognized ceremony and your English-only mass so you can meet your church requirements. There is one condition that must be met."

"What's that?"

"You must choose somebody besides Father Murphy to conduct our ceremony. I never cared for his holier-than-thou attitude when we went for church counseling. Remember?"

Her tears of joy and relief came fast and furious, but neither cared because Katey had the best cry of her life. She hugged and kissed and hugged and kissed Jerry some more. "Oh, Jerry, I hope you feel the same way I do right now…like a world full of problems and frustration has at last been lifted off me. My heart will sing a new song of love for you. Hope you feel the same way."

He smiled then held her close. "I do, Katey. Believe me, I do!"

"Carol is old history, Jerry. Let's leave her there."

CHAPTER 12

Late that afternoon, Jerry barbecued hamburgers while Katey went to the fridge to get her favorite potato salad along with watermelon and lemonade.

They dined in their own royal splendor on the picnic table, drinking in the evening rays of sunlight over the bulwark of mountainous stone behind them, sprinkled with the clean, crisp aroma of the nearby forests of pine and cedar. Indeed, God's blessing seemed to smile down upon them at long last.

That night, Katey tossed and turned as she reran the day's monumental events in her mind. Oh, how far they'd come. But their most important link was still missing…their wedding vows. And how she loved the thought of marriage, all the dreaming and planning and heartbreak. And yes, there'd been anger, hurt, and frustration all coming to a happy, happy ending no less! Her last thought was on the way they'd compromised to get what they both wanted—marriage and each other. It should be the sleeping pill she needed to fall into a peaceful and restful night's sleep.

"Jerry!"

"What, Katey?"

"I can't sleep. Let me lay down with you. No funny business, I promise." "Okay, as long as you keep your word."

It was like before. Oh, how she loved to snuggle with her back up against his body. There she found her resting spot and stopped moving. Next, she felt his arm drop over her shoulder. Gently, she moved it down to wrap safely around her, just under her breasts. Ah, sweet z's at last!

One, two, three hours drifted by. "Jerry!"

"Now what?"

"I'm awake again, and I can't sleep." She turned around under his arm and planted a juicy good morning kiss. "I'm just so excited about everything. The way we worked things out. And I don't think I could take another disappointment. Let's get married today. Please, Jerry?"

"Katey, there's only an hour or two left to get the deck job done. Tell you what. Let's do the deck this morning then run back into town and get our marriage license. And while we're in town, we'll do the ceremony then."

"No, I don't want to wait. Too much could happen."

He sat up and rubbed his eyes. "And to think that people who know me said I was stubborn. *Wow!*"

"You're the one that's stubborn. Me? Well, I'm just a bit persistent, that's all!"

"Yeah, until you get your way. Okay, here we go again. I'll compromise. We do the marriage ceremony, and as long as we're in town, we rent a sander so this afternoon, we might as well re-sand and put on the new deck stain. Then the job will be done right. Whatcha say?"

"Let's go. That's one better! Krissy and the folks won't be back for at least another four or five days. Does Ricco have a stepladder or two in his garage?"

"I saw one when I borrowed his pickup. What's on your mind?"

"Last night, you said our cabin needs a fresh coat of stain. We both have lots of vacation time piling up, so let's put it to good use and spend a few days or whatever it takes to get our cabin back in tiptop shape. This is the right place, Jerry, to figure out what we want to do with our married lives."

Now he was showing his old enthusiasm. "I couldn't agree more! If I could choose any place to start out our marriage, this would be it! And in the process, we put our cabin back in first-class shape. Let's take a week!"

"Done! Let's get going. I want to be first in line at the marriage license bureau!"

And first in line they were as hand in hand, they moved up the steps as fast as Jerry's leg would allow to the license bureau. Then one quick ceremony with Father Donovan presiding. They changed to shorts and T-shirts in the church restrooms. They hurried a wave of goodbye and were back into Ricco's pickup.

"Jerry, drop me off at Ricco's. I'll drive the Buick back home and pick up more food at Bettingers and make a stop at the Bon. I'll leave a note for Krissy and Dad and Mom. Boy, they'll be tickled pink that we finally tied the knot!"

"Okay. I need to stop by Ricco's for some extra duds. I'll pick up the stain and some brushes and then rent the sander. How much time do you need?"

"Meet me back at my home in about ninety minutes. That'll be enough."

Mission accomplished. The two newlyweds sped out of town by the time the rest of the employees at the headquarters of the California, Colorado, and Western Railroad (CC&W) reached for their coffee cups during the mid- morning break!

Katey's heart pumped a tune of love. Everything about the day was the kind of script Hollywood moviemaker's dolt on, with real down-to-earth couples in love. She kissed her ring over and over then beamed her message of love at her husband.

They finished replacing the worn deck boards by three in the afternoon. "That's it, Landis," Katey called out to him. "Let's enjoy life! Stay put! I'll go make some sandwiches and let's eat them out here!"

Ten minutes later, Katey returned with a tray loaded with sandwiches, iced tea, potato chips, and Krissy's picture album.

"I'm so hungry, Katey! I could eat the butt end out of a grizzly bear!"

She roared, "Landis, you do have a certain way of putting things! Try the sandwiches. They won't bite back!"

"Why the photo album? If I recollect, its Krissy's, isn't it?"

Katey couldn't touch a bite of her lunch. "There's a few new pages you need to see, my love." She slid in beside Jerry, adrenalin pushing her to the limit. "Please open it, my darling husband of six hours!"

He picked up a potato chip and opened the thick album cover. Katey never took her eyes off him, watching, waiting for his reaction. Methodically, with his usual Landis perusal, he let his eyes do the walking from snapshot to snapshot. "Katey, that's you. You look so young. Who's that with you?"

"Uncle Kevin and Aunt Rose."

"Always liked your hair shoulder-length. Still do. What? I can't believe it!

You look fat in these two. You're really puttin' on weight."

"Fat? Weight? Oh, my darling, do I need to draw you a map?"

He looked at her. He looked again at the first page of the album. "If…if I didn't know any better, I'd… I'd…"

"Say it, Jerry! Say it! What do I look like?" "You're…you're…you look pregnant!"

She waited no longer. She kissed him again and again. The stunning reality hit him harder than a mountain avalanche. He grabbed her, and they embraced. Katey had the best cry of her life.

"Oh, my darling. If you only knew how many times I've wanted to tell you.

How something always came up or else the timing wasn't just right."

He began to cry. "But you did tell me up in Madigan. Only after I pulled through, you backed away. Why?"

"I wanted you as my husband, not as Krissy's father because you felt you were obligated. I wanted our marriage to be because we loved each other, both of us free to make our choice, not because you had to. Can you understand my position maybe a little bit?"

He wiped the tears with his forearm and looked again. "See there, I'm nursing Krissy, and there's Mother holding our daughter. Oh, she was so proud. Said Krissy wasn't a baby. Said she was a real live doll! And she was!"

"Were you ever going to tell me? What if I'da stayed married to Carol?" "Dad and I talked about that when I brought Krissy home right after you left for Korea. I had a will drawn up just in case. There's also a stipulation that on Krissy's eighteenth birthday, if we were not legally married, you were to be notified so at least you wouldn't go through life not knowing."

He turned his back on her, closing the picture album and leaving it on the table. He walked away from her, still obviously troubled.

When he returned, he found his wife kneeling by the foot of the bed, eyes red, holding her rosary. "Why the big lie, Katey? Why couldn't you just come right out and tell me you were pregnant after it happened? Why, Katey?"

She came to him. "Jerry, we were just eighteen and so much in love, but we couldn't make it on love alone. Neither of us had any money to start our marriage in proper fashion. We both had more schooling to get out of the way. Dad and Mom convinced me the only thing to do was go back to Chicago to have Krissy and finish business college. There, I could take care of our baby till I returned, get a decent job, and then try to get us back together to make a good life for ourselves and for Krissy."

"During all these decisions, did the idea of giving Krissy up ever come up?" "No. I told Dad I would never give up my baby!"

He confronted her as never before. *"Did you ever consider giving Krissy up? Even for an instant? Katey?"*

"Never, Jerry! Never!"

She looked up in his face. "There's so much of you in her. Besides the eyes and hair, she's as stubborn and independent as you ever thought of being!"

They cleaned off the picnic table and carried the leftover food back into the cabin. Near the sink, they exchanged kisses and held their embrace.

Katey said, "Jerry, there can be no more secrets between us ever. Secrets eat and eat at the bond that holds people together until there's nothing left. First thing when Krissy gets back, I will tell her the truth about us. She's old enough to understand now."

Evening came with suddenness all its own, as though some celestial force conspired to yank down a huge bedroom shade from the rest of the world, separating day from night. Katey kept humming and singing. Jerry had never seen her sprits soar so high or feel so much warmth and love emanating from one person. They were both tired. It had been a long momentous and wonderful day. It was time to retire to their bed.

Katey dazzled him by modeling her very expensive and exquisite negligee purchase. She paraded around their bedroom, making sure his eyes didn't miss a trick, following every curve of her body, every indication she was ready for love with the full legal acknowledgment by the State of California and the unequivocal blessing of the Holy Roman Catholic Church.

With face and cheeks flushed, eyes darting and dancing full of expectation, she lay down beside him to wait for his passionate embrace and the ritual that was sure to follow.

The words came, the touch came, and the passionate kiss followed. Then everything stopped. Katey untied her negligee, letting it fall freely from her shoulders. "Love me. Please love me, my beloved husband. Seal our marriage with your love. Replenish our love within me. I need you like never before." With her body reeking with perfume and passion, she encouraged him in every possible way to be one. He turned away from their embrace, where she had cradled him. He moved away and sat on the edge of their bed.

His body shook, the scars on his back moved, and he sobbed out, "I can't, Katey! You said no more secrets between us! Well, here's one more. *I'm impotent!*"

CHAPTER 13

She lay there, still disbelieving his words. Her body was on fire, waiting for him to make love. Then Katey rose and sat down beside him and took him in her arms. "Can you talk about it? Tell me how it happened."

He dropped to his knees, buried his head in her lap, and sobbed. "You were right. You always seem to know, Katey. You warned me, but I didn't listen."

She lifted his head up and stroked his hair. "I'm beginning to get the picture, my dear. My ring and our commitment…that has everything to do with this, doesn't it?"

"Yes, you were right, Katey. Even on my wedding night with Carol, I had to pretend she was you before, before…"

"You made love to her?"

"It wasn't making love. I kept seeing your face and the wedding band I slipped on your finger and vows to each other and to God. I felt I'd committed adultery. We had a big fight. I moved into my own bedroom. I was so hurt, so ashamed."

Katey retied her negligee, got off their bed, and kneeled in prayer. Then she came to him in his hour of greatest need. They embraced. Amid more passionate kisses, Jerry sensed that he'd been accepted for what he was—her devoted husband.

Two days went by. The deck was sanded, and the new deck stain was applied. During this time, Katey never brought up the subject of Jerry's impotence.

On the third day, they set up the stepladders and brought out the brushes. It was time to restain their cabin. Both ends of the cabin were finished. It was time to redo the two sides. They worked side by side, enjoying each other's company, including a lot of good-natured ribbing and joking.

Then Katey brought out their lunch, sat down to enjoy it, and then disappeared into the cabin while he finished off the crumbs.

By the time she returned, Jerry was back up on his ladder, brush in hand, absorbed only in getting more stain on. She stood next to his ladder, patiently waiting for him to take notice. When nothing happened, Katey nudged his leg, holding up her empty paint bucket.

He turned to glance down to what she wanted. Surprise would hardly cover the shock that came across his face. His mouth was agape, eyes disbelieving what he was seeing. He almost dropped the bucket.

"Just checking, Landis, to see if your hormones are still alive." "You're trying to provoke me?"

"Well, now that I got your attention, let's see if you need glasses." She climbed her ladder and pulled her loose-fitting skirt above her thighs. "Well, do you?"

"Of course, I see your panties, and I don't need glasses!"

"Jerry, they used to turn you on! Said you could never get tired of looking at them!"

"They still do!" "Prove it!"

He came charging at her, bent on one thing—getting her down off that ladder. "I'm going to carry you inside, and I want to see jeans on, a bra, and a T-shirt, in nothing flat!"

"You're chicken, Jerry! Afraid you might just enjoy something more! Maybe a little love?"

He marched inside the cabin and headed straight for their bedroom, where he dumped Katey on the bed like a loose sack of potatoes.

"Don't leave," she begged. "The least you can do is let me give you some pleasure. We're married, you know! Or have you forgotten that too?"

"Don't, Katey! Please! You know I can't. I'll get professional help when we get home."

"Just kiss me and tell me how much you love me."

Their first kiss unleashed a torrent of pent-up emotion. She opened up to him, letting him suckle, kiss, touch, and caress to his wildest desire. "Think of only one thing, darling! How much you want me! Then let it happen! I'll help you all the way!"

Finally, he reached down to slip her shoes off then took time to drop his own off the edge of the bed with a soft thud on the rug. "Katey, I want you so bad. I don't know where to begin…or how anymore…"

She lay on her side with him still cradled in her arms, both still not fully undressed. "Jerry, don't hold back anymore! It's me, your Katey!"

"My brace. I might hurt you! I hurt you before. I can't, Katey!"

She finally bedded him down and calmed his fears about leaving his leg brace on. Soft whispers and little urgings here and there began to pay off. After, they lay as one, each so thoroughly satisfied, so completely absorbed in their moment of intimacy that the brevity of their lovemaking never once was questioned. Katey kissed him again and again. "Just think, we have the rest of our lives to practice up. And as you well know, the more practice we get in, the better the results."

He whispered he loved her then sat straight up. "Oh Lord! Oh Lord!" "Now what?"

"The paint brushes and the paint buckets! We left them out in all this heat!" "Tell you what, Jerry. You tend to them and get right back here."

He flashed a smile and looked down at her. The old Jerry Landis confidence was never more evident. "Suppose I'm too pooped to pop. What then, Katey, darling?"

"We'll just take a nap and rest up for tonight. You'll be ready to take my negligee off by then."

That day, that hour marked the beginning of a remarkable relationship between Jerry and Katey.

Early the next morning, they finished restaining the sides of their cabin before the heat came on. Jerry surprised Katey by fixing lunch for her.

Katey took a bite of her roast beef sandwich. "Anything else you want to get done before we head down to the valley?"

"We're low on firewood for next season. I noticed some cordwood stacked up at the country store at the turnoff. Bet we could get a pretty good deal if bought now. Firewood's not exactly the hot selling item with this heat wave we're going through. Ricco said no hurry in returning the pickup."

"No wonder you save money. Gotta hand it to you, every dollar they ever get out of you, they're gonna darn sure earn it!"

He snickered a bit. "Okay, so I'm a bit careful with my bucks, and from now on, they're your bucks too, Katey Landis. That's how people get ahead, by saving a few dollars and doing something with it. Look at your folks. They don't exactly throw money out the window."

"Yes, love," she said, giving him a good-natured jab to the ribs. "Know what? I wouldn't have it any other way either!"

"Have you given any thought on how you're going to break the news to Krissy when we get home?"

"Yes. I've been giving it a lot of thought. I believe I have it all figured out." "Go ahead. Try it on me."

"I'm going to tell Krissy that you and I have a special seed, and when we put that seed together in my tummy, with God's help, that's how we got her.

Then I'm going to say that sometimes people love each other so much that they can't wait to get married before God helps them put the special baby seed in the mother's tummy. That's what happened to us, and now because we loved each other so much, we had her first. Then we got married."

Jerry was impressed. "Katey, you should've been a schoolteacher. That was a beautiful story about love and babies. I'm sure she'll accept it, and there'll be no more wondering about why I arrived so late in her life."

"Thank you, sweetheart. It's true, every word. And I don't mind telling her that way one bit."

"I never asked, but I can assume from other things you had a very difficult time carrying Krissy?"

"I nearly lost her twice on near miscarriages. The last three months, I barely left my bed. I wanted to carry her as close to full term as possible. That's why they had to tie my tubes. It was just too risky to have any more. She's our blessed miracle baby, darling. She'll always be special to us!"

Jerry poured himself a glass of lemonade from the pitcher. "Speaking of family, I wish I'd done a better job of keeping tabs on my sisters. Stacey is God knows where. She ran away, and I have no idea where she's at now. Got mixed up with some scum and was hooked on drugs, last I heard."

"Any idea where Cheryl is?" Katey asked.

"Pretty sure she was adopted by a family near San Jose. Think it was a good move. I plan on trying to reconnect with her through the welfare agency."

"What about your mother?"

"She died last year. Alcohol related, I'm sure. Never shed a tear or attended her funeral. Happened right in the middle of my problems with Carol."

Katey held her husband close. "Too bad she never saw in you in what everybody else has seen. You're dedicated, responsible, committed, got your degree, and you're a war hero. Your mother's been wrong about you all her life.

There must have been an awful lot of hate between you two. Thank God, you don't carry that hate in your heart like she did."

"No, Katey, life's too short to put up with that. I've said it at least one hundred times. My life changed for the better the minute you stepped into it.

Thanks for being such an important part of my life."

They finished their lunch while the conversation drifted to their friends.

Katey said, "What do you think of Greg's new interest, Victoria?"

"As far as Ricco and I are concerned, the jury's still out on her. Oh, she has more money than she knows what do to with. But after I see her, I always come away with the feeling there's something missing in their relationship."

"There is. Greg told me she has no interest in starting a family after they get married. She likes the social whirl, and he does too, when you get right down to it. So maybe they're good for each other."

Jerry continued, "Ricco is the one I still can't get over! Man, oh, man, what a change! He squeezed through that election by only a handful of votes. He's a visionary...no, better make that a revolutionary!"

"What do you mean?"

"Ricco claims management's role is really that of being the caretaker for the railroad's stockholders, the real owners. He goes on to say that management will never assume labor's role. But doesn't mean that labor shouldn't try to assume management's role. He envisions a day when labor will fill both roles.

Then he says we'll have the most efficient operation possible. Everybody will have a direct stake in profits and losses, which will make for a truly competitive operation."

"How do you see it, Jerry?"

"He's right up to a point. Right now, it's a no-win situation. But if labor, management, and the stockholders were all the same people, think of the efficiency that would produce. It's exciting just to think about such a possibility. And you know what? Someday that's going to happen in certain industries. Then watch them grow!"

Katey got up to carry the lunch tray back. She stood, tray in hand, and took a good look at her husband. "You're a visionary too, Jerry. A bottom-line visionary. Tell me, what do you see?"

He got up and stood behind her, both arms encircled around his wife. "The merger was good for us, Katey. It bought us a lot of time. Time that you and I and Krissy are going to put to good use. We're going to be happier, more content than you can imagine. Our love will grow even stronger for each other until…"

She turned around, and for the first time, she saw a distant and far-off look cross his face. A bit of concern crept into her voice. "Until what?"

"Ricco was only half right. It could also go the other way too. Somebody from management could do the same thing that he thinks his union should do."

Katey still didn't follow Jerry's thought. "If that happened, wouldn't that be just as good as the union taking over someday?"

"Not necessarily. Instead of many, many owners, there'd be just one!" "How could that be?"

"Well, for starters, he'd have to be super rich, beyond anything we know. So rich that he'd buy out every stockholder. The worst part, he'd probably want to play God! On second thought, he'd be God! What an ego trip it would be for somebody like that."

"Oh, Jerry, I hope that never happens. Think of what he could do to all the employees, including us.

"He'd be so powerful, he could say jump and everybody would say, 'How high?' He'd be an enigma the likes of which our free enterprise system has never experienced. His monopoly would be that great and unchallenged."

"We'd be rubberlike people in a huge rubber room, wouldn't we?" "You got it, Katey!"

"You did say we have a lot of good years ahead, didn't you?" "Yes, my love. That I did!"

CHAPTER 14

Jerry brought in breakfast on the pizza tray. Katey sat up. "That's it, the end of the bacon, isn't it?"

"Yeah, this was our clean-out-the-fridge meal. There's two pieces of toast, one scrambled egg, half a glass of juice, and half a grapefruit section. We either pack up and head back down the valley or drive back to that mom-and-pop store at the turnoff to get some more groceries for another day or two. Take your pick!"

"Let's get in our firewood for next season, dear. Like you said, the price will probably be right."

He took a sip of juice and handed her the glass. "That wood should be well seasoned by this fall. Sure beats taking a chance on that high-priced green stuff they'll try to unload on us this winter."

"Okay, my darling husband, you're on! Two more days! Did I mention I love you?"

He laughed and tickled her. "Not in the last five minutes or so." He turned serious. "Katey, there's so much I want us to do. I have such big plans for all of us. Golly, I hardly know where to begin."

"Okay, Mr. Beancounter, shoot!"

"I've always wanted to learn to ski, and now with our own cabin up here near that new ski lift, you can't beat the deal."

"What about your leg, Jerry?"

"During my rehab, they showed us films. Skiing is one thing I should be able to do. Think you and Krissy would want to take lessons with me?"

Now Katey was excited. "Would we? Just try to stop us! Oh, Jerry, doing something together as a family would be perfect! I'm excited just thinking about it! You should be the one to tell Krissy about it."

"Got some more ideas, but I need General Katey Landis's okay. The other day, you said something about Krissy acting so much older than seven years old."

"Hon, there's so much of you in her, it's almost scary."

"Let's hear how it went with Krissy."

"Krissy met another new friend in school, a little girl from Lebanon. Her name's Salome. Anyway, once or twice a week after school, Mom let's her play either in our yard or over at Salome's home. Two weeks ago, she had Grandma all upset. She told Mom that she was going to stay up till nine thirty each night because Salome's parents let her stay up that late."

"How'd you handle it?"

"I told her in our house, her bedtime was eight o'clock. No exceptions!" "Then what happened?"

"She stuck her tongue out at me, stomped her foot, and dared me to send her to her room."

"Oh, oh, that was her Waterloo, if I know my Katey."

"You bet it was! She got her jeans pulled down, and, boy, I let her have it!

Then I marched her straight to her room to sit in her chair until she was ready to apologize."

"I imagine that took care of Krissy."

"Hardly! An hour passed, and Mother checked on her and motioned for me to come quick. You'll never believe what she was doing!"

Jerry set the tray on the nightstand then sat beside Katey. "Haven't a clue.

Go on!"

"That little stinker had Mr. Floppy over her knees and was whaling the stuffing out of her rabbit. After I came in, she told me every time she gets a spanking, Mr. Floppy gets one too! How do you like those apples?"

"Oh, oh, sounds like Krissy got some MOS. More of the same, right?"

"You better believe she did! Then I took Mr. Floppy away from her and set him up on the shelf for a week. After that blistering, I told her when she's ready to apologize, then she could come to the door and tell me."

"Bet she tried to wait you out, didn't she?"

"Yes. That took another hour, and I was beginning to wonder who would give in first. Finally, she came to the door, sobbing her poor heart out like it was going to break. I took her in my arms, curled lower lip and all. Then out of the blue, she says, 'Please hurry, Mommy, 'cause I want my supper!'"

Jerry roared. "Katey, you're right. She is a lot like me. An awful lot!"

"Okay, now try on this on for size. For weeks, she's been buggin' Grandpa to take her to Disneyland. Didn't ask me, 'cause she knows I'd be strict with her. So after two weeks of 'Please, Grandpa,' he finally gives in. End of story, you'd think, but not our Krissy. Not by a long shot!"

"So how did she get to you this time?"

"Two days before she goes to Disneyland, she really pulls a sneaky. She turns her head and refuses to kiss Grandpa good night. So I go in. Krissy tells me there'll be no good night kiss until Grandpa agrees to let her walk by herself at Disneyland. She's too grown up now to have anybody take her by the hand anymore."

"Oh, oh, here comes some MOS!" "Right on! Know what she pulls next?" "No, but I'll bet it's a doozy!"

"She knows I mean business! No holding hands, no Disneyland! Now she says that when she goes to the restroom, she doesn't want Grandma to come in to spy on her. That's the word she used. *Spying on her!*"

"Oh, oh, I smell more trouble!"

"I told her restrooms are the very places I worry about the most. I said, 'I know you feel all grown up, but this is definitely not the place to show it. Either Grandma is in the stall with you or *no Disneyland!*"

"So did that end the holdout?"

"Krissy ran out into the parlor and kissed Grandpa good night because her mommy explained there are bad people out there who might want to hurt her."

"Katey, you handled that very well!"

They finished breakfast. While Katey showered, Jerry did the dishes. When she returned, he poured her another cup of coffee. He leaned over the table to kiss her. "Thanks for being such a wonderful mother to Krissy, and thanks for having our daughter. I've never felt so relaxed and so happy with my life as I do now. At least I'm at peace with my lot in life. All we have to do with our lives is fill in the dots."

Katey watched him for a few minutes. "There's more ideas churning inside you, just itching to get out, aren't there, my dear? You're going to be just what's been missing in mine and Krissy's lives."

"How old do you think Krissy acts like?"

"My guess, probably ten or eleven. A lot like you were. Always seemed older than the rest of us."

Jerry went to the sink to rinse out his cup. "Let's put some of this independence and grown-up attitude to the test."

"Hon, she's still only seven years old, no matter how old she thinks she is or acts."

He turned and leaned with his back up against the sink. "Oh, Katey, I've got ideas I'd like to try on her. Of course, if you don't go along, then we'll leave 'em right here where they belong, in the round file."

Midafternoon found them hand in hand, walking down the Forest Service trail. They were two people in love, seemingly not a care in the world. Katey pointed to her right. "There, under that big pine tree. That's a good spot to spread our blanket! I can hear the gurgle from the mountain stream!"

They spread their blanket and then made short work of Katey's food. Jerry removed the cap from a bottle of orange pop, took a swig, and then handed it to Katey. "Katey, you're absolutely right. Up here, you're closer to everything." He pointed skyward. "See, even Mr. Hawk agrees. He's looking for his dinner too!"

They watched, fascinated by the hawk overhead, riding the down drafts, circling and gliding effortlessly, waiting for his prey to make one fatal mistake. Suddenly, the hawk swooped, talons bared, then the strike, and the rabbit was his. Katey shuddered. "Boy, Mother Nature doesn't fool around, does she? Up here, it's survive or starve. There's no middle ground or compromise, is there? Makes me feel awful glad we found a way."

"Yes, Katey. But did you notice how everything fits a certain pattern up here? It's all done with such efficiency and little room for error. This is where I really feel God's presence. This is where I feel close to him, and I know you do too!"

Both leaned with their backs up against the huge tree trunk, listening to the breeze shift in and out of the branches and pine needles. A fragrance of mixed pine and cedar filled the air. Katey rose then walked to the snow-fed mountain stream. She dropped to her knees to taste the crystal clear water. *"Wow, that's cold!* Makes your teeth ache!"

Jerry called out to her, "Come back and lay your head in my lap. Time to shoot the breeze…go over some ideas that've been kicking around in my head for a while."

She settled back on the blanket, head in his lap, and looked up at her husband. "One other thing about punkins," she said. "When she wants to still be my little girl, it's Mommy, Mommy, Mommy! But when she wants to act grown up, she puts her hands on her hips and stands straighter than a yardstick. Then she says *Mother* in the most easy, causal voice you've ever heard. Watch out when she tries to charm you for something she wants when she says, 'Daddy, Daddy,' and then switch to Father."

He bent down to taste her lips then sat up, shoulders erect. "Have you ever taken a real close look at the rooBine on your parents' house?"

"No, can't say as I have. Why?"

"It would sure make it easy to add a spare bedroom, bath, and walk-in closet. I've given this a lot of thought for a couple of days now. A lot of thought."

She looked up at him and put his hand in hers. "You've got something up your sleeve, Jerry. Okay, spill it."

"Your family is so close, so easy to get along with. Heck, you and Krissy have spent almost all your lives there except for Chicago. Set one more plate at the dinner table and basically, nothing's changed. Do you suppose your folks would listen to an idea I have about their home?"

Katey got up and lay her head on his shoulders. "Dear, when you talk about new plans and ideas, you really mean it, don't you?"

101

"I've had to face up to my limitations. Don't think we'd be happy in an apartment or duplex listening to my neighbor's dogs, cats, and kids. No, I'd like a small place with a small yard that I can handle. That's important later, 'cause we both know I'm gradually losing the use of my left leg."

"You figure we need a small house on a lot big enough to still keep the neighbors from camping on your front steps. Right?"

"Yes, your folk's place is ideal. There's even enough room to remodel the garage, too, for your Buick, Katey."

"But how would it work out for us if we lived there?"

"Here's my idea. If your folks agree to give us a trial period…say, six months, we live there and share groceries and utilities. And if that works out, we'll make them a buyout offer. Someday, they'll want to retire, and we put in a provision that they could live there as long as they wanted to."

Jerry's idea had merit in Katey's estimation. "Let's see if I got this right. First, we live at my folk's place for a trial period with their permission. I'd like to add a new wrinkle. You and me and Krissy do all the cooking for a month then trade off with them. We'd still be sharing the kitchen and laundry room with them. If that works out, we make them a buyout offer with the understanding that they keep the right to live there after Dad's retirement. How am I doing?"

"You got it!"

"Jerry, most young couples can't wait to get out on their own, away from their parents. What makes our situation so different?"

"You and punkins are the difference. We aren't starting a family. Our daughter is long past the baby stage. Face it, our habits and your parents are pretty well established. If you guys can accommodate one extra person, then I think this idea has a good chance to By. All any of us will have invested is a few months either way. If it doesn't work out, we use my GI loan and buy something similar to what your folks have."

"What do we do with all the new appliances and things still in my hope chest?"

"If we stay, we'll replace your folks'. Any more questions?"

Katey was optimistic. "Do you realize when we leave here, everything about your life, my life, Krissy's life, and even my folk's life will have changed? And that doesn't begin to cover our buying this cabin and fixing it up! Gerald Landis, when you change things, you really go whole hog!"

The subject of their daughter was brought up again. "Katey," said Jerry. "Let's cut Krissy some slack and put all that grown-up attitude to work where it will do the most good. Start her out with a weekly allowance to go along with chores to do. If she Bubs up, we cut her allowance. Great way to keep her discipline in line and save her little fanny from a lot of wear and tear."

"Oh, Jerry, just what the doc ordered. How much allowance to start with?" "Say a couple of bucks each week with the understanding that half of that

has to be saved. That'll plant the idea of her saving for something she really wants instead of always asking us to buy it for her. It's her money now…helps keep that attitude going."

She hugged him. "Oh, darling, you really have her pegged. Anything else?"

Krissy's artistic talent was thoroughly discussed. Katey really jumped on board when Jerry suggested that he had a project that everybody could do and share—build a full-scale playhouse for Krissy. One that would keep pace with Krissy all through her preteen, then teen, and finally her young adult years.

Their talk died down. Everything was settled for now until they returned to Rushton. They looked at each other, and both were on the same wavelength—the romantic one.

She was burning up with desire and passion. "Let me love you this time, my love. I want to so much."

He leaned back against the tree and let her work love's magic upon him. Gently, oh so gently, she took him to paradise, to another world at the base of the giant pine.

Two days later, their last day at the cabin loomed dark and ominous. There was no sunrise, only threatening skies. The cool, fresh pine scent had departed sometime during the night, replaced by a dry electricity that hung everywhere. All parts of Mother Nature's grandiose weather scheme for the High Sierras.

Katey sensed they were in for a real weather thrashing. Jerry doggedly maintained that they had plenty of time to get in their last load of seasoned cordwood.

They set off, Katey more apprehensive with each mile they covered. Both worked feverishly to load up the truck. There was no time to indulge in idle conversation with the old man who owned the store.

The return trip had Katey glued to the edge of her seat. She watched the ever-increasing cloud buildup, now so dark that Jerry was forced to turn on the headlights. He patted her hand, trying to reassure her they would reach their cabin well ahead of the brewing storm.

"Katey," he said. "It'll be all right. Lightning and maybe a sprinkle or two… nothing more. Then it'll be over. Bet we still get in a beautiful sundown to cap off our last day up here."

"I don't like it. We never should've left this morning."

"Must be a wee bit of Irish superstition roaming around in you somewhere, dear."

She leaned forward, eyes cast straight up, watching the ominous buildup all around. "Maybe so, but I'd feel a whole lot better once I see our cabin."

Suddenly, a mighty gust of wind sideswiped the truck, wrenching the steering wheel out of Jerry's hands. He fought the steering wheel, finally corralling the beast. He hit the brakes hard, pitching poor

Katey headfirst into the windshield. They sat huddled in Jerry's corner of the cab. All around them, the thick dark mass rolled, broiled, and churned in all its pent-up fury. Blasts of wind raked and buffeted them unmercifully. The lightning Bashed continuously between tremendous claps of thunder, so closely connected that it attacked their minds, till they wanted to scream just to relieve the pressure.

Jerry shouted, *"We can't stay here!* We're only a couple of miles from the cabin. Let's make a run for it!"

Katey never bothered to answer as they inched along between blinding Bashes of lightning, so close that Katey thought they'd been struck a dozen times. The intense Bashes played hopscotch on all sides of them, illuminating the darkness while the ground shook beneath them from the constant bombardment of rolling thunder.

He pointed. "That old snag! Can't be more than a mile to our cabin!"

One, two, three, four blinding Bashes seared the darkness. Jerry never heard the clap of thunder. Katey froze with terror as the snag disintegrated before her. Jerry slumped over the steering wheel, the horn blaring away.

"Jerry! Jerry!" she screamed, fearing he'd been hit by lightning. He never moved a muscle. Katey immediately touched his forehead. It was cold.

"Jerry! Speak to me! Are you all right?"

She then realized what had happened. He was in shock. An exact duplication of the battlefield in far off Korea where he'd been blown out of an old snag that had disintegrated beneath him. She rocked him slowly, sobbing away. "Please, please, dear Lord. Please, please make him whole. Bring him back to me!" She sobbed on. "He's my life! I don't want to go on without him! Please! Please! Dear God! Please!"

He stirred. His eyes Buttered, and he sat up as though nothing happened. "Katey, that was mighty close! What happened?"

With tears streaming down, Katey left them in free fall as she said a silent prayer. She turned to him, so sure of her words. "Now I know what happened my darling. No wonder you never talk about Korea."

CHAPTER 15

The railroad merger brought an infusion of new capital to the old and financially strapped CCR. It was time to recognize, promote, and install those deserving individuals who had successfully turned the railroad's fortunes around.

Thanks to the infamous Seelig-Landis finance proposal, Bill Seelig was promoted as the new corporate comptroller. Greg and Katey, along with a number of corporate council members, shared a far different view regarding Seelig's qualifications. No bailout would've been possible if one low-key financial wizard named Jerry Landis hadn't put in his nickel's worth.

Seelig's promotion opened the door for the next round of corporate infighting. Greg spearheaded a move to appoint Jerry Landis as the accounting department manager. Seelig countered with his own pick, his longtime friend George Jeffrey. He followed that up by demanding that Gerald Landis's personal file be reviewed by each council member. He patiently waited for Landis's resounding defeat once his memo had been circulated. All seemed in agreement. Jerry Landis was certainly qualified for the position.

Two hours of nonstop accusations and counteraccusations followed. A compromise was finally reached that neither side liked. The result: George Jeffrey was now the accounting manager with Jerry Landis as his deputy.

Seelig's first official act was to conduct his own behind-the-scenes investigation into the mysterious disappearance of his note condemning Gerald Landis. Not one shred of solid proof ever linked either Greg or Katey, but that didn't keep Seelig from harboring his own suspicions.

Outside of revenue sharing, the merger had little effect on the two railroad's operations. Each gained what they needed—valuable trackage rights into the others existing markets. Each line basically continued as separate entities under the new name as the California, Colorado, and Western Railroad (CC&W).

Two more years sneaked by, and Greg finally took the plunge. He announced to the world and the Sacramento Valley residents, in particular, that he would marry Victoria Grayson. It was a match made more in the world of preferred and common stocks than in heaven. For weeks, the society pages were filled with news about the upcoming nuptials.

Jerry, obviously tired of the whole business, finally confronted Katey. "For Pete's sake, why don't they just get married and get it over with?"

Katey took a woman's point of view. "Jerry, let them enjoy all the newsprint and pictures. After all, how many times in your life does one decide on such an important step?"

Jerry was not to be outdone. "According to statistics, about one out of every two of us will make that decision at least twice. We're right on par, Katey, with my first marriage gone down the drain."

Katey backed him up but good. "That was never a marriage, and we both know it. It was a terrible mistake, and I pushed you into it."

The night of the big wedding reception finally came. Katey was excited; Jerry could care less. Aaron and Mary treated Krissy to a puppet show while Jerry and Katey dressed for the formal reception. He stood in front of their full-size vanity mirror in his rented tuxedo.

"I feel like an overstuffed penguin in this outfit. Now if I could just learn to waddle a little, I'd have my disguise down pat."

Katey, seated on her bench in front of her dressing table, nearly cracked up over Jerry's imitation penguin waddle.

"Hey, Katey! Throw me a fish! Maybe I could slide on my butt long enough to get the hang of it!"

She pleaded with Jerry. "Please, no more penguin impressions. My side already hurts from laughing. I'll say this for you, Landis. You can be hilarious when you put your mind to it."

He stood a moment behind Katey, watching her brush her new hairdo, a little longer coffered look. "Like your hairstyle, lover."

She put down the brush and glanced in the mirror at him. "And you, my handsome husband, that tux does something for you. Makes you look distinguished."

He bent down and blew his breath on the nape of her neck. Then he kissed it. "That your new outfit? The one Theresa made for you?"

She reached back with one arm to bring his head down to her shoulders.

He kept kissing her neck. "Yes, I never knew black could look so chic."

"If chic means sexy, Katey, you sure got my vote." He raised up and, in a most solemn and businesslike manner, took a second look at his wife seated at her dressing table. "Yes, Katey, my love, there's something definitely missing. Now if I could just figure out what that lovely thingamajig you call a dress needs."

She turned around, eyes big as saucers. "Jerrrreee! You've been holding out on me. C'mon, what is it? Why all the fuss over my new evening gown?"

"Who, me? Katey, haven't got a clue what you're getting at. Honest!"

Katey was off her seat and into his arms. "Gerald Landis, where is it? What are ya hiding?"

"Close your eyes, and don't you dare peek!" "Or what?"

He loved to tease her. "Or it goes right back to the pawnshop where it came from."

Katey wrinkled up her nose. She squinted so hard, trying to keep her eyes closed.

He toyed with her again. He kissed her neck on each side then blew his hot breath down the cleavage of her exquisite dress. She reacted as he knew she would. He took out the diamond-clustered choker and gingerly draped it around her neck. "Okay, face the mirror. See what you think!"

With his arms draped around her, Katey dared to open her eyes. "Oh!" She squealed with joy at the beautiful jewelry around her neck. "Oh, how did you know I've wanted one of these for so long?" Before he could open his mouth, hers was on his, kissing him. "Oh, my love, you're so good to me. I pinch myself twice a day just to make sure our marriage is real. That it's happening to me!"

Pleased as punch at her response, he cracked. "Just check our savings account. It's real, all right. Wait'll you see that king-sized hit it took to pay for it."

She put her hand to her mouth. "Oh my gosh! Can we afford it? Jerry, maybe it's too expensive."

He answered like she hoped he would. "Nonsense, Katey. You deserved a present like this years ago just for putting up with me." Then he kissed her hand. "Without doubt, my wife will be the best looking, best dressed woman at Greg and Victoria's snob fling of the season. I'd better help even up the score a bit when it comes to the jewelry department. Just a reminder, my darling. You're wearing your Christmas present three months early. So enjoy!"

She leaned forward, looking in the mirror to center the jewelry piece around her neck. He'd never seen her look lovelier than she did at that precise moment. She surprised him by turning around and backing up. "Hon, help undo my dress and the clasp for the choker."

"What's wrong? Why are you changing your evening dress? Katey, you're absolutely stunning in that sexy black thingamajig. And the choker certainly complements your getup."

She had so much love in her heart as she confided, "Jerry, our love and our marriage has taught me one thing. Don't put off things that need doing now. Just go ahead and do the things that need doing."

"Like what, for instance?" "Me!"

They arrived at the country club and were surprised to find valet parking only allowed for all the reception guests.

Greg and Victoria rushed to greet them. Greg and Jerry shook hands and hugged each other.

"Hey, amigo," Greg said. "We were beginning to wonder if something happened to you two. Everything all right, I hope?"

Jerry, straight-faced as ever, couldn't resist a good one-liner. He winked at his wife. "Oh, a little something came up. Katey and I handled it just fine."

Victoria took one look at Katey and gushed. "Oh, my dear, you must tell me who your dressmaker is. That's such an exquisite evening gown. Is it an original?"

Kate was more than up to Victoria's level. "Why yes, it is! A Theresa original."

Victoria frowned a moment. "I don't believe I know that label. Is her shop in Rushton or in downtown Sacramento?"

Katey stood her ground with Victoria, who frankly was stunning in her own silver sequined original. "The Theresa I'm talking about is Ricco's wife."

Victoria didn't quite know what to say. Then she rescued the situation in her own way. "My dear, I'm so glad Greg gives you such a generous clothing allowance. Makes us the two best dressed women here tonight, if I do say so myself." Victoria's eyes feasted on Katey's beautiful choker. "And you're so correct. Diamonds definitely do go with that ensemble."

Katey had had enough of her snobbery. "I'm supposed to say congratulations on your marriage to Greg. I hope both of you will be happy. Now if you'll kindly show me where I belong, I'll thank you."

Victoria led Katey off toward a table occupied by Ricco and Theresa. With a graceful sweep of one hand, she gestured toward the two vacant chairs. "There, my dear Katey, is where you belong. Ta-ta. Now have a good time, you and Jerry."

Jerry slapped his old buddy on the back. "Congrats, amigo. Hope you two hit it off just great. Maybe this isn't the time or place, but thanks again for backing my nomination at work. At least Katey can accept and live with the situation now."

Greg pumped Jerry's hand hard. "No problem, amigo. Too bad you didn't get Seelig's job. Hands down, you were the best qualified. Next time, I'll push even harder if another opening comes up in your area."

Ricco and Theresa, like Katey and Jerry, felt they were definitely out of their element socially. They tried to make the best of the situation and enjoy themselves. In the midst of a crowd of social strangers, they ate, drank, and danced with each other to pass the time. Greg made a couple of appearances to claim dances with Katey and Theresa. It was his best effort to make up for the cold shoulder Victoria gave them.

The dance band symbols clashed, followed by a good long drum roll. The crowd quieted down. Greg rose from his table. The house lights darkened, and two spotlights focused on him.

"What the heck is he trying to pull off?" questioned Ricco. "I think he's about to level the playing field," voiced Katey. "Yeah? How?" questioned Jerry.

"Just watch him! They don't call him the great communicator for nothing."

Theresa, obviously very miffed at the treatment they'd received, echoed Jerry's sentiments to the letter. She said, "I no like Victoria. She…she thinks she so much hot stuff! No big deal! Is bargain basement lady, I think."

"Shhhhhh!" Ricco cautioned. "It's so quiet in here, she might hear you." "I no care. Is truth I speak. I tell her to her face."

"Shhhhhhhh!"

Greg's resonant tones over a hand mike broke up the foursome's conversation. "Ladies and gentlemen, may I have your attention!" He moved over toward their table and ended up standing behind Katey. "There are four special people here that I'd like you to meet tonight. Three of them have been lifetime friends with me." He motioned for Katey to stand up. "This lady is not only a dear friend, but she is also my executive secretary. For four years, I've been telling everybody that she's the best secretary a boss could possibly have. Last year, they finally listened and voted her the top executive secretary in management for the CC&W. Katey Landis is her name, and being my right- hand man is her game. Ladies and gentlemen, Mrs. Katey Landis!"

Katey received a very hefty round of applause and sat down. Greg moved over to Ricco. "This next gentleman and I have been through it all. We were on opposite sides of the bargaining table just last week. He's the chief labor business agent for our local railroad union. Next month, he'll also be the newly elected vice president of their union. Though we don't see eye to eye on many of the labor-management issues, we do see eye to eye on everything else. He's one of my dearest, closest friends."

Greg pointed to Theresa. "The lady seated next to him is his wife, Theresa. I don't know much about her yet, except that she's one heckuva seamstress. Had her own dress shop in Italy a few short years ago. That dress Katey Landis is wearing tonight is one of her creations! Need I say more? Ladies and gentlemen, I give you Ricco and Theresa Petrocelli, my amigos!"

Both rose to acknowledge a generous round of applause. Then they took their seats. Greg then stood behind Jerry. "This next gentlemen is something special, though you'll never get it out of him. He is one of a rare breed today. He's a genuine dyed-in-the-wool war hero. He's a recipient of the Silver Star Medal for saving his crew, not once but twice, mind you, on the battlefields of Korea."

A thunderous round of applause interrupted Greg's introduction. "Please, let me continue. Now ordinarily, that would be quite enough accomplishment for one man's lifetime. But not for this man! He also deserves silver-star recognition for his expertise as the financial wizard who saved the old CCR's bacon until ICC merger approval was granted. Over eighteen thousand jobs were at stake because of his brave and timely action. His name is Jerry Landis. He is also the husband of my executive secretary, Katey." He motioned to the couple. "Jerry and Katey Landis, please stand up and take a well-deserved bow."

The spotlight focused on Jerry and Katey while they stood up to acknowledge the thunderous applause.

CHAPTER 16

Krissy continued to grow and develop into a most remarkable young lady through high school. Her good looks came from Katey. From her father's side, she displayed his streaks of stubbornness, along with his careful-dollar ways. Her once glorious blond ponytail was long gone, replaced by what Katey would describe as her "Dutch boy rebel!" Even her deep blues now telegraphed a freewheeling spirit.

During her sophomore year at Sacramento State University, she switched majors. Fashion design became home decorating. Katey wisely stayed out of this decision, letting Jerry deal with it. Krissy bought her father's idea to take a year off, get a job in Penney's Home Decorating Department, and save some money. He thought it would be a good test to see if she made the right choice, he maintained.

Katey helped her daughter unload several boxes of clothing and personnel items from the Buick.

"Yes, Mother, Dad and I agree this is what's best for me. Then when I start my junior year, I'll really tear into my studies. My grades should improve, and I'll be focused on where I'm going."

Katey set Krissy up as only she could. She frowned for all of ten seconds, then the light bulb came on. "Your boss at Penney's will be expecting a full day's work out of you each and every day. So getting plenty of rest and sleep will be important. I can plainly see that, and I'm sure you can too! Better cut your social life to weekends only."

Krissy was crushed. "Good Lord, Mother, I'm not some sixteen-year-old who you gotta ride herd on every second! I'm twenty now! I can come and go as I darned well please! Nobody's gonna tell me when to hit the sack! Not even you!"

"Krissy," Katey said. "I'm doing you a favor. Get used to taking orders. You'll have to at work if you plan on holding down a job. Didn't you just tell me you wanted to save money?"

Krissy had stepped into the trap. "Yes, Mother." She sighed. "Go ahead. Lay it out. You're gonna anyway."

"You got that right! You can stay here and you will save money. I'll expect you to pull your share of the work around here too. If that doesn't suit you, then I suggest you take your problems to your father. My Irish is up, and there'll be no compromise. It's either my way, or you're gonna pay your own way somewhere else!"

Katey left no doubt who had won that round. Krissy put her arms around her mother. "Okay, you win, Mother. Lord, you can be a hard case when you want to."

Katey looked up at her daughter, now a good three inches taller. Her sternness disappeared as quickly as she put it on. "Welcome home, Krissy. You've just passed with your usual A for attitude adjustment."

Nobody was happier to hear such mature and comforting words from their blond-haired rebel than Mr. and Mrs. Gerald Landis. Yet there was also something disquieting, too, about Krissy's honest assessment of her life. This bothered Katey considerably. With Jerry, it was downright devastating, especially the parade of freaks, weirdos, and God-knows-what Krissy bought home to Sunday dinner.

After one such trying episode, Jerry blew his stack behind their bedroom door. "What the H is goin' on, Katey? Every Sunday, it's Halloween around our dinner table when Krissy trots out her latest. Some lowlife freak in his costume that's way beyond description. Getting so bad that Mom and Dad always make sure they're never around. Next time, I think I'll go join 'em!"

Katey approached her husband sitting on the edge of their bed. She helped him slide his leg brace off. "I'm sure it's just a phase she's going through." He handed her the brace.

She leaned it up against the wall opposite his nightstand. "Anyway, we should count our blessings. At least she's bringing them home. And she's not into drugs or alcohol. It could be worse! A lot worse!"

Jerry leaned back on the bed and watched Katey undress. "Remember three weeks ago? That was the worst by far! I swear, Katey, I couldn't tell just what we had pulling up a chair to the table."

Katey laughed out loud. "Jerry, that's ancient history. Boy, I thought you were gonna grab him or it by the hair and do a body check right then and there! Especially when he showed you his new leather shoulder purse."

"That did it! I was so upset, I had to excuse myself from the table. Noticed your father joined me outside too! In all the years I've known your dad, has he ever stepped outside to smoke?"

"No. Can't say I have."

"See, he couldn't stand him or it either!"

"Darling, we're going to have to be more tolerant with Krissy's friends. I know you can hardly stand them."

"Stand them? Heck, they're all losers! What's happened to this generation? And your folks used to worry and wonder about us! The men trying to look like women with that long stringy, straggly hair. Smelled perfume on that freak tonight. Some even wear makeup. Now it's big earrings. That's the latest!"

Katey pulled her thin nightgown down over her body. "The young women aren't much better. Wear little or no makeup. Haircuts getting shorter all the time…like the men used to have. And those terrible, terrible-looking sloppy, baggy clothes! They look like they've never been close to a washing machine or near an ironing board. Darling, we've got a sexual revolution going on right under our noses. Like it or not, this is 1972! You can bet there's more to come too!"

Jerry went in to brush his teeth.

"How long's it been since you were in to the VA hospital?"

He brushed some more then rinsed his mouth out. "Over a year, I guess.

Why?"

"Your foot drag's worse. Don't you think you better have your leg checked out and your brace adjusted again?"

That yearly question always brought out Jerry's quick retort. "I'm fine, Katey. Just a little tired. In the morning, I'm fresh as a daisy. Check me out. You'll see."

"I have, dear, and it's not a whole lot better. Jerry, we'd better talk about it. I know you'd rather face Krissy's friends than go to the VA hospital."

He gargled. "Katey, if I go, it's only for one day." He spit out the rinse. "Got more important things on my mind!"

"Such as?"

"I'm riding this out with Krissy. I'm not about to let her get hooked up with some sleazeball! He stood in the doorway then came to her. He knelt on her side of the bed. "Please, Katey, if you even suspect she's getting serious with any of those things, you gotta tell me. I'll put a stop to it! *Promise?*"

Katey looked at her husband. The worry lines were written all over his face. She knew he should be spending time in the VA hospital in Sacramento. "Okay, we'll put off your visit to the VA hospital only till Krissy sorts things out. Then you go in and take your chances. Agreed?"

CHAPTER 17

Six months down the line, Jerry and Katey recognized a big change in the selection of Krissy's new crop of Sunday dinner regulars. Jerry even tried treating a couple of them as human beings. Grandma and Grandpa McCray shocked everybody by sticking around. For in Krissy's mind, she had arrived. She knew there'd be less conversation about her friends behind two tightly closed sets of bedroom doors at opposite ends of the house.

One Sunday evening, a new regular happened upon the scene: Mark Stemple, a college classmate of Krissy's who held down a summer job in a commercial decorating and sign shop two doors down from Penney's. He wasn't exactly what Jerry had in mind as a suitable boyfriend for Krissy. He was nice-looking, about Jerry's height and build, had a very pleasant manner, had blue-gray eyes, and kept his dark brown hair neatly combed with a small tuft behind his head. This was tolerable to Jerry's way of thinking. Katey looked upon him in an even more positive vein. She now felt her payers had been answered to the best of his ability. Given Krissy's free thinking and wheeling disposition, that teetered on the brink of an all-out family war whenever the subject of Krissy's friends came up for discussion.

Following Mark's initial appearance, Krissy settled down to the point where she was a joy to have around. After three straight Sunday dinners with Mark, even Jerry had to admit Krissy's social life had taken a turn for the better. Mark and Krissy had just walked out the door that Sunday evening.

Still seated at their table, Jerry turned to Katey and his in-laws and triumphantly proclaimed, "I think the worst is over! Krissy's moved up from three Cs to three Bs. Now if we could just get her thinking more in line of three As, then we're getting somewhere."

Aaron and Mary hadn't a clue as to what Jerry was referring to. Their daughter played straight man. "Okay, Landis," she volunteered. "What are you talking about?"

"The three Cs! Those college campus clowns she's dumped. Don't you get it? She's traded them in for the bread-and-butter bunch, the three Bs! That's where Mark fits in."

Katey returned with the coffee pot. "Dear, Mark belongs in your three A category. Didn't you see the way they kept looking at each other tonight?"

Mary seconded Katey's observation. "Aye, Jerry, except for the blond hair and blue eyes, it coulda been our Katey showing the same kinda excitement all over again when you came a'callin'."

Jerry was still not convinced. "Hmm, wonder how I missed that about Krissy!"

Katey touched his shoulder before she sat down. "You were too busy getting a read on Mark."

Aaron looked at his wife then turned his gaze toward Jerry. "Son, I believe we all could stand a round of Irish coffee, eh? Lord knows we've earned it, what with all the shenanigans our Krissy's put us through!"

The bedroom conversation that night was strictly up-tempo as Jerry and Katey prepared to retire. Katey leaned hard into her vanity mirror, squinted a time or two, and then wrinkled up her nose.

"Jerry, there's wrinkles in both corners of my eyes! And I've found some more gray hairs. Guess that comes with the territory when you reach the big Four-O!"

Jerry took Katey's pronouncement in stride. Katey fussed and fussed, trying to cover her new wrinkles with an extra application of makeup. "Yup, I've let out my belt a notch. Need to get in more activity. Skiing season should remedy that, I hope!"

Katey said, "Nonsense, dear. All you need to do is back away from those second helpings at the dinner table. I'll see that you get only one serving from now on."

They lay in bed, not ready for sleep.

Katey sat up, so Jerry joined her. "Read an interesting article your father showed me couple of days ago. Written by some big-named sociologist back east. Anyway, this guy called our generation the change generation. Meaning that our country's traditional morals and values were inherited from mostly the strict, conservative European countries. That's now changed or merged into our more liberal ways of thinking. And that's why we're in the big social upheaval we find ourselves in. Then he goes on to say Krissy's generation represents the best thinking in modern society to date. That is, we should not expect people to be totally responsible for their own actions. We should be more tolerant of failure, more liberal in rewarding all instead of just those who've contributed."

Katey snuggled up to her husband. "So where does that leave us?"

"The way I see it, Krissy's generation is truly our first lost generation. Not society's best effort in any way, shape, or form."

"Did he say anything about God or Christian religions still playing an important role in our new modern society?"

"Yeah, this really upset me and your father too. This crackpot said God and the religions we practice in this country are a convenient crutch for the brainwashed and the uniformed."

Katey was outraged. "You know what really burns my toast about all this modern crap and permissiveness that we're supposed to go along with? I'd like to ask this so-called expert how come God's laws and commandments have worked so well for thousands of years before all this new thinking and social upheaval?"

They switched subjects. "Do you think Krissy will end up with Mark?" Katey mulled Jerry's question over carefully. "Yes, I do, but…"

"But what?"

"This same modern thinking you just talked about has her confused. She wants to do the right thing, but the peer pressure around her must really be something. It was all around us, but not the full blast she is getting."

Now Jerry was worried. "Katey, if I read you correctly, are you saying Krissy is already permissive sexually? I don't care for that thought *one little bit!*"

Katey's disposition did a flip-flop. "Hardly, my love! Our daughter's not so free-spirited as she would have us believe. Five years ago, she accidently watched us make love. Then she came to me with questions, lots of questions.

The upshot of our conversation is still very much embedded in her mind. She wants what we have. And she'll fight a buzz saw to keep her integrity that way. She may be a swinger in other regards, but granting favors sexually will never be part of her makeup. I only hope Mark will measure up to you, my love, in that regard, when the time comes. Anything less would be a big disappointment in Krissy's eyes after what she's seen, and I've told her detail by detail."

Both were resigned to let Krissy follow her own natural instincts regarding Mark's interest in her. Katey said her prayers and jumped back in bed. They kissed good night and snuggled up together, Katey, as usual, with her back fitting perfectly into Jerry's groin and hip cavity. "Jerry?"

"Yes?"

"Tomorrow is the day. No more stalling. It's off to the VA hospital for you." "Coming with me?"

"You know I'll be there! Why do you always ask?"

"Just wanted you to say it. It means an awful lot to me. Never want to stop thanking you for being my wife and supporting me in everything I do. I'm the luckiest guy in the world to have your love. Thought you should know, Katey!" Jerry's compliment struck a chord in Katey's heart. An oh so wonderful, welcome, lyrical song of love. A rhapsody in romance that rekindled each and every time they touched.

She kissed him passionately, trying, in her way, to convey the feeling, the affection she had for him.

CHAPTER 18

Krissy moved back on campus as she entered her junior year at Sacramento State University. She was totally refocused, and her grades shot up. It was an indication spending a year off campus had paid good dividends. The last Friday before Thanksgiving, she paid her mother an unexpected visit.

"Where's Dad?" she demanded. "Why isn't he here? I need to talk to him.

This can't wait!"

Katey tried to keep their conversation on a civil level. "Guess you missed those two messages I left at the dorm. Your father is back in the VA hospital. His new brace is giving him problems. He telephoned about an hour ago. Said I'd better figure on waiting another three days before I can pick him up. You know, Krissy, it will be the first time in over fourteen years he hasn't come home to me. Boy, do I miss him already!" She motioned for Krissy to sit down at the kitchen table. "Now what's so important that it can't wait for your father to get back home?"

Krissy fidgeted in her chair. "Can't seem to talk to you anymore. Well, I'm moving out of my dorm this weekend. Thought you and Daddy should know…need to give you my new address and phone number."

"Just you?" Katey asked cautiously.

"No, Mother. Mark's moving too…and another couple. We're going to rent a duplex…split up the rent so we should be able to get by."

"Krissy, is this other couple married?"

Krissy pointed and shook her finger at her mother. "See! You've done it again! At least Daddy would have given me the benefit of the doubt and listened till I'm finished instead of jumping on me."

Katey's rebellious daughter started for the door. "If you've already made up your mind, why do you need our permission?" Katey's question stopped her dead in her beat-up tennis shoes along with her loose baggy cream-colored pants and badly wrinkled light-green, no-wrinkle shirt. She stammered, "I… I just thought you two should know. That's all."

Katey went to her and put an arm around. "C'mon back and let's give it and us a chance. You still haven't asked me what I thought about it."

Krissy didn't budge. "What's the use? All I'll get from you is the same old tired jazz. It's morally wrong and the sin we're going to be living in. And have I forgotten God's law…"

"Have you?"

Krissy was totally exasperated by her mother's needle-sharp question. "No, not yet! That's got nothing to do with my decision to move out."

"I think it does, or you wouldn't be here. C'mon, sit down. I'll fix a pot of tea. Your favorite, orange pekoe."

Katey put a pot on to boil. "Okay, let's start over from the beginning. Surely you can spare me three minutes while we're waiting on the tea?"

"Mark and I have been kicking this around for the past month. It's called an open relationship."

"Exactly what does that mean?"

"We move in together, and if things don't work out, well…well, we go our separate ways. Or we can stay on together until we find somebody more compatible. Then one of us has to move out to make room for the next open relationship."

Katey was livid with rage at the mere thought of what her daughter was about to do. "Excuse me," she said. *"Don't you dare leave till I get back!"* She went to the bathroom to kick the living H out of her clothes hamper till her legs grew weary. She sank into her swivel vanity chair, her agony tearing at her insides, threatening to erupt any second. Her first thought was to go back out there and thrash Krissy within an inch of her life *and hope to knock some sense into her rebel.* Instead, she faced her vanity mirror and saw how crimson her face was, still cloaked in rage.

"Calm down, Katey," she told herself. "Calm down. Go back… sort it out. Krissy can still reason… I hope…try something! Anything!" About three minutes later, she returned, her fists half clenched, her knuckles white.

"Are you okay, Mother? You seem shaky, kinda out of control."

Her words came terribly hard, but she spit them out. "Okay, Krissy, where did this idea come from?"

Krissy got up to pour the tea. "You know, Mother, I misjudged you. Guess all those years, being around Daddy has kinda mellowed you out. Where was I? Oh yes, open relationships are really nothing new. Been around quite a while. Marriages aren't working anymore… no need for them. This gets rid of a lot of paperwork. Keeps the lawyers from getting fat too. No more divorce proceedings."

"Enlighten me, since I'm too old-fashioned to understand. How's it working?"

Krissy added a spoon of sugar. "Mark's buddy, David, has been in two relationships. Says number two wants a commitment, so he's gonna dump her 'cause that's not what open relationships are all about."

"Any other couples involved in this grand and glorious social experiment?" "Mother, you're whipping the life outa your tea! Sure you want me to continue?"

Katey set her spoon down. "Please go on, dear daughter."

"Another couple… Mark knows them… I don't. Switched partners about the time she got pregnant. Don't know who's going to end up paying for child support."

"Looks like this open relationship thing is going into the dairy business." "Dairy business? What are you talking about, Mother?"

"The guys get all their milk free without buying the cow!" "Oh, Mother, that's so gross!"

Katey took a sip. "As far as I can tell, your open relationship is just another new name for the guys playing the field. That's what we called it when I was your age." She pointed her spoon in Krissy's direction. "Now just who's been spreading all this social muck around?"

"My sociology professor, Dr. Lee Glazer. Our new textbook has over four chapters on open relationships and how they work. Come to think of it, he wrote the textbook."

"What really burns my buns is that these social nutcases are using our tax dollars to spread their dirty, sordid schemes around, and we're letting them get away with it."

Katey's last remark did not receive a reply in defense. Krissy seemed strangely silent. Common sense had tipped the scales in her mother's favor. "All right, punkins, what is it you really want? I get the feeling you're really not too keen on open relationships anymore?"

Suddenly, Krissy was in her mother's arms, sobbing away. "Oh, Mother, it's not out there anymore! I don't see it anymore! Everything I want is gone. I'm so unhappy."

Katey held her close. Wonderful, beautiful thoughts and memories formed a tried-and-true bond. "What do you really want out of your life? I think I can guess, but you'll have to tell me."

"You and Daddy! Such love! Such understanding! Such feelings! Romance that never stops…day after day! That's what I want! Mark doesn't even know what I'm talking about. He's so hung up on this open relationship thing. I'm just going along because I don't want to lose him. I love him so much. Why can't he see this?"

"There's so much peer pressure out there, Krissy. It's like a smoke screen. You've got to face it and fight it every day, but it's still there if you and Mark are willing to let your conscience and your faith in each other be your guide. Are you willing, Krissy? Really willing?"

"Oh, yes! Yes, Mother! But I need your help. I know how planning has been such a big part of your life."

Katey refilled their teacups. "C'mon, Krissy. We're a couple of sharp cookies. Let's put our heads together, and I'll just bet that we'll come up with a plan for you and Mark that will make you two happier and more content with your lives than either of you've been in a long, long time!"

"Okay, Mother. Where and how do I start?"

CHAPTER 19

Three long anxious days turned into three long and lonely nights before Jerry was ready to be discharged from the VA hospital. For Katey, counting the hours only accentuated the outcome. She wondered just how much more mileage could possibly be left in Jerry's left leg. Inwardly, she rejoiced that Dr. Novak at Madigan General had played God, allowing her husband to get as much use out of the leg brace and foot drag as possible. Would this be the last adjustment before amputation? She wondered how he would face the inevitable. This certainty he'd managed to put off one more time. She dismissed those thoughts, waiting for the hospital orderly to wheel him out. He waved to her then stepped away from the wheelchair. It was his Landis way of showing Katey his leg was good for at least another year.

They hugged and kissed and hugged some more. "Oh, Jerry," Katey said. "Seems more like three weeks instead three days." She eased the Buick away from the pickup zone and headed out the main gate.

"Hey, Captain," he teased. "What's up? How come we're headed west instead of east toward Rushton?"

"We're gonna celebrate! Our dishwasher needs a rest, and I've got the most incredible news. I can hardly wait to tell you."

"Me too! Katey, watch that lead foot of yours. Let's not spoil the start of our evening with a ticket. Where are we going?"

"Down to Templins, where the bill will always put your wallet into sticker shock."

"Must be pretty special, hon, to splurge like this!" "It is! Wait'll you hear!"

They chose a small table for two, off in a secluded corner, for a rendezvous of their hearts, minds, and feelings. The soft glow from the candlelight Bickered and danced across Katey's eyes, which brimmed over with good news and love for her beloved. They raised two wine glasses. Their voices were low and soft. Their touch ever so gentle, in concert with their love for each other. Jerry toasted first.

"Here's to you, my love, my darling Katey. And here's to the next fifty. May they be as good as the last sixteen."

They sipped, and then Katey toasted. "Here's to those fifty, my love. And as each year passes, it will be better than the one before because we'll have it no other way!"

The waiter took their order and disappeared after refilling both glasses. "Who wants to go first?"

"Let me, Katey. Got a hunch you've got a lot more to tell than me. You'll never guess who paid me a visit yesterday."

Katey knew, but she let him tell it anyway. "No. Who?"

"The old silver spoon himself, Greg. Come next month, you're looking at the new manager of the accounting department. It's a done deal! I'll be at the top of the heap in mid-management. Got Greg to thank for that. He's turned out to be one heckuva friend, hasn't he, Katey?"

Katey was in his arms in a Bash, hugging and kissing him. Even a spare tear found its way down one of her cheeks. "Oh, Jerry, I'm so happy for you! At last, at long last you're getting your just desserts! Why, why, you can run that department with one hand tied behind your back. You're still way overqualified. You know you'd be a shoo-in for Seelig's corporate position if Greg could've just swung the votes."

He looked at his very attractive wife. "Let's not get into that. Tonight, I'm just the luckiest guy alive to have both of you in my corner."

They held hands. Katey was absolutely radiant in her new blue dress, just purchased for this special occasion. The timing, the setting, everything about their intimate conversation added a cluster of love for her.

"Krissy and I have never been closer, my love. While you were gone, we really sorted things out, and she wants to have a baby and get married. Isn't that just the greatest! Oh, I'm so excited! Jerry, we're gonna be grandparents!"

"Hey, slow down! Bring me up to speed! What happened?"

"Your first night away, she and I had a real heart-to-heart. Seems she's always wanted what we have—a wonderful marriage and a great relationship. So she and I got our heads together, and voila! Everything's coming up roses!"

"How does this baby bit fit in then?"

"Krissy's not pregnant. She just wants to be! Had a close call awhile back.

Nothing that a wedding ring won't straighten out!"

He relaxed. "Okay, a close call I can accept up to a point. Fill me in!"

"Ever since you talked her into getting a job and saving some money, I could see Krissy was finally getting her act together. Now she knows what she wants. Which is Mark's baby and a career in home decorating."

Jerry took another sip of wine. "Fine, let her finish her degree, marry the guy, and then raise a family. Sounds pretty logical to me. Why all the sudden rush?"

Katey squeezed his hand and held it. "Jerry, life doesn't always happen just in that order. Sometimes, a woman's biological clock doesn't work that way. In Krissy's case, she's ready to have a baby. I… I…had to work like heck to figure a way to wrap a marriage around this so everything will work out great."

He thought on her words. "Okay, something like what we have. A love affair wrapped around your wedding band. Am I on track?"

"Exactly! Krissy's already talked to Mark about it. I helped her rehearse just the right lines. Took him these last two days to think about it. Typical man, you know. Don't dare bruise his ego. The bottom line is he's going to give her my old engagement ring. Jerry, let's put it to good use along with my old wedding dress in Krissy's hopeless chest. See where I'm headed?"

He smiled and shook his head in an approving manner. "Katey! Katey! Katey! I knew if it happened, somewhere, somehow, you'd be at the bottom of it. Okay, you've done your homework. Nobody enjoys planning more than you. It's your life. So when is the engagement?"

"Next week at Thanksgiving time. Ricco and Theresa are already invited. While Krissy and Mark are there, I'll have Theresa and Krissy slip off into her bedroom to try on my old wedding dress. Then make the necessary alterations. Simple, like one, two, three!"

"So far so good. How did you manage the wedding and baby bit?"

"That took some doing, but it should work out. Mark and Krissy get married Christmas Eve. Then they honeymoon up in our cabin and ski all day and make love all night. According to Krissy's cycle, she should be pregnant somewhere between the twenty-fifth and twenty-eighth of December. By the end of her junior year, she'll be six months along. She should have her baby just before she starts her senior year. After she has her baby, I plan on taking a year's leave of absence to babysit our grandchild while she finishes her degree. I'll train my friend, Mora Woodson, to be my replacement before I go on leave. Have I left anything out, darling?"

"Good thing I've only been gone three days. Hate to think what might've happened had I been away for a week or so!" With the Landis family business disposed of, it was time to wine and dine. Baked pheasant served under glass was a great change of food-fare for them. For dessert, they chose baked apples sprinkled with cinnamon and topped with a special house creamed concoction. It was a dinner fit for royalty and two middle-class Americans who'd come a long, long way in the scheme of their lives.

Once home, they made a beeline for their bedroom. "Katey," Jerry said. "I have to leave my brace on now…for good. Hope that won't change anything."

She gathered him up in her arms to put his concern to rest. "Never bothered before. Don't worry, lover. We'll find a way."

With their passion totally and beautifully spent, Katey went to her vanity to put on her nighttime facial creams. Jerry spoke first. "Lover, when I wasn't thinking about you, I did some heavy reading. The *Sacramento Star* has a new investigative reporter by the name of Jack Bailey. This guy really loves to dig deep! And what he came up with will blow your mind, Katey."

Katey laid her moisture pad down. "Must be quite the story to get and keep your attention. Now you have mine."

"This took place on campus recently at Sacramento State University. Let me back up a sec. When I attended, Mercer Hall was the hotbed for fruits, nuts, and every kind of social miscarriages man ever thought up. Bailey says Mercer Hall has gotten worse, a lot worse. Anyway, there's a Professor Glazer there who's a real piece of social change. He's bent on filling his young impressionable students with a real chunk of social misery which he calls open relationships. He does away with anything remotely connected with our legal system, including our social and God's laws. To make matters worse, he uses his own textbooks as his own guide to social destruction. Add in the fact that the academic community won't touch, censure, or remove him because he's tenured, and you see where this is all heading. One great big can of misery!"

"Jerry, this is terrible! So how does this all come out?"

He sat up on the edge of their bed and pointed. "What happened to our old clothes hamper?"

"I kicked it to kingdom come! It was either that or we would've lost Krissy for sure. Before she and I got on the same page."

He moved back with his head against the padded headboard using both hands to brace himself. "Why is it, Katey, each generation has to reinvent their own social wheel? Can't seem to learn a blessed thing from the previous generation."

She watched him in the mirror. "That's probably true for most young people. Krissy did learn from our generation. She now knows what she wants. All because you got her to take a year off, find herself, set new goals, and then go out and do it. You were the difference."

"Katey, that college crowd she was running with was bad news from the start. I had to get her out of there so she could think for herself. That's all she needed. The rest she pretty well put together with your help. One of Glazer's students gets pregnant just as she changes partners. Here is where Bailey says it gets sticky. Apparently, this gal has a change of heart. Or at the very least, she's consulted a shrewd attorney. Boy, is she now pushing for all she can milk out of our good old-fashioned legal system. She's named the college, the professor, and her so-called two partners as the legal father in her suit. There's no mention of a biological father. Bailey concludes she may have legal recourse here because the college has let this professor's teachings go on. And the students, per his instruction, are following his text to the letter, besides receiving direct encouragement from him! How do you like those apples?"

Katey's mind was awhirl. There was no doubt Krissy and Jerry were talking about the same incident with the same pregnant girl. "Can't the university do something about this kind of social muck being spoon-fed?"

"Bailey says that Glazer is untouchable! He's virtually given a free rein to inflict his social poison, no matter what the consequences. Bailey concludes that this lawsuit may force the university to take steps, whether they want to or not."

They dropped further discussion. Katey, punctual as ever, knelt to say her prayers then climbed into bed. She cuddled in her husband's arms then turned to brush his lips with hers. "Dearest, about that mess at college. This open relationship thing. Do you think Krissy or Mark could ever have gotten mixed up in such a degrading social experiment?"

"Still got you thinking about it, I can see. No, Katey, that's one area Krissy and Mark would steer clear of. Krissy's stubborn and hotheaded at times, and Mark's got too many smarts to get sucked up into something like that. No, not to worry, my love. Both of them would probably stand just outside the entrance to Mercer Hall to watch those mindless, thoughtless, brainwashed robots enter Glazer's classroom. They'd probably turn to each other and say, 'There goes the stupidest men and women that God ever created on earth!'"

CHAPTER 20

As general manager of the CC&W Headquarters Division, Greg Hibbard discharged numerous duties, responsibilities, and obligations. However, none could possibly have matched the pure pleasure he would derive from welcoming Katey Landis back. He'd come to realize just how vital she really was to his continued success.

He fussed around her enormous private desk, moving the vase of beautiful flowers twice, then stepped back to see if he'd placed them where Katey would really take notice and appreciate. Then he remembered. All flowers and family photos, Katey always placed on the left-hand side of her desk because she always worked from the right side. With that done, he retreated into his private office, leaving the door wide open so he could hear her friendly chatter long before he saw her pretty smiling face, her petite hourglass figure, or her shapely legs.

Greg sat behind his desk and waited. A first in over a year. He was usually the late culprit, exercising his executive prerogative. Minutes passed. Then he heard her familiar voice. He smiled to himself as her crisp Irish wit and charm already penetrated the plush carpeted hall long before she graced his presence.

Next, a familiar rattle. Katey had opened her top left-hand drawer to deposit her purse. Impatiently, he pressed the intercom button. In as mean and gruff a voice as he could muster, he bellowed out, "Katey Landis!"

A perky Irish lass, full of vim and vinegar, stepped inside his doorway. He rose. "Well, don't just stand there, Katey! For Pete's sake, don't I rate a welcome-back kiss or a hug or something?"

Katey, smiling as never before, rushed up and threw her arms around him. He bent down so she could finish their reunion by planting a firm juicy lipstick kiss on his cheek. "Welcome back, Katey! God, are you ever a sight for these peepers! Welcome back, amigo!"

They parted, each stepping back to see what changes, if any, were first noticeable. "Katey, you're wearing glasses! Since when?"

"Since about six months ago." She laughed. "Jerry said it was either that or hang a sign around my neck saying this lady stumbles over all curbs and pedestrian crossings!"

They both laughed. "Say, amigo, you've put on a few pounds," Katey teased. "Don't tell me, Victoria's gone domestic and found out you do have a kitchen in that mansion you call home?"

"Katey, that'll never happen. Her idea of a homecooked meal is stopping just long enough inside the swinging doors of our kitchen to ask the chef what we are having for dinner tonight."

Both roared. "Seriously though, amigo, Jerry and I have often wondered with all the money you two have, why do you work? Why aren't you two enjoying something like an around-the-world cruise for the rest of your lives or some such thing?"

Greg was Battered. "Here's the straight scoop, Katey. I love my job. And I think I'm pretty doggone good at it. At least when you're here to protect my rear. Victoria and I have discovered something about ourselves. It's not all like you and Jerry. After six hours around each other, that's about all we can take."

"You're serious, aren't you?"

"Very! In case you haven't noticed, Katey, in an awful lot of marriages, it's really about accommodation and companionship. With you two, it's love and romance day after day, year after year. Victoria and I have said it a hundred times how we envy you two!"

It was Katey's turn to be Battered. Never was a more triumphant smile an indication of how she viewed her marriage. "My marriage is the single most important thing in my life. Nothing will ever stand or get in the way of our happiness. I paid the price once. Never again! I know I don't need to remind you that in the order of importance is my marriage, my family, and then my job. I really think the difference is where we place our values. Now then, what do you want me to start on first?" Katey followed Greg to his desk, where he handed her two folders.

"The top one is our annual blurb, the one we hand out with the paychecks next payday about signing up for our annual community chest drive."

"Oh, yes, I'll retype and update it for your signature. And of course, follow up by phone after payday with our department managers and supervisors to impress upon them how important it is to meet our one hundred percent goal. Do you want me to get another contribution card ready for Jerry's signature?"

"No use, Katey. He'll never sign it. Just fill in the lowest contribution figure and leave it on my desk for a signature so we can meet our quota. But I will give Jerry this much. Our community chest committee has done a lot better job of screening our recipients since he threw a fit over what charities are still on our list. God, he can be exasperating at times!"

"He's my husband. And I do respect his views, even if I don't totally agree on why he'll never sign a pledge card. He'll never change, and that's okay with me. He's still the finest person I've ever known and loved. What's the other folder?"

"It's personal. I'm head of our high school's twenty-fifth reunion committee.

There's a list of our fifty-three graduates. The reunion will be held in Ormandy Park. Already got the park board's permission on that. I need you to draft an invitation letter for my signature and mail it out."

"Then do the follow-up too! Right?"

"You got it, Katey. Don't really know why I need to tell you any of this. Should've just handed you the folders and said take care of it, 'cause that's what you do."

"How did Mora work out?"

"She was good help, but she's not you! You take something and run with it. I never have to check or worry to make sure it gets done. Man, that's so comforting in my position!"

"Does it really seem like it's been twenty-five years since we were handed our diplomas?"

Greg pointed to the big CC&W calendar on the sidewall. "See for yourself, Katey. This is 1975! We're all pushing forty-three or so. Time's catching up with us. Speaking of reunions, any chance Molly might decide to come?"

"I'll send her an invite, but don't hold your breath waiting for her to show up. Still too much hostility out there between her and Ricco. Doubt if the hurt will ever go away. Both have good marriages now, and when you step back and take a real hard look, it's for the best. Never used to think that way. Do now."

"Meant to ask, did Ricco…did he ever meet his son, Little Ricco?"

Katey led Greg out to her desk. She set up her photos and pointed to one. "That's Little Ricco. He's the spittin' image of his father, and two inches taller too! After Ricco married Theresa, it took me five years, and Lord knows how many letters before Ricco ever got to meet his son. Since then, Little Ricco visits his father each summer. Molly and Ricco have never met, and they both prefer it to stay that way."

"As long as I'm out here, do you have any recent pictures of your twin grandsons?"

How proud Katey was when she dug out two eight-by-ten pictures. "That one's Jay, and the other one is Jon. Our family celebrated their first birthday just last weekend. Greg, they were a mess. Got cake and ice cream all over themselves. Oh, I just adore them. They're so precious!"

"How'n heck do you tell them apart since they're identical twins?"

"Jerry's got it figured out. First, he asks Krissy or Mark who is who. Then he takes a piece of paper and writes their name on it and pins it to their clothes. Boy, is he proud of our grandsons. Those two little pills can do no wrong in his eyes. But you know good old save-a-buck Jerry. He's talked Krissy and Mark into letting us buy good used clothes, like I did for Krissy when she was a baby."

"Speaking of money, our dear old amigo, Jerry, has come up with another big winner. I swear, that guy has nothing to do all day but think up these ideas."

"What's he come up with this time?"

"Heck, he's got four in the hopper just waiting for evaluation and cash recognition right now! Welcome to the high-tech age, Katey. You're husband has sold our cash savings committee on replacing the typewriters in all departments with word processing keyboards and computer storage and screens. Starting next week, you'll be going to keyboard class one hour a day for twelve weeks on company time."

"Any idea how much that suggestion is worth?"

"We've just completed our survey. The savings of storage space alone and not having to buy additional file cabinets will pay for the changeover in three years. He should get quite a chunk of change. Matter of fact, he's probably figured his cash award on this suggestion alone will more than pay for your years' worth of lost salary. Katey, I've never seen anything like that guy. Let him get within one hundred feet of a dollar, and he's got a way to get it or at least cozy up to it."

Katey was pleased, very pleased. "That's my Jerry! Lord, what potential he has. We both know he's barely taxing his brain to run the accounting department. Every time I walk by Seelig's office, I know Jerry Landis belongs there."

"At least he's as far as he can go in mid-management."

"I do appreciate what you've done. Do you ever think he'll get up there?" "Not likely, Katey. Seelig's only a few years older than Jerry. Told me last week he's here for the long haul, just like me."

"Your leave of absence was much more than just that, wasn't it, Katey?" "Yes, it was payback time for me. Time to square my account with my family. Time to re-thank my folks for really going out on a limb for me when I was pregnant with Krissy."

Greg turned to go back to his office. "Hey, boss, hold it a second!" He stopped and turned around. "Why? What's up, Katey?"

She reached in her purse drawer and pulled out a Kleenex tissue. "Here, better let me wipe off that lipstick smudge." Then she teased. "Wouldn't want you wandering around today getting a few extra snickers or stares or let Victoria think something's going on."

He let her wipe his cheek. "Heck, Katey, maybe you should've left it on! Who knows, the way things are going at home, Victoria might even take notice. And at the very least, it could've spiced up our evening conversation."

"Before I forget, thanks so much for the beautiful Bowers. What a lovely way to start my day."

Another three years slipped through time's sieve, and Katey saw the strain of Greg's crumbling marriage. He put on a good front whenever Victoria's name came up. But there was no hiding it. Greg was not a happy camper in the least. One day, out of the blue, Katey confronted him. "Hey, amigo, you don't seem to be getting much of a kick out of life anymore. If it's too personal, just tell me to butt out and I will."

Greg closed the door to his office and then sat down on the corner of his mahogany desk. Gone was the pure joy and excitement he used to bring to his job, his way of telling the rest of the CC&W management brass. "Forget about my social connections, forget about the fact I don't need my salary. Just judge me on what I do, what I contribute to this railroad."

"That obvious, huh, Katey?"

"Greg, I don't need a roadmap. It's written all over your face and in your attitude, too, lately."

He exploded. "Darn that woman! Dang her anyway! I told her to get off her hinder and do something constructive instead of playing footsie with her snobbish friends. Well, she did." He swallowed hard. "Wait until I tell you what she did."

Katey went over to him and put her arm around him. "Okay, amigo, what's up? You've been spending far too much time on the telephone lately. What's really going on?"

"This is just between us and Jerry. I've had Victoria followed by a private detective, and the news isn't pretty. I've got enough evidence on Victoria to sink a battleship! But that's not what I want! Not if she'll come to her senses. Last night, we had it out. Oh, it was something out of those daytime soap operas on TV. It got pretty ugly. Katey, she's slept with more people then I'd care to count. The latest! She's having an affair with our foreman on our new home construction."

"Why do you put up with it? You know I'm totally against divorce, but in your case, I'd make an exception!"

"Appearances, Katey. That's what my life's about. All my life, I've been written about and talked about, either pro or con. I've been in the limelight, and I like it there. I've never been a failure at anything I've tried, except my marriage. If I can salvage that, no matter what the cost, I will. It's that important."

"Knowing what you do about Victoria, how in the name of sanity can you continue even putting up with a phony appearance?"

"Quite simple, really. Once our mansion is completed, Victoria will live at one end of it, I in the other. I told her I'm going to have her watched twenty- four hours a day. If she needs companionship, so be it. But it will be in her bedroom, right under my nose. There'll be no loose talk, no gossip, and no one else need know."

"And you're willing to put up with that? Just for the sake of an appearance?" Greg put his arms around Katey's shoulder. "I know you'd never accept any part of this under any circumstances, Katey. Put yourself in my shoes for just one minute. I don't have a super relationship with my spouse. Never did! I don't have a family to worry about. So the only person I have to think about or consider is me. Victoria's promised to keep her affairs strictly limited to her bedroom. And as far as society's concerned, we have a good marriage because we've kept the proper appearance."

Katey was absolutely astounded. "This conversation is so, so unreal, Greg. I don't even know what to say or where to begin."

"Now do you see why I envy you and Jerry and what you've done with your marriage and your lives?"

Katey broke from under his arms and stood with her back to him, shaking her head. Slowly, she turned to face her longtime friend and boss. "I suppose the next thing you're going to tell me is that you plan on doing the same thing at your end of the mansion in your bedroom. Am I lukewarm?"

Greg never changed expression, nor did he back away from Katey's pinpoint question. "I told Victoria the next move is up to her. If she entertains in her bedroom, don't expect me to stay celibate or join a monastery. Katey, you'd be surprised what the right phone call to certain people and five hundred dollars will do nowadays. No streetwalker. No bar slut or pimply-faced teenage prostitute. I'm talking about a lady who looks, dresses, and acts the part. One who can hold a decent conversation on some subjects a lot of men would shy away from. And as you well know, money isn't my problem. Victoria is!"

CHAPTER 21

Greg and Victoria's marriage barely survived the two years it took to complete their dream mansion. It was the showplace in Sacramento's most affluent section. Their open house garnered rave reviews from all the regional society pages and construction journals. It was that pretentious! Katey still remained glued to her conviction that no marriage charade could withstand what was going on at opposite ends of that mansion. In her mind, it was all over. Only question left unanswered was when it would finally end.

It took another year for the Olympic-sized swimming pool construction to finally get completed. It was Greg's doing in order to rid his home of another of Victoria's many lovers.

The final phase was the installation of a hydraulic motor-driven roof. This roof would slide on its own track over the pool so that during inclement weather, the swimming pool would be completely protected from the outdoors.

January 1982 arrived before invitations were sent out to attend the very private pool party at 1214 Lancaster Lane. Meanwhile, Jack Bailey's "Soap Box" editorial had gone out on a limb, predicting the fall of the CC&W Railroad. There would be no merger with ICC approval this time to bail out the railroad and its many thousands of employees. The ripple effect, Bailey said, would devastate Rushton's economy and severely cripple the Sacramento economic base.

Bailey's mailbox was flooded with letters, notes, and cards from every doubting Thomas. Bailey's boss slapped him on the shoulder and said, "First- class job of journalism, my boy. Keep up the good work! Circulation's up by forty percent."

Jerry and Katey counted their blessings. They believed Jack Bailey had done his homework. Jerry said there was still time to avoid Bailey's dire prediction. If a corporate raider could be enticed, somehow, to take over, it would give him and Katey valuable time. Hopefully, five years' worth until they could draw their corporate pensions.

Three days before Greg's big pool party, Katey and Jerry received a surprise visitor, Theresa Petrocelli. Katey greeted her at the door. "Come in, Theresa. Where's Ricco?"

She'd been crying. Katey saw that she was very upset. She tried to hide her tears by putting on her best brave smile. In her thick Italian accent, she explained as best she could, "Ricco say we have to hurry. Is only time to say goodbye. This morning, I fly back to Italy."

"Oh, I am sorry to hear that, Theresa. Is your mother sick?"

"Alfredo say I must go back to my village…my…" The tears welled up. "Oh, Katey, I hurt so bad…my, my Ricco…he has dishonored me. He has been with *Victoria!*" She tried to control her sobbing. "Is true, Katey. He…he come to me last night to tell me. I close my bedroom door on my Ricco. He can never come in." She broke down, and a mixture of Italian and English poured out of her broken heart! She clinched her fist and spit on it. "That, that Victoria! I spit in her face if I see her! She force my Ricco to…to…they not make the love, Katey! Not the way my Ricco love me. She…she force my Ricco to do only little bit!"

Jerry came out of the bathroom and saw the two women holding each other. "Katey, what's up? Where's Ricco?"

"Ricco's outside in the car. Go with him. Play pool at Sam Moore's for a while! Wait for my call! I'm going to get to the bottom of this with Theresa."

Jerry was shocked. "What happened, Katey? Why all the tears?" "Victoria's struck again Jerry! Ricco's the target this time!"

Katey escorted a badly shaken and emotionally drained Theresa to the kitchen table. There, she comforted her as best she could with wet kitchen towels across Theresa's eyes and face. "Now then, start from the beginning. Tell…tell me everything you know."

Theresa quelled her sniffles. A minute later, the body shakes stopped. "Greg come to my Ricco and me. He say for big pool party, he like to have best Italian wine. So to ask me if I can get it for him in a quick hurry. I say yes. I can do for such a good friend. Last night, Ricco take our truck to deliver the vino. He ask where to put it. Victoria show Ricco where to take the vino."

Theresa suddenly stopped.

"Go on, Theresa. Go on!"

Theresa grabbed one of the wet towels out of Katey's hands. Her body went into spasms again. "Ricco, he is in wine room with Victoria. She tear her clothes…say she call police and tell them Ricco attack her if he not do little bit to her." Theresa began crying again. "Please don't he say. She say all right, then you have to make the love. What can he do, Katey? She tell him if he do not, she ruins his job, our marriage. But if he do it, then she no tell."

"What happened, Theresa? This is important. Every little detail!" "He not make the love like when he is with me. Is not the same." "What do you mean not the same?"

"I not know how to say it, but is different. Ricco do just a little bit with her.

Then he tell her to meet him someplace else. That way, he can get away from her. He swear to me he never go to that place to meet her."

Katey thought she had it figured out. "When he makes love with you, does he leave his baby seed in you?"

Theresa followed every word. "Baby seed?" Then her almond-shaped eyes came alive. "I see, Katey…the bambino seed! No, no, he swear to me he never do that with Victoria. Only to me he do that to. Like I say, Katey, only a little bit."

Katey got up and paced the kitchen floor. "I don't believe Ricco has been unfaithful to you in the normal sense. He had to do what he did so she wouldn't ruin his career. Ricco knew that a scandal would end his job and his career. Victoria undoubtedly knew that too. She had him just where she wanted him. That's not adultery in the strictest sense. It's really more like blackmail. Theresa, do you understand how important saving Ricco's job is to him and to you?"

"Yes. Ricco always say he has two loves. Me first and then his union job." "Exactly. You do see what happened? If he wanted Victoria, he wouldn't have come to you to tell you what happened. That's proof right there. It's only you he loves. Can you see that?"

"All night my body cry out to let him in. But I cannot. Then I cry to sleep.

This morning, my cousin, Alfredo, say our marriage is over. I must let him take me to San Francisco Airport to go back to my mother's house in Italy. Katey, I do not want to live without my Ricco. You are my best friend in America. Can you please to help me? Please, Katey!"

Katey got up and grabbed the phone and then dialed. "Father Donovan, please! This is Katey Landis calling. Please, please tell him it's *very urgent!* Have him see me at my house at once!"

Twenty minutes later, Father Donovan met Katey and Theresa. Briefly, Katey went over the situation and left him alone with Theresa. Thirty minutes later, Father Donovan and a smiling, much-relieved Theresa emerged from Katey's bedroom.

"This is a terrible situation this Victoria woman has put Theresa and her husband in. This woman certainly has no moral conscience or scruples."

"Can this marriage be saved, Father?"

"Yes, it can. Thank you for the call, Katey. You were a great help. I believe you're supposed to get a hold of Theresa's husband, and then he'll pick up Theresa and meet me as soon as possible. *This must be settled between them now!* I will do my best to council, advise, and guide. And with God's help, I can see a way out. Good day, Katey."

CHAPTER 22

The coffee vending machine down the hall from Jerry's computer room had only three customers at 4:00 a.m.: Jerry, Greg, and Ricco. For three straight days, they tried to do the impossible—find a way to leverage the right combination of labor costs, operating costs, and railroad assets into a package that would attract a big-time lender. That certain big-time risk-taker who could keep CC&W afloat with the right financial backing. No matter what assumptions they fed into Jerry's computer, the run always spit out the same answer: too big a risk to undertake!

Dead tired, Jerry arrived home late on Saturday night, barely half an hour before Greg and Victoria's pool party was to begin. Katey met him at the door. "You look beat, dear. Sure you want to go to the pool party? You know Ricco and Theresa won't be there. And the first chance I get Victoria alone, I'm gonna tell her where she can stick it. After that, we'll be leaving early too."

"Katey, we'd better show up for Greg's sake. Got a feeling he's gonna need all the support he can get. Don't be surprised if the lid to their marriage blows sky-high soon. Maybe tonight. He's been danged irritable lately. Think he's about had it."

"What marriage, Jerry? Greg told me he and Victoria haven't been sleeping together for months. It's so pathetic, my love! All that money, and yet they've got nothing. Absolutely nothing!"

He started for the shower. "I could've stopped for a sandwich, Katey. We're running late as it is."

"Jerry Landis, our supper is heating in the oven. We're going to sit down to enjoy our meal together. While you're showering, I'll go through the mail and pay the bills so we can have a decent conversation over our food. The Fuller Brush man has spent more time here then you have for the last three days. Now it's my turn to find out if I still have a husband or a computer robot who thinks he's my husband."

They sat down to eat. Katey was in no hurry whatsoever. "I looked at our last statement from the mortgage investment house, dear. Our balance is just shy of $100,000. I can hardly believe it! Can that be right?"

Jerry used a piece of toast to help slide his meat loaf onto his fork. "The old rule of seventy-two sure works, Katey. Getting a steady nine, which means that every eight years, our money doubles. When we said, 'I do,' we had just over twelve grand between us. That was twenty-four years ago! That's where it should be. Got both our cabin and your folks paid off…so were not hurting like a lot folks will be very soon."

Katey got up to refill his teacup. She kissed him on the forehead. "I'll say! Boy, when you started to manage our savings, you really managed. Any plans for our money?"

"Mark called me at work. He and Krissy want to start their own decorating business. They want to come out next weekend and run some facts and figures by you to get your reaction."

"How come you didn't say anything till now? I called you at work, and not one darned word about it. C'mon, Jerry, how come you're finally letting me in on it?"

"I had to run my own numbers on Mark's proposal first. If they didn't hatch, no use bothering you about an okay for their loan."

"All right, Mr. Beancounter. What did your precious numbers tell you?"

He downed another gulp of tea. "They can't miss, darling! Especially since we won't need any of our loan money back for five years till we retire."

Katey let him dangle a bit. "Got it all worked out, haven't you? How come I'm the last to know?"

He reached across the table to touch her hand. "'Cause you're always the hardest to sell. You'll never change, and that's one of a hundred reasons why I love you. If I can get it by you, it's a sure winner! That's what I told Mark."

Katey went to the fridge to get out the peach cobbler. "Dear, I had some plans, too, for some of our money. You know me, always planning."

"Okay. Such as?"

She put a dab of Cool Whip on the cobbler, and they started spooning the dessert. After two spoonfuls, she held her spoon high, and a dreamy and faraway look threaded its way across her face. "Always wanted to visit Ireland. See where all our family history came from. Visit some real castles and meet Dad and Mother's relatives over there. Then return to Chicago, introduce you to Aunt Rose and Uncle Kevin. They'd get a kick out of meeting you and maybe show you where I went to business college."

"Katey, no problem. We can do that and a lot more in five years."

"Got another idea, dear. How about inviting the home folks to go along with us to Ireland and Chicago too? It'd mean a lot to Mom and Dad to visit their old village once more. Mom talks about it, but they'll never go unless we go with them."

"Fine by me, Katey. Traveling with them should be a breeze. By the way, have you heard from them lately?"

"Not since that postcard from San Diego. They met a real nice couple from Arizona at Sea World. Don't be surprised the next time we hear from them, it'll have an Arizona postmark on it. Dad and Mom are really enjoying their retirement, and we're not far behind! Just five more years, my darling. Just five more years!"

Katey and Jerry parked outside Greg's mansion on one of the side streets, intent on only staying long enough to put in a proper appearance for Greg's sake.

"Don't forget, Katey. Keep your thoughts and your Irish under control, no matter how much you'd like a chance to tell Victoria off. Greg's still our friend. Let's make sure we leave on those terms."

"Okay. Just for you, Jerry, I'll go along. But she so much as looks sideways or says anything, she's fair game as far as I'm concerned."

Greg met them with open arms. "Man, oh man, am I glad to see you two, amigos." He pointed toward the dressing rooms. "Help yourselves. By the way, where's Ricco and Theresa? Thought maybe you two stopped to pick them up and that's why you're late."

Jerry and Katey exchanged glances. Jerry covered. "Ricco and Theresa phoned. Said they couldn't make it."

Greg took Jerry's remark at face value. "Oh, well, there'll be other pool parties. See you two later!"

The pool was everything as advertised and much more. With its luxurious furnishings and extravagant decor, even Katey found it impossible not to enjoy the chance to swim and frolic in such a surrounding in midwinter. She overheard one lady say, "The only thing better than this is that gold-leafed pool at Hearst Castle down the coast."

Jerry and Katey took a dip and then found themselves an unattended table and chairs. A maid approached them. "May I take your cocktail and sandwich order, please?"

"No sandwiches, but Mrs. Landis will have a small glass of Chablis, and I'll have a whiskey sour."

They spotted Greg talking to several of his country club friends. "Hmm, wonder where Her Highness, the non-Victorian, Victoria's been hiding out. Don't suppose she's entertaining in her bedroom again?"

Jerry jumped all over Katey's sarcastic remarks. "Knock it off, Katey! Don't worry, Victoria will make her usual grand entrance."

The poolside chattering stopped. All eyes were peeled toward Victoria's end of the mansion and the crowd of young people escorting Greg's wife. Katey lowered her voice. "Jerry, look! She's surrounded by young muscle-bound bodybuilding freaks! Not a woman in the bunch. Guess she likes 'em young. Can you beat that?"

Jerry couldn't resist. "Two to one, several of 'em have been pumping something besides iron, lately."

"Jerr-rr-rr-ee, that's enough now!"

Victoria made a beeline toward them. She sucked up Jerry in as clammy and superficial embrace as anybody could imagine. "My dear, dear Jerry, Greg's been telling me all about you. All that effort to save the railroad and no results!" She tossed a glance, like an old discarded chicken bone, in Katey's direction. "My dear, Katey," she mouthed dryly. "We must do something about your swimsuit. Come see me tomorrow. Must be something that can be done about you!" Her entourage of muscular admirers moved back to give her space to model her swimsuit. Off came her robe with the flair of a Mexicali bullfighter. Half the guests gasped in shock, and half applauded Victoria's daring exposure of flesh. No one took their eyes off what they saw. "Ta-ta!" She waved to those still glued to her scantiness. "Put your eyeballs back in your heads, gentlemen. Let's enjoy the swim!"

Victoria led her entourage toward the pool steps. Katey went crimson with disgust. "I've seen postage stamps cover more!"

"Did you see what passed for a halter, Katey? Or didn't you get up that far? Two big fat nipples stickin' straight out. Nothing covering 'em at all. Only two strings of fishnet to keep 'em from kissing each other every step she takes!"

"That's it! We're outa here! I've never been so disgusted in all my life!"

They gathered up their towels. "Never mind changing, Jerry. I've had it!" Greg broke away from a group of his country club friends to intercept the Landises. "Hey, amigos, I'm sorry! Can't control her anymore. She's getting way out of whack. Pretty disgusting, wasn't it, Katey?"

"You took the words right out of my mouth, Greg! Who needs this? C'mon, dear, let's leave before I really tell Victoria what I think of her!"

Greg grabbed Katey's arm. "Please, Katey. Please, Jerry, stay a little while for me?"

Victoria saw what happened. She came on high. Greg really tore into her. "For God's sake, Victoria, put your robe back on! And maybe, just maybe, Jerry and Katey won't be offended!" He turned to Katey. "If she puts her robe back on, will you two stay? Please?"

The three amigos looked at Victoria for the answer. Between overly painted lips, she said, "All right, I'll leave my robe on. And to show you two I meant no offense, let me give you two my personally guided tour of our private wine cellar." She jerked Jerry's arm and started leading him off.

"You go, Jerry. I have something I need to tell Greg in private."

Jerry read Katey's insinuation perfectly. "Okay. I'll only be gone a few minutes. Then we'll decide just how much longer we care to stay!"

Greg and Katey watched Jerry leaning hard on his cane, being escorted by Victoria. "Didn't mean to bring this up, Katey, but Jerry's having a hard time walking. Really dragging that left leg!"

"I've been trying to get him to check into the VA hospital. Boy, he's touchy about it! He's got it in his head that he'll be that much less of a man and husband in my eyes."

"Let me talk to him first chance I get. We're pretty close. Sometimes a man- to-man talk between the best of friends will turn the trick. Do I have your permission, Katey?"

"Sure, go ahead! He's downing a lot of pain pills, trying to make it through another day. Now let me tell you why Ricco and Theresa were a no-show. Victoria tried to put the make on Ricco when he delivered the wine Theresa ordered from her village. Darned near destroyed their marriage! I got Father Donovan to straighten it out in the nick of time!"

"Blast that woman! Now she's starting in on my friends! Ricco and I worked side by side these last few days, and he never said a word!"

"That's because Jerry got him to agree not to say anything for now because you three are such good friends. Greg, it can't go on like this. You're paying too high a price for appearances' sake. Don't let Victoria destroy you. Get out from under before it's too late!"

Greg said, "Oh my god, Jerry's down there in the wine cellar with her.

Suppose she's got sense enough to leave him alone?" "Jerry's not the one I'm worried about."

A small emergency arose. Greg's staff was shorthanded, so Katey volunteered to help pass the time waiting for her husband's return. Back in the kitchen, she quietly asked one of Greg's maids who doubled as a server, "Is the Hibbard wine cellar close by?"

The maid picked up a tray loaded with sandwiches and nodded. "When you push the coffee cart, go that way. There's a sign above the main door."

Katey wasted no time in wheeling the coffee cart out of the kitchen. Down the side patio she flew, her eyes searching for the sign.

She stopped abruptly beneath the entrance then abandoned her cart. She noticed an air vent toward one end of the temperature-controlled wine cellar. She knelt and listened. The first voice she heard was Jerry's, plain as day.

"Wait up, Victoria. My leg's killing me!"

She returned to her guest and slipped an arm though his. "I'm sorry, Jerry darling. I keep forgetting. There's a couch up ahead. Perhaps a break is what we both need."

He settled down on the couch. "Whew! This room is much larger than I supposed. Passed all the imported stuff. Now on to see the homegrown batches."

Victoria sat down beside him then placed her hand on his knee. Then she ran it up his trunks. *"Knock it off, Victoria!"*

"Jerry! You disappoint me! Don't you know how to treat a lady?"

"Hey, let's get one thing straight right here and now. You ain't no lady!"

Victoria's answer had a ring of sincerity in it, much to Jerry's chagrin. "I've always admired you, a real war hero. A make-it-on-your-own kind of guy. You know what you want, and you go get it. Katey's not half enough woman for you. You deserve better. Much better! I can satisfy you in every way. Have all the money you could possibly want and the connections you'll ever need. Name it and I'll get it for you."

"All right, hand me my cane! Conversation's over. Let's get the tour over *now!*"

He leaned forward, expecting Victoria to slip the cane in his hand. Instead, she jerked it away, pitching him headlong into her. He made a determined grab for balance, holding on to her. His cane bounced on the carpet runner ten feet away. He yelled, *"Now look what you've done!"*

Victoria yanked his trunks down till they caught on his leg brace, just above his ankles. He hobbled and had to hang onto her for balance. She pushed him down onto the couch and straddled him. "See, I knew it! You are a stud! Jerry, Jerry, listen to me! She can't handle that." Her dry laugh and her mock infuriated him.

Jerry gave it his all. It took one mighty shove to unseat Victoria off him. He dropped to his knees to retrieve his cane. Then he rose, pulled up his trunks so he could steady himself, and set out in slow, deliberate strides toward the wine cellar's back exit. "Get outa my way! Come near me and I'll christen my cane over your head!"

Victoria pulled her badly bruised pride together and hurried ahead of Jerry.

Then she turned to block his way, taunting him. "I'm gonna tell Katey we had great sex down here. She'll believe me 'cause I've seen everything! You have one last chance, Jerry! Do it now and I won't tell her about out little affair. Well?"

Jerry was livid with rage. "Go ahead. Tell her! See if I care! She'll laugh in your face, and then I hope she tells you where to go. Know why? Katey and I have something very special between us. Something you don't know squat about! It's called a real marriage with love and trust and commitment!"

Victoria stood defiant to the bitter end, blocking the last few feet to the exit. She ducked under Jerry's wild swing with his cane. She planted a most sickening kiss all over his mouth, smearing his lips.

CHAPTER 23

The ride back home was done in silence, absolute silence. Back in their bedroom, Katey and Jerry prepared for bed. Victoria took center stage in Katey and Jerry's minds. Katey stood in the doorway between their bedroom and the bathroom, waiting for his explanation. "First off, Katey, the lipstick you wiped off my face didn't happen the way you think it did. Hear me out…please!"

"I know, lover. No need to explain."

"No need? Are you sure? Thanks for trusting me. I know it looked pretty bad, Katey. Darned old heifer won't take no for an answer."

"Bet that was the first time any man ever turned her down! I'm so proud of the way you told her off and the way you handled her."

Now his curiosity was piqued. "How come you know so much about what happened?"

She doubled up with laughter and finally had to sit down on the floor. Her sides hurt so much from laughing so long and so hard. "Oh, Jerry, it was classic Landis all the way! Remember a few years ago when Don Ameche and Francis Langford did that radio show called the *Bickersons?* Dad and Mom never missed it!"

"Yes, Katey…so where's the connection?"

"Connection?" She rolled on the floor, trying her best to contain some of her laughter. "If I could've recorded you and Victoria's conversation, it'd put the *Bickersons* off the air! Why, it'd make millions! Really! I'd call it *Jerry's Joystick Hour!*" she screamed out with laughter. "Bottle up your boobs! Cover your snatch! Shove it in my face once more and I'll bite it off! See, I knew it. You're a stud! Where's my cane? Get off me! Now look what you've done! Bet you still want to kiss it, dontcha? Oh, Jerry, how do you come up with such gems?"

He was certainly far less amused than Katey, but he played along. "They just pop out, Katey. I just talk on their level. If it's highbrow, I go in that direction. If it's down to Victoria's level, I follow her dirty lead, kinda go with whatever I hear. Katey, you're never gonna let me forget this, are you?"

Finally, he saw the humor in that too. "All right, it was kinda funny when you stop to think about it. But at the time, I was fighting mad. She insulted our marriage. Tried to destroy it or at least get it down on her level in the gutter where her marriage has gone."

Katey thought deeply about his words. She squeezed his hand. "I know, and like you, that really hurt me. But it will never happen between us, because, Jerry, we won't let it happen! Good night, my love, my sweet, sweet, Jerry!"

For three more months, Jerry revised the weekly predictions on just how much longer the CC&W would survive. Everybody who was anybody or had any connection with the collapsing railroad had thrown in the towel and accepted the inevitable. Jack Bailey's astute editorial column, "The Soap Box," said it best: "The CC&W died today! Only thing left to do is hold the funeral."

"Better start checking the Help Wanted ads in the two Sacramento papers," he advised his spouse. "Don't think you'll have a hard time finding a job. I'm the one that'll really be hurtin'."

"Why is that, dear?"

"You've practiced your skill every day at work. Me, I've never really done any accounting in the true sense. You know all I did was use my accounting background to get my foot in the door. Go from there, solve problems, change things, make machines do more, people do less."

Katey was more upbeat. "Your background is exactly what many good companies would be willing to pay good salaries for. Those who can do what you've proved you can do are always in demand. You won't be out of work very long, I promise you!"

He started on his dessert without looking across the table at Katey. "Maybe so, but I'd give anything to squeeze out fifty-two months till retirement."

"Don't forget, Mark and Krissy will be dropping the twins off early tomorrow morning. They plan on spending the weekend in Frisco at the Cow Palace attending that big West Coast commercial and home decorator's exhibition. They're mighty serious about opening their own decorating business. Are we gonna loan them some money or not, Jerry? Krissy was hinting around for our answer when she called tonight."

Jerry picked up his first forkful of apple pie. "I reran Mark's numbers again tonight and inserted a worst-case scenario. Katey, they can't lose, even with only a slight to modest growth projection in their business over the next five years before they'd have to start repaying us. Let's tell them the seventy-five grand is theirs when they drop off Jay and Jon."

"You plan on keeping $25,000 for our emergency fund, right?"

"Absolutely! I'm not going to leave our cupboard bare, no matter what! I like the idea of having a nest egg. Money that we can get our hands on, just in case."

Katey started clearing the table while Jerry finished his pie. "Don't forget, next week is our busy week. Got the Catholic men's group again to advise on setting up their own halfway house for abused women and children. And next weekend, you and I help serve at the Gospel Mission in Sacramento."

"Oh, yes, Katey, last time I bathed Jon…or was it Jay? Darn it, I still can't tell those two apart! Anyway, whichever one I had, he said his brother didn't want you to be in the other bathroom with him. Said he's too big now. Doesn't want you seeing him when he takes his clothes off!"

Katey was having none of Jerry's conversation. "Just wait till they drop the twins off. Grandma Landis is gonna say, 'Hey, you two buckaroos! From the very first day your mother brought you home from the hospital, your grandma has diapered you, bathed you, fed you, and put you to bed for one solid year. Now since you two can't get along in the same bathtub without having two or three water fights, this is the way it's gonna have to be at Grandma Landis's home. Grandpa takes one of you, I get the other, and that is that! I've seen both of you naked plenty of times before. It doesn't bother me, so it shouldn't bother you. When you two get old enough to bathe yourselves, then Grandma will stay out of the bathroom!' How'm I doin', Grandpa?"

"Handled it like a pro that you are!"

"Now, Gerald Landis, it's off to bed with you. You look beat!" An hour later, Katey finished reading Jack Bailey's column then got ready for bed. She slipped in between the bedsheets and then rose up a second to plant a hurried good night kiss. Jerry stirred. Her aroma and her fresh scent filled his nostrils.

The odor of lilac aroused him. Suddenly, he was wide awake. "Katey?"

She didn't even bother saying her patented yes this time. She kissed him and murmured sweetly in his ear, "You were so tired. Didn't want to bother you. Ever since you've been working late, I've tried to stay away. Been over a week without you touching me, love. This weekend, the twins will wear us out. Its tonight or wait till Monday. By then, you may even find a little rust around the cap to my love tank!"

Seven days later, Katey was all aglow. She handed Jerry the editorial section. "Amigo, we're saved! Read Jack Bailey's column yourself!"

He put down the first morning cup of coffee. With eyes glued to the column, he drank in every word then managed to shift his gaze long enough to hold out his cup for a refill. Katey obliged. "Well, dear, what do you think?"

"This JD Silverman's no corporate raider. He's the genuine article! And for sure, it won't be a leveraged buyout either because Bailey says he's bought up every outstanding share of the California, Colorado, and Western stock. Get this, Katey. This guy has just paid $1.3 billion for our broken-down railroad!"

Katey poured herself a second cup of coffee. "I don't get it. If this Silverman has that kind of money, why in the world would he want to buy the CC&W?" She shook her head. "No, no, doesn't make a lick of sense, does it, Jerry?"

He folded up the newspaper and watched the bewildered expression cross his Katey's face change to one of concern. "Oh my gosh, darling. I remember what you said up at our cabin about the future of CC&W. You said the next owner would have to be super rich, which Silverman obviously is. Then you said something else about him wanting to play God with people's lives." Katey's anxiety built with each word. "And you also said we'd be lucky if he didn't start bouncing people and departments around like rubber balls in a rubber-padded room. Yes, that's it! *A rubber room!*"

Jerry reached across the table to hold Katey's hands. "Now look, let's give this JD Silverman character a decent chance before we go off on a tangent prejudging the poor guy. For now, he's saved our bacon,

Katey, and that's all I'm concerned about. If we can milk four more years out of this new owner, were in fat city, Katey! No more alarm clocks, no more worries. Just sit back and enjoy the good life we'll draw from our retirement!"

Three o'clock the next morning, Katey's safety net slipped out of bed. Their night-light said it all—a silent witness to more of the same. More and more pain pills to dull the unbearable pain. She stepped into their bathroom to lift the bottle from his hands.

"No more, my love! No more trying to make another day. Tell me what to pack 'cause we're going! You get up in the middle of the night, your pain so bad you can hardly think straight, let alone put in a half-decent day's work. No more, Jerry! I'm going with you to the VA hospital! Tell me what to pack 'cause we're going!"

CHAPTER 24

The amputation of Jerry's left leg at the VA hospital in Sacramento went better than expected with no complications. Katey was by his side the instant he was wheeled into the post-recovery room. After an hour's stay, she followed the two orderlies as they lifted Jerry into his bed in the hospital ward. She dashed out to the cafeteria for a quick snack, then back at her post, holding his hand, waiting for his first clear thoughts. He seemed unusually groggy. Then he blinked to clear his eyes just as two staff doctors made their rounds to check on the packing around his stump. Satisfied, they resumed their rounds and left Katey alone with him.

"Katey, Katey," he called out.

"I'm here, darling. Turn your head to the left so you can see me. The doctors said you're doing just fine, my love. Just fine." Katey rose to hover over him. "Feel like a kiss, love?"

He ran his tongue around the inside of his mouth. "Got that stockyard taste again. Let me have a sip first, hon."

She tipped the ice water in the glass toward his mouth while he sucked on the straw. Once the glass was back safely on his table, she found his lips. "Put some more feeling if you can into our kiss." He tried hard. "Hmm, that's better, dear."

"Man, you turn me on, Katey. And don't you dare invite. I'm not ready for that. Not today anyway."

A coy little smile invaded Katey's lips. "There'll be plenty of time for that when I get you home alone, where you'll be all mine. Then we'll see what happens. Anything special you want me to do before I leave tonight?"

"Tell Mark and Krissy to see me soon as I get to feeling better. Want to talk to them some more about that portable mock-up studio they ranted and raved about seeing at the exhibition in Frisco."

"Jerry, you can't be serious! Dear, that'd take our last twenty-five grand, and you're not one to risk our last dollars. Hon, we've helped them enough, don't you think? The remodel job on the warehouse'll be finished in four weeks, and I want you out of here on your new leg in time for their grand opening."

"Katey, we've got nothing to worry about if we decide to loan them our last twenty-five. Our jobs are protected under the ICC ruling back in 1958 when the merger took place. Mark says that the computer-operated portable mock- up unit is still available at the show price. That's a savings of over $5,700. Just think, with computer enhancement, one of Krissy or Mark's customers can see firsthand what their home or office will actually look like before they tackle the job. There isn't another like it in our area. They'll be the first to have this latest state-of-the-art feature. Be a leg up on all the competition. I think we should go for it! Boy, would that make a real difference if they had it to show off to their customers in time for the grand opening!"

Katey sat back on her chair, still holding his hand. "Jerry, you've just come out of the operating room, and here you are making big plans. Let's let it ride. If it still seems like a great idea after their grand opening, maybe then. Okay?"

He reached through the side rail to squeeze her hand. "I liked your suggestion about telling Krissy and Mark to keep names and addresses of all their old customers over the past two years. Now they've got a built-in mailing list of prospects to contact when they open. Also think it's a good idea about everybody registering for the grand prize drawing, which will provide another list of prospects to call on. Those ideas will generate lots of business, Katey!"

She was pleased by his compliment. "Now let's just concentrate on getting you ready to attend their grand opening. They'll do just fine, Jerry. Like you always said after you ran their numbers, they can't miss! Let's see how your numbers are doing!"

He turned his attention to her. "I miss you already, and this is only my first day. How in the world am I gonna do without you for three and one half weeks more?"

She kissed him passionately and then turned to pick up her purse. "You need to rest. I'll be in tomorrow right after work and bring you all the latest scuttlebutt on JD Silverman." She blew him a kiss at the foot of his bed. "Boy, your pillow is sure gonna get one heckuva workout each night till you're back home. Always remember, I love you with all my heart and soul, Jerry."

While Jerry recuperated, his world dwindled down to two things: Katey and his obsession with the computer-operated decorator mock-up. Katey had never seen him like this. So out of character, so out of the Jerry Landis mold she'd known since their first recess in public school way back in 1938. It was as though he'd completely abandoned his strict conservative ways for the sake of this technology. He had to have it, even though he'd never seen it. Bewildering and mystifying as it was, Katey also realized Jerry's stubbornness could turn their marriage into a verbal war zone if he didn't get his way.

Ten days later, Mark, Krissy, and the twins paid Jerry a long visit. Katey arrived late that evening, so she missed the family reunion at his bedside. She planted a warm welcome kiss and let him do the talking. He cranked the upper part of his bed and smiled. "Just missed 'em, Katey. You should've been here! I let the twins have a field day thinking they'd pull the wool over their grandpa's eyes by switching clothes. Boy, did I ever puncture Jay and Jon's balloon when Grandpa checked Jay's left ear like you told me to. That birthmark gave him away. We all had a great time and a great visit, Katey. Man, I think our two grandsons, those two pills are really something!"

"Anything else discussed?"

Jerry acted tentative. "You know me like a book. Katey, I... I went ahead and told Mark and Krissy we'd loan them the money to buy that mock-up studio. I know, there goes the last of our savings. Gosh, Katey, we were having such a good visit, and I wanted to give 'em some extra good news to take home. Please say you'll back me up? Katey? Please?"

Katey let him stew a bit. "By rights, I oughta make you get on the phone tonight and tell them you got carried away. You had your pride working overtime again, but I won't. I'll save your hide this time. Still don't know what's come over you lately. Dear, not like you at all. Usually you're the one I have to sell, not the other way around."

Jerry quickly changed subjects. "Hey, guess what? I tried on my new artificial leg for a few minutes today! It works by suction! Just slide my stump into it and it holds."

Now Katey was excited about some good news. "So soon! Aren't you real sore?"

He pulled back the bedsheet to show her. "Sure, but they want me to start exercising tomorrow." He pointed to the red coating at the end of his stump. "Katey, that's a tuff skin-like coating, not blood. It really helps put a thick scar on my stump so it will heal much faster. Then believe it or not, but each night, they soak my stump in an oil preparation. Makes the scab soft to keep from cracking as it heals. By next week, I should be spending quite a bit of time going for short walks around the ward here. Maybe even out in some of the halls."

Katey saw a change in her Jerry again; the same upbeat and positive attitude was back. "I'm so glad you're getting along just fine. Any problems?"

"My temperature has been a bit erratic. Goes with the territory. Not to worry, dear. I'll be outa here before you know it! Should be home in plenty of time for the grand opening! Mark brought some Polaroid snapshots. Their warehouse remodeling is right on schedule."

"Let's talk about us, Jerry! Miss me?"

He turned on his pillow to look at his wife. "The foods terrible. I'm getting horny. You're better lookin' every minute, and you've actually got the gall to ask me if I miss you?"

She was up on the side of his bed in a flash, smothering him with kisses.

Then she giggled. "Horny, huh? Now that sounds a lot more like the Jerry Landis I know, loved, and married. Landis, you do have a way of putting things in their proper perspective, I'll say that for you. Guess then there's no need telling you the gauge on my love tank is way past empty, is there, darling?"

He sniffed her hair, smelled her perfume, and brushed her breast ever so gently. "Lord, you are indeed some woman, Katey. Got it as bad for you now as when I was eighteen. And if I remember, that was pretty bad!"

She sat up beside him, sitting on the edge of his hospital bed. "Think we'd better change subjects again, lover."

"Been following Bailey's column again. He says Silverman did the same thing some years back when he bought out the old Denver and Southwest Line. Made some drastic changes, but he did put the road back in the financial black again. Ever see this JD up in corporate headquarters?"

"No. Even Greg's never met him. Understand he keeps to himself pretty much. Kind of a loner. Heard that he never grants the media an interview. Not his style, I guess."

"Well, has he officially taken over? There's nothing in the papers or on TV or in Bailey's column one way or the other."

"It all comes to a head next Monday morning, is what Greg told me. Silverman's having a meeting with the five division managers. Greg's already told me to block out Monday morning and to hold all his calls. He thinks it's going to be one heckuva round. Heads will probably roll. Said he feels sure this guy must be a fist-pounding, red-faced Texan, full of hot air, an overfat wallet, and plenty of bluff to back up his play. Greg's already got a nickname for the poor guy!"

Jerry laughed. "Yeah, leave it to the old Teddy Bear, Katey. He'd come up with something original, no doubt."

Katey snickered. "Greg calls him Little Jesus! Say's he must walk on water, or else how could he get to be so filthy rich!"

"Maybe he just uses the common sense and brains God gave him! Ever think of that, Katey?"

They heard clatter coming from the wheels on the hospital food service cart. Katey watched the server set up the portable table for Jerry. She removed the insulated jacket and smelled. "Doesn't look just so bad, lover. Sure you weren't a little hard about the food being so bad?"

He reluctantly replied, "Maybe a bit, dear, but it can't hold a candle to your cooking, Katey. Man, oh man, what I'd give to be sittin' across from you in our kitchen again. Heck, when I get out of here, I'm gonna move my chair around to your side. It's too far eating across the table from you. I wanna get closer to you, Katey!"

"Somehow, Landis, you've got bedroom duty mixed up with your food again. How about this? We move your chair just around the corner from mine.

That oughta be close enough for both of us. Then if you decide the food can wait, I'll be just that much closer so you can carry me down the hall." Katey glanced at her watch.

"Don't, Katey. Don't look at it. Stay with me a little longer! When you leave, everything stops! Even the time!"

"Okay, only fifteen minutes more. Then I gotta go. Shouldn't your nurse be around to check your temperature?"

CHAPTER 25

Monday morning came, and despite all the news media coverage, nobody had a clue as what to really expect from JD Silverman, the new owner and CEO of the CC&W Railroad. Endless days of speculation had come to a close. Five division managers looked around at what was left of the once plush conference room furnishings, now so bleak and bare. Greg Hibbard drummed his fingers incessantly in front of him, taking pains to avoid the nicks, scratches, dents, and old cigarette burns that marred its once spotless surface. He glanced down at the thin flimsy pad sticking out of the chair beneath him. Its frayed edges and missing stitches reminded him of the cheap chairs and cushions that littered San Francisco's skid row.

"I've heard of austere programs before," he blurted out. "This is ridiculous!

The army surplus store in Sacramento has better-looking junk than this!"

Several other managers were about to second Greg's remarks when the side door to the room quietly opened. In stepped an average built man in his late forties. He glanced around, taking notice of who was seated where. He proceeded to put his five-foot-eleven-inch frame at the head of the conference table. The managers rose to their feet.

"Gentlemen," he said in a soft monotone. "Please be seated."

He was dressed in a dark-gray business suit, which matched his hair. A neatly clipped pencil-thin mustache traveled an exact quarter inch above his upper lip. His suit looked to be of average material, less expensive than four of the five who faced him. His deep gray eyes commanded everybody's attention.

Their penetration, cold and relentless. They mirrored the man himself—hard and uncompromising. He pressed the button next to his chair. In came his private secretary carrying five packets, which she passed out among the managers.

He waited a few seconds for her to leave. "Please open your packets. The first item is your resignation form. Sign it so we can move on. There's much to cover this morning."

Greg glanced around. "Mr. Silverman, why are we here if the first order of business is our resignation signatures?"

"Mr. Hibbard, if you'll take the time to notice, none of the forms are dated. Should any of you decide that you don't want to join my team or you fail to meet your quotas, all I need do is date it. Eliminates wasting my time in useless discussion later on."

One by one, their pens came out.

"Now to the business at hand. Please follow my pointer on the slide screen.

The fastest way to get the CC&W back on its feet is to eliminate our diesel and electric locomotives, our most costly expenditure by far." He circled a figure in red. That's a savings of over $400 million."

Ed Cardenas, the Nevada Division manager, put in his nickel's worth. "How in H are you gonna move anything down the tracks without some locomotives?"

JD changed his stern disposition a tad. He addressed this man of Mexican descent. "Mr. Cardenas, I've just put the Denver and Southwest Road in the black last year without owning a single engine.

Allow me to continue." His pointer tapped the same figure. "This savings also includes fuel costs, overhaul and maintenance, and the biggest profit eater by far, eliminating the operating engineers' union contract."

Toby Garrett, the Utah Division manager, shook his head. "Excuse me, sir, but you can forget about your slice and dice program on your slideshow because you're gonna get your butt sued day and night taking on the operating engineers in court for the next umpteen years. Maybe you better appoint a deputy or somebody else to run your railroad. Their contract will bury you."

Four managers had a big chuckle over Garrett's tidy snippet of information. JD's pointer hit the table. Then he pointed it at Garrett. "My legal staff has done their homework. Without any engines, their contract is worthless because we no longer own the engines. Mr. Ricco Petrocelli's union has already been informed on this matter. I assure you, I'm on solid ground. Let's move on."

Another slide came into view before Gene Frey interrupted, "What are your plans for the operating engineers?"

JD never let the Wyoming manager ruffle him in the slightest. "Each engineer will be offered his job back at my new Denver location with a fifty percent salary cut. Those that refuse will be given my one-year buyout, along with my best wishes."

Ed Cardenas's big fist slammed down hard, sending his packet flying in several directions, startling JD and the other three. "That's it? That's all they get? You're screwing 'em, Silverman, and you sure as H know it!"

The room buzzed with an undertow of uneasiness as five managers realized they were pawns in a high-stakes game with million-dollar figures they'd never been around, much less comprehend. "Just find your resignation form, Mr. Cardenas, and hand it to me on your way out."

With the coolness of the polished pro that he was, JD had sent Cardenas packing. The burly man wadded up his resignation form and hurled it in Silverman's direction, along with some guttural Mexican that didn't need translation.

A minute passed before the four followed JD's pointer. "Effective immediately, there will be a thirty percent reduction in our total workforce.

Those still covered by the 1958 merger agreement are protected for now. If need be, I can and will find a way to get around that obstacle. In each of your packets, you will find a list of my employees in your division. You have forty- eight hours to submit to me only those you deem best qualified to keep. The rest will be placed in a pool for random computer two-week layoff notices. I must keep my labor costs under control."

The remaining four sat stunned to the core, wondering what slice and slash the next slide would provide. JD didn't disappoint. "My five years as CEO at Denver Southwest taught me one very important lesson. Middle management never pulls their weight, let alone justifies their salaries. Give the next in line ninety days to train on the job, and you'll never miss them. All mid- management will be replaced within the next thirty days. The savings alone here will run into the millions. Their replacements will get a ten percent raise once they complete their training period."

No matter what word or words JD used, it always boiled down to the two that breathed fire into the man's pointer—cut and save. "Within sixty days, our train marshalling yards, our dispatcher services, and our rolling stock maintenance and repair services will be moved to Ogden, Utah. Its central location in terms of track mileages and the latest state-of-the-art technology at our new facility will pay for itself within three years. Those who transfer will be retrained at reduced salaries. The rest will get my buyout offer."

Ed Marsden, the California Division manager, had been silent till now. He did indeed have something to add to the man in the dark-gray business suit.

"Mr. Silverman," he said, "you haven't saved this railroad, *you've just murdered it!*"

JD pressed on with another slide. "The next slide is a map of the combined operations of the CC&W and Denver Southwest." The pointer underscored an arrow touching a large black dot. "This is Denver, which will be our maintenance and operations hub, which will service both roads. Today we have access to the growing southwest markets, and we also have our fingers into the international trade pie because of our seaport connections in San Francisco and the Bay Area. The movement of raw, unprocessed material and natural resources from within our country will be the key to our profit picture. I intend to get our share and a bit more, now that I own both transport lines."

He waited a few seconds, watching their reaction, trying to gauge just how much his managers had absorbed. His pointer stroked back and forth along one dotted fine. "This line is temporary as of today. I'm negotiating for the sale of eight huge tracts of land in southwestern Wyoming. Millions of tons of high-quality unmined coal has been located there. It contains much less sulfur than the coalfields back east. Congress is about to put tighter clean-air restrictions and emissions into law. My new fields will meet those restrictions. We'll be just where we want to be. In terms of profit, sales from those coalfields will sustain our two lines until they can be brought into the black on their own."

Now the four were impressed. JD had lit the fire of understanding within. He pressed the remote and pointed to a box on the screen with no name. "Anybody know what name belongs here?"

Greg stood up. "Sir, with all that trackage you now own, there's bound to be valuable timber, mineral, and maybe even oil resources along those lines right-of-way. I'd label it Silverman Resources, sir."

"I see you've done your homework, Mr. Hibbard. And let's not forget those lines are easy access to skiing, boating, fishing, hunting, and camping. There's untapped millions there just waiting for sale to the right developers with good solid financial numbers. I'm going to staff a new resources department within the week to get going on all that potential just waiting to be picked."

"Why do you keep calling both our railroads CC&W Transport and Denver and Southwest Transport on your charts? Has the name *railroad* suddenly become a dirty word?"

"Good question, Mr. Garrett." JD moved around the table to better address the man and his question. He laid his pointer on the table and, with folded arms, closed his eyes, trying to visualize what came into focus. Then he opened those cold, calculated eyes that penetrated everything and everybody. "I don't think there's an old shipping customer around today who hasn't thought of this in one way or another. Know what he sees? I'll tell you what he sees! He sees an old broken-down locomotive that should've been in the scrap heap years ago trying to pull too many railroad cars down a pair of tracks that look like they've seen better days too! I'm going to change that image if it's the last thing I ever do. From now on, every new and every old customer is going to think of the word *transport* when he ships on my two lines. We're going to call ourselves by what we do, not how it gets to its destination. And that, gentlemen, is by transport."

It would be hard to tell if JD had won over any converts to his new thinking. One thing he did have was their undivided attention. Time to put the finishing touches to his search and destroy mission. "In your packets are lists of businesses that ship with another road, highway truck transport, or airfreight. It will be your job to contact three on your list each day to get them to ship with us. Your lists have been screened to cover only those who ship by bulk items, large tonnage, or volume. This is the only business that will make us a profit. You may deviate up to fifteen percent from our published rates. Anything over that, contact me immediately to see what it will take to get your customer shipping with us. Are we clear about this?. Yes, you're all going to be salesmen, *my kind of salesman!* One year from today, those of you who are left, those of you who have proved to me you have what it takes to be on my winning team, will meet with me in this very room. And I'll fill in your bonus *gladly!* I do reward success very handsomely. I do and will fire incompetence, poor results, and excuses. Make no mistake about that! You must meet your monthly quotas or else I'll fill your position with somebody who can deliver new customers. Questions?"

Four men exchanged glances. They had been prodded, provoked, and challenged by an average-sized man who sported a thin-clipped mustache and who spoke in soft monotones. But, boy, was he all business! Nothing but business! JD left them with his final thought. "I'm not here to let my transport business pass on into history. I'm here to make my own history with or without you!"

CHAPTER 26

Rushton's downed economy had its ripple effect on Sacramento. True, considerable belt tightening was felt in the capital city, but it was a mere drop in the proverbial bucket compared to the devastation heaped upon the bedroom commute community just fifteen miles away. Krissy's parents, collectively, heaved big sighs of relief when M&K Decorating enjoyed a very good grand opening. Now they could turn their attention to much more pressing problems at hand. Namely, Greg Hibbard and JD Silverman.

The strain of trying to keep his job and continue some semblance of marriage began to take its toll on Greg. JD hauled him into his office daily, demanding more and more out of him. Surely, as Katey put it, Greg's breaking point must be around the corner. The proof of it happened two days later, when Katey walked in on him. He was in the midst of an all-out, knockdown, drag-out call with Victoria. Greg slammed the receiver down so hard it's a wonder his telephone stood the abuse.

"Sorry, Katey. You had to listen to this when I buzzed for you. Didn't mean to prolong it. It's that I needed to have my say with her."

Katey approached his desk, steno pad and pencil ready. "Is there anything either Jerry or I can do for you, boss?"

Greg stroked his chin. "I'm strapped for cash…got a payment due for my swimming pool. My blue-chip market is way down. Don't dare unload now. If I do, I'll take a real shellacking, and that won't solve my problem for long."

Katey tried to be tactful. "Ever think about changing your lifestyle a little… maybe move down a step o' two on your social ladder?"

Greg turned around. "I've given it some thought, even considered putting my mansion up for sale. Victoria says if she sees one For Sale sign, that's the last I'll ever see of her. Katey, that's all I got left! My mansion!"

"If we had any spare cash, amigo, you know Jerry and I would help you." "Thanks, Katey, but my financial problems are way out of your league. But thanks again for your concern. If only I could count on her…if only. It'd be a start at least."

"Has she ever worked?" Katey blushed, realizing her inference. "I am sorry, boss. That's not exactly what I meant to ask."

Greg held up one hand. "No, no, that's all right. I get the point. Truth is, Katey, Victoria's never even had a nodding acquaintance with the work world. She's still living in la-la land where the money keeps rolling in just as fast as she spends it. Well, that's come to a halt! It's time to make some changes. If Little Jesus can, why can't I?"

Katey felt very sorry for Greg. "He's been pretty hard on you, hasn't he?"

Greg got up to pace back and forth. He stopped in front of Katey. "I can take the heat, Katey. Really, I can! I've surprised the heck out of JD so far by coming in way ahead on his quotas. It's the home front that's doing me in. Darn that woman!"

Katey was puzzled. "Hey, boss, fill me in. How in the world will Victoria's landing a job possibly help you if you own a big payment on the swimming pool?"

"Don't you see it, Katey? If she can get a job, then I'll sell out. For once in my life, I'll have somebody to come home to, and we'll have something in common! We each work! Not much to start on, I know. But just maybe, we'll learn to tolerate each other. Could even lead to better things, like…like a little mutual respect! Who knows, we even might try sharing the same bedroom again."

Katey wasn't convinced.

"All right, all right, Katey! Maybe I'm aiming a little high, but you gotta admit, I'm still in there pitching. Lord, what I wouldn't give to have the kind of marriage you and Jerry have…romance going on day after day, month after month all these years."

"Okay, let's get on with today. What's on JD's mind?"

Greg got out of his chair. "I've done all I can for Jerry. We both know it! Katey, this is it for Jerry! The divine one has decreed that all mid-management must go, and that includes him. Nobody's being spared! I argued with Silverman till my voice grew hoarse, but no dice! I've notified personnel to get out the notices this coming Friday. Little Jesus claims mid-management never pulls their weight. Claims they're living off the labor of others."

"It's not right! Jerry's given everything he has to this railroad! Why, why, even you said he pulled us through until the '58 merger was approved."

Greg tried to console his distraught secretary. He comforted her as best he could, putting his arm around her. "I know, Katey, I know! But Little Jesus isn't interested in history."

Katey broke away from him, sobbing. "Who's going to tell him? You? Or are you gonna let the computer run do the dirty business? That's all he is to this railroad, just another number! Never mind it's a waste of a brilliant mind!"

"I'll tell him myself come Friday, Katey."

She was blinded by her own tears. Katey was mad, fighting mad. "Oh, that's just dandy! Where do we go from here? What's going to happen to my husband?"

Greg gave Katey's pointed question extra thought. "Because he was here when the '58 merger went through, he gets thirty days to accept a one-year buyout offer. Katey, those not covered by the '58 merger protection get nothing, *just their termination notice!* Nothing more!"

Katey faced her boss. "He'll never sign it! He'll never trade thirty years for one year of severance pay! He'll never compromise! We both know it! He'll fight Silverman till he draws his last breath or spends every last dollar he can get his hands on taking him to court."

"And he'll lose, Katey! Nobody can beat Little Jesus! It's been tried in Denver. Silverman walked away with complete control of the Denver and Southwest Railroad under his belt. The same thing is in the works here too!"

Katey wiped her tears. "Then God help us, 'cause Jerry Landis is gonna start one heckuva war come this Friday!"

Greg put both arms around her. "That's what worries me most, little amigo. Talk some sense to him this Friday, Katey, after I give him the bad news. I've done a bit of checking on JD concerning the Denver takeover."

"And?"

"Can't prove it, but a couple of people who held out like Jerry's gonna do disappeared right into thin air. You, Jerry, and Ricco are my best friends. Let's make sure our foursome doesn't become a threesome."

Friday morning arrived, and Jerry found Greg waiting for him in the accounting office. Greg closed the door.

"Hey, amigo," said Jerry. "What brings you here so early? Looks like you just lost your last friend!"

Greg handed him two papers. "Hey, Jerr. I only hope to God you meant that as a joke!"

Jerry opened the letter, read it, and reread it. He exploded. *"What the H is this, amigo?* Must be some mistake, right?"

Greg put his hand on his friend's shoulder. "No mistake, Jerr. Your number came up. All mid-management is being laid off today. Wish to God I had better news."

Then it sank in, the full impact. Jerry fought back the emotion, the hurt, and the anger. "Katey know about this?"

"She's taking it pretty hard. Go easy on her, amigo, please. It's been a tough week on her too!"

He reread the layoff notice again. He got up and looked through the window portion of his office door separating the manager's office from his department. He exploded, punching the door, kicking at his desk, lashing out at everything near him. One swipe of his fist cleared everything across the top of his desk, including pictures of Katey, Mark, Krissy, and his two grandsons. "Worked my balls off for thirty years, and this is the payoff! Boy, Landis, you're nothing but a big-time loser!" He lashed out at Greg. "What's the other paper?

The I'm sorry-but-you-gotta-go letter from God almighty upstairs in his ivory tower?"

Greg waited for him to calm down before daring to approach his dear friend. "Jerr, it's a buyout offer. One year's severance pay if you sign within thirty days."

Greg had never seen Jerry so livid with rage. His eyes rolled, his body shook, and he had a dry raspy laugh. "Tell Little Jesus he can stick that buyout offer you know where. Silverman will die of old age before he sees my John Henry on any buyout offer." He turned toward his old amigo. "Can you see me signing away thirty years for one lousy, stinking year? Can you, amigo?"

"No, Jerr, I can't, knowing you the way I do. I can't even get you to sign a United Good Neighbor Pledge Card, much less this. And Katey's told me a dozen times you'll never sign a church donation pledge."

"Darned right, I won't!" he shouted. "There's only one piece of paper I believe in or signed, and Katey's got that tucked away in our safety-deposit box. *Our marriage license!*"

"Look, amigo, if you want to bag it and go home, I don't blame you. I'll cover for you, and take Katey with you!"

Jerry growled sarcastically. "Naw, wouldn't wanna screw old Ebenezer outa a full day's worth of warm meat. I'll stick it out and pick up Katey same as usual after work."

Greg got ready to go. "I'm leaving your buyout offer here on this corner of your desk. Do with it as you like."

"Don't worry one little gray hair over it. I'll put it right where it belongs— in the round file. Then tonight, just before I leave, I'll fish it out and put it in that nifty little box up in the right-hand corner of my desk. Any other good news today?"

Greg moved out of fist swinging range just in case. "There is one other thing, Jerry. I'd better let you cool off this weekend and ask you next Monday."

"Can't be any worse than the load you dropped on me already. Go ahead." "I'm supposed to ask you who'd make your best replacement in the department to take over your job. Now don't By off the handle, Jerry. I'm just doing my job."

Jerry shook his head in disbelief. "Ain't this *something*! Hand a guy his walking papers one minute and then has the guts to ask who's your best replacement? Only for you, Greg. And believe me, if it was anybody else, I'd deck him before he could get the question out! Give Andy Stephens a shot at managing my department. He's entitled. By the way, does he get my salary?"

"No, Jerr. Andy will get six-month probation and then a ten percent raise if he can cut it. Your old title as department manager will disappear."

"Yeah, I get it. Right along with me. Little Jesus is hoping! Right? Well, amigo, I'm here for the long haul too! Forty-four more months' worth, to be exact! I'm protected by the '58 merger agreement, and so Little Jesus will have to like or lump it! His problem, not mine! Got it?"

CHAPTER 27

That afternoon, Jerry drove straight home without muttering a single word to Katey. She watched, her heart nearly breaking, wanting to comfort him and hold him close. Something told her to stay away. He was a human time bomb about to explode at the slightest provocation. They parked in their garage. He turned off the ignition and looked straight ahead. His words were harsh and cruel. They were words he never used on her before.

"We weren't gonna have any more secrets, Katey. That's what we promised each other when you told me about Krissy being our daughter, remember?" She started to say something. He cut her short. "So you've done it to me again, haven't you?" He raised his voice. *"How come you never ever said one lousy, stinkin' word about the worst day in my life? Answer me, Katey!"*

She moved over to him. He pushed her away. She started to cry. "I… I tried to twice this week. Honest… Jerry. I… I just couldn't. It hurt so much. I… I didn't know how to start, what to say. Please, Jerry, it wasn't a secret. Not the kind you mean. There's no secret between us now. Never, I swear! Not since Krissy."

He turned away from her and mumbled. She thought he was saying something to her.

"What did you say, darling? I didn't catch it?"

He turned to face her with a full blast. *"I said my mother was right after all!*

Still not worth the spit on a public park bench!"

Twice she hit him hard across the mouth. Her second slap drew blood when her fingernails raked his chin. "Never, ever say those words, Jerry Landis! Understand? If I ever hear those disgusting words again, you'll get a lot more than a couple of slaps across your mouth!"

He shoved her hard against the car door. *"Get out!"* he screamed. "Get out before I do something we'll both be sorry for. Leave me alone, Katey! For God's sake, just leave me alone!"

Katey sat, stunned. Quietly, she opened her car door and stepped out onto the hard concrete garage floor. She walked to the garage side entrance and looked back again, fear gnawing at her heart, wondering just what state of mind he was in. Should she dare leave him alone as he demanded? Could he be suicidal? Should she call for help? She stood frozen in thought, her mind loaded with more questions than answers. Her legs felt like lead weights as she forced one step after another, gradually leaving him behind. Her beloved Jerry, seated alone in their car.

Inside her home, she stood at the kitchen sink, wondering what to do next. "Katey, get a hold of yourself," she said out loud, feeling the need to converse with anyone, even if it was only herself. "Jerry's gonna be all right. He just needs time alone to think things through. Go ahead, get supper on. Then call him in. He'll be ready to come in."

Mechanically, Katey went through the motions of setting the table and preparing Jerry's favorite broiled chicken in the oven. Then she made a fresh tossed green salad, making sure his dish had extra slices of tomatoes. "Garlic bread! Yes, that always draws a comment from him."

With their meal waiting on the table, she approached him again in the garage. Her legs were shaking to match her voice. She saw his side window was up, so she quietly tried the door latch. She found him slumped over the steering wheel, arms wrapped tightly around to give him support in this hour of crisis.

Katey stood next to him but made no attempt to touch him. Her lips trembled. "Jerry, can you hear me?" Again, she tried to raise him from his stupor. "Jerry, please answer me! Can you hear me?"

More time slipped by. Still no response. She realized he was in shock. What to do? She found his left hand partially open, fingers half relaxed. Without a second thought, she slipped off her wedding band and forced it into the palm of his hand. Then she closed his fingers. "Bring me the wedding band, Jerry! When you bring me my wedding band, I'll know you're all right! Never forget, Jerry. I love you with all my heart and soul! Remember that, dear!"

Tears burst down both cheeks. She made her way back into their home and sat down alone at the kitchen table. She tried a bite of chicken, telling herself he'd be in a few more minutes with her wedding band, acting as though nothing had ever happened.

Ten, twenty minutes, half an hour passed. Still no husband! The dinner went cold, and she had no appetite. Mechanically, she fixed him a plate as though he'd come busting through the door after working late, as he'd done so many times in their past. She covered his plate with foil and popped it into the oven, half expecting to feel his arms wrapped around her, blowing softly on the nape of her neck. A sure sign much more exciting communication was on the way between them before they said good night. She turned around and greeted nothing but silence. She brushed aside a salty tasting tear that somehow managed to find a corner of her mouth.

"I know, I'll call Krissy! They've always been so close."

She rushed to the phone. *Dumb idea, Katey,* she scolded herself. "Jerry'll be furious when he comes in to find out," she said. "The ring was a good idea. Jerry will see it and wonder what it's doing in his hand. He'll bring it in, and I'll make him slip it on my finger again. Then everything will be right between us. No, Katey, put your thinking cap on! Use your God-given smarts."

Bolstered by her own pep talk, Katey started to hum as she cleared the table to put away the rest of the unused food. That taken care of, she found herself washing her plate and silverware in the sink. She happened to glance down at the white band of flesh on her left hand, where her wedding band had been all those twenty-five beyond compare years. She rinsed the soap suds off her finger and thought back. Oh, what sweet, sweet sensual feelings when they'd last touched just two days ago. Then it suddenly dawned on her. She was standing alone at the sink, washing her dishes. My God, her dishwasher was less than two feet to her right!

She was in deep trouble, and she knew it. Two quick wipes on the kitchen towel and she rushed into her bedroom. Down on her knees, she prayed. She whispered, "Please, please, dear Lord, help me in my hour of need. Please bring my husband safely back to me. Please, please, dear Lord! Don't desert me!"

Katey returned from the bedroom. *How terribly quiet,* she thought. *Noise… yes, noise. That's it. That'll help pass the time till Jerry comes in…to me.* She aimed and pressed the remote. The TV sprang to life, giving her just what she needed. Noise! Lots of noise!

Another hour finally passed. Katey had made her decision. No Jerry by the ten o'clock news, it would be time to call for help.

Then she heard it. An engine cranking over. She rushed to the sink again. Her heart plummeted to rock bottom. *Jerry's starting the engine!* Her mind screamed! She rushed back from the sink to the front door just in time to see the double door to their garage come sliding down. Frantic with fear, she seized the telephone and pushed the 911 buttons till her fingers ached. The dispatcher came on the line.

"Hurry! Hurry!" she yelled. "*My husband's in our garage! The door's closed! He's started the engine!*"

CHAPTER 28

The dispatcher's voice had a calming effect. "Ma'am, I'll need your address. Help is on the way."

The next five minutes were as confusing as any Katey had ever experienced. Lights were flashing; people seemed to come out of the woodwork from everywhere. When it was over, Jerry stood outside their garage, shaking hands with two paramedics from the local fire department. He seemed quite calm about the whole episode, too darned calm for Katey's liking. He waved goodbye to the men and turned to walk toward the house. Katey ran outside and jumped into his arms, crying. "Oh, my Jerry! Oh, my Jerry! You're all right! You're all right!"

He kissed her and put her down. "Of course I am all right. Why shouldn't I be?"

Katey was dumbfounded. "Why shouldn't you be? Jerry, I heard you start the engine. I saw the garage door being lowered. What was I supposed to think?"

"Oh, that! Some jerk pulled into our driveway and killed his engine. On top of that, he flooded his engine before restarting it. That must've been the engine starting you thought was mine. He kept blinking his headlights so much that it annoyed the heck outa me, so I tripped the automatic switch on our double door, and that's what you saw. Anyway, the paramedics arrived about that time, so we pushed him back out of our driveway. I thanked them for coming. I can see how it must've looked to you. Thanks for your concern anyway, Katey. It was real thoughtful of you, even though it wasn't necessary!"

"And you're all right, dear? I mean really all right?"

"I just needed time to get my head on straight. Took me a while to sort things out in my mind and figure out what I'm going to do! You know, a plan of action! Say, hon, I'm starved! Hope you saved me a plate?"

Katey's Irish surfaced as sure as a breeze blows under the Golden Gate Bridge. She stomped both feet and shook a menacing finger in front of his nose. "Gerald Landis, you had me so worried, you nearly drove me nuts, and you've got the gall to tell me you're hungry? Don't you ever try to push me out of your life! When you hurt, I hurt! Got it? Just 'cause you're some super bean counter doesn't cut it with me. They apparently didn't teach you a darned thing in Beancounter 101 Class about empathy! Yes, Landis, that's what it is called! *Empathy*! Got it?"

Jerry saw his Katey in a far different light. "You're dead serious about all this, aren't you? It's not just my battle anymore, is it?"

She stood up on her tiptoes to him, trying in her small way to emphasize her point as much as possible. "We've always supported each other, dear, and that's the way it's going to be. Or else!'

"Or else what?"

"Or else you're going to want to go to work very early every morning to get away from the war zone at home if I'm not part of everything you plan or do. Got it, Landis?"

"Yeah, Katey. I read you loud and clear! Wow! You're sure touchy tonight!" "Okay, now let's sit down and I'll reheat our supper. We're going to talk it out no matter how long it takes. You mentioned you had a plan of action, so let's hear it!"

They ate their supper at ten o'clock that night midst Jerry's thoughts and ideas on just how he planned to counter JD Silverman. One half hour past the apple pie dessert, Katey was still asking questions. "I still don't understand leverage, dear. Explain it again, please!"

"Katey, it came to me while I was sitting there behind the steering wheel. Silverman's in the same boat we are, only on a much, much larger scale. He's buying time with his numbers game just like we are. Greg told me he's almost sure JD leveraged his buyout of the D&SW. That means he's had a silent backer somewhere who financed a huge chunk of the money he used to buy all the outstanding stock of the D&SW. Probably using the same backer right here too!"

"Let me see if I follow you. You're saying this man, this billionaire, didn't have enough money for both buyouts? Correct?"

"Absolutely! No matter how much money Little Jesus had to begin with, I'd bet my next paycheck he had a backer." Katey poured them a refill of coffee. "Okay, I follow so far, I think. Now how does that fit in with what you plan to do?"

"Just before I picked you up after work, I read a notice on our bulletin board. Ricco is holding an open meeting next Friday night at his union hall for all union and nonunion employees protected under the 1958 merger. They'll open our meeting with a couple of speakers who will discuss our options and then go on with their proposed plan of action."

"So how does that affect you?"

Jerry smiled, the first time Katey'd seen that all day. This was the Jerry she was used to being around. "Like I said, Katey, it's a numbers game. If somehow most of us can be shown a way to refuse to sign the buyout, Silverman's going to be hurtin' just like us. I'm betting he plans on tapping the pension surplus from this buyout to meet his obligation to his backer, just like he did with the Denver & SW. Follow me?"

Katey hugged and kissed her husband. "Wow, what a mind! But Greg told me JD got around his problems by eliminating them. Darling, I don't like the sound of that. That sounds pretty dangerous to me. How much risk, Jerry! C'mon, be honest!"

He put down his coffee cup. "I'd be less than honest, Katey, if I didn't tell you there's risk involved here too! Apparently, whatever problems JD had in Denver, he either took care of the problems or else had somebody do it for him so he'd come up with a clean show of hands."

"Are you gonna be a risk, Jerry? 'Cause if you are, I'm not sure about all this."

"It's still a numbers game. If we hang together, I truly believe this guy can be brought down to the bargaining table. His huge obligations will force it. We're both going to that meeting at Ricco's union hall next week. Then I'll know what's in store for you and me if we decide to take him on."

Jerry touched her hands. "I promise I'll keep a low profile as much as possible. But if the meeting's going nowhere, then I may have to step forward with my own plan. Katey, you must understand, I'm not about to flush my thirty years down the toilet. Nobody's going to shove that down my throat! Not even JD Silverman with all his money!"

"That's what bothers me, lover. Nobody can break you, and JD won't back down either. Somebody's got to give in. I'd better be around to make sure I still have a husband in one piece when the smoke clears!"

Their conversations tailed off, but that didn't stop the flow of communication between them. Their body language, those unspoken words of love. The little subtleties, the delicate but refined art of knowing exactly what each spouse is thinking mushroomed into one big desire. Jerry got up. Katey was ready for him. He scooped her up in one grand sweep of his arms and headed straight for their bedroom. Katey didn't even bother to close the bedroom door as they passed through.

"Darling, let me freshen up a bit first," she said. "Then I want your love."

He put her down, and she disappeared into their dressing room to put on a fresh pair of black lacy panties and dab her lilac perfume in all the right places.

Then he gathered her up and took her to their marriage bed. He began smothering her with kisses, the kind designed to move their love ritual. All part of their refined lovemaking.

"No, Jerry, *stop!* Please!"

Never in all the years of their marriage had she ever refused. "I don't get it!

Katey, what's wrong? I know you want me as much as I want you!"

She sat up. *"My wedding band!* You were supposed to bring it back to me and slip it back on before we got this far."

Jerry rose off their bed. Still in his boxer shorts, he went over to his pants draped over the back of Katey's vanity chair. He turned one pocket inside out. "This what you're lookin' for, love?"

"We need to repeat our vows, Jerry, when you slip my band on. I won't feel right any other way."

"Still a lot of Irish superstition roamin' around, I see. I'm way past ready, but if that's what it takes…"

"Another thing, dear. I've noticed lately we don't say how much we love each other nearly enough when we're one with each other. That's got to change too."

They lay side by side, still tightly embraced in each other's arms, a time for quiet reflection running through each other's minds. Katey wondered if she should say what was really on her mind. "Our lives are going to be tested again, aren't they? That's why it's been so special, so good between us all these years, isn't it, dear? I should've realized long ago it was part of his plan for us. I should've known, but I didn't. I thought—"

He quieted her fears and her concerns with his own kiss, searching her lips till he scored. "Katey, we can't be sure of anything, except we're going to go with the hand that's dealt us. The only thing I'm sure of is my love for you.

That will never change, no matter what."

She answered his kiss with her own sweet, delicate touch of lips. "You do know, dear, we're inseparable. And that's the way it's going to be for the rest of our lives."

A deep furrow crossed his brow. She picked up on it immediately. "What, my love? What's bothering you?"

He kissed her lips, her cheeks, and wound up wetting her nose with his lips. "In all our married years, Katey, there's something I've never quite figured out about you. I see you hang your black panties on our clothesline, right out in plain sight instead of behind the sheets and towels, blocking any view. Always directly across from Mrs. Monahan's wash. Why do you do that?"

Jerry saw his wife's coy smile spread slowly across her face. "It's my way of telling Mrs. Monahan that my love is very strong for my husband. That there's so much happiness in my home, and that I've satisfied my husband. And because of that, I'm so pleased and proud and happy!"

"All that from hanging your dainties out in plain sight for Mrs. Monahan to see? But you're so private, so very private! Why?"

"It's just a thing between us. She does the same thing for me to see and understand."

"You mean you actually know that about the Monahan's, and they know that about us? Katey, that's not your way. It's not like you at all! Have you actually talked about this with Mrs. Monahan?"

"Oh, heavens no!" Katey exclaimed. "I could never come right out and tell her. But she knows, and I know nonetheless. It's just our way. Much too personal for either of us to talk about."

He shook his head and sniffed her hair. "Will wonders never cease with you, my Katey? You're the greatest blend of old and new I'll ever know. Somehow, it always works for you. Don't think it would work for anybody else, but for you it does, and I love you all the more for your old Irish ways and your new world smarts and charm."

Their conversation turned romantic. "Da ole professor here is thinkin' 'bout takin' a sleeping pill, Katey. How about you?"

She snuggled up so close to his body that a cat's whisker didn't stand a chance getting between. "Do you want the one-pill or two-pill version?"

CHAPTER 29

Jerry sat alone in his office. He was seated in front of his empty desk with nothing to do, trying to keep his sanity. Ticktock, ticktock. It was so quiet, he heard the soft ticktock of the wall clock across the room. A first as far as he could remember.

Sharing his lunch breaks with Katey did nothing to bolster his sagging sprits. By Wednesday, she apologized twice for telling him about how busy Greg had kept her at the office. She reached across the table at the cafeteria to squeeze his hand. "I'm sorry, dear. Here I am rattling on about doing this and doing that for Greg, and all the while you haven't said one word about what you're not doing."

Landis's usual dry, sarcastic style of humor came into play. "Well, now, Katey, my honey chile, us out-of-a-job types ain't 'xactly kept on the cuttin' edge of anything like work, if 'n y'all know what I mean!"

Jerry's Southern rendition cracked her up for a solid minute before she came down to earth. "It's getting to you though. I can see it happening day by day." She touched his hand again, trying to reassure him she was behind him all the way. "Jerry, if you've changed your mind and you decide to take the one-year buyout, I will understand, dear."

His cheeks tensed. He gritted his teeth. "Doing eight hours of nothing is the hardest job I've ever done! Little Jesus will never break me!"

Katey's heart went out to him. It was tearing her apart too. "What is your day really like, dear?"

He looked away and tried shrugging his shoulders as some sign of despair and offered this thought. "I swore I'd never lift a finger to help this railroad again, but once, this morning, I actually begged Andy Stephens to give me something to do. That's how desperate I've become."

"Did he?"

"Didn't dare, or else he'd be fired, is what he told me." "Has Greg stopped by lately?"

"I know he means well, but he came shooting through my office yesterday, all a'dither over some new demands Little Jesus has put on his overloaded shoulders again. At least he's working his butt of doing something. After he left, I felt like all the air had been sucked out of my room. Katey, I need action. I've got to get involved. Come Friday night, if I see an opening or even just a glimmer of one, I'm gone! I'm gonna do whatever it takes to get hack into action again. This…this not doing anything is killing me!"

"You're going to try to make something happen, aren't you? Jerry, you promised me you'd keep a low profile. Not get too involved. You said there's risk!"

He read the very deep concern in her voice. "Katey, please! You gotta cut me a little slack. I know I promised, but I'll lose my mind if I keep it. Tryin' see it my way, just a little bit."

"Okay, but don't get too carried away. Remember, I'm going to be right there every step of the way with you, starting this Friday night."

He felt somewhat relieved. "Thanks, dear, thanks! Hey, know what the highlight of my work week has been so far?"

"No, but I'd bet a coffee refill you're gonna tell me anyway. Just a minute, darling. I'll refill our cups!"

Katey returned with two refills. "Okay, let's hear it, Landis!"

He paused, allowing the seconds to tick by to give his punch line the proper theatrical effect. "The highlight of my work week, my only highlight, has been trying to remember if you always wear color-coordinated bras to match your panties. Now that's some work week."

Ricco and Theresa stopped by on Friday night to pick Jerry and Katey up on their way to the open meeting. The union hall overflowed with a noisy, unruly crowd.

Ricco opened the meeting by introducing their union's top labor-management attorney, a lawyer well schooled in the legal aspects of what could be done. He candidly laid his cards on the table, explaining that their best approach would be to file a class action suit against CC&W Transport with a federal judge in San Francisco. Ricco and the attorney waved their hands and signaled for quiet. Then the lawyer further explained that this would be a lengthy process. Both CC&W Transport and their union would be given adequate time to prepare their case. In short, he offered his opinion that a final decision based on the merits of their case was at least two and possibly three years away.

The crowd's mood turned ugly. Some shouted obscenities, their frustration eating away because they felt the legal system was way too slow. They wanted something they could grab a hold of *now*!

Jerry bolted out of his chair, fearful that Katey might change her mind. "Gotta galvanize this bunch or it's all over!" he shouted back to Katey.

"What Jerry mean when he say galvanized?"

Katey clasped her dear friend's hand. "That's Jerry's way of telling me he's going to try to get this mob behind his plan."

"What plan, Katey? What plan?"

"I don't know, but knowing Jerry, you can bet it's been well-thought-out, and it's directed at JD Silverman's wallet, where it will hurt the most. Speaking of wallets, we're going to have to cut down on expenses too. I won't be ordering anymore new dresses from you, Theresa. Hope you understand."

Theresa returned the hand squeeze. "I understand, dear Katey, but I want to sew for you for free. I never forget you help to save my marriage, and because you my best friend."

Katey appreciated both the thought and the compliment. "Thanks, Theresa, but I've a closetful of nice new clothes. Enough to last me through, I'm sure."

"How long you think this be, Katey? Ricco say maybe long hard spell before anybody can win maybe something…anything."

"I'm afraid Ricco's right. That's the part that worries me the most."

Ricco introduced Jerry on stage as a decorated war veteran and a very concerned mid-management employee who'd gotten the shaft. That brought out a sprinkling of applause, nothing more.

Ricco took his seat with the attorney on stage. Jerry hung his cane over the speaker's podium and then raised both hands toward the ceiling. "*How many of you would like to do something about your problem right now?*"

The hall erupted into bedlam. "*Yes! Yes!*" came back the chant.

"*Good!*" He dropped his arms and opened them wide toward the mob. "All of you who would've retired in the next five years stand up!"

Chairs clattered, people stomped their feet, and many raised their fists in defiance. Less than two dozen still sat. Then those standing whooped and hollered and shouted till they were hoarse. Jerry patiently waited for all the noise and commotion to play itself out. "Good! I thought as much!"

He paused again, waiting for the last fifty to settle back down into their chairs.

Theresa nudged Katey. "Your husband… I never see him like this. He…he such a good talker. He know just what to say…what they want to hear. Is so, Katey?"

"That's what worries me. All I ever wanted is what we had. The best twenty- five years any wife could ever want and get. And now that's all gone! After tonight, it will never be like that. Jerry has just declared war on JD. He will never stop now!"

Theresa tried in her own way to finish Katey's thought. "Ricco, he say this, this Little Jesus, he no run into man like your Jerry before. Your Jerry one stubborn man. No can break him like he do to other men at railroad in Denver. What gonna happen, Katey?"

Jerry spoke out again. "JD Silverman will pocket millions if you sign. Yes, I said millions! Your millions! He needs us as much as we need him. Don't let him get away with it! Stop him now by not signing! If we stick together, we can beat him! Yes, I said beat him!"

Again and again, the right words at the right time came from the practiced lips, echoing the thoughts from one Jerry Landis. Thoughts and well-chosen words that translated into what he was after— *solidarity.*

Jerry flashed his V for victory symbols to his conditioned mob over and over again until he had them in a frenzy, his frenzy. "There's only one more thing left to do tonight to beat Silverman! Sign your pledge to stop Silverman! Do it, and you leave here a winner! Not a loser! Who wants to be first?"

Katey and Theresa could only sit back and watch the stampede lineup at the exit doors. Ricco shouted out, "We'll have tables set up in a couple of minutes!"

Ricco and his staff set up four tables in nothing flat. The union attorney seized Jerry's hand and shook it hard. "Great job, Mr. Landis! Great speech! You had 'em where they needed to be, rallying around you! Great job!"

Ricco made sure that his tables were being manned properly before he joined the union attorney and Jerry on stage. He hugged and hugged Jerry again and again. "You've missed your calling, amigo. You should've been a politician. You had 'em eating right out of your hand. They would've swallowed anything you cared to feed 'em! You pulled this crowd together. Now they have a common cause! What sincerity! What a speech!"

Katey and Theresa joined Jerry and Ricco on stage while waiting for the crowd to finish their pledges and file out of the union hall. They, too, offered their congratulations.

A medium-sized man in his late thirties, dressed in a dark brown suit, made his way on stage. The slightly balding man shook Jerry's hand. "Congratulations, Mr. Landis. My name is Jack Bailey. I'm with the *Sacramento Star*! Could we have a word in private?"

Ricco overheard the trim professional-looking man with the black horn- rimmed glasses who looked to be about Jerry's size and build. "Use my office, Jerry. Down the hall, first door to your right."

Jerry introduced Katey. "Mr. Bailey, this is my wife, Katey. She's my sidekick, and she goes everywhere I go. Our chat must include my wife!"

Bailey gestured toward Katey. "I certainly have no objections. Lead the way, Mrs. Landis."

They gathered in Ricco's office. Katey made sure the inside door was closed. Jerry spoke first. "Katey and I have read your feature articles and enjoyed your 'Soap Box' editorials from the very first time they appeared. We're big fans of yours, Mr. Bailey."

Jack unwrinkled his nose, reset his glasses up on the bridge of his nose, and faced his admirers. "Thanks for your kind words. Tonight, Jerry, you became public property. I dare say that nothing in your life will ever be the same. Even your marriage will be changed. Tomorrow morning, you will be the news! Your picture, along with a headline, will occupy the front page in the *Sacramento Star*. Depending on what we discuss and agree upon, your every move will make news.

Mr. Landis, I hope that you understand the full consequences of just what you've taken on this evening when you decided to rally all those CC&W employees. From now on, I will see that your story is reported accurately and treated fairly. I will do my best to see that it is done as professionally as possible. What I report is up to you, for you will be making news, good or bad, from now on. In effect, you are speaking for them from now on."

Katey could see where the discussion was heading already. "What if my husband chooses not to lead and decides to let someone else step forward?"

Jack smiled. "Let's all sit down and get as comfortable as possible. Now to answer your question, Mrs. Landis. That's already been decided after what happened tonight regarding your husband's action. No one else will be stepping forward. Since your husband will be making news, let me offer some advice."

"Please do," said Jerry. "We're both pretty new at this."

"Katey, get your telephone changed to an unlisted number as quick as possible. Next, get a box number at the post office. Do not have any more mail delivered to your residence. This will head off the cranks and the loose nuts and bolts out there roaming around looking for an excuse to disrupt what's left of you private life. There'll be very little left, I can assure you."

Katey was already upset. "I'm a very private person. Our marriage is everything to both of us, and we want our families left alone. Can you guarantee they won't be affected?"

Jack took off his glasses to clean them. "Nobody in the newspaper business can guarantee that, so don't ask again."

Jerry reluctantly nodded. "Okay, so what's your pitch?"

"First, let me tell as much as I can about the man you've decided to take on. JD Silverman is a behind-the-scenes type of guy. He has never tasted defeat and has no plans to do so now. He is an uncompromising sort of man who carefully plans each and every move and strategy down to the last detail. He is ruthless and will go to any extreme to make sure his every order is carried out. He will not tolerate anything less for himself or his immediate staff."

Katey smiled. "Gee, for a minute or two, I thought for sure you almost described my husband. Yes, even the behind-the-scenes bit would've fit my Jerry until tonight. Until he stepped out on that stage."

Jack turned to Jerry. "You, too, appear to me as a man who knows each and every move. Yet you did take a calculated risk tonight when you became their leader. You must've sensed some way to get to Silverman or force him into a concession, or else you wouldn't' have stepped forward."

Jerry now realized Jack Bailey had him pegged but good, the first besides Katey who could read his thoughts and know what made him tick. "You're not doing this all out of the kindness of your heart, are you? What's your angle in this? What are you really after? What do you really want?"

The two men had indeed sized each other up. One was going to be making the news, the other reporting it. "I can help you keep the pressure on JD. That will help you win your share of the battles, but not the war. Only you and JD can and will decide that, and that is as it should be! But I can keep you in the headlines. Give you at least a fighting chance to keep the battleground from tilting too far! You're going to need every advantage you can possibly get to stay with this man. I've done more than a little spadework on JD, and you come about as close to any real obstacle he's ever faced. Both of you will not break, but one of you will bend before this is over, and that's where I come in!"

Katey had a look of real concern written all over her. "Two men who won't budge, yet one will. Jerry, are you sure this is what you want?"

"It's too late for that," said Bailey. "Your husband has made his move, and you can be sure JD will counter with his. What I'm offering you, both of you, will be my reporting services. I want Jerry to make me his exclusive reporting agent. What do you say? Do we have a deal?"

"And you'll do everything to keep my private life and my family's out of it?" "Absolutely, Mr. Landis. But with no guarantees. You understand."

They shook hands, each satisfied he'd gotten as much as he could from the other. "By the way, Jerry Landis, do you really expect to win?"

Jerry was straight-faced with his answer. "If I take the buyout, I've just lost thirty years invested into this road. I'd settle for anything that resembles a full pension. That's all I'd ask, for myself and the others. A compromise is possible, but I'd have to run the numbers to see if it was acceptable to the corporate employees."

They got up. Jack shrugged. "At least you're willing to renegotiate. I doubt JD Silverman would even be so inclined."

Jerry smiled again as they started to leave the room. "That's where you come in, Mr. Bailey. It's your job to help me bring Mr. Silverman to the compromise table."

Ricco and Theresa wanted to go out to celebrate. Jerry and Katey only wanted to go home. Inside their home, Katey let her thoughts escape. "I saw two things tonight. If I hadn't been there, I wouldn't've believed neither were possible."

Jerry sat on the bed to take off his shoes. "I think I know one of them. You didn't think I could mold that mob into one common cause, did you, Katey?"

Katey started undressing. "That was a mighty big surprise, I'll admit. The other, I still don't hardly believe it, yet you did it!"

He slipped his pants off and hung them up in the walk-in closet. "Did what, Katey?"

"You had everybody sign a pledge, and you've never believed in them all your life. I didn't see you sign any pledge, but I'm sure you did, didn't you?"

He removed his shirt and put it in the clothes hamper. "No, Katey. That'll never happen."

She was flabbergasted. "Doesn't that make you a hypocrite? You know, telling them to do something you wouldn't be caught dead doing?"

Jerry, in his shorts and socks, took his beloved in his arms. "Ever hear of such a thing called the greater good?"

"That's when something is done on a large scale even though you may not personally believe in it yourself. Right, dear?"

He pecked her cheek. "Thanks, Katey. You just made my point!"

CHAPTER 30

The morning headline of the *Sacramento Star* exploded across its front page.

The brash, bold six-inch letters said it best: *"War Hero Takes On CC&W CEO!"*

Jerry became an instant celebrity. Everywhere he went, from the parking lot to the halls, to the cafeteria and back, employees gathered around him, shaking hands, slapping him on his back, wishing him good luck, urging him to hang tough, good things will happen, and just be patient. Silverman will negotiate!

Riding the crest of his newfound popularity, Jerry now took sitting alone in his office in stride. It became a point of honor, the place where he must endure the stark nakedness of his rubber room in exchange for instant recognition and resilience. The first trait was foisted upon him, the other as natural to him as breathing itself.

Two days later, Little Jesus retaliated. Greg came into Jerry's empty office with two men and a hand truck from the facilities department. "Better step back, amigo. Your desk is going bye-bye!"

With his jaw hanging on its hinge, Jerry watched his empty desk disappear down the hallway. "What the heck's going on, Greg?"

Greg took time out to mop some perspiration off his brow. "Little Jesus is on the warpath. He actually raised his voice to me. He's that steamed!" Greg laid a hand on his friend's shoulder. "From now on, I'd cut my lunch hour short by a good five minutes to make sure you're back inside this office. You'd better do the same with coffee breaks. Any excuse, any excuse at all, old pal, and you're history! That's how bad he wants you outa his face! I've got to post a sign outside your door saying that any communication with you while you're at this workstation is cause for immediate termination!"

"Workstation? Hey, this is CC&W's version of the old rubber room treatment and you know it!"

"I know it! Katey knows it! Pretty soon the whole world will know it if your writer friend, Bailey, has his way! Gotta go now. See you later!"

That night over coffee and pie, Jack Bailey interviewed his front-page news find. "How's it really going, Jerry? Let me turn on this tape recorder. Go ahead, pour your guts out!"

Jerry got up and circled the kitchen table, deep in thought. He sat down again, eyes focused. His mind was back in his empty room. "I truly believe it's no different than waiting for an execution. Once, this afternoon, I almost thought I heard a dungeon door being slammed shut on me and I'd never see daylight again. Never say another word to a human being. For a minute or two, I actually thought death would be an easier way out."

Jerry's words had a profound effect on both listeners. Jack pressed the recorder's off button. "I only wish there was some way to get a picture of you sitting all alone in your chair in the middle of that big empty room! Boy, that would be some piece of photojournalism. It would wring hearts and souls out across this nation. That's how powerful its message would be!"

"I could do it if I had a small enough camera!"

Jerry turned to his wife. "No, Katey, it's too risky! We could both be fired!"

Jack turned to his hostess. "Another piece of that homemade apple pie, if you don't mind, Katey. Let's think this thing out!"

Two days later, the *Sacramento Star's* front page had a blown-up photo of Jerry sitting dejectedly on a chair in the middle of an empty room. This classic piece of photography captured the minds, hearts, souls, and conscience of America. Every major news service, every major TV network carried that picture. Some carried the title caption under that photo. Its message was too powerful to deny its meaning or its implication. The *Star's* caption said it all: *"CC&W Rubber Room— 1982 Style!"*

No one could've guessed the full impact of that picture would have across America, not even Jack Bailey.

The next afternoon, every major news service, all three major TV networks, to say nothing of local radio and TV, had crews waiting for Jerry to walk out of his rubber room, out of the front door and into their interviews. Katey joined him just in time to realize something big was about to happen. Together, hand in hand, they were going to face the news media.

Down the steps, the couple appeared amid thunderous applause and shouts. Suddenly, Jack Bailey yanked the couple apart, holding Katey back as the mob of reporters and interviewers surged around Jerry. Shocked, Katey tried to give Jack a piece of her mind.

"What's the matter with you? I'm with Jerry all the way!" she shouted, trying to make herself heard above the bedlam unfolding a scant ten yards away.

He was rough on her purposely. *"Listen to me and listen goody, Katey*! It's your only chance!"

"Only chance? What do you mean?"

He cupped one hand and spoke right into her ear. "Jerry's hamburger with this bunch. They're not reporters. They're sharks on a feeding frenzy. He's their raw meat! They're going to chew him up, spit him out, and dissect him and his news any way they choose. People who are public property pay that price! You don't have to become part of that scene!"

"What choice do I have? Jerry and I are inseparable! It's always been that way between us!"

He led her away from the mass of TV cameras, TV communication vans, and reporters so he could be heard. "When they're through with him, you're all he has left. Give him something to come home to. Katey, if you go out there to rejoin your husband, they'll strip you of your dignity, your privacy, and anything else you hold dear to yourself and your marriage. Through slanted questions, half-truths, innuendos, and every trick of my profession, they'll pick you clean. You might just as well walk out naked, 'cause they've already raped you repeatedly without removing a stitch of your clothes. They're that good! Is that what you really want?"

"Why are you telling me this, especially after you're the one who set all this up?"

"That's my job. Remember my exclusive agreement with your husband?

Now take some advice. Don't question it. *Just do it*, Katey!"

"Do what?"

"Get away from here as fast as you can! Go home, pack a suitcase, and wait for Jerry out in the parking lot! That's your only chance to retain at least some privacy because your husband has just sacrificed everything else in the name of nineteen hundred others. I only hope someday, a few of them will come to appreciate it! From now on, always leave a suitcase packed in your car. It'll come in handy! *Now go!*"

An hour later, a word-worn Jerry, looking like he'd been put through a verbal meat grinder, managed to find his Katey patiently waiting for him out in the corporate parking lot.

As he approached, she started the engine and rolled by him, pausing only long enough to make sure he found the front seat. The door banged shut, and they were gone!

Ten minutes down the road, Katey pulled over to the curb. They flew into each other's arms. "Oh, Katey, I don't know which is worse. Having twenty- five shouting, screaming reporters in my face all at one time or no one to talk to for hours on end. Thank God, you stayed out of it! Lord, do I need a kiss!"

She covered every part of his lips then began to cry. "Oh, my Jerry, my precious Jerry, what have I gotten you into? I never should've taken that photo of you with Jack's mini camera. It's too late now, isn't it? Everything about our life has changed. I'm sick of it already!"

He took her face in both his hands. "We're both in too deep now to turn back. If you hadn't been there waiting for me, I don't know what I'd done."

She gunned the engine, and they sped off down the highway. "Hey, aren't we headed in the wrong direction?" He pointed back. "There's home, Katey. Where in the heck are you going?"

She floorboarded their Buick and looked straight ahead. "There's at least half a dozen Sacramento TV and radio crews camped out in our driveway. I had to park in front of Mrs. Monahan's home to escape being noticed. Then I sent her around to our back door with my key to pack a suitcase. Tonight, I'm registering in a Sacramento hotel under the first name that comes to me. Stay put in the front seat so you won't be recognized. Then we're ordering dinner brought to our room. If you dare turn on the TV or pick up a newspaper, I'm going to shoot you myself! Got it, Landis? Maybe there's still a little privacy left in our lives after tonight! I aim to find out! Any questions, Landis?"

"None that I can think of. You've about covered all the bases, Katey!"

Jerry's exposure to all the news media through Jack Bailey's intervention had a ripple effect on everything and everybody. Even JD Silverman. Two days later, he had Greg on the carpet as usual, expecting to see a humbled division manager.

"What's up, JD? Can't be my new business quota. I'm at least a month ahead! Must be another administrative directive, right, JD?"

JD had never seen him so cocky or so smug. That bothered him considerably. "How well do you know this Jerry Landis?"

Greg was in his own time zone. Believe it or not, Little Jesus was asking him for information. Oh, how he wanted to say, "What, your sources have failed you? And now you're asking poor little insignificant me?" He settled for the obvious. "I've known Jerry Landis a long time. Too bad you two have never met. Both of you have more in common than you realize. I can tell you this, JD. He's smart enough to checkmate you right now! What a team you two would've made. You the leverage master, and he the make-money-work-for-you master. Why do you ask?"

JD raised his voice. "*I want him off that newspaper's front page and out of that room now! Do I make myself clear?*"

Greg smiled, trying hard not to let his feelings escalate into unbridled laughter. "Well now, JD, we got us a bit of a problem regarding those instructions. What are you prepared to offer?"

"I'll go as high as fifty percent of his projected age fifty-five pension benefit, not a dime more. Offer him less to start with when you talk to him. He might take less if you start lower."

Greg could hardly believe his ears. The mighty railroad baron, the great one, actually willing to compromise. This was the man who never backed down, never lost, and always got what he was after. "That will never buy him out, JD, and you know it! He's committed for nineteen hundred others. What's your offer to them?"

"Nothing! They aren't the problem! Landis is!"

"Should've made this offer before he got involved. Maybe then you'd stand a chance. I know him! It's no sale, believe me!"

"Should you fail to get his signature on my offer in forty-eight hours, I'll date your resignation. Don't bother coming in to clean out your desk. Your replacement from Denver will be using the desk."

A Joe Louis haymaker to Greg's jaw would've hurt less! His knees buckled, his smugness wilted, and he gasped for breath. "But…but… JD," he protested. "Gerald Landis is my best friend. He…he…it'd be like Judas at the Last Supper! You're trying to make me sell out my best friend!"

"You have your orders. You're wasting my time."

Outside JD's office, Greg regained some of his composure. Katey noticed he looked unusually tired, his face drained to ash white. "Are you all right, Greg?"

He mumbled something about forty-eight hours then closed the door behind him.

Late the afternoon of the second day, Greg showed up outside Jerry's office. His old composure was back, loaded with confidence, brimming over with good news, about to embark on the selling job of his life. His words broke the silence in the room like a jet breaking the sound barrier. Jerry nearly jumped out of his chair.

"Hey, amigo, better watch it! You looked like you were getting ready to doze off! That's a no-no! Don't let Little Jesus's creep down the hall catch you sleepin' on the job. It'd be over, old friend. All over!"

Jerry stretched and yawned. "So that's why he keeps looking in every hour or so. Boy, Little Jesus doesn't miss a trick, does he? I'm bored to death! Can hardly keep awake!"

Greg hugged his dear old friend. "Hey, old buddy, got some great news! I mean great news! Let's rack up the snooker balls at Sam Moore's, hoist a couple of beers, and blow this joint!"

Jerry's jaw dropped a full two inches. "You're putting me on, aren't you? Man, oh man, could I go for Sam Moore's and a couple games of snooker right about now! I'll even spring for the beers!"

"You're on! I've already signed you out! Let's go!"

They started out the door and passed Jerry's watchdog standing bewildered in the hallway. Greg nudged Jerry and spoke to the man. "It's okay. I've cleared it with JD. He's off for the rest of the afternoon!"

"We'd better stop by to let Katey know what's up. Don't dare phone from Sam Moore's unless it's an emergency!"

Greg slapped him on the back and chuckled. "Not to worry, amigo. You're little missus knows all about it."

They played a very competitive game of snooker. Halfway through the second game and another round of beers, Greg motioned Jerry over to the storage room. "Hey, Jerr, come take a peak! That's where it all started in our fifth grade. Katey stood watch while Ricco and I filched case after case of empties and resold 'em to old Sam Moore so you could wear JC Penney school clothes. No more WPA specials after that, Jerry! Right?"

He was moved by Greg's remarks. "I'll never forget what you three did for me. And I never knew for sure who left my new clothes outside my door till you three owned up to it the night of our graduation ball. Thanks again, from the bottom of my heart!"

"Katey did all the wrapping. Said it would be the only present you'd get for Christmas that year!"

They continued with their snooker game. Greg squinted down his cue stick. "If old Sam Moore had caught us, I'm still willing to bet he wouldn't have pressed charges once Ricco, Katey, and I told him what a good cause we had in mind. You know, he's been dead over ten years now. Six ball, side pocket! Guess they kept his name anyway. Makes this place a landmark."

Jerry took his turn. "You know, if Katey wasn't behind me all the way, I think I'da chunked it. Had big retirement plans. Now they're on hold too."

Greg finished his beer. "Amigo, I'm so glad, so very glad you mentioned retirement." He hugged Jerry again and again. "You beat him, Jerr! Yes, you did, and they said it couldn't be done. I'm here as living proof to tell you Little Jesus has compromised! You figured right! He's hurtin', just like you predicted! He needs those big surplus bucks from the pension plan to pull off his railroad recovery! *Jerry, you beat him!*"

Jerry put down his beer and forgot about their snooker game. His eyes opened wide. He tried to dance a jig then grabbed for his cane to regain his balance. "You mean that's the good news, amigo? That's it, Greg?"

Greg reached inside his shirt pocket. "Get your John Henry on this offer quick before Little Jesus changes his mind! Start making those retirement plans, old pal. You're outa here!"

Jerry snatched the pen out of Greg's hand. "Wait a minute! This says I only get half of my projected age fifty-five retirement benefit! What happened to the other half? And what about the other mid-management types? What do they get?"

Greg sauntered up to his longtime friend. He laid a hand on Jerry's shoulders. "Come now, Jerry. It's time for some hard, cold truth. You and I both know ninety percent of those people would sell out their grandmother for a few extra bucks and to heck with you or anybody else. This great offer is for you, not for them! You've been their sacrificial goat too darned long as it is! Go ahead, sign it! It's the smartest thing you've ever done!"

"What kind of man is this Little Jesus? This, this JD Silverman? He's got the balls to offer me half a loaf of bread and thinks I'll suck it up like some wino down on skid row. Look, the rest of our guys don't even get a slice of bread or even a smell as it comes out of the oven. No, thank you. This conversation's gone far enough! Thanks for the trip down memory lane, amigo! Now let's head home! Katey's waiting supper for me, no doubt!"

The silence between them was stifling. Neither said a word while Greg drove Jerry home. Greg pulled into the driveway. Jerry started to get out. Greg grabbed him.

"Take your meat hooks off me, old buddy," Jerry snarled. "Let me thank you for your time today, and let's leave it at that!"

Greg released his grip. "Jerry, listen to me! I'm between a rock and a steel wall. You have Katey! A marriage made in heaven! I've got nothing except my job! I've had a nibble on our mansion, and I'm going to take it. I'll sign a contract with you. Guarantee I'll make up the fifty percent difference on your pension when my blue chips bounce back! And they will, Jerr. They always do!"

Greg started to break down while Jerry mulled over his latest offer. "Why didn't you come clean? It's you or me, isn't it, amigo? Little Jesus gave you an ultimatum. Either sign me up or out the door you go! Got it nailed right, haven't I?"

Greg made a desperate lunge for Jerry, grabbing him by the shirt collar. "All right! All right! But don't turn your back on me, old buddy! We can both come out of this smelling like a rose! Take his offer! There won't be a better one! Don't do something stupid, Jerr! Sign it!"

"Let go'a me or you'll get a knuckle sandwich. Let go, Greg! I warn you!"

Greg released his grip. Jerry slid out of his grasp and out of the car. "You told me you had great news. You tried to snow me! Me, your old buddy! *I'll never trust you again*! Get outa my face before I really tell you off!"

Greg beat him to the punch. "I told Little Jesus you were as smart as he is! I was wrong! You've got a deal, the best darned deal you'll ever get, staring you in your face, and you're too dumb to see it! Go to H, Landis! Who needs you?"

Jerry shook his fist. "Goes double for me, Hibbard!"

Greg took one last wild look at forty-six years of friendship. He gunned the engine, spraying rock pellets in Jerry's face and all over the small patch of lawn between the double garage and the house. Jerry watched him disappear in ten seconds flat, his fist still doubled up, still poised to punch out his best friend.

Katey had never seen him so angry, so livid with rage. "Hey, Mr. Beancounter! Boy, Greg sure left in a hurry! What was that all about?" She tried putting her arm around her husband. He was stiff as a board. "Okay, relax, will you? I'm not the enemy! Hey, I'm on your side! Remember?"

Halfway through their dinner, Jerry pushed his food aside. "I'm sorry. I'm not hungry, dear. Just so darned riled up over Greg that I can't eat." He made a fist so hard his knuckles turned white.

Katey picked up his plate and poured him a fresh cup of tea. "Here, drink this. Maybe that'll relax you, love. I've never seen you so tense. Now I know why Greg hasn't been himself for two days. JD's put him through all kinds of heck, and up to now, Greg's been able to handle it. He's a very capable man. He'll find a position with another company. I shouldn't say this because I don't believe in divorce, but in Greg's case, it's long overdue and then some!"

That night, Katey had to come into their front room twice to tell Jerry to come to bed. He was still unable to unwind over his altercation with Greg. On her second try, she coiled around his neck and smooched away. "Hey, Landis, I'm still your best friend and your wife and your lover, too, when you need one. How's that for doing triple duty, huh?"

His hard composure softened a bit. "Wish I hadn't said some things to him. Wish I could take most of it back. He's still my best friend. Look what he's done for me…tried to do."

"Sure, Jerry, I do know. Tell you what, how about I talk to him first thing tomorrow morning? I'll invite him to dinner tomorrow night. Give you two a chance to patch things up."

He smiled again. "Thanks, Katey. Just don't want all those years and our friendship to end this way. Think he'll be in tomorrow? Little Jesus gave him the heave-ho, you know!"

CHAPTER 31

Katey looked over at her husband, who finally settled down from his altercation with Greg. No more clenched fists or white knuckles. He'd be all right after she woke him for breakfast. Suddenly, the phone rang on the nightstand on her side of the bed. She quickly turned the night lamp on and grabbed the phone to make sure that there'd be no jangled nerves waiting for a second ring. A quick glance. Their clock read 3:49 a.m. *Who could possibly be calling at this ungodly hour? Someone sick? Hurt? Or worse?*

"Yes, this is the Landis residence…don't understand, this is an unlisted number. Oh, the police station…all right, what do you want?" Another long pause. "No, you must be mistaken, Officer. It was only an argument, nothing more." Another thirty seconds later, Katey's pitched voice shouted, "Who's filed a complaint against my husband?" More pause. "Victoria! That's the most ridiculous charge I've ever heard. And you can tell her that for me!"

Now Jerry was wide awake. "Hey, Katey, what's going on? Everybody all right?"

Katey rushed into her husband's arms, tears streaming down without end. "Greg took his life! Victoria has filed a complaint against you. You have go down to the police station to clear this up!"

The day of Greg's funeral was especially hard for Jerry. He sat out in the parking lot of the funeral chapel, refusing to go inside. At the end of the service, the funeral staff held the casket open for a few minutes longer while Katey made one final attempt to get Jerry to say goodbye.

"Jerry, listen to me! You and I are going back inside. Ricco and Theresa will be with us too! Now let's do the right thing for Greg. He deserves our respect.

That's the least we can do."

Ricco came out, and with Katey's help, they managed to get Jerry into the chapel. Jerry's knees buckled, his legs wobbled, but Katey and Ricco stayed the course with him.

They stopped alongside the open casket. Katey whispered, "Please, Jerry… please look down. You must…do it for yourself."

Victoria saw the hard time Jerry was having saying goodbye. She bolted from her group of friends and came at Jerry, screaming at the top of her lungs, "Greg told me what you did! You murderer! Some friend you turned out to be! Can't look down, can you? You should be lying there, not my Greg!"

Theresa grabbed Victoria, spinning her around. "Shut your mouth, you no good piece of trash! You put him there, not Jerry! You were never good wife to Greg! If we were not in church, I spit in your face. Come outside. I do it to you face!" She beckoned several times with a clenched fist. "Come outside! Come! I show you!"

Jerry wrenched free from Ricco's arm. Blinded by his own tears, he groped his way out of the chapel, bumping and stumbling as he returned to his car.

Ricco apologized to the funeral director for the disturbances. They closed the lid and wheeled Greg's coffin out to the waiting hearse. Katey and Theresa each offered a prayer for Greg's salvation. Ricco offered his own thought. "I hope Greg has found some peace within himself somewhere. Lord knows he deserved much better. Can't say for sure he'll find heaven, but wouldn't it be a just reward for a guy who's already been through way too much living H here on earth?"

Katey put her arm around Theresa and hugged her. "Thanks so very, very much for telling Victoria exactly what was on my mind."

The next morning, Katey found Greg's personal items already boxed up outside his office. Inside, she met a stockily built man in his early fifties. He had a receding hairline of salt-and-pepper mixture and a sharp and well- defined nose and disposition to match. His deep gray suit did little to hide a growing paunch around his waist. It was his cold, piercing dark eyes that caught her attention and made her feel uneasy. Try as she might, she couldn't shake the feeling that she was being mentally undressed. He broke their standoff by offering to shake her hand.

"I'm Vince Stoner, and you must be Katey Landis." "Mrs. Landis to you, sir."

Vince Stoner dictated three letters in rapid fashion and was pleasantly surprised with the professionalism Katey displayed. At the conclusion of his third dictation, Katey amazed him with her knowledge of the letter's contents. "Would you like me to include a personal note to Mr. Jeeters regarding your follow-up call now that you've taken over Mr. Hibbard's account?"

"Yes," he said. "I was told that you were on top of all Hibbard's files. Now I believe it. Also was told that you were the best secretary in this building. I'm beginning to believe that too."

No one felt the loss of Greg Hibbard more than Jerry. The guilt trip Victoria tried to lay on him nearly destroyed him. Day by day, he drifted into a deeper melancholy, which alarmed Katey to no end. She'd never seen her husband so drained of life. His pride, his independence, and even his own stubbornness seemed woefully lacking. He initiated nothing.

He answered only after her repeated questioning and contributed even less despite Katey's needle-sharp comments and provocation. Katey feared he, too, might choose to go the way of their departed best friend.

Two days later, Katey picked Jerry up after doing his eight-hour hitch in the rubber room. Jerry didn't even ask where they were headed or why as she drove to a meeting with Jack Bailey at a local Sacramento restaurant.

The threesome sat down and ordered coffee. Jack opened up the conversation. "I've a very good friend in Denver," he began. "This friend is a real bloodhound. Has a nose for digging into people's lives, finding out who they are and what makes them tick. Thanks to you, Katey, we now have some answers. Vince Stoner is JD Silverman's right-hand man. He's the enforcer of Silverman's empire, so beware of him from now on. I think after what I've learned, you'll agree there's more than mere coincidence that follows Mr. Stoner wherever he goes. When Silverman took control of the Denver and Southwest Railroad, there was considerable opposition. Much like what Jerry is putting JD through now. Two fellows bucked Silverman for a while. Then strange things happened. One guy got the holy heck beat out of him one night in front of his wife. He refused to press charges despite the fact his wife could identify both attackers. Stoner's thugs intimidated the husband and wife to the point that they left with only a token payoff to buy their silence."

Katey stirred her cup. "What happened to the other man?"

Jack paused and then looked straight at Jerry. "The second fella had an unbreakable spirit. He was willing to put his life on the line for his fellow coworkers rather than accept a partial pension for himself and nothing for them. Any of this sound familiar, Jerry?"

Jerry's void expression changed. "Go ahead, Jack. What happened?"

"Stoner had this fella moved into a railroad caboose…his so-called alternative work location. Each day, the switch engine would move him around to a different siding out in some remote location and then leave him there all day to think things over, shall we say."

"Okay, I can handle that if need be. What happened?" Jack's eyes shifted first to Katey then rested squarely on Jerry. "This is the strange part, Jerry. One day, the switch engine came to pick up the caboose. Wasn't any trace of this guy at all! He simply vanished! Of course, Silverman and Stoner vehemently denied any involvement or wrongdoing. It goes down as a lot more than just passing coincidence in my book. How about you, Jerry? How do you see it?"

Katey beat Jerry to the punch. "That's it, Jerry! You sacrificed your life for your country. I had to accept that! *But not this*! This is asking too much! Tomorrow, I'm going to talk to Stoner. See if their old offer can be reopened. If it is, you'd better take it! I'm not ready to be a fifty-one-year-old widow! Not by a long shot!"

Jerry remained surprisingly calm, considering Jack Bailey's damaging story. "How do you see it, Jack?"

"I believe you're headed very soon for a change of scenery. Probably a caboose dropped off each day on some remote siding out in the sticks where they can get to you anytime they choose. You simply won't come home some night. It'll all be over. You've hurt Silverman in the only vulnerable spot he has—in his pocketbook. Don't expect him to stand this big-time loss much longer. There's millions of dollars at stake and only one man standing in his way."

"I can beat them, Katey! Jack! I've done it so far, haven't I? All I need is a pair of friendly eyes and a long-range camera to protect me!"

Jack sipped his coffee then put down his cup. "I don't have the budget for somebody to tag along and record your daily moves to keep Stoner's thugs off you. What you're proposing would work, buy you time, and that item is going to be in awful short supply if Stoner has his way."

Katey confronted her husband. "You're dead set to tough this out, aren't you? If you can scour up somebody to watch over you with a zoom lenses?"

Jerry stood up. He clenched his fists. "We're too close to let this slip away, Katey! I can cut down the risk to almost nothing if they know I'm being watched no matter where they send me. All we need is one friendly guy to be my shadow."

Katey turned to Jack. "How difficult is it to learn to master the type of camera Jerry would need to provide this type of coverage?"

Jack mused a minute. "Anybody could do a decent enough job with, say, half a day's training from one of our photojournalists. You find a volunteer and I'll supply the camera and the instruction. Even throw in a little gas mileage for good measure."

Katey jumped up.

"Hey, where do you think you're going? This discussion's starting to get interesting!"

"Jerry Landis, you're the most stubborn man I've ever known, and since I'm married to this Missouri mule, Mr. Bailey, I'm going to make sure he comes home to me and his family each night. I'm going to call Yuma, Arizona. There's a special man down there soaking up all that sunshine, just itching to come north to operate your camera, Jack."

Katey didn't trust Stoner. While she waited for her parents to make the drive back to Rushton, she convinced Jerry that they needed a short vacation.

They reached their cabin in midafternoon. Katey carried in the fresh sheets, pillowcases, and towels. Jerry turned on the electricity and unpacked their ice chest. With that done, he went to the railing to view the vast panorama before him. Katey joined him shortly after making their bed.

"Never got enough of this place, Katey. The mountains, the trees, the quietness is overwhelming. Our parking lot could stand another load of crushed rock. I'll take care of that next trip up here."

She slipped her arms around him. "You always said we're closer to God up here, and I've come to understand what you mean. What dear, dear, wonderful memories we've stored inside these four walls up here. We've always been able to work out our problems. See things just a bit clearer and be just a bit closer up here."

"Best investment we ever made, you buying this cabin. Lost count of the number of times Mark, Krissy, and the boys have come up here. Gosh, Katey, with all that remembering, makes me feel kinda old."

She closed her eyes. "And when it's settled between us and the railroad, think of the wonderful days and weeks and months we'll have, just watching the seasons change up here after retirement. Oh, Jerry, we've truly had it.

Tasted the fruits of our labor and our good life, and there's so much, much more coming our way…isn't there?"

"There should be, Katey. That's all I can say for now. I've got my teeth into this battle with Silverman, and I can't let go. I don't think it's fair to you or my family, but that's the way I am. If I hadn't stepped on that stage, maybe I could've accepted less."

She turned away to hide a gnawing fear—a fear that no matter what precautions were taken, somewhere, someplace, somehow, Stoner would pick and choose the time to strike. "No, Jerry, you'd never accept less. That's what I admire and fear most about you."

He sensed her growing anxiety. He wrapped his arms around her. "Hey, cupcake, let's change subject."

She turned around and looked up into those deep blues that always captured her heart. "All right, there's something we need to talk about and put to rest."

He cut her short. "No, Katey, not that! I'm not ready… I'm not."

"Since Greg's death, we hardly talk like we used to. We don't touch like we used to, and we haven't made love once. When we talk, we touch, and that always leads to love, our making love."

"I can't. There's too much on my mind. You know how I'm still hurting." "Jerry, come inside and pray with me. God will help ease the pain. God can restore the harmony that's been missing in our lives. Give him a chance. Come with me. Kneel with me. Tell him about your pain…your hurt. Give yourself a chance!"

"You go ahead…maybe later I'll join you. Need time to sort things out.

Stay out here alone for a while."

Katey knelt at the foot of their bed, kissed her rosary beads, and meditated deeply. She lost track of time. She felt him beside her, his body heat next to her. Together, they prayed, asking their Lord to give them peace of mind. They rose as one and received comfort in their time of sorrow and need. Greg's painful memory had been put to rest at last.

CHAPTER 32

Jerry was his old self again. Bad Irish imitations and jokes to go along with his Jerryisms, his pearls of wisdom.

Katey, too, was her usual self again after seeing the dramatic transformation take hold in her husband. "Hey, Landis," she said to him when they reached the deck. "Are you gonna put those steaks on the barby or leave 'em out for the coyotes?"

He accepted her ribbing. "Katey, I'll have those steaks sizzling before you can whip up your special tossed green salad."

They enjoyed their meal out on the deck under a lazy late afternoon sun that just didn't seem inclined to set. Jerry now talked openly about Greg. "You know, Katey, Greg paid us the greatest compliment on his last day. Said we had everything, a great marriage, family, and things like that. Imagine that! And with all his money and all his potential, he had nothing in the end to show for his time on earth! Isn't that something? Still have to believe…"

"How I miss him, Jerry! That roly-poly teddy bear of a guy! Twenty Vince Stoners couldn't fill one of Greg's shoes as far as I am concerned. I'm going to remember all the good times we had and things he did and forget about his last day. How about you?"

"Same here, Katey. Speaking of Stoner, how are you two getting along?" "He's no Greg Hibbard, not by any stretch of the imagination!"

"Don't let him get to you, Katey. If he gives you any trouble, let me know!" Jerry got up to buss the dishes. Katey lifted one leg up to swing it over the bench. "Whoop! Hold it, Katey! Do it again!"

"Do what, dear?"

"Swing your leg up again like you did just a second ago! Only this time, much slower! Sure did like the view!"

Katey pretended to be embarrassed. Actually, she would've considered a hill striptease if that would've turned him on. "Jerrreeeee! You don't really want me to…do you?" Their love ritual was on. Any romance writer could've scripted the ending. It was the novel way that it always began that intrigued each other.

Jerry, ever the master of their mental foreplay, downplayed it to the hilt. "Guess it's more my imagination than anything else. But for just a split second, I swear I caught a glimpse of the sexiest, prettiest pair of black lace panties this side of the Mississippi."

Katey followed through just like both knew she would, letting her modestly melt into an all-out effort to get him to carry her into their bedroom in record time. "I might consider doing it again more slowly if I had the proper encouragement, Gerald Landis. Frankly, so far it's been sadly lacking. Do you hear me, lover? There's been an awful lot of dry days lately. Well?"

Three days later, Aaron and Mary McCray arrived back in Rushton. Mark, Krissy, and the twins joined them for a real family reunion, ala pan baked chicken. The three women set up a buffet-style serving line along the kitchen counter then watched Jerry, Mark, Aaron, and the two boys pack all the food they could carry.

"Hey, you guys!" Krissy called out. "Why dontcha put sideboards on your plates? Save coming back for seconds!"

Their evening wound up with a family picture taking session. Then it was hugs, goodbye kisses, handshakes, and see-you-later time. Katey and her mother cleaned up the counter and disposed of the paper plates and plastic spoons and forks.

"Gee, Dad looks great! Got the best-looking tan I've seen in a long time. Bet he could still outwork any of today's bunch of pansies they call our rail maintenance engineers."

Mary finished sweeping the floor. "Tell me the truth, Katey! Can Jerry really win?"

"Jerry says the next two months are critical. He's been right so far. Said there's enough surplus money in the pension fund to still operate the railroad for a reasonable length of time and still offer a decent settlement to the 1958 merger people. If he can hold them together for two more months, we have a chance for a reasonable settlement."

Mary untied her apron. "*If!* Such a little word, Katey, tied to such a big gamble! You know your father is the only man who ever backed Jerry down a wee bit."

"Well now, I'd say those two are more alike than either of us would care to admit, right, Mother?"

"Katey, you were a tomboy, and I guess it only stands to reason you married a man just as close to being like your father as you could get."

Both women laughed. "And your marriage? How's it going?"

"Had a couple of pretty rough spells. When Jerry was laid off, he was really down in the dumps. He gave me a bad scare out in the garage that first night.

The worst was when we lost Greg. Jerry and Greg got into it just before it happened. Jerry had a hard time accepting his death without taking part of the blame. Up at our cabin, we worked it out, and it's better than ever between us now."

"There's magic up there for you two! Whenever there's a problem or you need to be alone, 'tis the cabin that calls."

"Jerry says we're closer to God up there, and I'm not about to argue the point. All I know is it works for us, and we'll have it no other way."

Jerry and Aaron had an Irish coffee. Aaron looked at him long and hard. "Don't get a chance to say this often, son, but it's on your mother's and my mind, especially after seeing our granddaughter, her husband, and those two rambunctious great-grandsons of ours. What a wonderful family we have. Couldn't be prouder than we are of each and every one."

"Thanks, Dad! Coming from you, that's a great compliment!"

"I need to understand more about what you and this newspaper fella have in mind for me."

"I'm going to be shipped out in a caboose and dumped on different sidings each day. If you could see which caboose I'm in and follow me in your car, they don't dare try to get to me until this mess is settled."

Jack Bailey brought out his cameraman to instruct Aaron on how to use their special camera. They took off for a few practice shots in the countryside. An hour later, they returned. Aaron was smiling, and the cameraman told Jack that he was satisfied Mr. McCray could handle the camera without any problems.

Jack left Jerry with one final thought. "This is real important! Could save your life! Never, *never* step inside your caboose to meet or talk to anybody when you're out on that siding! Always do any talking outside, on either end of the car. If they get you inside, it's all over. There's no way Aaron's camera can help you then. Your protection will be worthless!"

Aaron added his own thought. "Tomorrow morning, I'm going to buy the best pair of binoculars I can find. It'll give me more range to see strange cars or people where they don't belong. If you hear me honk, be on the lookout! Somebody's out there!"

Jack turned to shake Mr. McCray's hand. "Great piece of advice for you, Jerry. You're in good hands!"

Katey appeared inside Stoner's office, ready for dictation. "Sit down. Let's exchange information. How much influence do you have over your husband, Mrs. Landis?"

Stoner's question was not what she had anticipated. "No more or less than most wives, I suppose."

"Come now, Mrs. Landis. Everything I know about your life tells me you exert a great deal of influence over your husband. Maybe up to now, you haven't thought of it in precisely that manner, but you do!"

Katey did not like his tone nor the direction his question and statements were leading. "If you think you know that much about me, why the questions?"

Stoner was ready to play the first ace up his sleeve. "I make it my business to know all there is to know about troublemakers who get in my way."

Katey got up to leave. "Are you discussing me or my husband? Seems a bit fuzzy!"

"Sit down, Katey, and I'll clue you in."

Katey, adamant as ever, shot back, "*The name is Mrs. Landis!*"

"Now, now, no need to get hostile." Stoner paused, waiting for Katey to settle down. "Let's see, where was I? Oh, yes, since you bought that used Buick to replace the company rental you had to turn in, as of last week's car payment, you have exactly $753.38 in your checking account. No savings now, but you're far from broke. Matter of fact, your husband has done a remarkable job of investing your savings in mortgage debentures. That's how you were able to set up your daughter and son-in-law in their new decorating business."

Katey was floored! Then she snapped back! "That's privileged information!

How could you?"

"I have my ways! Want more?" Katey refused to answer.

"You're active in two churches but remain a devout Catholic. You are a marriage and family-oriented person and have extremely close ties to your husband, your parents, and daughter's family. Undoubtedly, you've always maintained strict moral, religious, and social standards. Your marriage is rock- solid. However, if need be, I can and will change that. You had your daughter, Kristianne Marie, out of wedlock, but your husband had to be the father."

Katey couldn't believe her ears. She'd felt exposed before. Now she felt absolutely naked, stripped of her privacy. "How dare you say these things.

They're personal, very personal with me! How dare you!"

"I can see now I'm getting your undivided attention. Good! You own a very pretty mountain retreat, a cabin, also your own home, so you're not hurting financially as the other ninety-nine percent will be by this weekend. It's going to take a little extra work to get to your husband."

Katey interrupted, "What do you mean extra work to get to my husband?" "I like surprises, Katey. Don't you? No, on second thought, you really don't.

They tend to upset your best-laid plans. We'll just have to wait and see what happens, unless you decide to change it."

Katey was infuriated by what he knew and the threat implication. She charged at him, shaking her fist in front of Stoner's nose. "If you touch one hair on my husband, I'll have the police and the district attorney on your butt so quick, you'll think lightning hit you! *Get the message, Stoner?*"

"Mrs. Landis, I'm not going to touch one hair on your husband's head!

That's a promise!"

Katey wasn't buying it. "Maybe you won't, but you're going to hire a couple of sleazeballs to do the job, aren't you?"

"That's something we need to discuss when you've calmed down, Katey. Sit down and I'll tell what else is on my mind."

Still a word away from exploding, Katey managed to collect her thoughts and composure long enough to return to her chair opposite Stoner's desk.

"There now, that's much better! Let me compliment you on some things that I've noticed about you. You have impeccable taste in your clothes. Everything's just right. Not too flashy, not to drab or dull. Your makeup complements you, as does your hairdo. Immaculate, very, very professional through and through. Your clothes accent your figure which, for a petite build, gives every indication of being more than adequate in every sense. Your husband no doubt shares my thoughts and much more. I've taken the liberty of memorizing in my mind every inch of your panty line when you bend over, also when you stretch or raise your arms. I know where your bra straps belong, your cup size, and whether you're wearing a one, two, or three-snap hookup."

Katey got up to leave.

"You step out of my office and I'll can your pretty little butt!"

"Not without just cause, you won't! I'm on my way down to personnel to get a transfer. Who needs this?"

"Shut up and sit *down,* Katey! That's an order! By the time you step off the elevator on the first floor, I'll have personnel on the phone, busy typing your termination!"

"On what charge? You have *none!*"

"Don't worry, I'll find a reason if I really want to! Who do you honestly think they'll believe? You or me? Anyway, *sit down!*"

"Think I'd rather take my chances down there! I can always file for job protection under the 1958 merger guarantee! Try getting around that!"

"I can and I will if you don't *shut up*! If I fire you, you lose twenty-nine years of service with a one-year buyout at best if you even win your case, which is doubtful under the circumstances. I can put up in court! Is that what you want? Is it?"

Stoner's logic hit home, harder than a right cross to her jaw. He had the advantage, and she knew it. Oh, how she wanted to finish this conversation by telling him to go to H and walk out and never look back. She walked to his door and paused, still unsure which way to go. He beat her to the punch.

"Katey, you have two choices. Either work for me or out the door you go! I can and will make fighting me in court a losing battle. It'll always come down to your word against mine. Now you're a darned good secretary, the best by far I've seen around here! Come sit down and hear me out!"

"Is that an order?"

"Only if you give me no other choice. Please sit down! Katey, *please*!"

Katey came back only as far as her chair and stood behind it, making sure as much of her body was behind it as possible. "I prefer to stand, and I promise you'll never catch me crossing my legs in front of you ever again!"

Stoner gave in just a tad. He shrugged his shoulders and cocked his head slightly in an "I could care less pose." "Fine, suit yourself!"

Katey snapped right back, "I intend to!"

Stoner, too, stood up behind his desk. He moved to one corner, trying to get a better view of Katey. She turned the chair, still trying to shield as much of her body as possible from Stoner's penetrating stare. He stopped moving, so Katey stopped.

"As I said before, your whole life's thrived around planning, commitment, and control. You don't like surprises because they're not planned and you can't exercise any control. This situation with your husband can't go on. Surely you must recognize that too, Katey. There's nothing but surprises ahead for you two. You can't win!"

"Is that a threat?"

"Take it any way you want to, but I will resolve this problem. That's why I'm up there!"

"Like you did in Denver? Beat a man almost to death and make the other disappear?"

"Katey, I had no hand with those unfortunate incidents. I was absolved of any connection or wrongdoing."

"Tell me another fairy tale, Stoner."

"At least now we both know where we stand, don't we? I'm prepared to sweeten the offer for your husband. I'll go seventy-five percent of his projected age fifty-five pension!"

"And the others? What about them?"

"We're going to reinstate the one-year buyout off for another thirty more days. That's it!"

"You know darned well there's enough surplus pension money to make a decent offer and still leave enough for Little Jesus to survive on till his scrooge tactics turn his mess around."

"So that's what everybody calls JD. Hmm! I'll bet your old boss, Mr. Hibbard, had something to do with hanging that handle on Mr. Silverman."

"It's old history now. But for the sake of your ego, you're right. Are you through?"

"Not quite! I've measured your hip size mentally, and I know your husband and I are approximately the same size. Given what I know about you and your personal statistics and your absolute desire for commitment and control, I'm not even going out on a limb when I tell you this about yourself. Because of your small frame and hip size, there's just enough space to accommodate a medium-built male like your husband or myself."

"So what are you getting at?"

"You're a person who must control everything, even your bedroom activity. It fits your character and your disposition. Your husband has to be in heaven when he touches you. Everything so snug, so tight all the time! Wouldn't it be a shame if he never saw your bedroom or your exquisite sexy black panties?"

Katey couldn't believe her ears! Then she exploded. "*How dare you*! It's impossible for you to know! It's a lie! You're guessing! You can't possibly know! No way!"

Vince Stoner, calm as ever, retreated behind his desk, oozing with confidence. He opened a drawer. And with one finger, he lifted up a pair of dainty black lace panties. "This one look familiar, Katey? Like the pair you've got on right now?"

CHAPTER 33

Katey sank down in her chair outside Stoner's office. Her mind was numb from the avalanche of personal and intimate information Stoner had buried her with. She felt sick and had a terrible urge to vomit, but couldn't. She was beyond rage, beyond the seething, loathsome feelings she harbored against him. Her body jerked. She felt dirty, unclean, had a tremendous impulse to walk out and go home to shower. She felt violated, horribly violated. Stoner had raped her of her dignity, her self-worth, and worst of all, her sacred privacy. She raised one hand and elbow upon the desk in a futile effort to rest her head, to stop the dizzy merry-go-round in her brain.

Stoner stood in front of her again. Instinctively, she looked up and tugged away at her short skirt, trying to keep him from seeing more.

"You've nice shapely legs," he said in a low voice. "Goes very well with your thighs."

"What do you want?" she managed to blurt out.

"Just stopped by to tell you I'll be at JD's, errr… Little Jesus's office. I'm expecting callbacks from Telco Steel and Boysen Plastic. Take a message." He moved closer and peered down at his secretary. "I apologize for upsetting you. A woman should never turn down a compliment, even if it's not from her husband. I've a feeling he compliments you often. Right, Katey?"

That night, Katey stood in the doorway in her sheerest negligee, brushing her hair. "Notice anything different, lover?"

Jerry rose and cradled both hands behind his head against the headrest. "Let's see, you look sexier than ever. You're brushing your hair more than usual, and I'm getting a real eyeful checking out your black panties…wait a minute! Your panties, Katey! They're different! Still black, but they look different! C'mere. Let da' old inspector have a real up-close and personal look!"

"We have to start over dear…about everything. I almost changed colors tonight when I bought these in a different women's intimate shop in Sacramento. I'm going to let my hair grow out a little too. Wear less makeup and just a trace of lip gloss. Have to change everything, Jerry. Have to get my personal life back. I can't live this way."

"What way, Katey?"

"Stoner! He's dug up every little scrap of information about us. He knows everything! From what's in our checking account, what we own, right on down to some very personal stuff. I can't let him do that to us. I won't let him get away with it! I have to get our lives back together the way it was, before he showed up. I need to know where you are, what time you're coming home for supper…things like that…so I can plan. Then I'll feel safe and secure."

Jerry kissed her panties and then moved up to her lips. "Stoner threw you a curve today, that's all! Those kinds of guys will spend a small fortune gathering personal, intimate stuff so they can feel all powerful. They're playing God, or so they think they are."

"But, Jerry, he knows too much about us. Far too much already!"

"Guess we'd better get some sack time. Gotta get up extra early.

Remember?"

"No, Jerry! Not another surprise! You know I don't like surprises!"

"Didn't you hear your father at the supper table? Your mind was somewhere else tonight, that's for sure. Had to nudge you twice to get you to please pass the spuds. And Mom asked you if you wanted to pack lunches or get breakfast. You never answered. Had the darnedest blank expression I've ever seen, Katey."

She lowered her head and pecked him on the lips. "I'm sorry. I must've missed a lot. Try again, please, dear!"

Jerry lifted her off to one side of him. "Jack Bailey must spend a lot of time picking JD's brains, or else he's camped out in his hip pocket 'cause Stoner paid me a visit just before quitting time. Says he's decided to move me to…get this, Katey, an alternative work site! Ha! Ain't that something? Says to show up at six in the morning sharp at the dispatcher's office. Of course, I'm to bring my work along with me, all five out-of-date railroad timetables and schedule books! The same kind of manuals I used to work out of in the clerk's office back in 1950 and '51 when I started clerking and freight rating! From now on, just call me the CC&W Caboose Kid!"

Katey gasped. "Oh my gosh! Oh my gosh! Stoner promised surprises! Jerry, listen to me! You have to be extra careful from now on!"

"Hey, I got all the bases covered! Your father's going to be my shadow from now on till we take Little Jesus down another peg into a final settlement!"

Katey put her hand to her mouth. "Oh my gosh! I forgot to tell you. Stoner upped the offer. Seventy-five percent of your age fifty-five pension. The rest get a rerun for another thirty days of the same one-year buyout!"

"See, what'd I tell you! Katey, we got 'em just where we want 'em. Got a hunch another big payment is about due to Little Jesus's backer! Let him make another one or two more out of his own pocket, and the hurt will hit him big- time! Then, Katey, our lives will be back to normal, just the way you like it! Hang on a little longer. It'll pay off!"

They fell asleep in each other's arms instead of Katey's usual backing and nestling into Jerry. Early next morning, Katey was up, busy packing lunches for both men. Mary sauntered into the kitchen, half asleep. Katey poured her a cup of coffee.

"Thanks, Katey. Thought these days were behind me. Now 'tis plain as table salt they're far from over. You go wake the men. I'll see to the breakfast."

Katey gave Jerry an impassioned embrace and matching kiss to send him off. Mary held her own too. The two women scraped the pates and loaded the dishwasher. Then, Katey, in her nightgown, disappeared to get dressed for work. Mary poured herself another cup of coffee, waiting for Katey's return and another cup.

Mary took one look at the way Katey was dressed. "All right, lass, what's troubling your heart? I've never seen you dressed like this to go to work. Full dark-blue skirt, loose light-blue blouse! Aye, lass, you got trouble perched on your shoulder. I can see it!"

Katey rushed into her mother's arms for comfort. "It's a mess, Mother! I lied to Jerry this morning. Never done that to him in all the years we've been married…not since I was pregnant with Krissy!"

Mary patted her daughter on the shoulder. "Time to get to the bottom of it!

The sooner the better!"

Thursday morning dawned bright and early, and for Jerry, more of the same rubber room treatment. This time, Aaron followed Jerry's caboose east of Ruston, some sixty miles into the first ridge of foothills. Because of the hilly terrain, Aaron had difficulty finding a location to get a good unobstructed view of Jerry's caboose. He finally settled on a low bluff about five hundred yards from Jerry. That done, he set up is camera on the tripod and kept his binoculars strapped around his neck. Just in case.

It turned out to be a hot muggy day. The sun beat down on the tracks and caboose unmercifully.

Twice, Jerry stood on the back of the caboose, waving to Aaron that he was all right. Aaron waved back, making sure Jerry knew exactly where he was standing up to his neck in the weeds on the bluff. His car parked some fifty yards behind him, as close as he dared drive.

Aaron stood there, hidden from view except for the weeds and brush he'd knocked down in front of his tripod-mounted camera. What bothered him was the closeness of a patch of scrubby brush and stunted jack pines immediately to the north side, a scant thirty feet away from Jerry. He took some comfort in the fact that he had a scouted that area before deciding on the bluff, which provided a much better overall view. There were no trails or paths near. The only way to approach Jerry from that side would be by foot as the brush was too thick to penetrate by vehicle.

High noon came, and Aaron retreated to his car to pick up his lunchbox and thermos. He was glad he thought to bring along a hat. Without that, his face, forehead, and neck would've been sunburned hours ago. He stood there, munching on his sandwich. It had to be at least forty degrees hotter inside the wood and metal coffin on the tracks. The only good thing he could say about Jerry's situation was that during the hottest part of the day, the sun would be casting a shadow, enough possibly for him to find some relief, sitting out on the back door entrance deck.

By three o'clock in the afternoon, Aaron wished Jerry would take a chance and leave his bake oven. It was that hot! Yet one slip of company work rules and Jerry would be history. He opened the thermos and poured the Kool-Aid drink into his cup. He downed it without stopping to pause. How good the cold cup felt in his hands. He thought again on Jerry. Katey was indeed right about him. This man, this decorated war hero would not allow himself to be beaten. He was just that doggone stubborn! He smiled, remembering his own sweet Mary's version.

"Well, she says, 'tisn't hard to come to the quick of it. The poor lad came from nothin', so he'd as soon part with his life 'afore he gives up one single shilling of somethin'."

He turned his back to the caboose to relieve himself. Then he thought about what Jerry had to endure inside to do the same thing. The stink, the smell radiating from the covered pot the minute he removed its lid must be unbearable, especially on a scorcher such as today.

Outside the open doorway, Jerry sat, soaked in sweat, hoping a slight breeze might come his way. He mopped his forehead with his shirtsleeve, trying his best to keep the beads of perspiration from draining into his eyes. He heard footsteps, a scuffle from someone's boot on some of the old roadbed cinders. He jerked his head, his senses attuned, honed in like warning radar.

"What the H!" he exclaimed. "Where'd you come from?"

They had covered their faces with bandanas to protect their identity. With a knife blade out, the short stocky one made a lunge at Jerry. He jumped aside, deflecting his attacker's thrust.

Jerry stood with his back up against the caboose wall, wielding he cane, ready to deal out his own punishment. They might get a full meal outa his hide, but he was going to make them pay for lunch!

"*Do what?*" he sneered.

The tall one produced a paper out of his hip pocket. "Sign it or you're dead meat!"

"The buyout, you stupid *son of a B*!" screamed the short one again. "You're kind never learn!" He lunged at Jerry again. Jerry went down, screaming in agony, blood spurting out from a stab wound in his left side.

Both attacked him. One, two, three kicks to his stomach by the short one.

The tall one shoved his foot hard across Jerry's throat. Jerry was pinned. "*Sign it!*" demanded the tall one, waving the paper in front of Jerry's eyes.

A steady blast from a car's horn interrupted the brutal attack. "We've been spotted!" the tall one yelled. *Poof!* They were gone!

Two minutes later, Aaron knelt down over Jerry, who was writhing in excruciating pain. "Hang on, son. We'll get help!"

CHAPTER 34

Aaron floorboarded his car once they reached the highway, oblivious that his camera-mounted tripod was banging incessantly against a partly closed rear door. Jerry sat doubled over beside him, holding his ribs, trying to stem the blood from a nasty gash on his left side. Five minutes later, he was met by a highway patrol car and immediately received a personal escort to Rushton's hospital.

An hour later, Katey, Mary, Krissy, and Jack Bailey were gathered in the waiting room outside the hospital emergency room. Dr. Sloan appeared before the anxious group as Aaron rejoined after changing his clothes.

Katey rushed up to the doctor. "Is he all right? How bad is he?"

"Your husband's lost quite a bit of blood from the stab wound, but I'm happy to report no vital organs were damaged. The gash looks bad, but we've stopped the bleeding, and he's on a blood transfusion hookup right now. He has three cracked ribs. They're causing a lot of pain. We're going to keep him for another forty-eight hours as a precaution."

"Can I see him now?"

Dr. Sloan fielded Katey's question and knew from her concern she wasn't about to be denied admittance to his room. "Okay, but only a minute or two. He's under mild sedation and needs his rest. Now all of you go on home!"

There's nothing more any of you can do for now! I know you're deeply concerned, but I assure you, everything is under control."

Katey disappeared through the emergency room doors with Dr. Sloan on her way to Jerry's room. Jack Bailey looked for a public telephone while Krissy and her grandparents found seats in the lounge, waiting for Katey's return.

Five minutes later, Katey reappeared, much more relieved. She went to her father and hugged him deeply. "I've been so worried about Jerry, I've forgotten to thank you…to thank you for being there. For saving Jerry's life."

"Now, now, Katey. I only did my bit. I only wish that I'da set up closer to him so I could've been some real help. Your old dad hasn't forgotten how to use his Irish dukes, daughter. Not yet, anyway!"

Jack Bailey returned and pumped Aaron's hand. "Just talked to my guy at the photo lab. Your roll of film turned out great! Wait'll you see tomorrow morning's photo and headline! They'll have some explaining to do, all right! By leaving the automatic button on, we've got our pick of the best! We're turning over all your film to the police for their investigation. Aaron McCray, *you were the difference!*"

Tears surfaced in Katey's eyes. She was so proud and so grateful for her dad's effort. She dabbed at her eyes and smiled.

Krissy saw the change. "Did Dad say anything? If he did, bet it was a doozy!"

Katey motioned for them to group around her. "You're not gonna believe this, what my Jerry said. When I got ready to leave, I kissed him. Now he's wide awake, and he lays this on me. 'Katey,' he says. 'Those robin redbreasts got nothin' over meadow larks. I'll take the meadow lark call any day over that chirp, chirp from a robin as he goes bob, bobbin' along.'"

It was hard to find a dry of pair eyes or, at the very least, a snicker or two among Jerry's relatives at that precise moment.

Dr. Sloan appeared. "Hey, everybody, time to clear out! Thought I made that perfectly clear five minutes ago?"

Katey squared herself in front of the good doctor. And then with her distinct, undaunted tone, she said, "Doctor, I'm not leaving my husband for a single second. Now you have two choices. Either I camp outside his room or you can do the right thing and have another bed moved into his private room because I'm not going anywhere. Are we clear on that?"

Krissy chipped in. "You don't know my mother. She and my dad will not be separated. She's going to have her way or else!"

He smiled and gave in. "All right, I'll go along with Mrs. Landis. Now this time I mean it. The rest of you clear out! Let Mr. Landis get some rest!"

Katey turned to her mother. "Would you go home and pack an overnight bag for me? And also a fresh change for Jerry so he'll have something decent to wear when they release him?"

Mary's coy smile came into play. "We're one up on ya, lass. I had your father do just that when he went home to change. Your rosary is packed along too. Hug Jerry for all of us, and you might toss in a couple of extra prayers too! No tellin' the good that'll come of it!"

Jack hugged Katey. "They'll be posting a sheriff's deputy outside his door till they're finished with the investigation. Make sure you identify yourself with the deputy, or you won't be staying in Jerry's room. Heard the doc say even the on-duty nurse and doctor will have to identify themselves. They're being extra careful. Tell Jerry I'll be checking with him when he's up to it. I have plenty to keep the ink wet till then."

Late that night, the on-duty nurse opened the door and motioned to the deputy. "Psst! C'mere and see this!"

The deputy and nurse stood at the open door and looked in. "Look at his wife," she said. "Nestled under his arm, under the hookups. That's devotion! You read about it, but until you see it, you never quite believe it."

"Yeah," observed the deputy. "I'm around the wrong element a lot of the time. When you get to see something like this, makes you think that it's not really so bad out there after all."

The Star's sensational headlines rocked the news media and the nation: *Sign It Or You're Dead Meat!* The clear pictures of the bandanna-covered face with the attacker's cowboy boot resting on Jerry's throat sent shock waves from ocean to ocean. The telephone lines to the corporate offices of CC&W Transport rang off the hook. Jack Bailey had really upset the establishment with Aaron's photo and his scathing article detailing the botched assault.

The implication of CC&W's involvement was so clear-cut, so linked, that JD Silverman was forced to call a press conference to rebut the news media charges and establish some semblance of damage control to his already badly tarnished corporate reputation.

The minute Vince Stoner stepped into CC&W's conference room, he was the media's dead meat!

"Mr. Stoner, why isn't JD Silverman out here to defend his action?"

Stoner faced the hostile TV reporter. "Mr. Silverman does not give interviews. I have complete authority to field your questions."

Flashbulbs popped, and cameras rolled. Stoner acknowledged another TV newshound. "How can you possibly deny any involvement when the photo clearly shows one of Mr. Landis's attackers waving your buyout offer in his face?"

A chorus of muttering drowned out Stoner's first words. He patiently waited for the rumble to subside. "There were hundreds of buyout offers mailed. Mr. Landis's attackers used one such offer to try to implicate CC&W.

Gentlemen! Gentlemen, let's be fair about this! It's circumstantial at best!

There's no solid evidence against us, and there won't be!"

"How in the world can you possibly justify shipping Jerry Landis all over your so-called alternative workstations when we all know you've been giving him the rubber room treatment since day one?"

Again, the catcalls and grumbling drowned out Stoner's first try to respond. Finally, he had his say. "Mr. Landis has been transferred to these sites to keep just this kind of publicity out! As for this so-called rubber room treatment, we categorically deny such accusations. CC&W Transport will always seek an honorable path to negotiations whenever there is a major disagreement. If that doesn't work, we're willing to let the courts decide."

That drew a chorus of boos and more catcalls. Stoner acknowledged another TV reporter. "Mr. Landis was manager of your accounting department before he got the shaft. What kind of related work can he possibly do out in a caboose parked on some remote siding?"

The question brought handclapping and more hoots.

Again, Stoner took the unfriendly heat. "We're in the process of redefining what duties he might take on while our labor-management disagreement continues. By the way, we've made two fine offers to Mr. Landis, which he has rejected. So, gentlemen, we are trying to do our part to bring all this hostility and misunderstanding to a peaceful resolution."

"Oh, really? And what exactly have you proposed for the rest of your employees covered under the 1958 merger agreement?" Three minutes of boos, catcalls, and more handclapping racket brought the house down.

Again, Stoner bided his time. "We're in the process of reevaluating our position on that and will announce a new proposal this week which we feel opens the door to a lasting settlement."

"About the assault on Jerry Landis! Since he's still technically your employee, what are you doing to protect him from further harm?"

"Mr. Landis has been given a week's leave of absence to recover from this most unfortunate incident. We hereby announce today that CC&W Transport will offer a $25,000 reward for any information leading to the arrest and conviction of his attackers. We don't condone violence! Never have! Never will! We are behind Mr. Landis one hundred percent regardless of our differences in the labor-management ranks. Now good day, gentlemen!"

While Jerry was healing his stab wound and cracked ribs at home, Stoner kept his word about sweetening the pot for the other employees protected under the 1958 merger. He upped the offer from a one-year buyout offer to two years with thirty days in which to comply.

Jerry had an early morning visitor on his first day back. Stoner walked into the rubber room to personally hand him his paycheck envelope. Jerry took one look inside but refused to comment, spoiling Vince's confrontational plans.

The afternoon edition of the *Sacramento Star* screamed, "1958 *Wages for Merger Employees* in 1982!"

That night, Jerry was still livid about Silverman's latest tactic. The talk around the supper table was about one thing, but what to do about it! After the meal, Aaron and Jerry drifted into the parlor, leaving Katey and Mary to finish up the supper dishes. Mary watched her daughter clear the table and start to load the dishwasher.

"You've been awful quite through all this. Cat got your tongue?"

Mary put away the salt and pepper shakers. "Jerry said his check was less than thirty percent of what he's been drawing. Suppose you got more of the same, too, eh, Katey?"

Katey didn't answer at first. Instead, she got her purse and opened it and reread her check. "What is it, Katey? What's goin' on, lass?"

"Stoner never cut my pay. It's still the same as always."

Mary wiped her hands on her apron. "Could there be some mistake, perhaps?"

"No, he's got something else in mind for me."

Mary went over to her daughter. "Your father and I have never given you all your rightful dowry. One thing led to another, lass. And before we came to our senses, here we are today. It would pleasure us considerably if you would allow us to pay off your car."

"Oh, Mother, you and Dad are the greatest!" Katey hugged and kissed Mary. "Make sure Dad tells Jerry it's all part of my dowry from way back, or else he'd never go for it. You know how touchy he is about such things."

"I take it nary a word about your full paycheck to Jerry, eh?"

"No, Mother. Jerry would come unglued if he knew. Right now, all I want him to think about is getting well. No more active role in his fight against Stoner and Silverman. I won't allow it! I love him too much to see him risk himself anymore. It's all over for him!"

"Might just as well cut off his two hands, Katey! He'll never be the same if you do that to him. He's too full of fight! He can't stop! It's his nature. It's what God gave him, sure as he put a saw or hammer or a carpenter's pencil in the next man's hand."

"Dead heroes are a dime a dozen! Making sure mine stays alive is all that matters to me!"

CHAPTER 35

Ricco and Jerry decided to hold another rally to counteract JD's latest tactic. It was time to count noses again and reaffirm each employee's determination to stick it out for another sixty days despite the drastic pay cuts. Both reasoned a major concession was just around the corner if only enough employees could be convinced to hold on.

The minute Stoner learned of the upcoming open rally, he pressured Katey again. "Don't think for a second that all this media pressure is gonna protect your Jerry. He's living on borrowed time! Accidents can and do happen every day! As for you, my little Catholic sweet, your days as a one-man woman are numbered too! It's just a matter of time till I get you where I want you! Right under me!"

Katey turned the tables on him. "Got some more advice for you, Stoner. Pick up the telephone. Spend $400 or $500 like my former boss did whenever he wanted company in bed with him. He got stimulating conversation, a good dinner companion, and ten minutes or so to do his huffing and puffing. As for my fat paycheck, the only thing you've earned is exactly what it deserves, my thanks and nothing more. Now if you have some corporate work for me, *fine*! If not, me and my long loose skirt will be parked out front behind my desk where I belong!"

The sheriff's investigation concluded with one inescapable fact. Aside from only a circumstantial connection to CC&W Transport, there was no direct link with Jerry's attacker.

On the night of the open rally, as Mary feared, Katey had it out with Jerry. "You'll be going to that rally under one and only one condition, Jerry Landis, and that is you keep a low profile! Let somebody else lead the charge! You're sacrificing days are over, or I'm out of your life!"

Jerry sat on the edge of their bed, stunned, still trying to put on his pants. "For Pete's sakes, Katey, this is great, just great! We're within shouting distance of getting a decent settlement, and here you are trying to pull the plug on twenty-six years of marriage. *What's going on?*" He stood up and tucked his shirt in. "Katey, you've backed me all my life. That's why I've been a winner.

There's too much between us!"

Eyes blazing, Katey stood her ground defiantly. "I'm not walking out on you. I'm only getting out of your life till you come to your senses, Landis! If you put one foot up on that stage tonight, don't bother coming home. Just phone and I'll have your suitcase packed, ready for Dad to drop it off. And don't even think about divorce, 'cause there won't be any! We'll be separated, that's all!"

He was steamed! Oh, was he ever steamed! "When I need you, when I really want your love, what am I supposed to do? Get on the phone and say wish you were here?"

"If you insist on me sleeping with you, you'll think an iceberg just moved into our bedroom 'cause you'll never touch me! When you chose tonight, Jerry, make sure it's the right choice! I've had my say. Now let's go to the rally!"

Ricco and Theresa had never seen Jerry or Katey so quiet or so distant with each other. At the rally, Jerry and Ricco excused themselves to go to the men's room.

Theresa turned to Katey. "Something is wrong between you two. I never see you like this before. Can I help?"

"I had it out with Jerry tonight. He's not a happy camper. He had to make the hardest, toughest choice of his life. I did it to save his life."

Jerry returned to his seat beside Katey just as Ricco introduced the first speaker, the union attorney. Amid a sprinkling of applause, he raised his hand to quiet the packed house. "Good news, my friends. We're going to have our day in court next year at this time!"

That was *not* what most wanted to hear. Two men stood and tried to drown out the speaker. Then, one by one, others rose as if on cue to disrupt the rally.

Jerry took one look around the noisy confrontation. "It's a setup, Katey!

These hecklers were planted by JD and Stoner to throw this rally into chaos!" Ricco joined the attorney on stage, trying to quiet the rabble. "Please, please, Mr. Zuckerman is on our side! Let him speak!"

Chants of "sit down" were directed by the rest of the crowd at the hecklers. It took five minutes of frenzied appeals by the attorney and Ricco to restore enough order so Zuckerman could continue.

"I know that all of you are trying to live on thirty or forty percent of what you're used to drawing! Hang on! We must stay united!"

Again, the hecklers rose on cue. Fistfights erupted all over the hall, turning the rally into a free-for-all. A donnybrook designed to do one thing—destroy the meeting!

Jerry gritted his teeth and clenched both fists. It was tearing him apart to stay put and not get up on that stage. Andy Stephens, Jerry's replacement in the accounting department, found Jerry and shouted in his ear, "Jerry, get up on stage and lead us! We're behind you one hundred percent! We thought you'd be up there! We're ready to demonstrate for you! You gotta lead us!"

Jerry wrestled with his promise to Katey. She could see he tried valiantly to respect her demand. "*Jerrreeeeee*! You promised!"

He rose amid the confusion like a man possessed. A man no human could stop! He turned to Katey and shouted above the din, "There is no one else, Katey! Can't you see?" He jerked her hand to make sure he had her undivided attention. "I must go up on that stage! This is my hour! My time has come! Never, never think I love you less! It's because I love you more than you'll ever know, even if it means losing you!"

With his cane on the floor, Jerry winded his way behind Andy, who ran interference. Theresa watched him get swallowed up in the mob. "Never, my dear friend, Katey, do I see such love in a man's eyes than he has for you! Only my Ricco come close. How can you not see it?"

Up onstage, Jerry was a totally different man. He was in complete command of every move, every gesture. He was polish and perfection rolled up into one! He had Ricco and Zuckerman take their seats. His stage presence was uncanny, to say the least! He motioned for the overhead stage lights to be dimmed. Another nod and the spotlight shown on center stage and a fold-up chair. With one foot on the chair, he slowly unbuttoned his shirt. His deliberate movements slowly quieted the unruly crowd in utter amazement as the pantomime artist did his thing. He refolded his shirt, turned sideways for all to see, and preceded to remove the dressings over his stab wounds. He did not tug or rip away at the tape strips on the perimeter of the dressings. Instead, he gradually worked deft fingers along the tape until he had succeeded almost effortlessly! With the flair of a rehearsed butler in a Broadway stage play, he let the entire dressings flutter to the stage floor like a dainty hanky. Fifty flashbulbs popped, the only noise in the vast crowd. He had so completely mesmerized his captive audience.

They saw what he wanted them to see—the ugly gash in his side and the strips of tape still heavily wound around his ribs. For a solid minute, he struck this pose, letting each and every one fill his or her eyeballs to the limit. Then in a mannequin-like performance, he turned his head to utter these words. His words were electric, his audience spellbound.

"This…is…what… I…did…for…you! It's…your…turn…to… do…for… me!"

Five in the audience rose as if on command too! "*Tell us! Tell us!*"

Jerry motioned for the stage lights to be turned on. He held the crowd in the palm of his hand. It was time to deliver the message. "We're all living on a paycheck that looks like it's been starved to death. Go talk to your mortgage lender, your banker, your credit union officer, Sears, Wards, Penney's, or whoever you owe money to. Ask them to give you a forty-five-day extension. By then, we'll have Little Jesus whipped!"

Then he raised both hands and clenched his fists over his head in a victory gesture. Pandemonium broke loose. The people rose as one and chanted, "*Jerry! Jerry! Jerry! Jerry!*"

Jerry signaled with his index finger toward the back stage. Right on cue, Andy marched out with two dozen of the accounting department to form a half circle behind him. Each wore a gigantic campaign-sized button with the words "Don't Sign! Don't Sign!" emblazoned across the glossy button surface. Again, the flashbulbs nearly blinded Jerry and his old accounting crew as they raised their voices, chanting the same refrain over and over again!

Theresa leaped to her feet! "Come, Katey! We go back to meet Ricco and Jerry."

Katey hesitated. Theresa wouldn't take no for an answer. "Come, Katey!

Jerry, he look for you!"

By the time the two women worked their way around to back stage, Jerry was mobbed by a group of admirers. Ricco was in the midst of them, hugging the life out of poor Jerry. "Amigo, you sure know how to percolate in front of an audience! Man, I was sweatin' bullets till you did your bandage striptease act!"

Theresa pushed ahead to greet Ricco. Katey stayed back, watching her husband absorb the handshakes, hugs, and good wishes.

"Kind of leaves you wondering just where you fit into his life after all, doesn't it?"

Jack Bailey's question startled Katey. She hadn't expected him to be standing on the perimeter with her. "I… I don't know what you mean exactly."

He took Katey by the hand to lead her away, to keep from shouting. "Sure you do. Ricco told me about your demands on Jerry. Credit me with the natural nose of an experienced newshound, Katey. I don't miss much, especially what you must be going through at this very instant."

"I don't think it's your business to interfere, no matter what."

"Your daughter paid you two the greatest compliment I've ever heard when you told the doctor you weren't leaving Jerry, the day your father rushed him into the emergency room. She said you two are so close that you're the only couple she's ever seen who could sit across from each other, anywhere in the world, and have a pretty darned good conversation without ever saying a word. Now that's close!"

Katey was moved by Jack's words. "I didn't realize it showed that much.

Our marriage up to now has been more than I could've dared dream about." "It still is, Katey, if you'll listen to your Uncle Jack. You've trusted me till now. Trust me a little longer. You're so worried about keeping your husband alive that you're missing the obvious. Katey, believe me when I tell you Jerry could never be safer than he is right now. Silverman knows it, Stoner knows it, and so does your husband! CC&W can't take more bad publicity. Guess you have me to thank on that score. Anyway, the point is, Jerry won't be parked on remote railroad sidings anymore. They can't afford to have anything more happen to him, accidental or otherwise, than you can! I'll stake my professional reputation on that. And if, Katey, mind you, I said *if,* Silverman should get a wild bee in his bonnet to try farming Jerry's rubber room out on the tracks again, I'll personally hire a longtime friend of mine. A retired Sacramento police detective to go right along with your father for double insurance. And I'll plaster that fact all over the front page of the *Star.* How's that for ironclad guarantee? That's as close as anyone can get in today's world!"

Katey thought long and hard about what Jack had told her. She grabbed him and hugged him. "Thank you for opening my eyes to the obvious. I threatened to leave Jerry if he set foot onstage again. I could never leave him. God, how I love that man! Almost feels like it should be some sort of a sin the way I care for him. Think he still knows that?"

Jack let out a long hard cackle. "Knows it? Katey, that last thing he said to me before he took the stage was, 'Tell Katey I had to do it! She's never let me fail before, so I'm not about to start now!'"

"But when Jerry's out here onstage, I don't know my husband! I swear it! He's…he's a different person! I know that doesn't make a lick of logic, but that's the way I feel!"

Jack took Katey's hand and patted it. "That's the other side of Jerry Landis even he didn't know he had until he got pushed into it."

They started to work their way back to the throng still milling around Jerry. "Think of the irony of this, Katey! Little Jesus and Jerry are both numbers men. Their whole lives are built around with what those numbers can and will do. Think of the millions of dollars Silverman could've saved if only he had the sense to put Jerry to work instead of trying to shaft him."

Katey finally had a smile on her face. "My old boss, Greg, tried to tell him that. But no, Silverman wouldn't listen."

They moved closer to the circle surrounding Jerry. "Corporate America doesn't know how to handle the Jerry Landis types. They're a throwback to our old roots as a nation. They're as honest and independent and stubborn as the day is long. And they can't be bought! Their corporate counterparts can only figure out one way to deal with them—destroy them, no matter what it costs! Depending on how you look at it, you had the fortune or misfortune to love and marry one."

"I count it as the best decision I ever made. I'm not about to change my mind about the man, our marriage, or our love for each other. I'm going to tell Jerry that the first chance I get…when we're alone."

"You're so private, Katey. This being around your husband in public must really put you in a bind. I know now that you'd do about anything to have your privacy back again. You've been in control all these years. Making this adjustment must really come hard for you."

"I'm paying the price for only one reason. When this is over, I'm going to put our lives back again the way it was. I'll never be satisfied until that happens. I can't live this way much longer. It's against everything I believe in."

"You won't have to, Katey. That number Jerry threw out tonight wasn't the ham in him searching for a short-term answer. It's the figure Jerry's worked and reworked in that computer he calls his brain. Only two men know those figures, Katey. Little Jesus picked on the wrong man at the wrong time. Jerry's got his number, and he won't let go. He knows JD has no more than forty-five days to come up with some sort of reasonable compromise. No man's ever done this. Beat him or at least made it a draw on each and every round like Jerry's done to JD. It's a whole new experience, and Silverman doesn't care for it *one little bit!*"

Jerry continued talking and continued answering questions until he found her, his Katey. The back stage filled with people didn't matter one iota to him. He found what he'd been searching for. No one else was there, just the two of them. Separated by numerous transparent bodies, attached to voice boxes that meant nothing. They were alone with each other's thoughts, feelings, and emotions. Jack Bailey saw this marvelous communication, and he thought about what Krissy had said. Now he more than understood and believed.

Jerry moved between the newshounds, the reporters, new acquaintances, and total strangers until he took Katey by the hand. They found the nearest room as Jerry glared hard at several reporters and then closed the door behind him. "I've been a regular H… A about some things, Katey. I know how much you've hated every minutes of this, yet you've never left my side until now. Please, somewhere, somehow, can you find it in your heart to take me back?"

"What's an H… A?"

"A regular horses butt, Katey! That's what I've been. I can only say I've marveled at you putting up with me and all this publicity crap when this entire mess is enough to make you puke!"

"You got that right, Landis, especially the H… A part!" Neither said another word for a few precious seconds, their minds locked into each other, telegraphing their thoughts on their next move. With one joyous effort, they leaped into each other's arms, Katey kissing him while Jerry was trying to keep their lips apart long enough to tell Katey how much he loved her.

"Don't…don't invite unless you mean it, Katey," he begged. "You told me to pack and now this. Katey?"

She returned his kisses with an extra measure of passion mixed with all the body language she could possibly move into him. "The only packing you're going to be doing is helping me get ready to spend our vacation time up at the cabin the minute this is over. Jack says that'll happen soon. I can hang on till then. When that happens, you have to promise me we're going to get our lives back together like before."

"You got it, Katey! Gonna take a while to simmer things down, but we'll make it."

"Good! I never want to pick up a newspaper, turn on a TV or radio, or see Jack Bailey, bless his soul, into our lives ever again. That understood, Landis?"

"What about Ricco and Theresa?"

"Tell 'em to follow us. It's time those two Italians found out the Irish know- how to celebrate with their own brand of Irish coffee! Then after I shoo them back out over our welcome mat and Dad and Mom retire, we're gonna close the door to our bedroom where we're gonna have one more night of honest-to- goodness privacy. Got that, Landis?"

Jerry winked, and his one-liner caught Katey off guard. "You know, Katey, we can't get much closer than we are now. At least that's the way Ricco sees us!"

"Oh, really? And how does he see us?"

"He calls us the Siamese couple. Said we're so close that when I brush my teeth, you have to bend over to do the rinsing and spitting in the sink."

Katey jabbed him. Jerry winced in pain. "Oh, I'm sorry. I forgot about your sore ribs. I'm sorry, darling!"

Jerry blinked a bit to hide his pain. "You mentioned you want a lot of privacy tonight, Katey. Hope that you keep my ribs in mind."

"We'll work around that. We'll find a way or two, always do, especially when I tell you my sad tale of neglect."

Jerry bit on Katey's one-liner. "What neglect?"

"When we're absolutely alone, my darling, I'm going to tell you the saddest tale you're ever heard. It's about my love tank. It's been so long since its had any action or been touched or filled, I doubt it can remember what it's like anymore. Got any suggestions, Jerry?"

"Yeah. Make sure Ricco and Theresa don't overstay your famous Irish coffee hospitality!"

CHAPTER 36

The early morning edition of the Sacramento Star blazed its front-page headline: *"One Scar! One Stab Wound! One More Victory!"* Underneath the six- inches letters were two photos of Jerry onstage in his now infamous profile pose, showing the scar and his bound-up ribs.

While Bailey brimmed with confidence, JD was outraged. He retaliated with one command to Stoner. "Eliminate the accounting department! We can do very nicely without their display of loyalty!"

Jerry returned, as Jack Bailey predicted, to his usual spot, his lonely vigil in his one-man rubber room. This time, he was more alone than ever before. He stood silently, reading the notice taped to the main entrance door: "Due to economic necessity, CC&W Transport can no longer afford to operate its accounting department. This function has been subcontracted out. We suggest those eligible for our generous buyout offer, contact personnel as soon possible!"

A quarter million readers of the late afternoon edition of the *Sacramento Star* knew better when Jack Bailey posted the same notice on the front page.

The first payday after JD's drastically reduced paychecks to all 1958 merger- affected employees started to take its toll. Mortgage payments, car payments, credit card payments, and all other debt obligations thinned Jerry's pledge card ranks considerably. Aaron summed it up: "Just too many people living from paycheck to paycheck, never thinking about saving for a rainy day. If you live by credit, sooner or later, you must pay the piper, even if he is JD Silverman!"

Jerry, Ricco, and Jack got together in Jack's office. It was their turn at damage control. Jerry borrowed one of the calculators and refigured their position. Ten minutes later, he returned to Jack's office with his new calculations. "I've re-crunched the numbers! If we can keep our pledge count to around twelve hundred, we've still locked up considerable pension monies that Little Jesus needs to get his hands on. Below that figure, we're in deep trouble!"

Ricco poured himself a cup of coffee. "How do we do that, amigo?"

Jack shook his head. "I'm just the reporter, remember? I'm doing all I can to keep the pressure on. You guys come up with some gimmick. Run it by me, and if it will By, I'll do my best to keep it alive in the public's eye."

"Gotta keep this thing going," said Jerry. "Katey's counting pretty heavy on it all ending within the next forty-five days. She's about had it with our present lifestyle. She can't wait to get back to the way it used to be between us."

Jack got up from his swivel chair to get a drink from the water cooler. "I told her the same thing. About the forty-five days bit, I mean. Of course, that was based on you being able to keep the troops from bailing out. Still think forty-five days is still realistic, Jerry?"

"Yes. One way or the other, it'll all be over by then, if not sooner. Both sides are hurting. It's down to who can hold out the longest."

Ricco thought a while on Jerry's statement. "How about me paying a visit to Little Jesus? Never know, maybe he's thinking along the same lines. I'd like to feel him out, see if negotiations are possible at this point. Anybody got a better idea?"

Jack looked at Jerry and then shrugged. "Go for it! What have we got to lose?"

The meeting with JD started out cordial enough. He assured Ricco that none of their conversation was being recorded, so he should please speak freely, as the meeting was strictly off the cuff. Ricco opened with his best shot. "I've done my homework, Mr. Silverman. You ran the union out of town in Denver by undercutting the wage scale, cancelling existing labor contracts on a technicality or two, and buying your way into the existing union leadership before you destroyed it. That won't happen here, I can assure you."

JD turned around in his chair, facing the wall behind him. "How's your wife, Theresa's health lately? Good, I hope. And your four daughters and their families? I imagine they're all doing fine?"

Ricco knew JD was trying his best to intimidate him. "It won't work, JD, so let's cut the implication and deal with the issues at hand. You're hurting, and we know it. Question is, are you willing to meet in good faith to resolve the buyout offer to the point where both sides can live with it?"

JD turned around. "Mr. Petrocelli, you're in no position to demand anything! Fact is, your boy Landis is hanging on the ropes. All I have to do is finish him off! All his rally produced is some pictures and large, oversized letters printed on the front page. Do we understand one another?"

"You touch one hair on Landis's head and your days here are numbered!" JD chortled. "I hope that wasn't meant as some kind of a threat, Mr.

Petrocelli. I don't take kindly to threats!"

"Neither do we! Now do we have something to talk about or not?"

JD scratched his chin. "I'm glad we're having this little chat. Saved me the time to hunt you up. Listen up, Petrocelli! This is how it's going to be! I could break you in less than six months. It would cost me a few bucks to buy my way in, but in the end, you'd be out and I'd be in. I plan on keeping the union here. I'm not going to repeat the same mistake I made taking over the Denver and Southwest. Of course, it'll be a company union, and that's where you come in. Interested, or should I get somebody else?"

Ricco was seething with rage. "*You can't buy me!*" he shouted, emphasizing his point.

"I just did. You took the time to answer instead of telling me to go to blazes before you walked out my door. Like I said before, I'm glad you're concerned about your wife and your family's health. That's good thinking, the kind that you and I can build on. Now then, this is what I want, and this is how it's going to be, if you plan on drawing your big, fat retirement pension from your union. Remember, Petrocelli, I call all the shots. You keep the union name, I keep you in my hip pocket."

That evening, Jerry telephoned Ricco. "Hey, amigo, did Little Jesus come across with anything we can take to the bank?"

There was a long pause on Ricco's end. "No. Nothing we can count on." "What's wrong? What happened?"

"It didn't turn out the way I expected Jerry. Not at all!"

Jerry didn't quite know what to make of it. "I don't understand. I was so sure he was hurting just like us. I can't be that far off! Tell me what really happened."

"It's like what you said a few years back, Jerry. You told me figures don't lie. It's the way liars do the figuring that changes things. Silverman's got all the aces still up his sleeve. We're nowhere near where we thought we'd be!"

Two days later, Katey telephoned Bailey. She was worried, plenty worried. "You better get your retired police detective on the job. They're shipping Jerry out tomorrow morning at daybreak! I thought this wasn't supposed to happen!"

"Calm down, Katey. I still believe Jerry's numbers are right on target. This will be a series of dry runs, Katey, that's all! More harassment which he can stand, nothing more!"

The caboose-style rubber room treatment on Jerry began with one big difference. Two people sat in their cars, keeping careful watch out on some desolate, unused siding. Katey, ever fearful that Stoner was not playing games, parked each night at the main gate to the switchyard to wait for her husband's safe return. Her father and the retired detective's job was to tell her the engine number that pulled the caboose into the switching yard before they were allowed to go home.

And so the vigil began for one solid week. The monotonous routine that could spell the difference between life and death for Jerry Landis. Day by day, tempers grew a little shorter, nerves a bit more frayed and fragile, and conviction and determination somewhat short in supply. Doggedly, Aaron, Katey, and the retired detective continued their routine without so much as a hint of anything suspicious out of the ordinary, the very thing that scared Katey the most.

Friday night came, and Katey parked again near the main gate to the switchyard. She waited and waited and waited some more. Still no sign of either her father or the detective. By the time the yard lights were switched on, all the crews had long since completed their day's run and gone home.

Katey waited alone in the darkness, eyes smarting from the strain of trying to pick out a set of headlights that were friendly. Either her father's or the detective's. Finally, she recognized her father's car as he drove alongside.

"Katey, it's engine 058 tonight that picked up Jerry's caboose. They've just entered the switchyard. I'll tell your mother to get supper on. The detective followed me in, so I told him to go on home and enjoy his weekend."

"Do you see anything or anybody today?"

"No. You're newspaper friend did the right thing by putting the word out about the extra protection. They won't come near Jerry!"

"This is the latest they've ever kept him out."

"Yes, lass. I was beginning to think they intended on leaving him out there.

Finally, 058 came along to hook up!"

"See you and Mom in a few minutes. At least I'll have Jerry for another weekend before the same old routine on Monday. *Will this ever end?*"

"Soon, Katey! Soon, lass! I trust Jerry's numbers!"

Aaron drove away, leaving Katey to pick up her husband. Finally, she heard the steam engine's huffing and puffing and saw the rotating headlight on the huge locomotive as it came lumbering into view. Katey sprang from her seat and ran up to the security guard at the gate. She Bashed her ID card and stood by the guardhouse, anxiously waiting for the engine to hiss, sputter, belch and then come to a complete stop so she could welcome him up in her arms.

The guard called out to her, "Are you waiting for that celebrity fellow, the one I saw on TV and read about?"

"Yes, that's him! But not for long. It'll soon be over!"

Her body jerked as her mind spoke before she was ready. She shouted, not realizing what she'd said for an instant. "Where's Jerry? Where's the caboose?"

There was no caboose! No Jerry waving to her! Nothing except a hot, smelly steam engine and darkness! She waited for the engineer and brakeman to step down then pounced upon the engineer. "Where's my husband?" she demanded. "What have you done with him?"

"Lady, we dropped him off at the old entrance to the yard just like the dispatcher told us to!"

She turned and ran out the gate, screaming at the top of her lungs.

Dog-tired, body aching, mind exhausted from endless mind games to keep a reasonable amount of sanity, Jerry made his way from the caboose across two dozen sets of tracks that separated him from the rusty, old, and unused turnstile. All that remained of the old main gate. He was puzzled why the switchman had dropped him off here; they'd never done that before. Oh well, he was too darned tired to care or worry. All he could think about was the sweet smell of lilac perfume, cherry lips, hair that smelled so fresh and clean, and an embrace that melted their bodies together.

In the semidarkness, he gingerly picked his way across the tracks, making sure he didn't put all the weight on his cane until he was sure he hadn't stepped into a hole or stumbled over an old can or bottle. At the turnstile, he had to push hard to make it revolve. Its creaking sound gave ample evidence it'd been quite some time since another human had trod this way.

"You Gerald Landis?"

The voice to his left startled him. Jerry tried to draw him out into the light, but the shadows of the old guard shack hid him.

"Who wants to know?"

"We do!" That voice came from his right side. Instantly, Jerry knew something was wrong, so very deadly wrong! With his cane raised high to defend himself, he tried to retreat to the turnstile, where he could see who belonged to what voice. Down he went. Somebody had tackled him. He punched away in the darkness then was blinded by a flashlight stuck squarely in front of his face.

"Sign it if you want to live!"

He still couldn't pick out his assailants with the flashlight blinding his eyes. *"Sign what?* I can't see anything!"

He never knew who or what hit him. He doubled up in pain, positive his bandaged ribs were cracked again. *"Please! Please!"* he screamed. *"I'll sign!* Just show me where to sign!"

He felt two strong hands jerk him to his feet and slam him hard against the side of the guard shack. "Okay, cripple, here it is. *Sign it!"*

The other man grabbed him by the hair and shoved his face into a piece of paper. Then he held the flashlight on it. "Here's a pen! *Sign!"*

Jerry cleared his fuzzy mind. These were not the same two who'd worked him over. Their voices were different. "Out-of-town boys, right?"

He got two punishing kicks to the stomach for his question. His knees buckled, and he fell down into an agonizing heap. The one holding the flashlight yelled, "Now I gotta raise you up again, you worthless cripple! One more stupid remark outa you, Landis, and I'll beat you to death. Forget the paper!"

"I'll sign! I'll sign! Show me where."

Again, the paper was shoved in front of his face, and a pen was pushed into his hand. Jerry bought time, precious time, pretending to slowly read the buyout offer. Could Katey realize something was wrong? Be on her way? Could he stall long enough for help to arrive? Dare he risk another terrible beating? Or death? "Oh! Oh!"

"Now what?" snarled the man holding the flashlight.

His two attackers looked at each other. This was not the reception they had expected. The man without the Bashlight spoke up. "What's wrong?"

Jerry did the greatest con job of his life of trying to buy more time. "Hand me your Bashlight." The attacker obliged. "Look! See the date printed on the bottom? That's the old date for the one-year buyout! Should have the new date for the two-year buyout. Sorry, no use signing. Won't hold up in court!"

The two looked at each other.

Jerry felt the strong pair of hands that had bulldogged him relax from a split second. He made his break. The Bashlight fell, and the paper hung in midair. Down along the fence he ran as best he could in his race against death.

For thirty feet, Jerry had his freedom. Then he was knocked down from behind. Seconds later, the second man caught up and pinned both arms behind his back while the first attacker went to work on him, kicking, beating, and kicking him some more.

They took turns, kicking his head like a football. The screams, the cries of pain and agony gave way to a bloody pulp. Then all was quiet. There was no more resistance.

The other man stood over the body, seething with rage.

Katey was choked with fear. Her body jerked and spasmed, but she gamely held on. Twice her foot slipped off the gas pedal, and then she connected, jamming it to the Boor. The Buick bucked and lurched forward, tires screaming, spraying loose gravel for twenty yards. Down the frontage road she sped, weaving all over it, trying to control the steering wheel between blinding tears. Three minutes later, she located the old guard shack and the turnstile beside it. Both were empty.

She sobbed, slumping over the steering wheel, not knowing what to do next. She sat up, bravely wiped her tears away, and eased the Buick over the curb into the weeds. She did not care if she ran over nails, broken beer bottles, or anything else. She had to find Jerry and be quick about it!

Down along the fence line she drove, the headlights bouncing off into space each time she hit a dip or ran over a rock. No Jerry! Which way? Maybe she was driving in the wrong direction? She clung to her original decision, sure that if he was walking, this would be the shortest path to the main gate!

Her headlights picked out a lifeless form crumpled against the fence. She hit the brakes and shot out of the driver's seat. In the beam of the headlights, she knelt beside him and tried to lift his head. She couldn't even recognize his face. It was a bloody mess.

Blood, blood everywhere! All over his body, all around him in the weeds, and on the ground. She screamed to the heavens; her agony shattered the night. Two dogs barked somewhere down the street, from some old sheds used by the local winos to sleep off their ninety-cent apricot wine.

Then she heard it, the grinding of gears, the double clutching as the big freight truck meandered up the frontage road toward her. With blood all over her hands and in her skirt and blouse and shoes, she made one frantic leap in front of the truck, wildly waving her hands back and forth.

The brakes hissed, and the truck came to a grinding stop. "*Lady!*" shouted the driver. "*What's the matter with you? Dang near ran over you!*"

"*My husband! My husband! He's by the fence! Help me, please!*"

CHAPTER 37

They gathered in the waiting room down the hall from the emergency operating room, these concerned family and friends of Jerry Landis. All eyes were on Katey, her clothes caked with blood, dirt and grime.

One, two, three hours of unbearable agony drained the life out of those who waited. Finally, a small man in white came to them. "Who is Mrs. Landis?"

"I am," volunteered Katey, who stood up in front of him.

He took one look at her, shook his head, and then rolled out the news. "Your husband will probably not live through the night. Massive head and brain injuries, hemorrhaging in the abdomen, along with related respiratory and circulation problems will take their toll. He's in a coma, on life support. We've done the best we could under the circumstances. If he does somehow survive the night, his long-term chances are not good. This you need to know and understand. There's little hope in either case."

"I'm going to stay as close to him as I can. Don't even think about trying to order me out of here!"

"But, Mrs. Landis," protested the doctor. "Look at yourself! Go home, get some clean clothes, take a sleeping pill, and stay there. When any change comes, good or bad, we'll call you. I have your number. There's nothing more you can do!"

Katey would not be denied. "Yes, there is. I will be here regardless, and we can all pray. Now, Doctor, where am I going to stay? Come! Come!"

Mary came up to the doctor. "I'll fetch the clean clothes, Doctor, for my Katey. She's not going to leave! Aye, she needs to be here, and that's the way of it!"

The doctor was annoyed. "Look, there's nothing anyone can do at this time!

Don't you people hear? Where's your ears?"

Aaron approached the doctor. "You're the one with the hearin' problem, Doctor. My daughter is not leaving, and my wife will see to it she has plenty of clean clothes and whatever else she needs. Now let's get that room number and help her get settled!"

Krissy barged into the conversation. "You don't know my mother, sir. My mother will not leave, so get used to it!"

He threw up his hands. "All right! I get the message!"

Katey, Krissy, Ricco, and Theresa followed the doctor. Aaron went over to Jack. "Your detective friend, get him on it this very minute! I don't care what it costs, but get him on it now! I hope the trail leads to this Vince Stoner or that big shot JD Silverman. Tell him there's an extra ten grand in it for him if he does! We both know they're behind this!"

For the next seventy-two hours, Jerry's life hung in the balance as he drifted into a deep, deep, deep coma. It was one that most of the staff of doctors predicted he would not come out of. Midnight came, and it was time to change his round-the-clock nursing help. Claire Jerrod was just ending her shift, and it took a few minutes to make sure her replacement, Betty Hopkins, was brought up to speed on all the specifics. They conversed in low tones at the entrance of the private room.

"These are your new instructions, besides watching all the monitors. You'll be busy all night long."

Betty pointed to Katey. "Shouldn't she be outa here?"

"She's no bother. Let her stay. Now there's one spunky, determined lady. Insists on holding his hand and reciting her rosary beads. Nothing seems to faze her anymore. Told me her husband pulled through a mighty close call up in Seattle during the Korean War, and she was right there, doing this very same thing."

"She's dropped the beads and fallen asleep!"

"Yeah, but notice she won't let go of his hand," said Claire. "You believe in the power of prayer?"

"Never put much faith in it myself," Betty replied. "Will admit I've been around these hospital walls long enough not to discount it entirely. One thing always gets me, though."

"What's that?"

"Take a case like this. Okay, suppose he does pull through by some miracle.

Then what? We ship him out of here to some nursing home to be cared for the rest of his life. There's no dignity left, no quality of life, only a near brain-dead human being that I'm not all that sure if he had his say would want to live out his days like a vegetable."

"Aren't you playing God a bit ahead of time, Hopkins? First off, I've seen patients in deep comas use their coma as a protective shell to gradually recuperate. I've also seen them rehabilitated to the point where they can join society again. Not the people they used to be, but productive, nonetheless."

"How many have you actually seen that? I count less than four in my twenty-two years here."

"That's where the power of prayer and God-granted miracles come into play!"

Hopkins could only shake her head. "And that doesn't even begin to take into account the brain damage or all the rest of his internal injuries."

A long agonizing week passed. Jerry clung to life by the barest of threads. Most of the community tried to hide the shock of the brutal beating which the *Sacramento Star* had so soundly publicized in its headlines, feature articles, and scathing editorials. Signed two-year buyout offers flooded the mailboxes. Nobody wanted to stand up to replace Jerry Landis. JD Silverman had his day, though it remained for the police investigation to completely clear or implicate him. That was pending.

Aaron, Mary, and Krissy paid Katey a visit in her hospital room early one morning. Aaron brought a copy of the Sacramento Star. He rolled it up and smacked his hands again and again. "Look at this, Katey! The nerve of those big shots! Read this! It'll make you sick!"

Katey unrolled the paper. CC&W Transport had taken out a full-page ad.

It read:

> We are conducting our own investigation into the vicious attack on one of our employees, Gerald Landis. While the assault took place off company property, we cannot let this hideous crime go unpunished. Therefore, we are offering a reward of $100,000 to anyone who supplies us with information or leads that will arrest and convict the guilty party or parties.
>
> Signed, JD Silverman,
> President and CEO, CC&W Transport

She finished reading and handed the newspaper back to her father. "There was another man in Europe who tried the same thing and got away with it for quite a while. He told and retold the same lie enough times until he had his followers believing him. Those who opposed him, he either murdered, executed, or had them put in concentration camps. It took a while, but they finally caught up to him and exposed his big lie. His name was Adolf Hitler!"

Mary spoke her mind. "Yes, and may Stoner and Silverman get run over by a dozen locomotives for what they did. Katey, Jerry was right. He was that close to winning. No one would order such a terrible thing to happen unless he was about to lose!"

Krissy hugged her mother. "Let me take your place for a while Mother. You need to get away."

"Come home with your father 'n me. Have a good homecooked meal, sleep in your own bed. It'll do you good. Aye, lass, you need a change!"

The tears finally showed. They came hard and with much pain. "Oh, Mother, Dad, Krissy, I'm so tired. The fight's gone outa me. Please, Krissy, always hold your father's hand. I'll be back in a day or two. If there's any change, you *must* phone me right away!"

Slowly, ever so slowly, Jerry's vital signs improved. He was making progress, much to the relief of Katey and her family. He remained in a coma, but the signs were there. Any day he would open his eyes to see a different world of strange faces, strange voices, and strange surroundings. Jerry's doctors tried to prepare Katey for this eventuality. They told her that he'd sustained permanent brain damage to the extent most of his memory was gone. Irreplaceably gone.

Late one evening, Jerry opened his eyes, stared out into space, rolled his heavily bandaged head to one side, and stared straight into Katey's eyes. For what seemed like an eternity to Katey, the two exchanged glances. There was no recognition whatsoever from him. Katey let out a scream and ran from his hospital room, devastated by what had happened. She spent the rest of the evening crying her poor heart out. Gone was the Jerry she'd known, loved, and treasured for these many years. In his place was a man, a total stranger, who might one day look like the Jerry of old but who surely would be different, far different from the man she'd loved so very, very much.

Her heart, mind, and soul cried out for salvation, compassion, and some recognition of what had once flourished between them. A love, a marriage unmatched in depth, in closeness, and in understanding. Could any of this ever be salvaged? Would any of this ever come to pass?

Jack Bailey's detective friend completed his investigation about the same time the local police department filed its conclusion report with the district attorney's office. Both basically said the same thing—assault by persons unknown, with no eyewitness, and no tangible evidence linking the assault to anybody. The engineer and brakeman were thoroughly interrogated and could shed no real light on why the dispatcher had given the order that morning to drop the caboose off just inside the switchyard at the old main gate location. A careful check of all dispatcher log sheets indicated no one from the dispatcher's office had issued that order. Somebody had, but who? That mystery remained hopelessly lost in what happened on that fateful day to Jerry Landis.

Katey had missed work for five weeks now and had no real desire to return to work as Vince Stoner's secretary. Enough was enough. Yet it was Krissy who lit the fire of curiosity and revenge in her mother's heart one afternoon in Jerry's hospital room.

"It's so sad to come in here and see Dad this way. Not a spark of recognition or remembrance. It's tearing me apart! How do you stand it, Mother?"

Katey tried to hide the frustration and hurt. "By remembering that we had all those wonderful years when we lived on the outskirts of paradise."

"Will Dad ever get back any of his lost memory?"

"The doctor says it's very unlikely. The best I can hope for is a fragment or two. Maybe a feint recognition now and then, but no more."

"What are you going to do with your life, Mother? Don't you think it's about time you got on with it? Dad could be here for months or even a year or two!"

"I've given that a lot of thought lately. I think I'll try to find another position with a local law firm and let the upcoming 1958 merger proceedings fight for my pension rights, and your father's too!"

Krissy was surprised at her mother's answer. "You mean you're going to let Vince Stoner and JD Silverman get away with this? Mother, I'm surprised at you!"

"If they're too smart to make a mistake with the police department and a crack retired detective hot on their heels, what chance have I?"

"Plenty! Go back to work for Stoner. You'll be right under his nose. He'll make a mistake, and when he does, nail him good!"

"That's what your father would say. You two are so much alike. But I despise the man. I hate him beyond all words! I wouldn't feel right working for the man we both know ordered this done to your father!"

"All the more reason to nail him! Face it, Mother! You've got the rest of your life ahead. Probably without ever rekindling the flame between you and Dad. If I were in your shoes, I'd devote my best efforts to getting some satisfaction at Vince Stoner's expense. Where's that McCray and Brannigan Irish smarts and cunning I've heard so much about?"

"You mean Irish planning and persistence, don't you, daughter?" "Whatever! You're the only person who ever made Dad bend a little, and nothing could've been harder in life than that! If you really apply yourself, Vince Stoner's goose is as good as cooked."

CHAPTER 38

One bright early Monday morning, Katey Landis walked back into Vince Stoner's life at work as though she'd just come off a long extended vacation. Stoner stood in the doorway to his office and watched Katey put her purse away in her desk drawer.

"I'm in the process of interviewing another secretary, Katey. Didn't know if you planned on returning or not."

Katey withdrew her purse and started to leave. "Good! I'll be on my way back down to personnel to see if they have any other openings."

"No need to, Katey. I'll call down and tell them the position is filled again." Katey wheeled around to face Vince. "I wouldn't think of depriving some lucky lady of the rare opportunity of working for you! You could do a number on her, just like you did on me! All that exhaustive snooping around into her family's and her personal life. Mustn't let that new secretary pass up the chance to tell you to go to you-know-where! No, we wouldn't want her to miss out on all that excitement now, would we?"

"Can the sarcasm, Katey! You either work for me or out the door you go!" "Why, boss, what a nice welcome back! How thoughtful!"

The confrontation was on again between the two. Stoner tried to get in the parting shot, always his trump card. "By the way, Katey, that was a very nice gesture on your folks' part to finish paying off your

Buick. I'm sure you will rest a lot easier now that you have one less thing to worry about. Especially since your late afternoons are going to be busy checking at the hospital on that food processor that was once your husband!"

"You low slime! How can you say such a thing like that?"

"Easy, when it's the truth, right, Katey? Isn't that about what he amounts to nowadays? They put a little food into him, he processes it, and then he has a great big bowel movement, and they diaper him up again for the next round!"

"I won't dignify that remark, no matter how much I'm tempted to!" "One other thing, Katey. We need to get together about this right away." "I can't imagine about what!"

"Don't buy your black panties at that new shop anymore. They are not near as nice as the ones you used to buy. Matter of fact, let's talk about changing to a new color. I like a light shade of blue. It's always been my favorite!"

Two weeks somehow dragged by. In Katey's estimation, it was one tiny step forward and two big steps backward on Jerry's good days. Yet some progress was there. At least that's what the specialists kept telling her. By the time Katey learned to pronounce their correct medical specialty along with their name and what they did, it was on to a new doctor, and the process would start all over.

This frustration reached its peak late one afternoon while Katey waited patiently in Jerry's room for his return. The orderly wheeled him in. Jerry's eyes lit up, his mouth opened, and he pointed to Katey. Though his speech was slow and he slurred his words, Katey had no problem understanding.

"I…kn…kna…know…y…ya…you—"

Katey never gave him a chance to finish his thought. She was all over him with as much emotional display of affection as she'd let herself do in public. She kissed him and hugged him, nearly squeezing the life out of him. "Jerreee! Jerreee, you do remember! Oh, I'm so glad. Oh, I'm so glad! Thank the Lord!"

Just then, in walked his speech therapist, Mrs. Codington, a middle-aged redhead in her late forties. "I'm glad you approve, Mrs. Landis. Now let him finish his sentence. Jerry, go ahead and tell Mrs. Landis what was on your mind."

Katey stepped back. She was all smiles. "Jerry, go ahead. Tell me again, darling!"

He labored hard with his words. At times, his mouth was contorted. The muscles of his jaw appeared in direct opposition to his thought. "Y…ya… you…a…are…the…th…the…n…na… niceeeeee…l…la…lady…that…c…ca…com…comes…to…sa… sa…seem…ma…me!"

Katey gave out an agonizing scream. Down the hall she went, with Mrs. Codington a step behind. "Mrs. Landis! Mrs. Landis! Wait up!" The therapist finally caught up. "Let's get a cup of coffee at the cafeteria." Betty let Katey settle down before she offered a word. "Let's start at the beginning, Mrs. Landis. As far as your husband is concerned, his world started the day he opened his eyes in this hospital room and saw you as a total stranger. Forget the past. It means nothing to him now, and for the rest of your life, it will mean next to nothing to him."

"Nothing at all?"

"Mrs. Landis, stop resurrecting the past. Just concentrate on the present so maybe, just maybe, there'll be some kind of future for you two."

Katey held her cup between both hands. "Where do I start? And please, call me Katey."

Betty raised her cup to her lips then put it down. "I'm only a licensed speech therapist, Katey, but I'm willing to work with you all the way if you agree to put your trust in me. That's the key to your husband's recovery. *Trust!* You have to earn it again from him! How committed to your husband are you? Stop and really give that some thought before you give me an answer: Let me back up a bit and tell you about another case I had recently. Science tells us a lot of our brain capacity goes unused because we've never learned to tap it. Had a recent brain-damage case. Husband married thirty-five years and was on the road to a good recovery. Katey, he made a lot of mistakes, did bizarre things, yet his wife understood and accepted that, knowing those would lessen with time. One thing she couldn't or wouldn't accept was his crude bedroom manners. She forgot or refused to understand that. Guess he'd been the perfect lover prior to his accident. She now has his best friend service her on a regular basis. She's filed for divorce, and he's been dumped in the custody of a noncaring convalescent center for the rest of his life. All my work has been Bushed down the toilet. Where along this scenario do you fit in?"

Katey looked the speech therapist right in the eye. "I don't believe in divorce, and I will do anything, *anything* to keep my husband and my marriage alive. Oh yes, I've known my husband all his life, and we've been best friends, sweethearts, lovers, and husband and wife. I won't have it any other way! My conscience, my commitment, my vows, and my God would never allow another man into my life, regardless of the circumstances. My life and my marriage are wrapped around the best man I've ever had the pleasure of knowing and loving!"

"Good girl! How old are you two?"

"We're both fifty-two now."

"Katey, there isn't time to do this like it should be done. Are you ready for a crash course?"

"Yes, I want my husband back in my life, no matter in what limited or restricted capacity."

"Here's the three key words to always remember: *repeat, repetition,* and *redo.*

Those three words will become your motto in everything you're ever going to do, say, or think regarding your life with your husband from now on. Now the first thing you must do is gain his interest, then his confidence, and finally his trust. Without his complete trust in you, your marriage will go nowhere from this point on. Katey, what I am about to say will shock you, but I'm sure somewhere down the line, it will happen. And when it does, you must reject your husband's advances to save your marriage!"

"I don't understand. I… I will welcome any advances he makes. Always have."

"Listen, I'm ahead, way ahead of myself, but I assure you it will happen. Katey, have you ever been somewhere, met somebody, or seen somebody and said to yourself, 'I swear we've met before, but I know it can't be true?'"

"Yes, several times. It's a strange feeling!"

"Right! That's going to happen to your husband sooner or later regarding you. Right now, he'd swear, and correctly so, that he doesn't know you. Yet there'll come times something will trigger his old feelings. Maybe a certain phrase, a catchword, or even a gesture, or going by or driving to a certain place or building or even a certain food. Anyway, you get my point. The trick is to make the first day he came out of his coma yours and his past, and build your life together from that point on. Believe you me, it's far easier said than done!"

"I noticed Jerry is having a difficult time with his speech. Will that improve?"

"Right now, his mental capacity is about at a sixth-grade level on his good days. Give me another three months and I'll have him reading and talking at the high-school level. Katey, your husband already has shown a hunger and thirst for learning and knowledge that exceeds most of the patients I've worked with. With most, they develop up to a certain level, and then stay at that level. It's too early to tell for certain, but I do believe he'll develop into a fine person again mentally and physically. I've checked his charts and talked with several of his specialists. In two more weeks, all the bandages come off, and you'll be amazed at how far reconstructive surgery has come. Given the scars and tissue matches that will gradually change and disappear into normal Besh tones, your husband will pretty well resemble the man you once married. But that's as far as they can go. The rest is up to him and you."

"Okay, basically, I do understand what's ahead. What about now? Where do I start?"

"You start by devoting four hours each evening after work being with him right here. You must be patient with him. Don't expect too much to happen too soon, because it won't. However, you must become a part of his everyday routine. And then little by little, I believe good things will happen between you two."

"How intimate do you want me to be around him?"

"Not at all! This is so hard for wives to understand, but it must be followed! Do not touch, caress, fondle, or kiss unless—and this is so key—*unless he invites first!* I'd be willing to bet you won't be faced with anything remotely connected to those situations for weeks, even months! Remember, he regards you as a total stranger, and until you've completely won over his trust again, you must not proceed with any advances or intimacy!"

Katey was filled with remembrances, and a slow smile drifted across her lips. "It wasn't easy, believe me. Took me seven years and our darling baby girl and some big changes between us to get him to the alter, and it's been dynamite between us ever since! My daughter, Krissy, likes to say I'm the only person who ever dented my husband's iron-clad constitution! No one's ever been able to break him!"

Betty laughed and then turned deadly serious. "Your husband's strange assault case is not so strange to you, is it? When you said no one could break him, I can only assume he was an obstacle that had to be removed one way or another?"

"Yes, and I have to work for the SOB that did it in order to keep our medical insurance in force. They kept giving him the rubber room treatment. His class action case comes to trial next year."

"Well, with an awful lot of hard work by you, me, and your husband, maybe he'll be able to attend that trial. At least it's a goal worth shooting for!" Betty noticed the full-length skirt and loose-fitting blouse Katey had on. "I'd say there's some other problems brewing, too, between you and your boss. Katey, you've got a full petite figure you're trying awfully hard to hid. No doubt your boss probably figures you could use some attention since you're vulnerable now with your husband out of circulation and you stuck to your job. Am I lukewarm?"

"Red-hot! I've never hated a man before I met this lowlife. It's a real hassle just to put in eight hours around him each day. He undresses me every day, if you catch my drift!"

"I had the same problem a few years ago when my husband had his accident falling off some construction scaffolding, hitting his head on concrete thirty feet below."

"How'd you handle it?"

"Probably the same way you'll have to Katey. A fist in his face and an extra hard knee or foot into the family jewel pouch! That more than got his attention! I thought about sexual harassment proceedings, but with no witness, it boiled down to his word against mine!"

"Thanks for the tip. Only hope I don't need it! Can I ask you a personal question?"

"Depends on how personal it gets. Go ahead, try me!"

"Did you have a great marriage? I think you know what I mean."

"Couldn't really come right out and ask, could you, Katey? Okay, I'll save you the infringement on my privacy bit and answer. As far as I was concerned, our marriage was second to none, in or out of our bedroom!"

"You said was!"

"That's right. We're working on that now, the same thing you'll be faced with someday. You're months away from this discussion at best! Look at it this way, Katey. I'd rather have my husband at home waiting for me each night in whatever limited capacity, sexually or otherwise, than sleeping alone thinking about what used to be. If you can accept that, you've taken the first real step in the right direction."

CHAPTER 39

Katey's twenty-six years of wedded bliss had somehow dwindled down to sorting out the smaller problems from the much larger unsolvable ones. Doubts were everywhere, and nobody was coming in to rescue her on the tide of trouble that threatened to drown her in her own expectations, goals, commitment, and marriage.

At home, she laid her problems squarely before her parents. "Katey, if we had the money, surely, lass, you could count on us. We'd gladly give it to you, no questions asked."

Katey tried her best to smile, but it wouldn't come. "I know, Mother. You and Dad have never let me down. There's no way out. When the insurance money is gone, I'll have to sign over everything we own to the state and hospital."

Aaron pounded his fist on the table and kicked the empty chair, his mind in a real Irish stew.

"Careful, Father," cautioned Mary. "That's Katey and Jerry's till they have to give it up!"

"Darn it, Mrs. McCray. It's our place too!" He walked over to the wall next to the refrigerator and ran his hands up and down it. "This part came from the first raise at work, and that wall over there came after we paid the bills and had enough left for Katey's first Christmas here when we moved in." He pointed to the parlor. "And that furniture came after your mother saved in a cookie jar after two years of scrubbin' and sewin' and doing the washin' for the extra gang." He wandered around the kitchen. "And this all came about when Katey and Jerry took over, when Jerry used his brains instead of his back to change things for the better. Each generation should leave something better for the next, like we passed it on to Katey and Jerry. And they helped Krissy and Mark, and then they're supposed to help our two great-grandsons. That's what family and hard work, saving, and sweat is all about. When you pay for something, it's supposed to be yours to keep because you saved and earned it! Lass, it's all haywire now!"

Mary shook her head in disgust. "Katey, after this is all over, come as soon as you can when Jerry is able to live with us down in Yuma. At least you two will be away from the heartache, the pain, and the longing to keep what was rightfully yours."

"Thanks, Mother. That's the best offer I've had in a long, long time." "T'aint right, daughter. Even the law's no help these days. Look what

happened to Jerry, and they can't even lay a finger on this Stoner or that railroad big shot, Silverman."

Mike Dutton, managing editor of the *Star,* was inclined to be a nervous and impatient type of guy. To him, increased newspaper circulation went hand in hand with good writing and investigative reports, supplemented by hard-nosed editorials and spiced with plenty of ammunition to spark enough controversy to boost circulation. When his newspaper contained these successful ingredients, his daily supply of Bromo-Seltzer and peptic acid pills went virtually untouched. Lately, he'd began twisting the caps off those bottles in his desk drawer earlier each day, a sure sign that change was most definitely on the way. He summoned Jack Bailey.

"What's up, boss? You look like you've just checked yesterday's circulationfigures!"

Dutton chomped on his unlit cigar, another dead giveaway he was unhappy. "Circulation's down another ten percent. We've milked all we could outa Landis and the CC&W snarl. Time to switch gears and go for another point of view. Maybe call it something like 'The Flip Side of the Coin,' a new editorial column. Use your imagination. We're gonna replace the 'Soap Box!'"

"With what, Mike?"

"With some serious in-depth interviews with Vince Stoner, JD Silverman's chief honcho! I figure since Stoner's his mouthpiece, he's the next best ticket!"

Jack opened Mike's upper left-hand drawer and retrieved a bottle of Jack Daniels, which Mike affectionately nicknamed the Dutton Holy Water. He dispensed with the shot glass and took it straight. "Care to tell me what this is all about?"

"Need new blood, that's all! Time to get off this righteous kick and give CC&W a chance to have their say!"

"New blood? Righteous kick? Let CC&W have their say? C'mon, Mike, what's really behind all this crappola?"

Mike borrowed the bottle from Jack and took a good healthy snort. He wiped his lips with the back of his hand. "You're too good of a reporter to let go! It's either write about CC&W, or I hand you your walking papers!"

Jack was in shock! "Who got to you, Mike? Bet it had to something to do with Vince Stoner or Old Lady Meecham's visit last week! Right?"

"She owns the paper, so she calls the shots."

"Want me to do my own snooping, Mike? I've already got this sick feeling that when I dig deep enough, I'll come up with Vince or JD! Wanna save me the trouble!"

"I'm sorry, Jack. Can plainly see this conversation's been pigeonholed. I'll be glad to write you the best dang reference this side of the Rockies! Anybody special I should address it to?"

"Never mind, I've got my own contacts. C'mon, Mike, how'd they do it?

How'd they get to the widow Meecham to sign over the paper?"

"Don't know all the details myself, but CC&W apparently made an offer old Lady Meecham couldn't turn down. I hear she cleared a cool million and will buy back the paper in two years as part of the agreement. By that time, Silverman figures he'll have mended his reputation to the point he'll be a respected, reputable community and civic leader. Amazing how a check in the right hands can restore about anything nowadays. Even communities like Ruston develop short memories quite conveniently!"

Jack took the bottle back and took a long swig. "Well, we've covered all the late breaking news except for one little item tucked away in the corner that needs a little clarification!"

"By whom?"

"*You!* You're too good an editor, Mike, to sell yourself, along with the paper, to be under CC&W control! What was the asking price? C'mon, you owe me that much!"

Mike fidgeted uneasily in his chair. "Never thought much about retirement till about a month ago. The wife and I were having dinner at the Sir Francis Drake in Frisco when she said something to me about what our plans are for retirement and if we have enough money… things like that. Jack, I've been an editor, and a pretty fair one, for over forty years! Always planned on salting away a few bucks. Just never got around to doing something about it. We stayed at the Drake that night. Good thing the newspaper picked up my tab, 'cause I sure as heck couldn't have afforded it. I'm sixty-three years old without the proverbial pot or the window to throw it out of."

"How much, Mike? How much was the agreement if you stayed on?"

"My mortgage gets paid off when I retire at sixty-five, and there's two hundred fifty grand set up in a trust account to be turned over to me upon retirement!"

Jack handed the bottle back to Mike and started to leave. "Hey, where are you going? I can keep you around for at least another payday or two!"

"Thanks, boss, but I'd better be on my way out. My conscience won't allow me to work on a newspaper controlled by Little Jesus. I'm gonna clean my desk out, make a couple of calls to some contacts, and pay my respects to a plucky little Irish lady who's had one heckuva run of bad luck. Her leprechauns have deserted her, and a new crop of four-leaf clover is nowhere near ready for picking. Only thing keeping her going is her daily hospital trips and her almighty faith in God."

Katey was shocked to learn Jack was leaving and about the circumstances surrounding his sudden departure. Over a cup of tea at the kitchen table, Jack got ready to say his goodbye. "I'm sorry it turned out this way, Katey. I know it's no comfort to you now. I can only say I believe more than ever, Jerry had the right numbers. JD had to be hurting. I should've realized camping him out on those sidings that last round was a dry run for the real attack just outside their own switchyards."

She smiled bravely. "We'll never know for sure now, will we? Any job prospects?"

"As a matter of fact, yes! That publicity Jerry received helped me too! I have two job interviews this coming week. I'll drop you a note when I decide where I'm going to hang my hat. Is there anything else I can do for you?"

She turned away and swallowed hard, fighting to keep it in.

"C'mon, Katey, out with it! Been around you long enough to know something's eatin' at you!"

"I have nowhere to go for financial help to keep paying Jerry's medical bills.

His insurance is about used up, and my boss is pressuring me for…well…"

"I get the picture! Sounds an awful lot like sexual harassment to me. It's a hard one to take to the law 'cause if you do, your boss can always argue you consented. Without proof, you're going nowhere! Say, wait a minute! Three years ago, I did a series of articles about secretarial pressures in the nine-to-five world. One of my articles was about an interview with a married lady who was being pressured. She nailed her boss but good with the help of a lady police detective who specialized in those cases. Her name is Ann Archer, and she's with the Sacramento police department. Look her up! Can't hurt!"

Katey followed Jack to the front door. "Katey, this comes from the heart. In all my years of news hounding and reporting, I've been around every kind and description of human being that calls earth his home. I've met governors, one vice president, and more congressmen and senators than I'd care to count, including most of the local, state, and quite a few national celebrities, and none of them can hold a candle to you and Jerry. Both of you stand head and shoulders above the crowd. You two are that special! I also know what I'm about to add will mean nothing to you now, but Jerry was right on target.

That's why they had to take him out!"

She vainly tried to smile. "Thanks for the testimonials, but we'll never know for sure about Jerry's figures, will we?"

"That's the sad part, and I'll always feel somewhat responsible for not covering all the security bases. I never thought they'd get to him right under our noses. Always thought it'd be far out, along one of those old abandoned railroad sidings!"

"You were partly right. The first attempt was way out!"

He opened the door, stepped out, then changed his mind and stepped inside again. "A bit of info for your consumption, Katey.

Vince Stoner's going to be called back to Denver to answer grand jury questions concerning his possible implication in the disappearance of one of the rubber room employees out of a caboose, when JD took control. They've decided to reopen the case. Wouldn't it be just desserts if they nailed him after all?"

"It'll never happen. We both know it! Stoner and Silverman cover their tracks too well!"

"Gotta go!" He paused again. "Please take this as its intended, Katey, but I'd be honored and tickled pink if you'd hug me goodbye. That is, of course, if you feel Jerry wouldn't object."

She graciously complied with his request. After their embrace, he stepped back, happy as a lark, and winked. "I know there are no secrets between you two. That's one of the many reasons for your successful marriage. Do you suppose one small indiscretion like this would matter at all in your lives?" He knew before Katey answered.

"I'll mention this to Jerry someday when he's able to understand. Just to keep the slate clean between us!"

"Goodbye, Katey Landis. I'll drop you a note when I decide where to unpack my pajamas for my next job!"

CHAPTER 40

Vince Stoner was summoned into JD's private office. "I'm not at all happy 'bout this Landis business. Wasn't handled properly. We overcame our problem, but it was botched, nothing professional either time!"

Vince strutted around JD's office as though he had seating privileges behind JD's desk. "That's what happens when local talent gets involved. Should've let me take care of it the way we handled the Denver deal."

"You're not out of the woods yet, Vince. That grand jury might have some sticky questions. Then what?"

"Not to worry. You're in the clear regardless. Stop carping about what can't be changed. I'll tell 'em the same story as before and the dust will settle, and I'll walk away, just as before."

"I suppose you'll pay Mrs. Downey your usual visit while in Denver?" "Wouldn't miss that for anything! You know me, that's private stuff! *Ha!* I'll never forget when I drove out to her house to give her the bad news that her husband was missing. Of course, I assured her I was conducting my own investigation into the disappearance. She poured out her grief in my arms while I took her into the bedroom and poured everything I had into her. Man, oh man, what a woman! They're real pushovers, JD, when grief strikes 'em. Can't think straight at times like that. Called me real regular, wanting to know when I'd pay her another visit so I could personally give her the latest scoop on her husband's investigation. By then, she knew the only investigation I ever conducted was to see how fast I could get her into the bedroom. Been great ever since!"

"You should find a real nice steady companion, Vince, like the lady attorney I socialize with. Get off this hit-or-miss stuff!"

"My thoughts exactly, and I have just the right little lady waiting in the wings ready to be plucked!"

"Who?"

"Mrs. Landis! JD, I tell you, this is gonna be super prime! I've got her boxed up so tight she's gonna have to come across. She's fought me every inch of the way, but when I bed her down, it's gonna be that much sweeter! When ole Vince gets to 'em, they stay in his stable from now on!"

JD swiveled around his chair, watching Vince gloat over his conquests. "I've done some checking into your private secretary's life. She's very religious, comes from strict upbringing, and is totally committed to her marriage, her God, and her family. First generation women over here are hard to crack. Still too much of the old country in them. Take some advice, forget her and move on."

"I want her, and I intend to have her!"

"You're running out of time! Since our newspaper deal, I'm going to start mending fences and come up with real PR work, first class all the way. Starting tomorrow, the Star is doing a series of articles on what it takes to run a railroad today. Give the public a real insight into the problems, competition, operating, and labor expenses. A real layman's story in their own words. Then next week comes out my full-page announcement that CC&W Transport is going to retire Gerald Landis with a full pension and pay all his medical expenses for life. Won't that be a magnanimous gesture in the public's eye? They'll eat it up, and we'll have taken one giant step toward respectability once again. Exactly where I want to be, and this mess will gradually fade into the Western sunset!"

"Okay, but give me a week more, and we'll both get what we want!"

"You have ten days starting tomorrow, and then I'm going to run my announcement!"

"I hear you, JD! By the way, let me offer you a little advice. Next time you get the itch to add another railroad to your empire, take time to thoroughly investigate middle management. That's where Jerry Landis came from. Think of the millions you could've saved by keeping him and promoting him to the job he was most definitely qualified for. End of speech, JD!"

Katey had run out of options. It was either submit to Vince Stoner's advances or let the hospital and the State of California take control of all the Landis assets. Everything she and Jerry had worked and saved during all their married years would be gone. True, Stoner did offer a way out of the quagmire of never-ending medical expenses for Jerry with JD Silverman's signature on a contract. Jerry's medical expenses would be covered for life.

The hospital business manager's words still haunted her: "*Two days left, Mrs. Landis! Remember, only two!*" With knees shaking and butterflies churning in her stomach, Katey turned the doorknob and glanced around for one last look at her own independence and respectability. She entered Stoner's apartment.

Stoner waited until the door closed before rising from his lounge chair. He was dressed only in a bathrobe tied with a sash. He strutted around like a barnyard rooster, so cocksure that Katey was now his for the taking. "On the coffee table"—he pointed—"you'll find everything in order with JD's signature."

Katey took her own sweet time carefully reading every word while keeping her coat buttoned. The minute she put the two signed contracts back down, Vince handed her a negligee. Instead of changing before him, Katey disappeared into the bathroom. He heard the distinct click. Katey was still safe behind the locked door.

A minute passed, then two, then three. Stoner pounded hard. "I'm not going to wait a minute longer! And you'd better have only my negligee on!"

No answer, then a faint click. Katey reappeared with her coat still on. "Take it off, or I tear up the contract! That what you want?"

Katey teased him with only a fleeting glimpse then closed her coat quickly. "Time to talk trade, Stoner, or else I walk out that door for good!"

He shook with rage at the cat and mouse game being played on him. "Remember, the deal was only one time. I might make it more for some information."

No man ever coveted another man's wife more than Vince Stoner. "How many more times?"

Katey opened her coat fully. Stoner drooled over what was about to be his. "Depends on the answers I get. This is just between you and me, so I want to hear you say, 'I, Vince Stoner, personally ordered two attacks on Gerald Landis.'"

"Take your bra and panties off right now or it's no deal!"

"I'll do that in bed after you say the words. Come, come! Haven't got all day." Katey went back to the bathroom once more. This time she returned carrying her clothes, and she walked to the front door. She opened it then looked back. "Last chance, Stoner, or else it's goodbye."

He salivated worse than a junkyard watchdog. The words came out. "Again, Stoner. I didn't quite catch them all."

Stoner repeated them with raised voice. *"Satisfed! Now are you satisfed? Knock off the stalls, Katey!"*

Katey came back into the room. She pulled back the sheets and lay down. "Everything comes off under two conditions."

"You're stalling, Katey! What conditions?" Katey sat up in bed and lowered her coat. Man, oh man, did Stoner like the view. "What conditions?"

"You must go into the bathroom to put on your protection. Don't want to see it any sooner than I have to. And tell me, was Silverman really hurting as my husband suspected?"

"All right, since you're so darned interested, JD had a mighty big payment due. Now I expect to see you take everything off, and I'm going to leave the bathroom door open so I can keep an eye on you."

Two policemen walked straight to the bathroom and handcuffed Stoner. He leveled a barrage of profanity at Katey as he was escorted on the way out. Ann Archer entered with a most satisfied smile.

"Here, let me unhook the wire from your bra. Stoner's admission came through loud and clear. Look for a settlement. The scandal would bury Silverman, and the trial publicity would finish the job! Make sure you get a sharp attorney to represent you during negotiations. Great job, Katey! Boy, you can really dangle bait when the time comes!"

Katey finished dressing then picked up her purse. Ann Archer saw the great rush of relief across Katey's face and shoulders. She closed the door behind them. "Stoner was a dead duck before he knew what happened."

"I only hope that Jerry will understand what I had to do…when he's able." Ann hugged her. "He will, Katey, when the right time comes."

CHAPTER 41

JD Silverman sat alone in his private office awaiting the announcement he knew was coming—the newsbreak over Channel 11, Sacramento. He stirred his tea, added two lumps of sugar, and then stoically watched the television program in progress. He was the absolute emperor over two railroads he had personally resurrected from the ashes of bankruptcy. Twenty-five thousand miles of track linked the two gasping electric and diesel-fired transportation businesses with their combined thirty thousand plus employees under this thumb. They were dependent upon him for their paychecks, in tune with his every whim and command. The stark realization that one husband and wife team had nearly wrecked his dream and brought his empire crashing down was the most humbling experience of his lifetime. The investigation ended just before it touched his office, but he'd been badly shaken. Mr. Untouchable had been all but reached!

The TV program switched to the Channel 11 newsroom. "We interrupt our regularly scheduled programming for this important announcement," the reporter began. "We now switch you to our main studio where Mr. Harold Baines, newly appointed general manager of CC&W Transport, will read from a prepared statement. Mr. Baines."

"We at CC&W Transport would like to take this opportunity to publicly announce that an out-of-court settlement and agreement has been reached with Mr. and Mrs. Gerald Landis. Mr. Vincent Stoner's employment with CC&W Transport has been terminated He is awaiting civil and criminal indictment charges of sexual harassment concerning Mrs. Landis. He is also awaiting criminal conspiracy charges related to the horrible beatings administered to our employee, Gerald Landis.

"We at CC&W Transport sincerely regret these unfortunate incidents and hereby serve notice to all our employees that actions of this sort will *not* be tolerated, and our company will make every effort to expose and prosecute any employee found guilty of such violations to the full extent of the law!

"In recognition of these terrible offenses, Mr. and Mrs. Landis will be compensated for these crimes, and both will be fully pensioned as of today. Mr. Landis's medical expenses for life will be underwritten by CC&W. Thank you!"

The TV program switched back to the reporter in the newsroom. "Mrs. Landis has declined all interviews and photo sessions on behalf of her husband and herself. While no exact compensation figure was discussed in today's announcement, reliable sources have estimated the amount was in excess of $2.6 million. This is Dan Dibble reporting. We now return you to our regularly scheduled program."

He finished sipping his tea and then swiveled around to find his wastepaper basket. Upon his desk, he deposited its contents. Twenty seconds of sorting satisfied him he'd left no scraps of reusable paper, so he brushed the paper scraps back into the basket. It seemed so apropos and fitting for just the kind of day he'd been forced to witness and endure, given the horrible circumstances he created in the first place.

Katey wasted no time hiring Betty Codington full time to oversee Jerry's speech therapy along with his physical conditioning. And what better facility to continue the efforts than at home in Krissy's old decorator room? The privacy was there, away from the new flock of snooping reporters at the hospital after the compensation announcement over TV.

The two women developed a kindred relationship, one that blossomed into a full-blown personal as well as professional comradeship.

A year went by, and Katey saw the benefits of full-time effort. Jerry's progress was nothing short of spectacular considering the severity of his mental and physical condition. However, the bond between them remained distant at best. He seemed to trust the "nice lady," and he did acknowledge at long last that he indeed felt married to this "nice lady." But that was about the extent of their contact, even though Katey conveniently placed photos of Krissy, her parents, and their two grandsons in conspicuous places as reminders and reinforcement that he, indeed, was first a husband, and second a family man.

At Betty's urging, they slept apart, Katey in their master bedroom while Jerry occupied Krissy's old bedroom. Even the photos of Krissy as a baby and as a seven-year-old, when Jerry came into her life, did little to rekindle the closeness the two had shared. Something was still missing. That certain spark which needed to be found to reshape the close personal relationship Katey prayed so earnestly for each night, before clutching his old pillow and falling into a restless sleep.

One day, Katey was busy sorting her mail as Betty entered the kitchen. Katey looked up, pointed to the coffee pot, and said, "Help yourself. You know where we hang the coffee cups."

Betty joined Katey at the table. "I'm going to let the physical therapist go after today's workout. Jerry's where he's going to be for the rest of his life. No need spending any more money. He's about seventy percent where he used to be. He's graduated from the walker to total reliance upon his cane. His balance will never be what it was, which means he'll walk somewhat slower than before. His artificial leg will always have a more pronounced drag. No more standing his cane in the corner for short distances, like you told me he used to get by with." She raised her cup. "Anything new with the pony express delivery?"

Katey picked up a sorted stack and ditched them in the kitchen wastebasket. "Still getting hounded by investment counselors, mutual fund dealers, and various con artists. You'd think they'd give up after a while!"

"Money attracts those types, Katey. They know you have it, and it's their job to separate you from your money as soon as possible. Anything else?"

Katey handed Betty a pretty picture postcard. "It's from Mom and Dad!

They're in Ireland, having a ball! Sure glad I splurged so that they could go first class! They want me to come join them!"

"Why don't you? The change away from Jerry might do you both some good. I'll hire a competent round-the-clock person to look after him till you get back!"

"No, I won't leave Jerry, no matter that he'd probably never miss me!"

Betty put her cup down. "You two are closer than you think, Katey. I know you don't believe it now, but I can see the response in his face when you're around. He really does appreciate you!"

"Appreciate me! I want him to love me, I want—"

"Stop it, Katey! What you want has to be put on the back burner just awhile longer!"

"How much longer?" snapped Katey. "*C'mon, tell me! How much longer?*"

Betty didn't have an answer at first. "I can't name the exact hour, the day, or even what month. You know that! Tell me this, and before you answer, give my question some real deep thought. Are you willing to risk your relationship now in favor of a quick shortcut, one guaranteed to put you two together or else pull you apart probably for good?"

Katey stewed and stewed over Betty's question. "What'll happen between us if your idea doesn't work?"

"He'll retreat into a shell because he'll feel he's committed adultery! Katey, that perfect marriage you worked so hard to have and control has a downside. He's scared to risk involvement with you because he knows he used to care so very deeply about someone else."

Katey protested, "But that someone was me! Why can't he see that?"

"You just said the key word—*was!* He's not ready to take you on now unless you force him."

"How would I go about forcing him? I mean, what or where do I start?" "It's another variation of the old carrot-and-stick approach. Get him to do something for you and then reward him. Keep doing that until he either initiates his own action or refuses to play your game."

That night, Katey prepared a delicious supper. Afterward, she asked Jerry to clear the table and load the dishwasher. He obeyed without question as Katey pretended to be busy in her dressing room. About the time he finished, she sashayed back into the kitchen, reeking of his favorite perfume, and planted a thank you kiss on the cheek.

"What was that for?" His innocence was still much in evidence.

"When you do something I like, Jerry, well, it just makes me feel good, and so I want to show you my appreciation. Hope the kiss was all right?"

"It was fine. Really, it was." "Did you like it?"

He looked around as if someone were spying over his shoulder. "I shouldn't say this, 'cause I'm married to somebody else, but I liked it just fine, Little Lady. Just fine!"

Katey retreated to her bedroom in tears.

The next thing Katey tried was the jewelry approach. She paraded in front of Jerry with the chic black evening dress that Theresa had made for her.

"Jerry," she called out. "I forgot to wear my diamond-studded choker. How about you be a dear and go into the top right-hand drawer of my dressing table and bring it to me?"

Again, he obeyed and returned with the choker. "Oh, this is beautiful, ma'am! Who bought it for you, Little Lady?"

It took all the willpower Katey could hang onto not to scream into his face and shout, "You *did! Why can't you remember?*" Instead, she politely turned to him and said, "Why, thank you, Jerry. Would you mind putting it around my neck?"

She worked her body back into him, as he was all thumbs trying his best to snap the choker's clasp at the back of her neck. Her body language was having a noticeable effect on him. Katey smiled inwardly and then softly complained, "I wish I had some other piece of jewelry to wear. This is so nice, but I've had it such a long time."

"Golly, Little Lady, I read in the newspaper that you have lots of money! C- could I…maybe we…spend some of it and buy you some jewelry?"

Katey turned to him and gave him a seductive glance. "Why, Jerry, what a wonderful idea! Tell you what, just for that, I'm going to let you buy me something special tomorrow morning! And for coming up with such a good idea, I'm going to kiss you for your reward!"

She didn't wait for a yes, no, or maybe! She gathered him up in her arms pulled his head down and gave him the kiss of his new young identity! Then she moved into him with a grinding body language that all but undressed him right on the spot! Katey held him so tight, she could've sworn she was standing inside his boxer shorts!

Suddenly, he backed away. "You shouldn't do that, Little Lady. There's an Irish lady. She'd blow her stack over what you've just done."

Katey couldn't believe her ears. "Who, Jerry, who? Tell me about this little Irish lady with the temper! Don't stop, Jerry! Tell me!"

He looked puzzled and slowly scratched his head and went into deep thought. "I dunno, Little Lady, who she is. I just know she's there!"

Oh, how great it was, the first breakthrough! The first possible connection!

Oh, sweet Jesus! At last, at long last! Maybe, just maybe!

That night, Katey lay wide awake, going over the chain of events in her mind that triggered Jerry's response. She felt she was on the threshold of what she'd been waiting for over two years—a touch with her past! It there's one connection, one tiny remembrance, why couldn't there be more?

The next morning, Katey proudly escorted Jerry into one of the local jewelry shops. She picked out a beautiful gold inlay broach, got Jerry's approval, and started to get out her checkbook. Jerry offered, "Why don't I write the check, Little Lady?"

The checkbook! Of course! Oh, thank God! She thought, *Why hadn't I thought of that before? What he did and the way he said it was as natural a thing for my husband to say and do, as was his infamous Jerryisms.* "Fine, dear. You go ahead and take care of it!" She handed him her checkbook. "I'm going to watch this nice lady wrap the jewelry while you go ahead and give the store manager our check."

The manager could hardly wait to hand Jerry his gold-plated personal pen for such an extremely expensive purchase. "Over here, please, Mr. Landis! Please use my desk! Recognized you the minute you and your charming wife walked in!"

Mr. Landis? Recognized you? These questions played havoc with Jerry's mind. He sat down at the manager's desk, rubbing his forehead. His headaches were coming back! Katey saw the danger signals immediately. They always started when he tried so hard to recall, to remember things, people, names, or places that escaped his memory.

She rushed over. "Dear, why don't I write the check? It's been quite a spell since you've written one!"

"No," he said. "I'll write it! I can do that."

Katey watched in horror and agony while he fumbled, first with the checkbook then with the pen. He'd forgotten how to write a check! Jerry Landis couldn't remember how to write a check! Her Jerry! She found it incredible! Her husband, a man whose middle name should've been money, finances, and more money! His forehead broke out into a sweat, he squinted hard, and his fingers turned white from the pressure he squeezed, trying his best to remember how to write a check.

Get Jerry out of situations he can't handle! Betty Codington's words and warning hit Katey like a sledgehammer! She took the checkbook out of his hand and smiled sweetly at the astonished manager. "He's had a touch of arthritis in his knuckles and fingers. Perhaps I'd better write it!"

They left quickly. Jerry was having a hard time keeping up as Katey did her best to get him back to their car. Inside, she opened her purse and handed him two pills.

"Here, darling. You'd better take those. You'll feel better in a few minutes." He gulped them down without a water chaser. "Thanks, Little Lady, er…

Katey… I mean! Say, that checkbook sure had a lot of zeros in it! Are…are you that rich?"

Katey wasn't quite sure how much she should divulge. In the back of her mind, rule number two stood out like a sore thumb. *Always keep your answers short and simple. Never elaborate or go into detail. It will only confuse Jerry!*

"Yes, we are, dear. Now let's get going! Say, how about me treating you out for coffee and donuts? Got just the right place in mind, and we won't have to write any checks!"

"Gee, thanks, Little Lady. You know, I feel sure that I used to write checks. It all seemed so natural. Don't remember what happened… why I can't write them anymore. How about you teach me how, Little Lady? Er… I mean Katey!"

CHAPTER 42

Betty squeezed her hand. "Katey, you're almost there! He's going to start having a lot more headaches as he wrestles with his mind. There's a real war going on between just who you are—that sweet Little Lady or his Katey. The double- name dilemma forces them to accept one or the other. Good things are about to happen, but you'll have to play God to make them happen the way you want them to."

Betty's friend turned serious, deadly serious. "I can't do that, Betty. Playing God isn't right. It's against everything I believe in. No, it's not right! I can't do that!"

"You must, Katey! Look, God put the tools in your hand. He gave you the power! Use it! A doctor, a surgeon, or a medical specialist. They all play God every day of their trained lives! From what I know about your life, you've planned, and I give you credit, because you carried out a remarkable life between you two! You told me yourself in no uncertain terms that you set the standards for commitment, marriage, and yes, even your lovemaking. Now maybe you never quite looked at it that way, but that perfect marriage that you and Jerry had just didn't happen. Katey, you made it happen! You did play God with the tools he gave you. Respect, dignity, and a carefully trained mind that allowed and controlled just like a skilled surgeon. Katey, you're a professional every bit as much as any person I've ever known! Use those tools again, and I guarantee you'll never regret it!"

"You mean you want me to take control again, but start over?"

"Exactly. You took the words right out of my mouth!"

"You mean I can remake our lives all over again? That it'll be that good again between Jerry and me?"

She touched Katey's hands. "Listen to yourself, Katey! You're back to livin' on cloud nine again! No, it won't be like it used to be, but it can be mighty good and rewarding! Question is, are you willing to settle for something less than perfection? From what I now know about your life, you had that! Katey, that's gone! Accept it for what it was, but don't overlook a new start between you two. Yesterday means absolutely nothing except lots of headaches from your husband. His past and yours still started that day in his hospital room when he didn't know who you are! Build from that!"

There came an excitement back in Katey's eyes, yet she allowed herself a minimum of hope. "Where do I start? I want a relationship with my husband, no matter what!"

"Good girl! Next time he needs his headache and tension relaxer pills, lay down with him! Try it and see if after he's relaxed, he doesn't respond. His sex drive's not dead, not dead by a long shot! Give him encouragement and help him, but make sure he initiates the action!"

"Why can't I start it between us? I used to invite a lot of the time!"

Betty stood up and walked around the kitchen. "Let him have an accident. I mean it, Katey! An accident all over you and him! Do you know what I'm trying to tell you?"

Katey's face reddened like a Santa Claus suit. "Boy, do I! When we were dating, Jerry really had an accident! I mean an accident all over me! Had to stop by an all-night dry-cleaning place before Jerry dared to drop me off at home. Always embarrassed him to no end. Hurt that big I'm-in-control ego of his!"

Two days later, Katey's first opportunity came. Jerry had been helping do simple little chores around the home as Katey gradually gave him more and more slack. It was a watch, wait, and worry type of process. Indeed, at those times, she felt more like an observer or a mother or a watchdog than ever his wife. He made clumsy mistakes and terrible errors in judgment, but patience fast became Katey's virtue, which she found was so indispensable if she harbored any expectations of resuming any kind of normal relationship with him. He'd just finished dusting the photographs of her parents. Without warning, he sat down, the pictures of Aaron and Mary still clutched in his hands. The dust cloth dropped to the carpet. He started shaking his head and rubbing his forehead back and forth.

"I know these two," he said. "I know I should know them. He smokes a pipe all the time. I can smell the tobacco…some kind of special blend…yes, that's it…special blend. And she talks different… always did. Yes, that's right. Who are they, K… Ka… Katey?"

At first, she couldn't believe her ears or what they heard. He'd separated the Katey part from the Little Lady dilemma in his mind. "Come sit down on the davenport, darling. I'll bring your pills."

She sat down beside him. He took the two pills along with a glass of water. "Jerry, you've done enough for now. How about a rest? Maybe a nap would help. Give you a chance to relax, and you'll feel better after."

"Well, okay, Katey, if you think that'll do some good. But just for a few minutes. Then you can give me some more to do. I want to help more!"

He still cradled the pictures in his arms while she slipped off his shoes. He'd forgotten his questions about Aaron and Mary, but Katey didn't let on.

She let him snooze for a while before she slipped inside, under his arms, his protective arms, her security blanket for all those wonderful, wonderful beyond compare years. She gradually backed into him and waited for nature to take its course. She felt his response still under heavy sleep, but it was there! Oh, God, it felt good, even if they were fully dressed. She raised her skirt and slid back into him and wiggled just a tad.

Jerry mumbled a bit then stirred. Her perfume, her body, her warmth worked their magic. He was wide awake, his senses on fire, his passion set to explode. Katey lay there, pretending to sleep, desperately praying he'd make the next move so she could take control.

He rolled her over and began kissing her, forcing his lips hard upon hers. She responded with her own passion. Soon he was lost in her cradle as Katey worked her body into his.

"Tell me you love me, Jerry. Tell me! Go ahead, darling, you know you want me! Tell me! Tell me, Jerry! Just say it! Then everything will be all right between us! Say it, Jerry!"

She watched his tears come. "I can't, Katey. This other lady…oh God, I hurt…she's my wife." He sat up suddenly. "I want to, but it's not right. I've never cheated on her…but I want you."

Katey felt the terrible torture his mind must be going through. She heard Codington's words and warning. *This is the crisis you've put your Jerry through. He's about ready to commit adultery with you because he can't decide if you're the same person or not. Help him! Reassure him!*

Never in all her life did Katey Landis ever get a better indication of how strong their marriage had been till now. She took him in her arms. "Do you trust me, Jerry? Do you, Jerry?"

He gazed deep into her eyes, her soft, lovely, loving eyes. "Yes… yes, I do.

Don't know exactly why I do, but I do… Katey."

"Jerry, it's all right between us. It's okay! I'm that other woman, the one you remember but can't quite see because the shadows block out her picture. Look at me, Jerry! I'm her! Trust me, Jerry!"

Katey cradled him again. Yet she would not help him, no matter how much she wanted to. He tried clumsily to make love while she made no effort to help him in his big, passionate buildup. His breathing came faster and faster when he finally got ready to make love. Oh, how he wanted her!

"Katey! Katey!" he cried out. "Oh God, Katey…look what I've done. I got in too big a hurry. I made a mess."

He got out of her cradle and sat up, tears streaming down both cheeks, thoroughly embarrassed to the point he could no longer look at her. His Katey had him exactly where she wanted him. She made no attempt whatsoever to clean up the mess he'd made all over her. Instead, she kissed one wet cheek then the other. The she softly whispered, "It's all right, my love, my darling husband. Next time, everything will work out just fine between us. I'm going to help you, Jerry…help you every step of the way. And I promise you this won't happen again, because next time, I will be ready when you want to do this to me, when you want to love me, when we need to make love."

He felt as if a thousand-pound weight had been lifted away. He turned to her, his innocence radiating like never before. "Oh, I'm so glad you said that. And…and best of all, you're not disgusted or angry with me…about what happened…right, Katey? Right, Katey?"

Her response gave him the reassurance he needed and wanted to hear. "Dear, you had just a little accident, my love. And you know what you just proved to me, Jerry?"

"No, what?"

"That you must love me an awful lot when you did this to me, even if you got in too big a hurry! Next time I'll help you slow down so we can both enjoy it much better next time. That way, it'll be much better for the both of us."

Katey could see she'd rekindled the passion in him once more. Crude to be sure, but his love, his desire was sure there, and that was most gratifying to her. Now she could take it one step further. It was time to plan and make it happen her way!

CHAPTER 43

The next thing Katey did was to try to convince Jerry that they needed to repeat their wedding vows. That was the proper place to start their new life and relationship. It took more than a bit of doing. A sliver of the old Landis opposition surfaced until Katey reassured him that it was the right thing to do, and then she ended with her not-so-subtle request, her patented catchall, clear- all obstacle phrase: "If we do, it'll be good for the both of us!"

The minute Father Donovan pronounced them man and wife, Katey sensed their brief ceremony had a double-edge effect. Jerry seemed to accept his new role as her husband, and it gave substance to the reason for Krissy, Mark, and their twin sons to be spectators. Once outside the Catholic church, Jerry was surprised to see Mark drive up with a new Buick, open the door, and hand Katey the keys. Mark then turned to shake hands with Jerry.

"Dad, Krissy and I and our two sons wish you and Mom the best of health and fortune. When you two have had enough honeymooning, please come see us."

Jerry gave a faint smile, but no hint of recognition whatsoever. Krissy then kissed him on the cheek. "Daddy, Daddy, we're all so happy for you and Mom. We know you're still trying to figure out who we are and how we fit into your life. Please don't shut us out. Come see us as often as you can."

He held her close, using both arms to look, to search Krissy's face, hoping somehow, some way, her deep blues would reveal their secret and tell him who she was…really was. He made no effort to return the kiss or even give her a hug. Instead, he shook her hand. "Thank you, dear lady, for such nice thoughts. I'd like to come see you…but what would we talk about?"

Krissy turned away; her lips quivered. Katey rescued the emotional tug-of- war between Jerry and Krissy. She waved at them. "Thanks, Mark, Krissy, Jay, and Jon. Thank you for coming!" She turned to him. "Jerry, dear, let's see if this new Buick knows the way to our honeymoon cabin. I'll drive. You can be the copilot!"

He accepted that and opened the car door for Katey to get in on the driver's side. Katey started the engine then waited for Jerry to put his cane in first before climbing in on the passenger side. Katey eased the sleek new Buick out of the parking lot and headed east, out of town. Neither spoke, each alone with their thoughts.

Ten minutes later, Jerry seemed ready to burst at the seams with some good news.

"Go ahead, love. I can tell something's ready to come! You remembered something or someone!"

He seemed almost giddy over his newfound discovery. "*Katey! Katey! I know them! I know who they are!*"

She was tempted to pull over to the side of the shoulder of the highway. Instead, she patted his hand. "It's Krissy, isn't it? Oh, love, you two used to be so close! Now you will be again!"

"Not the blond lady…that man!" "Who? Mark?"

"That man! He…he smokes a pipe…always carried it in his shirt pocket… smokes special tobacco. Yes, that's it! And…and she's got a brogue, a real Irish brogue! Yes, yes, it's them, all right! His name is Aaron! And her name is Mary! I should know them, Katey! Who they are!"

This time, Katey had reason to stop, to rejoice with Jerry and his breakthrough! His most significant one yet! Two less shadows had finally emerged out from the darkness! She pulled off onto the safety of the road's shoulder. It was time to celebrate! Time to kiss him. A tear refused to stay put, so she let it ride down one cheek while she hugged and kissed him.

"You're right, Jerry! That man, Aaron, is my father! And Mary is my mother! Now take a good look, darling! I'm their daughter! You must know who I am! Who I really am! C'mon, say it! Tell me who I am! C'mon, love! You're so close!"

"Sure, you're Katey! 'Cause that's the name you told me to use after I woke up…in that hospital! Why did you want me to say your name?" He looked around. "Say, Katey, sure do like your car! Even smells new! Did you buy it with some of those zeroes in your checkbook?"

Betty's words loomed larger than life in Katey's mind. *Remember, Katey, Jerry's memory will always just be that—bits and pieces. Rarely, if ever, will he be able to complete the missing links. Accept it for what it is—remarkable progress— and go from there.*

Her words cleared their last hurdle in Katey's mind. She smiled and hugged her husband. "Yes, love, this car is brand-new. The man who gave me the keys at the church parking lot is the husband of that blond lady who called you Daddy! And, Jerry, all those zeroes in my checkbook belong to you too!"

Jerry seemed to accept the explanation. It eased most of the quizzical look from his face.

Katey pulled back onto the main highway and headed into the foothills to the High Sierras, hoping against hope that the day might promise more breakthroughs for Jerry, maybe even some slight recognition of who she was.

Jerry remained silent, almost too quiet. He touched some of the buttons on the dashboard, running his fingers over them, and then looked at Katey as if he needed her approval to continue. For his effort, she smiled at him and said, "Go ahead, dear."

As soon as they reached the approaches to the mighty mountain range, he seemed caught up in the magnificence of the awe-inspiring panorama that unfolded before them. "I… I feel I've been here before, Katey! Have I?"

She touched one hand and said, "Yes, you have many times, love. You always said up here, we're closer to God, and I couldn't agree more!"

He turned to her, eyes full of wonder and want. "Katey…why can't I remember more? All I get is more headaches, and then you give me a pill. The pill helps stop the hurt in my head, but I don't get any closer to what I want to remember. Why, Katey?"

Again, Katey's warm reassuring smile paved the way. "Dear, you're doing fine, just fine. All we have to do is enjoy this beautiful day and whatever it brings to us. You know, Jerry, it's just possible once we reach our cabin, some more wonderful memories will be waiting for both of us."

"Good! I can hardly wait to get there! How much farther, Katey?" "Another forty minutes! That's all, my love!"

They arrived at the cabin, and to Katey's dismay, Jerry showed no signs of recognition of being there before. Instead, she had to completely oversee every effort to unpack their suitcases and unload the groceries. He seemed lost in each and every move. She thanked him for his help then dutifully told him, "Jerry, go out on the deck and take in the great view! I'll make some coffee and join you out there."

She watched him hesitate, lost as to which of the two doors he should take, the kitchen door or the front door, the one they'd just used a few minutes ago from the parking lot. He finally chose the kitchen door because it was the closest. Leaning hard on his cane, he looked back at her then reached down to grasp the doorknob.

Fifteen minutes later, Katey found him leaning over the deck rail at the farthest corner of the deck, peering down the mountainside toward Lake Tahoe, its jewellike waters sparkling way off in the distance. Gaze fixed, he appeared lost in two dimensions, time and space.

"Jerry, dear, I brought out fresh coffee! Come sit with me at the picnic table!"

He reached for his cane hanging on the rail beside him and slowly came toward her, his gait slow and quite stilted. Once he sat down, he held the cup with both hands, elbows perched on the table. Suddenly, he dropped the cup, spilling its hot liquid over himself and the table in his rush to get back up again. He put forth a burst of speed that amazed Katey. Back and forth he paced the full length of the deck. He stammered and he stuttered, trying to get the words to match his unbridled excitement.

"I... I... I... I... I...know I've been here! I can feel it! I... I... I...really do, Katey!" He came back toward her, his face all aglow with such good, good news. He dropped his cane, extended his arms toward her, and continued, "I... I... I...hear things in my mind that tell me I should know or remember this place. And, and I smell things that should help me remember too."

Suddenly, most of his newfound energy and excitement disappeared from his face and body. He seemed lost again in his warp of time.

Katey picked up his cane and helped him sit down once more. A new excitement bubbled from within. "Jerry, Jerry, my love, coming up here was the best possible place for us! You're starting to remember! Maybe more will come later!"

He turned to her, eyes pleading, and his words flowed even this time with his most profound statement about the new Jerry Landis. "I look and then I see…but I really don't. It's worse than a blind man who has lost his cane…or can't find his Seeing Eye dog. That's me!"

Katey sensed his futility but would have none of it. To her, he'd made good progress. It was not the big breakthrough she'd hoped and prayed for, but progress nonetheless. "Come, love. Let's take a nap. It'll do both of us a lot of good!"

They lay down together with Katey backing up, snuggling into her usual safe haven, the spot reserved for her, the cavity between his thighs. She mulled over the day's events, waiting for her husband to drift off into sleep so she, too, could gather her Zs without worrying about him getting up to wander off somewhere. Her thoughts came on strong. *Would this be the day? The day when some sliver of recognition between us fnally happens? Maybe enough to relight the touch of passion and love once more? Right now, I'd gladly settle for even a little smolder. Nothing big, mind you, but like an electric burner left on its simmer setting.*

Sometime in the late afternoon, Katey felt a draft on her back. In an instant, she shot out of bed, her senses telling her she'd better find her husband *now*! One quick check of the deck produced nothing except a gnawing feeling that he must have wandered off. But where? A slight afternoon chill told her to go back inside to grab a light jacket.

"Better bring one for Jerry too," she observed outwardly. No telling how long it might be before she spotted him leaning hard on his cane, heading down the trail to Lord only knows where. She snatched two jackets from their closet and passed by the bathroom door. A small stream of light held steady beneath the closed door. She knocked softly. "Jerry… Jerry…are you in there? Answer me! Please, darling!"

No answer.

She began to think that he'd probably left the light on before heading out, something he'd done countless times during the past three plus years. Then she heard a slight movement and small squeak. He must be at the medicine cabinet mirror. That squeak gave it away.

She rapped again. "Jerry, Jerry, I'm coming in to see it you're all right." She walked in on him and found him leaning over the washbasin, face pressed within two inches of the mirror on the cabinet door. He appeared absorbed in examining where his hairline met his forehead.

He caught Katey's reflection in the mirror. "Never noticed this before," he slowly began, continuing his examination. "When did this happen?"

She slipped her arm around his waist and kissed his back, wondering just how much detail she dared part with. "Love, four years ago, we both worked for a very bad man. He hired some people to hurt you…very badly. What you see is what's left of the skin grafts the doctors gave you at the hospital. In another year or two, those hairlines will disappear entirely."

He turned around, satisfied so far with her explanation. "You said we both worked for this man. Did he hurt you too?" He clenched both fists. "If he hurt you, Katey… I want to find this man."

"No, no, my love. This very bad man is in prison now, where he won't ever hurt you or me again!"

"Show me your scars and the places he hurt you! I want to see!"

"Jerry, my scars are inside where you can't see them. And with each passing year, I think less and less about what he tried to do to me. Now that you're back in my life once more, I know that in time, you'll help me to make those scars disappear forever, just like those lines on your forehead."

Again, he seemed to accept her words. Suddenly, he twisted around to check on the many scars on his back. "Did he do this to me too?"

Katey turned him around. Her eyes were full of warmth, admiration, and love. "Those scars come from a terrible, terrible war that you were in."

"War? What war?"

"It was called the Korean War, Jerry. You barely survived a terrible injury!

That's why you walk with an artificial leg while your back took a terrible pounding from the exploding shells." He blinked hard and tried to visualize just what she'd said. "Korean War… Korean War…" He looked away. "Funny thing…can't seem to put any of what you said together." He shook his head then rubbed his forehead again and again. "All that comes out…comes out for sure, Katey, is Poolis…yes, that's it! Poolis! Does that mean anything to you? Me? Maybe he can help me remember."

She looked up into his eyes, such wonderful deep-blue eyes, chalked full of the innocence and trust she'd earned by pouring every waking minute, hour, day, and year back into him until the results even staggered anything her friend Betty Codington had ever seen. "Love, Sergeant Poolis never made it back from Korea!"

"Oh…thanks for telling me."

The balance of the late afternoon was spent out on the deck where, for some reason, Jerry seemed to fit in better than inside their cabin. Katey thought about this for quite a spell then decided this was another of the many quirks and nuances Jerry would forever be saddled with for the rest of his life. Accept it and go on from there, she surmised.

Just look how far he's come since that terrible, terrible beating outside the abandoned turnstile and gate at the railroad switchyard. She smiled to herself, remembering what Betty Codington had said just the week before: "I've never seen anyone like your husband, Katey. Sure, I expected progress up to a certain point then a tapering off! But not with your Jerry. There's no dead end, no stopping once he reached that point. With him, it's more headaches, more pills! He will never give up the fight that's going on inside him to salvage every scrap of information he can possibly gather. I've never seen such determination to conquer the unconquerable!"

Katey smiled again to herself as she remembered her answer. "Well, Betty, you've just met a truly remarkable man. There's so much fight and stubbornness and pride locked up in him that nobody can or will ever break him! Too bad, you never knew my Jerry before! Then you'd have a real appreciation of what today's Jerry Landis is all about!"

Katey left Jerry alone out on the deck while she started supper. The large picture windows in the front of their cabin gave her a clear view so that she could get on with meal preparation and still keep a watchful eye on him.

She turned her back on him while she opened the pantry door. She snickered to herself as to what Jerry had done unpacking their canned goods. He'd put all the large cans in front of the shelves while hiding all the small cans in back.

"Here, Katey, let me help you. You're looking for the cut green beans, right?"

She turned around, simply amazed. "Why, yes, love! How in the world did you know I was looking for a small can of green beans?"

He motioned toward their table then the oven. "Well, there's bakers in the oven. Felt the heat as I came by. And earlier, out on the deck, you mentioned we were gonna have broiled pork chops. And we both know that green beans go nicely with the chops and baked potatoes. So it has to be the green beans you're looking for."

She hugged him over and over again. "Oh, Jerry, Jerry, Jerry! It's been a truly amazing day. Your thoughts, even some of your old Jerry Landis logic and reasoning, have come back! Welcome home, my darling!"

"Thanks, Katey, for those kind words! Most of the time, the reason I look lost is because I am…until you bail me out one way or another."

Katey released their embrace. She moved several tall cans, reached in, and found the green beans. She held the can up and said, "How about opening this can for me? Remember where we always kept our can opener?"

He thought long and hard. "No…no, I don't. But once you tell me which kitchen drawer to look in, I'll remember from them on."

Over oven-broiled pork chops, cut green beans, baked potatoes, and garlic bread, they sat down to supper. Even their conversation had reached a new level. No more force-feeding it or enduring long periods of silence, hoping against hope that Jerry would say something, anything at all. Tonight, it was different. He responded wonderfully. Even a word or two of dry humor got loose from somewhere, much to Katey's pure joy and amusement.

"Know what I am going to do tomorrow?" "No, love. What?"

"I am going to mount that can opener on the outside of the cabinet so I won't have to look for it. That way, it'll always be in plain sight for me! No more opening all those drawers trying to remember which one!"

She patted his hand and squeezed it with delight. "Good idea, Jerry! Oh, my love, some of the pieces of our life are coming together once more. I can feel it, love! Can't you?"

He didn't answer her. Katey sensed that he was deep in thought, perhaps too deep to really understand that a big breakthrough was oh so close at hand. Had too much happened too fast today? He turned his back to her, leaned against the kitchen counter, and began to rub his forehead.

Katey recognized the danger signal immediately. "Jerry, let's take a break. I'll get your pills. They're in my purse. I'll be just a minute."

By the time Katey returned, Jerry had pulled out a chair from the kitchen table to sit down, still rubbing his forehead nonstop.

"Here, love," she said. "Take two with this glass of water."

Jerry looked up and seemed genuinely glad she was his helpmate. Then he swallowed the pills, helped along by the water chaser. He set the glass down. "Every time I get to thinking so hard…trying to remember, my headaches start again. Why is that, Katey?"

She pulled out another chair beside him. This was the first time he'd ever asked such a pointed question. She took his hand then kissed it and gently rubbed it. "Remember that man I told you about? That very bad man that you and I used to work for?"

"The same man who hurt you, but you can't see the scars?"

"Yes, dear, that man! He hired some men to hurt you. They hurt you so bad, Jerry, that you were in the hospital a long, long time. Most of your memory is gone now, but some of it is starting to come back. Not all at once, but small bits and pieces here and there."

"Will I always have headaches because I'm trying so hard to remember?" "That's a hard one to answer, love. Because you've been such a proud person and so independent, most of the doctors who treated you believe you'll always be trying to gather and hold onto any scrap of memory that comes to you. And you know what, love? That's just one of the many, many reasons I love and will always love about you!"

Katey's explanation appeared to satisfy him. He stopped rubbing his forehead. A small smile drifted across his face. He seemed upbeat once more. "You know that new car you're driving, Katey…it's got all the latest whistles and bells. After I get better…maybe not so many headaches…do you think I could learn to drive it?"

She hugged him. "Don't see why not, my love! There's a lot of knobs and push buttons on that dashboard just waiting for you to push in, slide, or turn." "But where would we drive to? I don't know or remember any places or how to get there!"

"Well, love, for starters, there's that jewel of a lake you've been looking at ever since we arrived here today. All you have to do is drive back on the road we came in on, and once you hit the main highway, turn right and it'll take us straight to the shores!"

"How long are we going to stay here, Katey?"

"Just as long as we want to. Why, we could even watch the seasons come and go, just so long as you're happy and content. That's all that matters."

"No problem! I already like it up here, and today is only my... I mean our first day! Right?"

She got up. "I'm going to do the dishes. Got a little job for you to do.

Think you're up for it?"

"Yup, I think so. If it's not too hard...or I don't have to remember too much!"

CHAPTER 44

Katey couldn't believe her ears. That was the first "yup" she'd gotten out of him in over four years. She pointed to the front door. "Go out on the deck, dear. To your left under the far corner, there's dry wood stacked up. How about bringing in an armload? There's still enough of a chill here in the evening that a good warm fire would sure feel good."

He followed her directions. Happy as a lark, Katey turned to do the dishes. She squeezed the liquid soap bottle, waiting for the hot water to make the suds. She heard the front door close. She turned to keep a momentary eye on Jerry. Oh, how far they'd come today. He looked ready and eager to join in. No more prompting, suggesting, or taking the lead to initiate or continue any exchange of thoughts or ideas. Her jubilant thoughts took a nosedive. Jerry had reentered without one stick of wood. Oh well, she surmised, he's probably forgot where the firewood is or what she sent him out there to get.

"Couldn't find it or remember, right, dear?"

He approached, his face a calendar of good tidings. "I… I just remembered something, Katey. I'm pretty sure I used to help do the dishes up here…didn't I?"

A feather could've floored her. "Why yes, love. We haven't done dishes together in over four years. Third drawer down to your right is where we keep the dish towels."

Never were soapsuds, hot rinse water, or clean dish towels a more potent mixture of togetherness than what happened in the cabin, snuggled upon the bench land surrounded by the High Sierras. They touched, they smiled, and a bit of electricity passed between them all under of the guise of domestic peace and tranquility. When the last dish was wiped and put away, Jerry topped it off.

"You know, this was fun…wasn't it?"

"Yes, love. We used to get such a kick out of doing things together, dishes included!"

"Got a suggestion. Care to hear it?"

Another breakthrough after a four-year lapse of getting nowhere. Katey was all smiles. "Go ahead, love. I can't wait to hear it!"

He started slowly taking his good old sweet time picking and sorting the words he planned on using. Katey could see and sense his flashback, the Jerry Landis of old, carefully laying the groundwork. Everything had to be just right, in perfect order, and in logical fashion. Four years of rust was about to be removed and stripped from the gears that moved the wheels that one Gerald Landis called his brain. "Some of those zeroes in your checkbook, all they'd need is a gentle nudge and—"

"Don't forget, Jerry. They're yours too!"

He accepted her interruption. "There's a new Buick in the parking lot, and I read back somewhere that the newspaper said you're loaded. Couldn't you loosen up a bit and think about putting in a dishwasher?"

She rushed into his arms. "Oh, my love! Oh, my love! What a great suggestion. What a wonderful idea! See! See, Jerry! All this time this cabin has been waiting for you to come back to me. To us! Anymore thoughts or ideas, lover?"

He thought hard on her question. "No, nothing more…and I didn't forget to bring in some firewood. I'd better do that now before I do forget!"

Katey's anticipation had reached a new high as she watched Jerry amble out on the deck once more. With his cane in hand, he was the picture of hope eternal. There'd never be the complete picture. She realized that. But from what had once been complete hopelessness and helplessness, a new person had emerged from the shadows. Not the Jerry Landis of yesterday but a pretty darned good substitute, the one Betty said was definitely worth caring about and loving. Now it was beginning to happen! Really happen!

Before each realized what was going on, Mother Nature had her say in their lives. Night fell with a quiet rush and suddenness, forcing the two to think about and prepare for bedtime, their first night together as husband and wife. Jerry seemed apprehensive, even though Katey had spent a considerable time reassuring him that everything was under control. She dutifully led him into their bedroom and pointed to one of the pillows.

"Dear, I've laid out a clean pair of boxer shorts. You never used to wear pajamas. Starting with tomorrow when we wake up, let's start dressing in front of each other like most married couples do. Be good for the both of us."

Jerry was down to his socks, shorts, and artificial leg. Katey was down to her bra, slip, and panties. Suddenly, Jerry turned around. "Could we talk a little while, Katey…first?"

She read him perfectly. He was more than a little apprehensive about the physical needs to their marriage. She smiled then blew him a kiss. "Sure, love. Let's prop our pillows and lay down the way we are. It'll give both of us a chance to have a real good heart to heart, and I'm sure it'll be good for both of us."

Several worry lines disappeared from his face as if by magic. He seemed a lot more at ease now with both hands cradled behind his head, much like in days long past and sweetly remembered by Katey.

"Let me go first," he said. "First off, I'm glad we said our vows this morning. That way. I feel more like we're married…even though you told me we've really been married for more than twenty-nine years."

"Do you believe we were first married that long ago, love?" She watched him wrestle with his answer, torn between what he knew to be true now and what she'd told him was true.

"I believe what you told me…because I know now how much you love me…and that I trust you. Ever since we first met in my room in the hospital… that's all I can say. Maybe someday it will come back to me…enough so I can remember how it was…how it used to be between us."

She smiled at him, pleased beyond punch at the progress they'd made up to this point in their reconstructed relationship as husband and wife. Dare she hope for more? Possibly the real breakthrough, the one thing she wanted more than anything else in life? Recognition by him as to who she was and is?

"Jerry," she began sweetly, her eyes aglow with such caring, such pride, and yes, such love for this man, her husband. "I know this won't mean much to you now, but I feel it needs saying because it came from you. Many years ago, you said something that will be with me always. The night you first proposed to me…you said you didn't have much to offer me except your love. But if I were patient with you, give you a chance to prove yourself to me, that you'd never let me down…and you haven't, my darling husband. You haven't, ever!"

He turned to her, his eyes, his lips, and his heart telegraphing his passion for her—his new Katey. They held each other close as in days gone by but no longer remembered by him. He kissed her again and again, his need to bond with her now more pressing than ever. She returned this hunger with a want of her own—her need to convince him to make love, to consummate what their bodies were telling them to do.

Jerry parted from their embrace to reach down to touch then feel the delicate lacework on the hemline of her half-slip. He lifted it up gingerly, his eyes drinking in its exquisite design. For a precious few moments, he seemed lost in time, the garment capturing his full attention. He raised it higher and higher till Katey's soft thighs and lace panties lay exposed for his viewing pleasure alone.

Katey sensed they were on the verge of something special between them once more. She felt his hand and fingers move, touch and excite both. He was on fire.

"Love, let me freshen up a bit. I won't be but a minute or two."

Jerry moved enough so Katey could get up. His eyes pleaded with her. She knew what was on his mind before his lips ever voiced his big concern. "Hurry, Katey. Remember now, you're going to help me… all the way, right?"

She blew him her best hot kiss yet. "Don't worry, love. I'll help you in everything that we do. And don't worry about your leg. Never got in the way before, so there's no reason to even think about it now." Most of the worry lines left his face.

Once inside the bathroom, Katey quickly changed into a fresh pair of panties. She applied liberal doses of lilac-scented perfume all over. She removed her half-slip and hung it up on the clothes knob next to the shower stall. Next to the slip hung the most exquisite see-through sheer negligee money could buy from Sacramento's best woman's intimate shop.

"Not tonight," she heard herself say. "Maybe in a day or two. Too many distractions for Jerry. Tonight it's back to basics…then we'll see."

She primped in front of the big vanity mirror. Satisfied, she was ready for intimacy at any level. She gave herself one last parting pep talk. "Now, Katey, come back down to earth where you belong. There's a fifty-five-year-old virgin out there who's come a long, long way back. He's going to be in a hurry! Probably his bedroom manners will put you in shock. But no matter how it goes, you make sure you let him know how much you enjoyed it. To him, he's waited a lifetime for this, while you've only waited four years!"

Suddenly, she dropped to her knees to offer up a prayer. "Please, dear God, grant me this one special miracle. I now know and understand your plan for us. That's why we had those beyond compare and perfect twenty-five years.

You were trying to tell me…tell us that we were to be tested again. Lord, look how Jerry has responded! No one, not even I, could've believed just how far he's come back into my life. I ask only this of you, dear God. Please find a way to have him know me once more… and the rest of the days of our lives will be truly blessed. Amen."

Armed with a new determination born of necessity, Katey opened the bathroom door and made her entrance back into their bedroom and Jerry's life.

He caught the sweet fragrances of her perfume. It aroused in him a desire to have her no matter what. He forced his lips upon hers, hard.

Even Katey was a bit startled as he showed no inclination to slow down. She finally moved her lips slightly to one side. "Jerry, my love," she pleaded, whispering in his ear. "Let's take it easy. That way, we can enjoy this and each other that much more. It'll be good for both of us."

He rose up. "I… I… I'm sorry. All I can think about is you and how much I want you."

She reached up to gently pull him back down. "I love you, my wonderful husband. Can you tell me how much you love me?"

He looked down at her, his vision of everything a man could possibly want or need. "I'm… I'm ready! You were gonna help me! Remember?"

It was time to interject Katey's leveler, the one catchphrase that produced the desired results. She had fervently hoped that he might reign passionate kisses on her lips or any place else he cared to, whispering those words she longed to hear. "Do you love me, darling? Say it, please, for me! It'll do us both a lot of good."

He bent down to kiss her. This time, she made it count—with their first French kiss. Finally, his words came. "Wow, Katey, that was some kiss. Took my breath clean outa my mouth!"

A tiny tear of pure unadulterated joy found a pocket in the corner of her eye. "Oh, darling, we used to French kiss a lot…and enjoy it so much!"

"And…and I do love you, Katey. I didn't forget to say it, Katey. Katey, you'll have to help me on this…anything else we used to do… before…you know?" He spent what seemed like an eternity. He looked down. "Prettiest panties I've ever seen, Katey. All so smooth and silky like…lots of frilly places around them…more especially next to… your legs."

Again, decision time came for him. He looked first at his sweet, sweet, wonderful little wife beneath him and then down to those sexy black silky panties. He slid down slowly, ever so slowly.

Katey was on fire. *Oh, thank God, he's responding. He's responding.* A voice within her shouted out such glad tidings. Suddenly, he froze. He stood up, his eyes riveted on those panties.

Katey was by his side in an instant. "Jerry, Jerry, my love, it's all right! Come lay down with me! We'll make love! I'll help you! I promise!"

He turned to her then reached down till he felt the delicate material. He ran his fingers inside the top of her panties. The words came in torrents, with the rapidity of an auctioneer. "I, I, I, I, know these panties! I, I, I, I remember! Yes! Yes! Yes! I do! I do, I do, I do, I do! You always wore them! Just for me! Always! You're Katey McCray! No, no, that's not right! Katey Landis! Yes, that's who you are! I know who you are! Katey Landis! Katey Landis! *Katey Landis, my wife!*"

Such hugs, such kisses, and yes, such wonderful, wonderful tears of joy! It was the reunion of all times, this special blending of minds, hearts, and togetherness for all eternity. At last, at long last, they were indeed husband and wife.

Katey looked up at her husband. "Love me. Please love me, my husband!"

Their bed barely moved. The bed covers were never pulled back, nor were there any indents on their bed pillows.

They lay cradled within each other, a contentment beyond anything each had ever experienced now would be their master and mentor. They drifted off into a deep sleep, drained more by the momentous day's events then by the natural give and take to complete their union.

Somewhere during the night, they awoke. Both took showers then got ready to go climb back into bed. Jerry sat up in bed with his pillow propped behind his head, both hands cradled, quite reminiscent of times long past. Katey had left their bathroom door open so she could keep their conversation going while applying cleansing cream.

"Jerry?"

"Yes?"

"Now that you really know who I am, do you have any other thoughts or maybe another remembrance or two?"

He thought about her questions for some time then finally answered, "No, Katey, nothing comes to mind right now…unless you wanna count some LTIA? Don't think that would qualify."

For all of twenty seconds, Katey sat on her vanity stool. Then all of a sudden, she came charging out of the bathroom, her face still covered with cleansing cream. *Oh my Lord! Oh my Lord! An honest-to-goodness Jerryism!*

One solid minute of mock attacks and roughhousing between the two produced the desired result—one sweet surrender kiss. "Oh my love, my love, if you only knew how many times I've wanted to hear one of your patented Jerryisms. I'da given $50,000 if I could've gotten one outa you four years ago. By the way, what does LTIA stand for? C'mon, love, you gotta tell me! Please, Jerry! Please!"

A bit of the old Jerry Landis wit and charm surfaced in all its theatrical glory. "Didn't mean to ham up such a good day between us, Katey, but da old professor here got in too big a hurry…so anytime you're ready, all you gotta do is say, 'Jerry, sweet darlin,' sho'go for some more LTIA.' Let's try it again!"

ABOUT THE AUTHOR

Ivan Bosanko's critical research has produced his fifth novel, *The Rubber Room, Volume 2*, which exposed the railroad industry's "century-old, out-of-the-closet secret." Set in the 1950s, the story gives you a nostalgia tour unlike anything ever experienced. His considerable writing talent and wide range of unforgettable characters are truly showcased for your reading pleasure and enjoyment. His epic is loaded with *change, commitment,* and *challenge.*

Ivan's writing talent has been duly recognized by the national and international literary community. His online series of articles have earned him two most prestigious awards. Who's Who names him their 2009 Member of the Year. That was followed up with being selected into their 2010 Hall of Fame.

All this from a lad who first published his own newspaper at the ripe old age of twelve.